Bo + Susan

Enjoy!

Fred OA

Ambivalent about his religious, social or political beliefs, Andy is passionately over-opinionated about everything he knows nothing about. Contemplation of life's important questions such as religion, creation and karma, are key to the mix of this author's ramblings.

Married to Emma, the emotional keel to his life and teacher of all things 'female', Andy is approaching middle-age with an air of nervous excitement as their relationship embarks on the next stage of maturity – children.

THE ANSWER
Part 1 of the Tatlaue Trilogy

Andy Bacon

THE ANSWER
Part 1 of the Tatlaue Trilogy

Vanguard Press

A CIP catalogue record for this title is
available from the British Library.

ISBN-13: 978 1 84386 311 3

*Vanguard Press is an imprint of
Pegasus Elliot MacKenzie Publishers Ltd.*
www.pegasuspublishers.com

First Published in 2007

**Vanguard Press
Sheraton House Castle Park
Cambridge England**

Printed & Bound in Great Britain

Emma, you are my world and the answer to my everything.
Thank you for completing me.

Preface

Despite having seen it thousands of times, Cass still found himself stunned by the site of The Chun. He had spent most of his waking life around the gravity-poised, colossal object, which hung inches from the ground in front of him. Floating like a magical trophy on God's mantelpiece, the huge testament to a greater but long-gone race, hovered solidly in the air. From the ground, The Chun looked like a vast inverted pyramid, hundreds of times the size of even the most ambitious of mountains, suspended like a zillion-ton puppet from the skies, but without the obligatory strings. Rarely did you actually get to see the whole of The Chun. Only on very clear nights, when the moons were full and bright, reflecting the sun's rays onto the sides of the immeasurable object, could you appreciate its true immense presence. Only then could you faintly make out the rim at the top of The Chun, rising far above the atmosphere of the planet Vacchion, and into the beginnings of space. It was solid, very solid. You didn't need to know what it was made of to know that it was probably more solid than anything you could imagine. It reflected light like chrome, but added an element of distortion that made the reflections look slightly tormented. And there seemed to be a very small time-delay, as if the image was being processed before being beamed back out again.

Cass leaned back and raised his head upward, his eyes scanning the vast, solid structure in front of his humble and very mortal being. The Chun, despite being seemingly inanimate, had an uncanny knack of making all observers feel very insignificant indeed. No matter how important the onlooker, no matter what standing in society, a few minutes gazing at The Chun soon brought their egos crashing back to microscopic proportions. His eyes followed the smooth surface up and up, as he had done so many times during his many years in the city, ever since he had reached the qualifying age to enter the realms of the bustling citadel, at ten years old.

He remembered the first moment he saw The Chun, twenty years ago, as if it were yesterday. When his eyes first befell the inexplicable item, they were still fifty miles outside the outer walls of the massive global capital, slowly travelling along the bumpy rural roads in a wheeled people carrying vehicle. He was prematurely stirred from a light, dreamy doze by the other children's sudden silence. He sleepily awoke, looked around the vehicle at his fellow ten-year-old passengers, all of whom had ceased their noisy babble of childish banter in exchange for calm, awe-struck serenity. Cass turned his gaze towards where all of his peers were looking. There, through the trees, far off in the distance, was a dark shadow in the sky. It was an inverted triangle, thin at the base (which was hidden by the distant horizon) and wider at the point it disappeared into the haze, high up in the summer's sky. It was awesome. Incredible. His eyes widened with the wonder of it and his mouth slowly dropped open. As his childish eyes travelled up the monolithic object, he followed the shadowy structure into the wispy clouds. Gradually the faint outline disappeared completely, but went so far into the sky that it seemed it would continue forever. After a long period of staring, it dawned on Cass that The Chun was so large it would have always been visible to him, all of his life, even though he had grown up in the community pre-life school, hundreds of miles outside the city walls. All those years he had known the colossal object existed – had been taught all the facts the Vacchions knew about it, which was very little indeed. All of his young life he had dreamt about seeing it, desperate to know what it looked like, impatient to realise its true unimaginable size. He felt cheated that no-one had told him he could have seen it on a very clear day if he'd known in which direction to look. He felt angry – betrayed by his tutors. Resentful of all those wasted years imagining the object, when all along he could have seen it. He felt… grown-up, almost. The awe-struck silence and intense personal anguish in the people carrier gradually subsided and was replaced by polite, adult-like discussion and gentle contemplation about the awesome sight. It was a cruel but deliberate lesson the Vacchions considered essential for all.

For his first ten years of life Cass had wondered why the law made children live hundreds of miles outside the Citadel walls. But, as with every inquisitive ten year old who asks such naïve questions, he soon forgot them when his eyes fell upon The Chun. The awesome spectacle had the ability to stop a person querying such topics ever again. Somehow, due to its sheer size and unbelievable poise, some things just didn't seem worth asking anymore. Especially when there were real questions to be aired, which usually formed themselves in sentences like: "What the ffff...?!". Despite its heavily disguised form – veiled by the camouflage of wonder and a somewhat shameful display of poor vocabulary, this succinct question was probably the most commonly asked question in the universe. The fully-extended version of the same question would look something like:

"Considering the vastness and totally ludicrous way that the five-hundred-mile high object is poised no more than a hand's thickness above the ground, at its lowest point (which, quite literally is a point, as the object in question appears to be an upturned pyramid), and then considering that beings such as us, or any form like us in a previous, but now extinct race, could have ever been capable of such an awesome achievement, especially when the only thing keeping it in such a position is the gravitational pull of the planet of Vacchion and its three moons in the greatest scientific state of equilibrium ever displayed in the universe..., who or what the hell put it there and if such awesome creatures existed that could display such immense knowledge and strength to create such a masterpiece, where the hell are they now?"

Roughly transposed, this is the Vacchions' equivalent to the more traditional and universally accepted question: "What is the meaning of life?" Otherwise know as: 'The Question'.

Apart from the odd few fanatics and all ten year olds, who had just become of age to enter the classless society of The Citadel, most Vacchions tried their hardest not to think of 'The Question'. It was all a little too daunting when you had such a stark reminder of your pathetic, tiny, frail existence in what was quite simply, without doubt, the much vaster scheme of things. The Chun was truly the greatest social leveller.

Preface II

Cass's eyes strained to see as far up the side of The Chun as they could in the bright, clear blue sky. Even with powerful telescopes, the Vacchions could only see as far as the distant lip of the vast upturned pyramid. Before flight was possible, people speculated that the rim marked the edge of an immense, square, plateau atop The Chun. Many people believed that a supernatural world existed there, spawning many diverse religions – as do all inexplicable features of life throughout the universe. Civilised societies the galaxy over have always used religion in some form as an explanation for all unexplained phenomena. It allows them to neatly arrange all their ignorance under one titled package and gives them an almost endless supply of reasons to go to war, or simply to dislike people who don't believe in the same things.

Who ever invented religion must have been kicking himself, thought Cass. He could have registered the invention for a patent and made a very healthy living off the massive royalties he would earn for eternity.

Once flight had been achieved, three hundred years ago, the Vacchions first and foremost aim was to discover the hidden world at the top of The Chun. They could make contact with the beings, which must surely be of a god-like nature, as they had obviously built this structure in order to observe and protect their planet-dwelling children from atop. Or so the vast majority of the religions had speculated. However, the first exploratory flights to investigate the surface of The Chun, simply increased the dismay and frustration of ignorance. The Chun was actually a great deal taller than was first thought. From the ground it looked as if the rim (and therefore the assumed 'top') was inside the planet's atmosphere. Once flight had been able to take the explorers much closer to the outer reaches of the atmosphere, the truth had been realised. Only a tenth of The Chun was actually within the atmosphere of the planet. The truth about The Chun's secrets would have to wait hundreds of years until space travel had been achieved.

For many decades the people of Vacchion remained peaceful – with all races and classes forming a totally division-less society in an attempt to devote all resources to the advancement of space travel. The answer was at the top of The Chun, and the Vacchions were getting more and more anxious to solve the mystery with every day that passed. As each small technological hurdle was overcome, the desperation to get past the rim got worse.

One hundred years after flight was first achieved, space exploration was made possible. After a further fifty years of fine-tuning, it was developed far enough to also allow the survival of the crew during the flight. Eventually, after many more years of adjustments, the safe return of the Vacchonauts to the planet's surface was finally achieved. This fundamental enhancement of space travel (i.e. survival) meant the reality of The Chun could finally be known.

Would the top of The Chun reveal the guardian angels that many religions preached? Would it expose gods, heavens, hells, the creators of The Chun themselves? Pessimistic religions predicted horrors atop the giant structure, whilst those that revelled in more jovial rituals assumed it would unveil treasures of relational synergy with the beings that reside there, allowing the Vacchions to advance and evolve beyond their wildest dreams.

As it transpired, much to the dismay of thousands of people (many of whom had made very wealthy livings preaching about the gods that inhabited the top of The Chun), there was no flat, inhabitable surface to the object. Beyond the rim lay another pyramid shape, much shorter than the base section, pointing upwards towards the stars. It was made of the same strange material and completed the single, solid shape which hung like a giant diamond between the planet and its three satellite moons. All of this made the planet of Vacchion, when viewed from a distance, look like a rather extravagant engagement ring fit for a Goddess! Luckily, the Vacchions would never travel far enough away from their planet to discover this rather embarrassing fact about their home world.

Hundreds of thousands of years of religion and tradition smashed to smithereens and then swept, quite heartlessly, under the rug of time. The entire fabric of society was under the most extreme strain, and the Sixth Jut – ruler and counsellor of Vacchion, when asked his opinion on the seemingly huge mistake of commissioning the flight to the top of The Chun, merely commented; "Sh*t happens!"

This quote gradually, over the following decades, became the foundation for a new religion, which believed in fate and destiny, rather than false hopes and awkward assumptions. The religion became known as Shitappen, and its believers were referred to as the Shitappians. Strange, how religion can be spawned by the most simple of events, and take on a snowball effect to encapsulate millions of people over a relatively short period of time. Across the universe exist thousands of examples of magicians, conjurers and illusionists immortalised in the faith of their disciples by their abilities to cure the ill, turn water into wine and saw people in half.

But now, in Cass's time, the biggest catastrophe of all had taken place. His race was paying for it dearly with the maximum penalty – extinction. It was an accident, as are so many of the discoveries made by civilisations across the universe. Some of these discoveries take civilisations forward in giant leaps on their planned evolutionary journey, some take them back. Others are lethal. Right now, millions of Vacchions were dying, almost inexplicably, as an unrelenting disease rapidly spread throughout their society. It was no ordinary disease. It required no physical form, it had no organisms or cells upon which a cure could be attached. It needed no bodies on which it could travel, no wind to carry its poison. All it required was conscious intelligence and the natural pattern of societal chaos that allowed it an erratic path through to every one of the planet's inhabitants. The disease killed people through enlightenment.

The discovery upon which the Vacchions had stumbled was the answer to life. The deadly disease it brought with it was the realization that they had succeeded in their eight million year quest. It gave each of its victims the short piece of information that they had always thought they wanted to hear. But in this moment, following the greatest example of anti-climax the universe had ever spawned, the need to live was removed. Suicidal lethargy engulfed each victim as the words "is that it?!" appeared in the subconscious of every cell of the sufferer's body. They had discovered the answer to life and that meant it was time to go. It took away their desire to live. Once they knew 'The Answer', there was no point to their existence. After all, when you find what you are looking for, you stop looking. That is why the missing object is always in the last place you look. This was the knowledge that allowed you to stop searching. After this, there was no need for life.

The Answer did not spread itself by touch, word of mouth, or bodily fluids. It had a life and an existence of its own, it could breed 'Knowledge' from one person to the next in the blink of an eye. The information travelled from one sufferer's depressed, suicidal mind to the next unsuspecting victim. And yet, The Answer had no destructive tendencies, no malicious intent to destroy the race on Vacchion. It should never have existed, if truth be known. But the Vacchions' endless search for The Answer – fuelled by the questions raised by living in the shadow of The Chun for tens of thousands of years, not to mention the events hundreds of years ago when they discovered that The Chun did not hold the answers – had finally succeeded. And now the Vacchions were paying the ultimate price.

The prize and the price was all rolled into one. The new found knowledge gave its victims the ultimate answer to the ultimate question, but at the same time took away all reason for existence. They had, in effect, reached the end; 'Game Over'... 'Congratulations – You Win!'... 'now please leave the rat-race in a calm and orderly manner (no pushing!)'... It was nobody's fault, not really. Just society's unrelenting characteristic to keep everyone shoving each other to move forward all the time.

The Answer raged through the citadel, breathing its fatal knowledge on everything that had conscious belief in its soul. It entered each victim's mind through a form of unknown telepathy. Eye contact between a carrier and a new host was enough to create the connection. Once inside, The Knowledge spread itself rapidly throughout the parts of the Vacchion's brain that were yet to be unlocked. Over a period of minutes, days, or weeks, The Knowledge would gradually dawn on the subconscious of the 'enlightened' individual, who would then begin to realise that the reason for their existence had simply reached a logical end. A few tried to escape the citadel, but in doing so merely aided the spread of the new found knowledge to all other areas of Vacchion.

Within weeks, the entire planet had been touched by the stark reality that was 'The Answer'. Everything that had a conscious understanding of its own existence, slowly prepared to die. They had completed the task and had achieved what races of beings the universe over want to achieve. Nobody knew that these were the consequences of such new-found knowledge. And once they did, it didn't matter as it was too late anyway. The Vacchions had found... TATLAUE – The Answer To Life And Universal Existence.

Preface III

The entire Vacchion race had lost their need to live but they still had a sense of duty to the remainder of life in the universe. They could see the devastating effects of The Answer and knew that it would destroy life throughout the entire cosmos if it was not controlled. They decided it was imperative that they use their modern micro-technology in an attempt to contain it. They had to try to stop it from travelling away from the planet, wreaking the same suicidal havoc it had spread across Vacchion throughout other innocent civilisations. To the scientists' underwhelming surprise[1] they succeeded. Only minutes before the last few souls gave up the struggle to continue living, they completed the final stages of a miniature self-managing microchip prison cell in which The Answer would spend its eternity. Moments later the last few scientists lay down and gave up the tiresome habit of breathing.

The remainder of life on the planet (i.e. those species that chose not to indulge in the complicated matters of conscious self awareness) thrived over the thousands of years that followed. Animals, plants and insects that had never considered the universal conundrum that was 'The Question', continued to scurry around searching for the next meal rather than the answer to life. This made them safe from the wrath of The Answer. Maybe there was a moral to this expensive lesson. Maybe the motto to learn from this was: "Seek and ye shall find – Mind your own business and ye shall live". Either way, the humanoids' reign on this planet was over and it was the turn of other beasts to exploit the rewards that were on offer on this rich and fertile land.

Flora and fauna took over the planet and the constructions the Vacchions had left behind. Carnivores of all shapes and sizes thought all their birthdays had come at once[2] when they suddenly found millions of humanoid carcasses to feed on. For

---

[1] life was simply too much of a chore in these latter stages

[2] or at least they would if they had that kind of conscious thought process

21

the first few years a huge plague of scavengers developed, then for the next few years small predators dominated the planet as they preyed on the abundant scavengers. Finally, large meat-eaters flourished due to the volume of smaller, overweight, predators available. Eventually the universal laws of natural equilibrium took over and the planet's species quickly settled into a standard seasonal pattern of existence. Despite the early sequential plagues encountered at each level of the food-chain, nothing ever compared to the infestation of humanoids that had dominated and deformed the planet's existence for many thousands of generations. The galaxy-wide rule sowed its seed back into the fabric of Vacchion's remaining animal and plant societies. A natural balance was restored as the only ruler. 'Survival of the fittest' was once again the only law.

Existence on Vacchion had returned to true normality. The course of survival was no longer perverted by the supercilious society of humanoids who considered their extensive dominance the 'norm'. Their infestation of the planet had ceased and that allowed all other life to resume their rightful positions in the tried-and-tested hierarchy of the food chain.

Preface IV

Deep in the undergrowth, the microscopic electronic components of the tiny prison soundlessly carried out their invaluable task. It had been constructed to last. To survive all the elements. It had built-in artificial intelligence, and more environmental monitoring software than you could shake a large stick at. It even had a fail-safe. A last stand on which it would only rely if all else failed and there was no hope left for its survival. The Vacchions could not be sure it would stop The Answer from spreading, so it really was a last-ditch attempt at damage limitation: the thermo-gravi-nuclear melt-down would only begin if the artificial intelligence of the tiny machine had weighed up all the alternatives and come up with nothing. If this occurred, it was highly advisable not to be in the immediate vicinity of the device.

What the Vacchions didn't realise when they built this total containment capsule was that they had actually compounded the devastating effects of The Answer. Extending the destructive capabilities of The Knowledge ten thousand years into the future. Instead of helping the universe escape the wrath of The Answer, they had aided its survival. The Knowledge would only have existed whilst it had conscious minds to feed on. But the Vacchions had actually provided it with a sanctuary in which it could dwell, once it had annihilated the entire conscious society of the planet. Had the miniature, personalised prison not been generated, The Answer would have had no host in which to survive. It was to all intents and purposes a parasite whose existence depends entirely on the constant supply and consumption of conscious minds in order to 'live'.

Once its food was exhausted, it would have died. Like any creature. Except it wasn't like any other living creature. There was only one. Only one true Answer. But it can spring up anywhere in the universe. Every few million years a race would venture too close to the edge of inquisition about TATLAUE and would find themselves falling over the cliff of ignorance, into the depths of knowledgeable extinction. The Vacchions

23

weren't the first to discover it. It had been exposed thousands of times before, perhaps millions. Entire races had been destroyed all over the galaxy. Each time it happened, all that remained were the remnants of their bodies for a future race to excavate with small brushes and ponder: "why was this species wiped out millions of years ago?". On almost every planet across the fabric of the universe, entire species of intelligent beings had spent millennia investigating possible reasons for the extinction of ancient creatures, native to their planets. In each case, the only clues they had to help resolve such a riddle, were fossilised remains and a strange desire to blame the inexplicable annihilation on a theory about a large meteorite hitting the planet's surface!

The Answer was a well-known fact amongst the "Elders" of the universe. These conscious beings sailed around the Universe on their pre-set courses in an ice-white incandescent flurry of self-awareness. Each Elder dragged behind them a huge white tail, boasting the depth of knowledge they had obtained, and the level of omnipotence they had acquired throughout their endless existences. They had proven to be the only conscious being in the whole of the universe with the ability to survive The Knowledge. Largely because they formed a major part of the content of The Answer itself.

The universe often breathed a metaphorical sigh of relief that the Elders never lowered themselves to communicate with any mere mortal race. That would be catastrophic. The Elders existed purely to contemplate the existence of the universe and to absorb knowledge continuously until they outgrew their own tails, wrapped themselves around a nearby star and caused it to go supernova. The fact that they carried The Answer with them at all times was the prime reason for not communicating with other races. They could potentially wipe out all conscious existence throughout the universe if they were to go around letting it slip that they had the answer to everything! There was one Elder, who had once attempted to allow itself to be communicated with by a planet of comet worshippers. It was rapidly demoted to a meteorite. She played out her short remaining existence burning through the atmosphere of their planet whilst trying to spell 'hello' in a language so advanced that not only would it have been impossible for any intelligent life to decipher the burning scrawl, but it would have actually proved impossible for any mortal creature to be able to see the range of colours that completed the image. Once these sad facts are known, it seems almost disrespectful to point out that when this Kamikaze form of communication was attempted by the disgraced comet, the only creature on the planet to notice anything at all of the last few seconds of a supposedly immortal 'god-like' being's final moments of existence, was a single small marsupial, who happened to be cleaning its genitals at the time!

The Answer's prison cell, lay for ten thousand years in the shadow of The Chun. Small rodents passed it frequently, occasionally giving it a quick sniff before moving on to more interesting and nutritious things. Very slowly, the world in which it sat silently changed. Flora seeded, grew, died and decayed, and fauna was born, grew-up, died and was eaten. Generally speaking, 'life' went on.

The most interesting thing to happen to the tiny electronic prison cell during the thousands of years following its creation was that a society of insects decided the device would make a fantastic assembly hall display. A huge swarm of the microscopic creatures chattered frantically as they lifted the monstrous object into the air in unison and began the many nanometres trek back to their underground city. After twelve hours and hundreds of casualties, the monolith was installed in the huge chamber known as the assembly hall. Countless numbers of the minute creatures filled every square millimetre of the massive hall for the grand unveiling of the new religious idol. Insect religion was born.

Over the next few millennia, the object gained a name and god-like status within the religion that thrived amongst the tiny insect race. They worshipped the giant structure and attributed all good things to its very existence.

Then one day, not a good day, everything went wrong for the insect race. The walls of their underground city tumbled down as their world was turned upside down by a giant being. Huge boulders of earth and debris were strewn everywhere, claiming the lives of thousands of the creatures. As their crumbling city collapsed around itself, maiming and crushing the tiny insects, it gradually began to rise up. Slowly, out of the sanctuary of the depths of the ground, the metropolis rumbled upwards. Walls and ceilings buckled, light streamed in through the cracks, piercing the dust and devastation. The insect capital ascended, higher and higher, disintegrating as it accelerated towards the clouds. Huge sections of the city broke away from the rising mass, tumbling endlessly towards the ground, claiming countless more lives as they crashed into the earth, smashing into hundreds of smaller neighbourhoods, sending homes and families spinning into the air. Entire districts were crushed instantly as they impacted the planet's surface at high velocity. Surely none of the inhabitants could survive this horrific catastrophe. It was carnage. Death reigned… literally.

As the city's seemingly endless acceleration towards the sky began to slow, some of the insects that were still breathing gradually came to. Those who were lucky enough to be left in the open, rather than being crushed beneath the many layers of the earth-city below them, gradually began to look up. Squinting towards the bright sky, their unaccustomed eyes strained to see what the monolithic shape was that held the remains of the urban mess high in the air. The insect race knew of colossal creatures that once roamed their planet, but this one's outline was unknown to them. Never before had any of them seen such a shape.

Tuk-tuk looked out over the remains of his home, his neighbourhood, his district, and into the distance at the adjoining borough where so many localised disputes had been instigated, it was all so trivial now. All were barely recognisable as they had been reduced to rubble and dust. Some of them were even missing entirely as they had broken away from the main section of the city and plummeted towards the ground far below. Bodies of the dead and injured were everywhere, exclaiming the hideous extent of the devastation. Tuk-tuk was in extreme pain. All six of his legs were broken and bleeding badly, half of them were still trapped under large sections of his destroyed home. His gaze continued past the mass carnage and unrecognisable remains around him, and up towards the sky. He narrowed his eyes in an attempt to see far off into the distance. There, too far away for him to be able to focus, was a monumental silhouette, many times larger than his entire city. A long shadowy shape protruded from the distant monster towards the ruins of the once impressive metropolis. It was somehow holding the entire remains of Tuk-tuk's 3-million-strong colony high up in the air. Tuk-tuk had heard the stories of ancient existence, when their race used to live in much smaller, simpler dwellings. History taught of a time when lives were short and the future uncertain due to huge beings, the size of planets, who used to roam the land. There were ancient accounts of entire towns being wiped out in one go by these clumsy giants with their boiling floods that scorched and drowned simultaneously. But this had not happened for millennia. Why would it suddenly start happening again?

The planet-sized being started to move. The floating city began to shake again. Another vast protrusion, which dwarfed Tuk-tuk's entire district, appeared from the main body of the shape and gradually moved towards the floating insect capital. Five long appendages at the end of the massive limb lowered themselves towards the city. Two of the five extensions were the first to impact heavily into the earthy remains. Heart-stopping shockwaves penetrated deep into the foundations of the devastated metropolis, causing further mayhem and structural collapse, claiming yet more lives.

Moments before the black veil of death took over Tuk-tuk's limp and useless body, he glanced up at the retreating hand. Pinched between the hard rippled surface of the two lowest appendages, held delicately like a tiny petal, was their god. The giant assembly hall centre piece which had been the focal point of the race's existence for so many thousands of years, disappeared into the clutches of the monster that had so carelessly and disrespectfully torn Tuk-tuk's home world to shreds, callously murdering its inhabitants.

Then… nothing. Tuk-tuk went to a better place. Well, maybe not better. But different. At least, that's what his religion had convinced him when he had signed up for a lifetime of relentless worship.

Actually he hadn't gone anywhere. Except down. His breathing consciousness had ceased to be, and his soul died along with his physical being. Tuk-tuk's lifeless body tumbled effortlessly towards the earth with millions of other lifeless bodies and thousands of partially maimed 'survivors', whose only benefit to not dying when Tuk-tuk had, was an exhilarating journey through the air which not many non-flying insects ever get the chance to experience.

Life for this huge insect tribe was over. None could survive the one million nonometre plummet towards the ground[3].

Just as the doomed survivors of the excavated citadel were about to strike the planet's surface with fatal impact, the giant shape boomed out a slow and resonating sound of victory. Totally undecipherable to the insect race, but loud and meaningful enough to be etched into their memories for the rest of their lives (which, at this point, was about one fiftieth of a second).

"'ere, Dyla, look what I've found!" boomed the planet-sized oppressor.

Dyla came bounding over, through the knee-high grass towards his work-shy colleague. It can't possibly be anything related to what we're supposed to be looking for, thought Dyla as he drew up along side the motionless figure.

There in his fat, gloved hand was what looked like a minute circuit board, less than a millimetre in width.

---

[3] Actually, that was not strictly true. Many of them could easily survive the massive drop – it was the phenomenal impact at the bottom of the drop that would crush them to pulp.

Chapter 1

The Landing

K always felt nervous at this stage. He felt as if at any moment he could lose all control over his bodily functions. Then he wouldn't only be sh*tting himself in a metaphorical sense. He sat, rigid in his seat. Bones and muscles tensed at the prospect of the unknown experience that was about to unfold before him and his colleagues. His face stared straight ahead at a faceless fellow co-worker who stared back, unemotional and relaxed. K tried to avoid his eyes, more through embarrassment at his own lack of courage than anything else.

Anxiety ran rife through K's mind as the cabin raced through space towards the unexplored planet. Nobody knew exactly what to expect. Most of K's colleagues were eager to get down there and start exploring the unknown – mainly because the sooner they started the job, the sooner they could get back to playing cards and drinking, but also because the ship's entry into any unknown atmosphere was by far the most dangerous part of their work. K, hadn't started to think about what was on the planet's surface yet, he was too anxious to know that his life was not in danger of being incinerated. They all had their own idea of what was about to befall them, based on past knowledge and the briefing they had been given before the adventure had begun. Most of K's colleagues had many years of experience on which to draw their preconceived conclusions. K was relatively new to the role and therefore created his presumptions from his anxiety and nervous disposition. This showed in his face.

During the last few days of the long journey from the previous exploratory landing, briefings had taken place regularly to provide all TAKers with as much knowledge about the planet as possible. Many experiment results, graphs and photographic images provided by dozens of probes and landing droids that had been sent to this quadrant over the past few decades were revealed to the TAKers. Each probe sent back millions of bytes of information about all planets within range of its trajectory, many of which happened to be within this unique solar system. One planet in particular intrigued the Republic, due to its unique giant diamond shaped protrusion and its three equally sized moons. The 'Diamond Planet' as it had become rather lamely referred to, held the evidence of some incredible former race, but had no obvious signs of any intelligent inhabitants now. This kind of planet was like Sincha dust[4] to the universe's exploratory civilisations.

K's ship had already explored four of the eight planets identified as being potentially useful within this solar system. Some planets were investigated for their ores and precious stones, others for their fauna and flora. Very occasionally the planets were also inspected with a view to colonisation – an act that allowed the Republic to expand its viral-like spread across the galaxy even further. Not satisfied with plaguing their home planet with their extensive presence to the point of virtual self destruction, the Republic's race now felt it necessary to expand their reign of terror over less developed species of plant and animal life on planets all across the reachable universe.

TAK regiments were never given the full details of what use the planet had been provisionally short-listed for, in case it impaired or influenced their reports and feedback. The Republic's exploration council believed that if the TAK teams knew a planet was destined for colonisation, they might well view their investigations with that fact in mind. The council concluded that this could cause problems 'if the TAK investigators were to allow strange things like morals and ethics to taint their views, especially when there may be delicate existing races inhabiting the planet. And that just would not do. To have an undeveloped and weak race of beings, as yet undiscovered, ruin the Republic's plans would simply not be acceptable. To keep the TAK teams in the dark was far more logical.

K thought about this for a second, as he had done many times in the past. He recalled the cynics in the squadron who

---

[4] Sincha dust – one of the rarest and most expensive forms of precious stone in the universe – a single grain would buy you half a standard sized star.

often speculated that the real reason the Republic only gave them limited information was because the council didn't want the 'TAKers' to know when valuable ore and rocks were being searched for. Some investigative 'specimens' may accidentally get mislaid and the Republic might suddenly be faced with a great number of early retirements to Kaser6[5]. The cynics would continue; declaring that TAKers did not have morals and ethics anyway, so why would the council presume that menial things such as weak inhabitants of a planet influence the validity of their reports? This cut K to the core. He joined this elite scientific military squadron to do good for his race. For the first two years of his final rookie training he firmly believed that he was helping to mix and develop races and cultures to better the universe, to spread genes and to allow new and improved creations to take forward a mixed-race civilisation. After his third rookie training year, his colleagues had long since destroyed that rather naive and patriotic view, turning him into half the cynic they had already become. K was beginning to realise that the TAK teams were simply the sharp bit of a poisonous dart that was slowly spreading the plague of the Republic across the galaxy. He had recently started to realise that all they were doing was making the rich guys richer and spreading the disease, social problems and greed of the Republic further into the outer reaches of the universe. But he still had an obligation to at least try and make it right… didn't he?

K had planned his entire existence around doing this job from a very early age. This is all he had ever wanted to be. He had studied for five years to be highly qualified in investigative sciences. If truth were known, he was massively over qualified to be a TAKer. But K wanted to be the best TAKer in the Republic – studying new life forms and analysing the best ways his species could harness the riches of a planet without destroying its life-balance. He wanted to be a pioneering

---

[5] Kaser6 – a planet colonised and inhabited purely for the pursuit of ultimate and continuous hedonistic pleasure. Anyone found not to be at the peak of pleasure at all times would be relegated to the planet of Kaser5 – a planet dedicated to mere over indulgence.

scientist, not only for his own, personal sense of well being, or for his 'king and country'. He didn't even want to dedicate his life to this cause for his planet. He did it for his entire race – the Human race.

That feeling made K want to cry. He had dedicated his life, his mind and soul to doing good for the Human race. It had been his childhood dream to be a hero of a different kind – a hero of scientific investigation. He had been betrayed. Not by the fact that the job wasn't everything he expected it to be, but by the false image that was portrayed by his race to itself about what it was they were doing. It had always been promoted as being about the expansion of knowledge, learning and Human evolution. The reality was, just as it had been thousands of years ago when they were still investigating the various continents on their own home planet, that it was really just about greed and selfishness. Powerful humans just wanted to be more and more powerful, no matter what the cost – especially if the brunt of the cost was suffered by lesser creatures.

K no longer felt proud about the work he was doing. He felt frustrated that his years of hard work and study had been for a role that could be viewed (especially in the eyes of inhabitants of a short-listed planet) as destructive and malicious. But he did feel proud that his own personal intentions for being a TAKer were honest and good. K's motivations were not just based on patriotism to his race, they were loyal to his own values. That was very important to K. He was so proud of his reasons for wanting to be a TAKer that he had recently started to view it as everybody else's fault that the job was actually destructive and corrupt, not his. However, knowing this unavoidable fact made K feel very small and insignificant. In the grand scheme of things, he realised that he really didn't matter at all, and that he was unlikely to be able to make a difference. That upset him, because that's what he had always wanted: to make a difference and to really matter. He wanted to change the way the Republic viewed a new planet as a treasure trove to be ransacked, raped, pillaged and deserted.

But if K didn't do this job, some other poor git with a slight aptitude for science and handling small fire-arms, who had a childhood dream of making a difference to the human race, would end up sitting here. Then that unsuspecting fool would be sh*tting himself in this plummeting landing craft, suffering this anguish, excitement, pent-up frustration and nail-biting tension. That same poor git would be the one discovering new plants and animals, analysing their distant paths through an ever-evolving ecological journey. The poor bastard would be setting foot on planets where no human being had ever been before, instead of K.

Right now, K wouldn't change places with anyone! He was a mixed up mess of emotions and contradictory feelings.

A sudden heart-stopping jerk bought K's surroundings back to his attention in a single flash. This always happened, but it never ceased to scare the oxygen out of K. The atmosphere of all planets had a violent effect on the lander. After the deceptive motionlessness of smooth open space, the brutal jerking and shaking of the atmosphere always came as a bit of a shock to the system. The planet's natural defence system tried its hardest to incinerate the mechanical meteorite invader, heating its metal exterior to near melting point. The intense buffeting served as an excellent cocktail shaker, waking every sense in K's body and increasing his heart rate to a healthy one hundred and fifty beats per minute. All TAKers refer to this entry period as the 'happy hour'. It started the blood pumping as the nervous system was kicked into action, preparing itself to be ready for anything. K felt his blood rush around his body and head. His heart pumped hard as his glands worked overtime to release adrenalin and other stimulative hormones to create a fox-alert, cat-nimble, bear-powerful, human, ready to... investigate rocks, soil, flora samples and possibly even some animal cr*p, if he was really lucky!

That wasn't K's entire job though. He did have to be a genuine soldier too. True, they had the elite front-runners to secure the area and hold off any unexpected attacks from local beings, which rarely happened, but K still had to be aware of his surroundings and be prepared to use his weapons and hands in self-defence, if ever it came to that. It never had, much to K's relief, but he always wondered how he would fare. Would his many years of training jump immediately back into place when they were needed, making K a fighting machine to be reckoned with? Or would he curl up like a baby girl and start to suck his thumb in a panic stricken pool of his own waste products? K (and most of his colleagues, including his commanding officer) suspected the latter. K knew he was a lover, not a fighter. But in all honesty, he was pretty diabolical at the former as well!

Now past the outer reaches of the planet's atmospheric self-defence, the lander rocked and jolted slightly more sedately as it found its way through the uncharted sky, smashing through huge pockets of rising warm air, only to be suddenly released into a plummeting pocket of cold. The roller-coaster ride made K feel nauseous, but he knew he could not be sick. The embarrassment would be too much to bear. There were no windows where K sat, so he could not view the horizon to stop the stomach-churning motion of the craft making him turn green. He decided to look around the familiar surroundings of the craft's interior, concentrating on specific details in an attempt to take his mind off the pending reappearance of his last meal. Opposite him, strapped into heavy-set padded flight seats were a number of his colleagues. Each deep in their own thoughts, lost in their own worlds of memories, musings and mild anxieties. Each man dealt with the excitement and anticipation of the journey and task ahead in their own way. Some were contemplating what may be encountered on the ground, others were quietly thinking about what should have been said last night in that argument with their wives. The most cynical of all were wondering if the planet held as many riches as the Republic was banking on, and whether this would be the trip in which they would die a horrible and painful death.

Next to K sat Two-eye, so called because of his three eyes. Two-eye was a unique individual, with an exceptional background to his scientific education. When he was a youth, dabbling with experiments as a crazed yet advanced biologist, Two-eye and some of his equally twisted college friends at the Tower Hill University of Species Science had experimented with the growth and attachment of all manner of additional body parts onto their own bodies. Most of the operations proved successful, making Two-eye's social circle a strange array of self-mutilated advanced scientists with a droll – and simply not very funny – sense of humour. Two-eye's best friends, Forearms and Oneear, had never truly recovered from the trauma experienced by the social problems of their late friend Three-cock. Three, as he was lovingly referred to by his closest friends, and many of his open-minded mistresses, had died four weeks after recovering from one of the group's many experimental operations. Three's student peers speculated as to the cause of his sudden death. Some concluded that it was due to over-indulgence, others said that sustained heightened pleasure was as lethal as severe depression, and that's what got the better of him. The coroner declared that Three had died of a massive cardiac arrest, where his heart had virtually exploded. Three's body was found after a five-way, eight-hour sex session, his face contorted into the strangest, most perverse grin anyone had ever seen. The corpse's eyes were wide open and no facial features could be moved. It was as if rigor mortis had set in immediately – freezing his face and highly twisted body into a picture of rapturous ecstasy for eternity. At the funeral, the truly unique shape of Three-cock's coffin provided welcome light-hearted relief to what was otherwise a very sombre occasion.

K smiled as he recalled some of the wild, yet rather cruel stories Two-eye told of his student experiments. Visions of half goat, half pig creatures, an elongated horse with twelve legs, capable of carrying 20 people (a bit like an equestrian bus), and for some strange reason, an ant-leaf. Two-eye was extremely proud of that one as he claimed it as a social victory for ant society – a lazy ant could get away with not carrying any leaves as he had one permanently attached to his body. Two-eye had a very distorted view of life.

K's attention returned to the scene in front of him once again. He noticed a fellow TAKer looking in his direction. He smiled the half-hearted all-knowing smile one worker gives to another, the universe over – head rising up slightly with one eye-brow raised, which roughly translates to 'here we go again – business as usual'. The reply, as expected, was an equivalent wry smile and sharp upward head movement, acknowledging K, giving the automatic response of 'Yeah – same-old, same-old'.

As the landing craft descended through the buffeting air, K's ears began to pop as the atmospheric pressure changed. He continually pinched his nose and blew hard through his nasal passages to release the pressure in his head. Failure to do so at this speed of descent could mean that his ear-drums would implode. They had been falling through the bumpy atmosphere now for well over half an hour. By K's rough calculations, it would only be a few more minutes of shaking and shuddering before they made their final approach and landed on the surface of the undiscovered world. Then the excitement really started. Eventually, after what seemed like an age, the bone-crunching juddering subsided as the descent slowed. After a few more moments of smooth, decelerating flight, the lander came to a sudden jolting halt as the heavy weight of the vehicle impacted the planet's surface. The cacophony of noises and motion sensations gradually died down as the engines were switched off. The mandatory ten minute settling period went by, as slowly as ever, as the preliminary landing area checks were made by the cabin crew via a complex array of high-tech equipment which scanned the immediate surroundings for imminent danger. Very rarely was an exploration called off at this stage, as so many pre-landing investigations and tests were carried out from the distant safety of the mother ship.

Only once to K's knowledge had an expedition been aborted after landing, and that had been due to human error. The hugely embarrassing legend, although somewhat embellished by the story tellers over the years, told of a ground observation specialist who had called off the mission due to some rather strange ground chemical readings. The reading had shown a rather high level of AV359F2G, a known and extremely volatile bog gas that had been used many times throughout history in chemical warfare – highly effectively. As it happened, they later discovered that the lander had set down in an area largely inhabited by pig-like creatures. Through pure, unfortunate fluke, a part of the landers undercarriage had succeeded in pinning a live pig to the ground by its ear, whilst the environmental testing probe had entered the pig in a truly undignified manner. Much to the anguish of the hog, the investigative gadget proceeded to prod around its innards to reveal extremely high levels of dangerous gases which caused the panic-retreat– much to the pig's relief.

A simple and innocent mistake, but one which had repercussions for many a year and for many a TAKer. Never had the TAKer academy been so humiliated. For months after the incident was leaked to the general public, pigs of all types were found attached to a variety of poles. Live, stuffed, inflatable, it really didn't matter – the joke was the same. Some were placed atop flagpoles, others to trees, fence posts and lamp posts. There seemed to be no end to the inventive combinations a professional society could be ridiculed for accidentally sticking a probe into an alien pig's arse. Provided the equation consisted of a pig and a pole, anything went. For many months, these self-proclaimed practical jokers had a field day at the TAKer academy's expense. It had taken decades to live it down, and even to this day, at prestigious events and gala gatherings where the senior members of TAK staff were present, you could still make out distant pig-like squealing noises from the crowd.

The wait was over. The front-runners were given the order to stand, check their equipment and disembark. The doors opened, sending in a wave of warmth, light and smells that sent K's senses racing. The front-runners quickly exited the craft, shouting commands at one another. K's heart was still racing, but his adrenalin was no longer induced by the death-defying drop through the sky, or the possibility of a horrible demise from a massive native predator. It was the excited child in K, anxious to see the wonders of the new planet that drove his adrenalin release and pounding heart now. He wanted to get out there and discover new plant life, investigate new minerals, document new species of animal. He couldn't wait to understand their survival needs by prodding around in their faeces to see what they ate. The excitement was almost unbearable, but K had to keep it contained. If he didn't keep his enthusiasm covered under the shroud of his bored 'business as usual' exterior, he would stick out like a French kiss at a family reunion. That would have dire consequences, as K had discovered many times in the past. If you let-on you were still excited about the work you did, colleagues would allow you to do all of the terrible jobs. K assumed this was the same in any industry, the universe over, and therefore did not fight it. But he wanted to do everything within the vast array of interesting tasks that were required of TAKers, so he continued the charade that he was as disinterested as his colleagues. He often wondered if any other TAKers felt this way, but quickly discarded this line of thinking, as there would be no way of finding out without blowing his cover, and that could mean months of clearing up his colleagues' messes. It was simply too risky.

After a few more moments, the front-runners had established that the area was secure and safe for the TAKers to exit the craft. Orders were given to K and his fellow scientific pioneers to stand and prepare their instruments, weapons and collecting devices. K found it difficult to contain his excitement and let out a little yelp, like a small puppy about to go for 'walkies'. Coming to his senses quickly, he covered it up with a series of small coughs. It didn't matter how many times he faced this situation – it still filled him with anxious glee. Being amongst the first human beings to set foot on a planet to investigate its usefulness for future generations was a great privilege, and one that should not be taken lightly. The experience never lost its interest and novelty. Not for K, anyway.

Once TAK A4 had collectively secured their equipment, they were finally given the command to disembark. K walked down the short central aisle of the lander, following the single-file line of his fellow TAKers, and turned left at the doorway into the bright orange sunshine that streamed in through the large opening. K took in his first view of the warm new world, as he stepped out onto the sun-kissed metal gantry. Unlike his colleagues, he took a moment to bask in the awesome sight. It was beautiful. The sun was bright, the trees were huge and the sounds were incredible, varied and rich with life. Strange woops and whistles could be heard all around. It was alive with strange new species. All for K to discover – he mentally rubbed his hands with excited anticipation. A few seconds later he took the necessary few steps down the steep ramp to the thrilling new terra-firma, and again took a moment to look around. The wonderful new surroundings bombarded his impatient senses, as K struggled to keep his nonchalant exterior composed.

He smiled conspicuously at the prospect of investigating these new specimens of flora and fauna, logging their habitat and behaviour. He only wished he could go beyond the realms of ticking boxes on a multiple-choice questionnaire, to specify whether the creatures were passive or dangerous, edible or poisonous, four legs or two. But that was the unfortunate mundane aspect of his job. All jobs have to have a boring part to them, and this restrictive practice was K's.

Chapter 2

The Stirring

The small mechanical prison stirred. A number of its tiny lights, barely visible to the naked eye, started to flash and flicker. It felt the presence of conscious, animated thought. It had been dormant for ten thousand years, but now the time had come for it to start replenishing its power. It was running low on many reserves and detected the presence of greed. Danger was therefore imminent. The prison began its preparations to ensure The Knowledge remained locked within its complex electromechanical labyrinth. The tiny Alcatraz had been designed to survive for many millennia without requiring supplementary power, but there was an excellent opportunity to recharge its depleted energy, so it decided to take it.

TAK A4 had deliberately landed two hundred miles away from the giant mystery object that dominated the planets' sky-line. The purpose of A4's expedition was to investigate flora and fauna, not to wonder in awe at the phenomenal engineering prowess of the previous residents. Other, more experienced geologists and social scientists had been dispatched to investigate that colossal monument to a former race.

Dyla's team had been assigned a segment of land four miles away from the landing zone. It was their task to investigate life within the allocated sector, the results of which would be amalgamated with all other teams' results to form an overall view of this area of the new world. This in turn would be added to the results of the other TAK teams to form a view of the planet as a whole.

After receiving the preliminary speeches from their superiors about 'being careful out there' the pre-assigned TAK A4 sub-teams, each consisting of three men, picked up their allocated equipment and formed themselves into small mumbling groups. Gradually each team disappeared into the thick forest around the landing zone clearing to find their allotted piece of land.

Dyla and his two subordinates set off on one of the small land vehicles assigned to such journeys. The vehicle was less of a mode of transport than a test of endurance. It consisted of a central anti-gravitational device, powered by a noisy rattling motor, which screamed its continuous complaint at having to carry such a heavy load. Four very uncomfortable threadbare seats punctuated the corners of the small square craft. They had no padding left in them and had obviously been designed for the most distorted and mutated bottom anyone could ever imagine. As with the majority of work vehicles, it had only been designed to be tolerated for the first few seconds of use. The rest of the painful experience was used to remind you that you were using work property during work time to carry out work related activities and that you certainly shouldn't be enjoying it.

K didn't feel the pain quite as much as his two colleagues, despite their advantage in the padding department. K's buttocks were filled with a racing concoction of rushing blood, excitement and adrenalin, which made for a comfortable alternative to the non-existent stuffing on the seat. Jay-jay and Dyla felt the vehicle's masochistic design for every god-forsaken metre of the journey. This was all old-hat to them. Nothing new. Except that 'nothing new' in this job actually meant that everything was new and as yet undiscovered by human beings. Just the same old new stuff. They were used to being surrounded by the strange, the weird and the wonderful. Their excitement and enthusiasm had not completely subsided over the years, however, as each expedition had its interesting moments. There was one particular occasion that had been recalled over many a drunken evening, where one of Jay-jay's colleagues had been eaten alive right in front of him by a giant eggplant. It was an amazing sight, and one that always made Jay-jay chuckle. He especially remembered the way the plant spat out the man's shoes after digesting his body, in the satirical manner described by unoriginal novelists of poor second-hand comedy for many years. He recalled nearly wetting himself when that happened.

41

The journey, in spite of its continuing agony, offered breathtaking views of forests, mountains, waterfalls, valleys and a beautiful orange-blue sky. The overall effect of the stunning countryside, was that of a montage of greens, blues, pinks, reds, golds and yellows, all mixing to provide a huge undulating and unrealistically picturesque environment. It was straight out of a fairy tale scene of old. K took in the captivating surroundings, whilst his colleagues chatted and joked about other members of the A4 team, oblivious to the stunning backdrop.

Eventually the trio arrived at their sector. Jay-jay stopped the vehicle, and brought its noisy engine to a clattering halt. The relative silence was a welcome break from the constant rattling of the poorly maintained vehicle. It took a few moments for K's ears to return to normal, after the four-mile journey of constant eardrum abuse. The ringing slowly subsided, and K became increasingly aware of the many wonderful noises around him, just as he had been when he first stepped out of the landing craft. Unidentified animals of all shapes and sizes were chatting, squawking and chirping all around him. To K it was a symphony of nature, a wonder of evolution, enchanted music to his naturalist ears. To Dyla it was a minor bloody annoyance. And Jay-jay's opinion was quickly summed up when he bellowed into the surrounding undergrowth "Shut-up!" He was truly a man of few words. But when he did speak, he usually did so with a complete lack of grace and elegance. He gave the impression of being completely classless – not in the form of him being able to seamlessly transcend the multi-layered social levels of society… more that he simply had no class whatsoever. It would be insulting to sewage and sludge to pigeon-hole him as gutter-trash!

After a few commands had been blurted by Dyla to his two lower ranking officers, the trio separated, safe in the knowledge that they would only be a few seconds away from each other, should anything untoward happen. They had always been trained to remain within one hundred metres of their colleagues to ensure that each member of the team was able to come to the rapid aid of a colleague, should he get into trouble. This way, even if the situation was unsalvageable (i.e. it was too late to stop the team mate from being demoted to the ranks of 'unfortunate victim'), at least the colleague would witness the event and know what not to do in future. Such information would then be communicated to the remainder of the ground forces so that the victim's life was not lost in vain. That was the principle behind the ruling, anyway. In practice, when your team mates are Dyla and Jay-jay, it might not work quite the same way. K knew that a blood-curdling scream would be unlikely to get a raised eye-brow from a less than enthusiastic Jay-jay, who would no doubt saunter over, just in time to see his colleague's feet disappear into some giant creature's mouth. Dyla on the other hand had slightly more work ethic and coupled with the responsibility of a small amount of superiority on his side, he would be far quicker to respond. The chances are, he might even get there in time to witness the bowels being chewed. It really depended on the depth of his slumber at the time of the incident.

Once in their designated positions, work began. K studied the flora around him, delicately attempting to understand the plants without disturbing their ongoing life-long activities. He knew that he took a great deal more care than his colleagues, who were quite happy to disturb as much local life as it took to get their work done as quickly as possible so that the obligatory nap could take place after a swig or two of the mildly hallucinogenic Cagnaf Juice. Each member of Dyla's team gradually worked their way back to where the trio had left their land cruiser. Every metre offered a new and interesting sight (for K at least) and a new challenge of identification…which box should he tick on his multiple choice questionnaire about this particular plant? Despite his nurtured cynicism, which had grown significantly in recent months since he had been working with Jay-jay and Dyla, K enjoyed what he was doing. He loved looking at new plants and creatures, never knowing whether they were harmless or deadly. He loved the excitement of what the new life forms he came across were capable of. The unexpected was always exhilarating and this job offered an everlasting over-dose of the unknown. Often, the cutest little creatures were the most dangerous, whilst the huge menacing looking beasts were the most friendly, docile animals imaginable. He truly appreciated beauty and form in every living thing, no matter how capable the object might be at tearing him limb from limb, or poisoning his body into a twisted heap of tortured pain. It was all part of the colourful tapestry that is 'life', thought K.

K's standard issue protective clothing was changing colour around the knees and ankles, where various plants rubbed against the specially designed, chemically reactive material. The colour depicted what effect the substance would have on a human's skin, should it come into direct contact. Various colours illustrated the many levels of pain that would be experienced. Bright red indicated that the chemical was capable of killing an average human male, whereas pinks would indicate various levels of agony. By the time the other end of the colour spectrum was reached, light blues and greens showed side effects no more serious than occasional allergic reactions such as hay fever. The colours on K's clothing were a mixture of soft yellows, blues and lilacs, making him look like a psychedelic hippy from ancient history, whilst indicating that the best defence the plants here had was to cause a slight rash.

The planet felt ideal. It seemed to have no flaws. It felt like a wonderful place to colonise. If asked, K would happily become a member of a ground team who would remain here to conduct extended experiments after the TAK team were rounded up and shipped to the next planet short-listed to be violated. But K knew that was unlikely. He was still very excited about the prospect of getting closer to the massive up-turned pyramid, as were all of the TAKers who were exploring this solar system. Even the most cynical and experienced TAKers were openly admitting that the sight of the monolithic structure was the most awesome they had ever seen. K stood up and looked up through the branches and leaves of the nearby trees to see the faint outline of The Chun rising up into the sky and far beyond the planet's atmosphere. He knew the site from space must be even more breathtaking, but so far he had not had a chance to see it, mainly due to the windowless design of the landing craft on which they were bundled to the planet's surface, very soon after the mother ship had arrived.

His attention was suddenly jerked back to his local surroundings by Jay-jay's shouting in the near distance, "'Ere, Dyla, look what I've found!"

Despite not being invited, K decided to see what his work-shy colleague had discovered and ran the short distance through the colourful undergrowth, treading carefully so as not to damage any delicate ground plants, to where his two colleagues stood in mildly confused contemplation. Standing above the lip of a fist-sized hole in the ground, his two colleagues stared with squinting eyes at something in Jay-jay's heavily gloved hand. Around their feet was a spattering of earth, where Jay-jay had carelessly discarded the contents of the hole. K moved his gaze to the tiny object in his colleague's palm. It was less than a millimetre in diameter, but looked electronic and mechanical in design.

"What d'ya think it is?" asked Jay-jay.

"Dunno," replied Dyla, "It looks like a memory chip of some kind. It's probably nothing, but we had better catalogue it, just in case." Dyla looked up and saw that K had come over to join them. "Here, make yourself useful and document this." K knew that he had just been the victim of the effects of rank. Dyla was the leader of this small and rather pathetic little team, and Jay-jay was his lazy, good-for-nothing friend. Combine this with K's youthful enthusiasm for his job (despite his attempts to camouflage it), and it created the perfect recipe for Dyla and Jay-jay to take advantage of K at every opportunity. No matter what the job, no matter how dirty or disgusting, K got it. It was a situation that all three of the men were happy with. K got to do his job, his way, which was far more rewarding than watching the ham-fisted efforts of his two colleagues, who were both designed more for their destructive powers than their investigative ones. And Dyla and Jay-jay got to sit around chatting, whilst drinking and smoking their mildly hallucinogenic, but legal, drugs.

K walked back to the land cruiser, delicately turning the tiny object over in his fingers, examining every side of the miniature piece of unknown technology. At one stage he thought he saw a tiny light blink on, but that would be impossible. This planet had been uninhabited by a technically advanced race for thousands of years according to the Republic's preliminary reports. It must have simply been the sun reflecting off one of its tiny components. Yes, that had to be it.

Something in K's mind made him nervous. This object did not fit here. Somehow it did not belong. But then again, neither did he.

Chapter 3

The Cell

The tiny machine prepared itself for a manoeuvre it had not attempted before. A manoeuvre that would allow it to rejuvenate its power supplies and best protect the secret of its sole prisoner. Despite its power levels still being over quarter full, there were things occurring which meant it had to raise its self-protection status to that of level 4. The explosions and screams that it had registered beyond the thick walls of cloth in which it was now imprisoned meant there was a level of panic in the air that could not be ignored. The cell had to prepare itself for the possibility that it may have to gradually escalate its self-protection level through three and two, and finally to the point at which thermo-gravi-nuclear melt-down was instigated. And that took a great deal of power. It had to be prepared, whilst all the time learning how to survive. That's what it was programmed to do.

The giant walls of the cell's new environment pushed against both sides of the device as the entire world shook and swayed in an irregular fashion. The new surroundings were a great deal less glamorous than the idolised position of godliness it had obtained over the hundreds of years it was in the company of the insect race. The tiny electronic unit bounced around uncontrollably, bashing into large pieces of fluff and grit that had accumulated in the neglected cloth cavern. It must stabilise itself before attempting the delicate operation. Two minute arms with sharp pincers extended from either side of the tiny machine. Each clamped themselves onto the white fabric wall. A third arm extended from the centre, revealing a sharp, rotating cutting instrument at its end. The cell started the process that would enable its escape from the cloth cavern. Pieces of the prison wall gradually began to give way to the small, but incredibly sharp instrument that sliced away at the microscopic layers of the cloth. All the while, the wall moved and jerked as the environment was thrown this way and that by what ever was going on outside. The explosions and strange zapping noises

47

continued to be monitored by the object's listening devices, and were diagnosed and catalogued in a continuous effort to analyse the current situation and the chances of self-preservation. Level 4 should suffice – for the time being at least.

Eventually, the cavern wall had been successfully dissected, and a neat opening, big enough for the unit to pass through, was being held open by its two pincers. Beyond the cavity was another wall, of a very different type. This was the target of the device's self-preservation manoeuvre. Luckily the environment had stopped its erratic movements and was now stationary, making the next operation much easier to perform. The unit pulled itself forward, closer to the light-tan, pitted surface. A number of cylindrical dark brown branch-like protrusions allowed excellent anchorage for the machine to ensure it was not moved during the next phase of the ambitious project. The central extended cutting arm began its dissection once more. After a few moments of precise, careful slicing, a huge, thick globule of red jelly-like substance began to extrude from the depths of whatever lay behind the tan wall. Though the substance was increasing in size and fluidity, the device continued un-phased. It was imperative that it reach its ultimate goal. Eventually, the opening behind the think globule of dark red jelly was large enough to squeeze itself through. Carefully the electronic device began the difficult task of forcing its tiny form through the jelly-filled gap into the dark mass that filled the space on the other side of the pitted tan exterior. Moist blackness was all that awaited its arrival.

Once inside, the cell turned its attention to carefully repairing the damage to the outer wall. It was made of a malleable substance that would best be repaired with a needle and thread. But all the device had to complete its task was a form of high-bonding glue, which it strategically placed at various points along the edge of the incision, and then using its two strong pincer arms, began to force the opening shut again. Soon the bonding glue had taken hold and the device was happy that the evidence of its 'breaking and entering' had been minimised.

The darkness enveloped the device as it found itself in a warm, wet and very cramped pitch-black environment. Soft, dense fibres pushed at it from all sides and the thick jelly-like substance, which now appeared to be more liquid, engulfed everything. The cell had been programmed to recognise this type of environment. Its journey to safety, however, was far from over. In fact, it had barely begun. A long and arduous expedition must be completed before power could be restored and the device could allow itself to rest. Due to the increased dangers of the new environment, the device decided to be cautious and raised its alertness to protection level 3 – just in case.

Chapter 4

The Attack

K nearly jumped out of his skin as a massive noise took place behind him, far off in the distance. It was very loud and one that he recognised, but had not heard for a number of years. The last time he had heard such a noise was way back in his training years on Kajuk. What was it? He racked his brains. There, it happened again, only louder this time, and much closer. It was an unmistakable noise that seemed to initially consist of the extraction of all noise around you, before developing into a deafening boom that almost ruptured your ear-drums. More thunderous eruptions took place as shards of trees began to rain down all around K. But for some reason K's mind wouldn't function enough to tell him what it was. His brain cells had frozen. Billions of tiny charges of electricity whose job it was to race around K's head with various messages and instructions, all stopped dead in their tracks. Like an army of rabbits staring into the headlights of a giant oncoming vehicle, the noise had made K's brain momentarily redundant, frozen with adrenalin-induced fear. As quick as they simultaneously stopped, the mass of cells and electrical pulses suddenly came back to life... Every single one of them carrying the same message: RUN you idiot – RUN!

K launched himself into a sprint that any top one-hundred-metre athlete would have been proud of. His body leant forward at such an angle that most of his speed was derived by his legs trying as hard as they could to get back underneath K's torso. At least that's how the first few steps of the impressive sprint were. After that, gravity caught up with K and kindly informed him that it could not possibly allow him to cheat it any longer. K made contact with the soft ground, using his face to break the fall. He sprang to his feet as another of the unmistakable loud whooshing noises filled the air all around him. At this stage his sub-conscious mind had recalled exactly what the noise was and had decided to let K's conscious brain in on the secret. This rather risky decision would have one of two possible outcomes;

1) stop K dead in his tracks as adrenalin and other natural internal drugs overdosed his body with total fear, or; 2) propel him faster out of the noise's range than K could have ever wished for. K's mind was banking on the latter. It paid off. He found speed that a rocket strapped to his back would struggle to emulate. He ran like the wind. He had no idea where, but at this moment in time, that had no relevance. The important thing was that it was away from where the noise was coming from.

K still clutched the small electronic device between his thumb and forefinger. He had nearly dropped it, and as his colleague had said... it might be important. K doubted it, after all, it was found by someone who cared less about his job than a pig cares about soap. He rammed it into his right pocket, hardly breaking his phenomenal sprinting stride.

Laser-cannon fire! Thought K, as the information slowly filtered through his brain cells (half of his brain's electrical pulses were reluctant to carry the message as they were not in favour of the decision to inform K of the whole truth and believed that the conscious mind shouldn't be controlled as an equal rights democracy with each pulse getting a vote on all key issues). A second wave of panic finally set in. This wasn't friendly cannon fire, thought K, it was someone else's! (Not that 'friendly' cannon fire would have made any difference to K's pace – after all, death by cannon fire is not made any less terminal by it being a colleague's mistake). But K's mind had protected him from the truth for a moment, in case the noise was simply the actions of his trigger-happy (and slightly inebriated) colleagues. His mind wanted to be certain that K's only reaction to the noise would be to run away from it as fast as possible. Despite not being the bravest man in the universe, K was far too caring to leave his colleagues behind in a situation that sounded like they needed help to stop themselves from behaving like drunken fools and hurting each other. But the majority of cells in K's body had unanimously voted for a fleeing tactic (much to the annoyance of the more totalitarian electrical pulses), and K really had no choice but to go along with it.

He ran as fast as he could, back to the land cruiser. Once there, he jumped onto the small vehicle and tried to start it up by pressing the green button. Then he tried again. And again. His panic was getting worse, he almost couldn't see any more as his eyes began to flood with salty water and adrenalin began to rush his nervous system. A huge bolt of bright light flashed past his head into a group of trees a few hundred feet past his present location. Milliseconds later came the impact, followed by a huge explosion and a shower of bark, wood shavings and leaves. K found himself on the floor, a few metres away from the now over-turned land cruiser. He nearly burst into tears with fear, and to make things slightly worse, he felt a sharp pain in his right thigh, like a heavy-handed booster injection. It made him grimace momentarily. He guessed he must have been hit by a piece of shrapnel from the explosion. But he had bigger things to worry about right now, like getting back to the landing craft to warn the others about the attack. Warn the others? Warn the others! What was he thinking, they could hear the massive explosions and laser cannon fire as easily as he could, he needed to get back to the landing craft to escape and to stay alive – screw warning the others!

Another near miss occurred flipping the scarred land cruiser right side up. K jumped aboard, started the engine successfully and sped away from the ensuing attack. He accelerated at maximum rate towards where he believed the lander would be. Dodging trees and bushes at break-neck speed, barely staying on board the vehicle as it jerked from left to right through the undergrowth.

Unfortunately, in between dodging trees and making bodily adjustments to keep from falling off the speeding contraption, he found a few moments to contemplate the recent events. It didn't help – it simply confused and panicked him even more. How was this possible? All relevant preliminary checks had been carried out before they were even in orbit around the unique planet. It was an uncharted solar system, by all known interstellar races and was free of all signs of advanced civilisation. There was nothing down here but flora and fauna – at least, that's what their highly sophisticated instrumentation had told them. Maybe this was a race as yet unknown to the Republic. Maybe they had some special device that meant they couldn't be detected. Maybe they were not alive by humanoid standards at all, maybe they existed outside the confines of what humans called 'life'. Maybe... K made a conscious decision to stop contemplating all such unhelpful thoughts, as a couple of near misses with large examples of native flora highlighted the need for him to stop his mind wandering off on tangents. He had never been a strong multi-tasker, so he decided to concentrate on the priority one task – staying alive! And right now that consisted of one thing – getting back to his colleagues and the safety of the heavily armoured landing craft.

The loud whooshes of the cannon fire, and the deafening explosions they created seemed to be a little further away now. K relaxed enough to take a well-deserved breath, but not enough to release his buttocks' vice-like grip on the seat of his overalls. He slowed down a little to try to get his bearings. Having not driven the land cruiser to their designated investigation sector, K had paid little attention to the direction they had taken. He was far too busy on the outbound journey admiring the beautiful surroundings to notice where he was going. He had observed the stunning flowers, the towering trees and the small creatures that scurried around in the undergrowth, he had even noted the fluttering birds and scavenging insects, but he had not paid attention to the route. Now he wished he had. As he sped through the trees and occasional clearings, he looked around for sights that he might recognise. The problem was; he thought he recognised everything. All the trees, every clearing, each and every bush suddenly looked the same. Very quickly, K began to feel incredibly lonely. More alone and scared than before. Except that time when he first went to Kinder1, when his mother had dropped him off at the huge building and he had to talk to strange new people and find his own way to the toilets. But this was much worse than that, despite the vivid memory of hysterical tears. 'Oh my god!' thought K. Is that my life flashing before my eyes? Isn't that what happens before you die? A new wave of panic engulfed K's conscious mind.

Finally, he remembered the huge upturned pyramid, which hung in the sky hundreds of miles away, far beyond the horizon, was on their left as they travelled to their designated sector. That meant, if he kept it directly on his right, he would be heading in roughly the right direction. He stopped the vehicle and peered through the trees, trying to see the faint outline of the colossal hanging rock. There, there it was. K's face illuminated with a small spark of hope. The lander must be this way, thought K, as he moved his attention to the thick forest slightly to his left. He had been going more or less in the right direction. As he viewed his surroundings momentarily, a familiar noise attracted his attention. It was coming from the forest directly in front of him. The deep rumbling was recognisable to K through his experiences of previous planetary investigations over the years. However, it was very slightly different this time, in one very distinct and gut-wrenching detail. Usually K would experience the noise from the INSIDE! "Oh god no. No. No, no, no. Please no!"

His heart sank even deeper when he saw the slowly rising lander craft clear the trees in front of him. He was so close to where it was situated, and yet it was taking off in front of him. He was going to be left behind. He did what any self respecting, panic-stricken castaway would do, he yelled and screamed at the thundering craft as it rose high above the trees. "Help! Don't leave me here! Help me! Come back you bastards!" K waved his arms and screamed in blinding fear for his life. He knew they couldn't hear him, but he had to try. He was so scared. Tears streamed down his cheeks, creating small canals of clear pale skin between the fields of dust and mud that had gathered on his panic-stricken face over the past few minutes. The craft turned in mid air, preparing itself to accelerate through the atmosphere and into the skies above. K would give anything to be on that ship. It would have saved his life. But now he was all alone and was bound to die.

The lander's engines roared as it increased its thrust into space, and just as its momentum was about to speed it to safety, a huge bolt of light streamed through the air from the forest behind K. The lander exploded into a billion pieces, instantly swapping its solid shape for a more modest cloud-like design.

K nearly threw up on the spot at the sight of the explosion. His feelings were instantly torn between extreme and sudden relief at not being on the lander (only seconds after being willing to sell his sole to the devil to be one of its passengers), and massive sorrow at the knowledge that some of his colleagues had just been turned into rain. K sank even further into a state of stranded depression as he realised his chances of survival now were only marginally higher than those of his colleagues who had just been vaporised. What was he to do? He was not cut out for this sort of thing. He was a nervous wreck when it came to being in a room of colleagues he didn't know very well, let alone being stranded on an uncharted planet under foreign laser-cannon fire!

A deep, ground-shaking trundling noise dragged K's thoughts, kicking and screaming back to harsh reality. It was coming from the forest behind him, from where the lightning bolt had been fired into the landing craft. K knew he must flee again. But where to? Who cares, he thought – he simply had to get out of here. This natural subconscious reactive thought was abruptly opposed by the conscious side of his brain. 'First we need a plan' thought his conscious brain. 'No we don't, we just need to get the hell out of here you blithering idiot, now move!' Conscious thought stepped in once again and froze K to the spot. 'A plan, if you please' it insisted. K's subconscious mind gave up and retired to the recesses of K's mind – deciding to flick through a few of his life experiences, as it felt sure this would probably be the last chance it got to do so.

K looked up. Above the tree tops he once again saw the distant silhouette of The Chun. Nearly two-hundred miles away, it was the only thing K recognised. The only land-mark he could see. He knew that TAKA3 and A6 were investigating that area and there was a good possibility they were still there. K may even be a hero, if he managed to get word to them in time. He might be able to save their lives as well as his own. K decided to head for the massive object, in the hope that the other TAK teams were still on the ground there, investigating the mysterious structure, oblivious to the incidents that had taken place here. As the deep rumbling noise got closer, K's subconscious thoughts finished flicking through his life history and concluded that there really wasn't enough interesting stuff in there to allow K to die just yet. "Get out of here now" he shouted to himself out loud before starting the land cruiser and speeding off into the trees.

As K sat atop the noisy craft, dodging trees at high speed, images of Dyla and Jay-jay sprung to mind. "Oh my God, I deserted them" thought K out loud. I took the land-cruiser and left them stranded. Guilt ran through every cell in his body (well, every cell except one).

Whilst re-running the manic events over and over in his mind, K reached two conclusions. Number 1: They must have both been killed by the huge explosion that flipped the land-cruiser over the first time. Number 2: The quicker K got help from the other TAK teams, the sooner they could send out a search party to save his two colleagues, if they were still alive.

There was a third conclusion that K's mind head reached, but it was too awful to admit to. He knew that it existed though and it proved a bitter pill to swallow: Neither Dyla, nor Jay-jay would think twice about leaving K behind. Although that fact shouldn't make it any easier to desert them, somehow it did.

Chapter 5

The Escape

Nothing but trees. Trees in every direction. Even here, half way up a small mountain, there were trees everywhere. K had been lucky to find a clearing that allowed him an unspoilt view of the surrounding countryside all the way to the massive pyramid in the distance. But it didn't help him plan a safe route to the colossal structure as all around him were trees. The only things that broke the monotony of the forest that lay before him were the occasional small clearing, a large river, and specific areas of even more densely populated forest (populated by trees, that is). K was a big fan of flora, but even he was beginning to wish there was less of it right now. It wasn't helping visualise a successful outcome to his quest to be saved by the remaining TAK teams at the base of the monolithic upturned pyramid.

K listened intently. He couldn't hear the cannon fire anymore, nor could he hear the deep rumbling noises made by the vehicles that presumably carried the highly destructive cannons. He still had not seen any of his assailants, but he figured it was a pretty safe bet they weren't far away. They had destroyed his landing party and left him stranded and all alone. Uh-oh, here come the water works again, thought K. I must remember to stop thinking about all my colleagues being killed and me being left all alone on this strange planet. It simply upsets me and makes things worse. A tear ran down K's face as he forced a smile onto his red and blotchy exterior, in the hope that his interior would follow suit and allow him to be more positive about his possible fate. Briefly, he remembered one of his teachers at college, who always had a very positive outlook on life. The scholar's face appeared in K's mind and spoke to him briefly, reminding K of the one thing he tried to drum into his young student's mind from the very first day he met him; "You are the sum of your own thoughts" he had preached, "think positive thoughts and your outcome will be positive. Think negative thoughts and you will get exactly what you think you will." He always thought Jack was a bit mad, as did everyone else at the college, but that was mainly due to the fact that Jack was always smiling – no matter what was going on. This meant that society presumed that Jack was a cup and saucer short of a tea set. But what it probably meant was that he was right. This was the first time K had thought about Jack since leaving the college. Positive mental attitude was the new order of the day. Right, thought K, I am simply going to head off in that direction (he nodded towards the distant giant object) and I will get there in good time, without incident. K didn't believe these thoughts for a second, but he realised that they were making him feel better already, so he went with the flow.

He felt a little safer as the noise of the forest seemed to have returned to normal. Chirps, squeaks and howls once again filled the air, giving K the reassurance that he so desperately needed. His journey to The Chun, far off in the distance would no doubt be an arduous one, which would take many hours. He prepared himself mentally for the quest ahead, reminding himself that he needed to remain vigilant. But all the time, with a new positive twist to his thoughts. No longer was the unknown enemy a risk that could possibly mean agonising death, but instead, merely an acknowledged challenge that K would successfully avoid.

A sharp tickle deep inside his thigh caught his attention and reminded him that he had suffered an injury during the first explosion. Before returning to the land cruiser to continue his journey, he decided to take a look. He didn't want to die of tetanus, after all the other challenges and dangers he had faced so far – that would be embarrassing! He undid his trousers and pulled them down enough to reveal the offending area on his upper right thigh. But instead of seeing what he expected to see – a small cut or burn from some flying splinters or debris from the explosion that had very nearly vaporised him – he witnessed the impossible. A tiny scar had appeared where he had first felt the pain less than an hour ago. But the scar appeared to have been healed for years. He prodded the small dark line, which was less than half the width of his finger. There was no pain.

That was impossible. There was no way his skin could have healed in that short space of time, and he knew that he did not have a scar there before – he'd always been so proud of his soft unblemished skin. After a few moments of thought, K decided that there must be something in the air that allowed human flesh to heal at massively accelerated rates. That must be it – there was no other explanation. This gave him a little hope for the future, as it made him realise that if he did get injured on his long journey, he was unlikely to bleed to death as his flesh could obviously heal very quickly on this planet. Things were looking up already! He pulled his trousers up and prepared to begin his long journey.

But before he had finished doing up his belt, a tingling inside his hip twinged at his subconscious mind. He raised his upper garments to check the area near his right hip bone. Maybe he had been hit by a second fragment during his escape. No, there were no abrasions, scars or marks of any kind. Besides, the twinge felt as though it was coming from far below the surface of his skin. He had no explanation, and no choice but to ignore it, so he put it down to a muscular twitch and decided to make haste. Sitting here worrying about unexplained twinges was likely to get him killed. Time was of the essence, so he started the land cruiser and headed off down the side of the mountain in the direction of The Chun, carefully picking his way between the giant trees and thick undergrowth. It was going to take him hours, possibly even days.

Chapter 6

The Journey

The journey was a slow one. The device was effectively blind as it did not have any imaging equipment. Even if it did have it would not have been aided at all by the gift of sight in this dark, claustrophobic environment. It was pitch black. The cell navigated using pre-programmed biology software and a lot improvisation. Much of the information in the device's memory banks did not tally with what it was experiencing. The journey was never going to be a simple one, but had been further complicated by a lack of biological knowledge. The device had been programmed to learn and adapt to almost any environment and so it concluded that its current situation did not require any increase in its self preservation security level. In fact, the noises from outside had ceased for a significant period of time now, which meant it could reduce its level of awareness back to level four.

It dragged itself forward, one tiny step at a time, cutting and slicing its way through the cramped, hot and wet total darkness, mending any significant damage it caused behind itself with the healing glue. The next incision into the fleshy darkness had bought the unsuspecting unit to a rock hard wall. It tried a number of incisions, but the white rock-like smooth surface was not going to give way as easily as the surrounding fleshy substance. It would have to travel around this obstacle, despite not computing that it should even be there. As far as the device was concerned, it should have been going far enough to the right of this object to avoid it. But as it had already admitted to itself, this anatomy was not as it had been programmed to expect.

After a long period of diverted cutting and slicing, the mechanised unit came to a wall of a different consistency. This was right. This meant it was back on track and that the mission was going according to plan – well almost according to plan. Other than everything being different to the pre-programmed memory the cell had of all the creatures of Vacchion, things were fine. It made slight adjustments to its calculations and, as was its designed intention, learned each lesson as it continued its path. The next incisions would be far more delicate than those before. This operation must be done very carefully, and must be repaired even more vigilantly than all previous incisions. Things were about to get far more exciting, at least they would have been, if the mechanical device of pure logic had any concept of excitement. After slicing through the gristly wall, the opening revealed a large cavernous area on the other side. A huge tube-like cavern that twisted into the distance in both directions. There was much more space here, which should make movement a great deal quicker and easier for a while. This was important as energy reserves were being depleted fast. The device had happily existed for thousands of years only needing to use the bare minimum of its energy reserves, and yet in the last two hours it had managed to use a fifteen percent of its battery power. The opening was made large enough for the tiny device to clamber through, and it did so, making sure to hold tightly onto the side of the tubular wall. Far below, a yellowy sludgy pool bubbled and slopped at the sides of the cavern. Movement here seemed to be much more exaggerated than in the close confines of the muscly flesh from where it had emerged. The bursting bubbles of thick liquid threw up huge pieces of debris into the acrid air of the cavern, each capable of damaging the device if direct contact were made. It was imperative that the cell stay well away from the acidic liquid below and from any other ominous looking objects. It knew it was a foreign body in this environment and was therefore fair game. It must stay vigilant.

The device carefully repaired the opening it had created using the high-bonding glue and then took a moment to gain its bearings before clambering its way along the wall and ceiling of the vast twisty cavern. The device used all of its sensors to constantly detect flying objects thrown from the acid pool below, predicting their likely trajectory and taking evasive actions to avoid collisions. A number of near misses had occurred but no damage had as yet been sustained. It was slow going, as the path was constantly blocked by natural activity all around. Another hour had passed and the journey was about to get far more dangerous. Although the device had a great many defence mechanisms up its proverbial sleeves, it had been programmed to be ultimately respectful to any host, and would therefore only use its tiny arsenal in the most desperate of situations. Besides, it needed this vessel to stay alive, if it was to replenish its power supplies. Then it would be able to leave and continue its sole responsibility to protect the secret of its single prisoner for eternity.

The next twist in the cavern led to a huge opening, much more space here than any other part of the journey so far. But the device detected the danger instantly and it knew it had been spotted. The cavern was host to some of the most dangerous and unforgiving organisms known to the universe, all of which were heading towards the cell, with one sole aim: to destroy it. Hundreds of small clumps of white fleshy jelly started to make their way towards the cell, hell-bent on its total biochemical break-down. The tiny prison cell knew from its programming that it had only one choice of action before it had to adopt protection level 1 – thermonuclear melt-down – resulting in the demise of everything within a very large radius of itself, and that was to adopt protection level 2! It did so, which seemed to kick in some additional programmes that had as yet remained dormant. Reserve memory and processing power joined the fight for survival, revealing to the device that its best chance of escape was up, across the ceiling of the massive cavern and towards an opening near the centre of the roof of the hostile cave.

It fired a microscopic grappling hook up into the fleshy red ceiling of the cavern, and then started its miniature winch system, pulling itself away from the wall and up into the air of the cave. It let go of the walls just in time, as thousands of white organisms reached the spot where the device briefly resided and were busy attacking each other in the empty space. It took a few seconds for them to realise the alien object was no longer there, by which time, the device had reached the roof of the cavern. It detached its grappling hook from the flesh and begun its journey across the ceiling, towards the opening using its powerful, but tiny pincer arms. The device made note of all that had happened in its memory banks, hoping that the information need never be used again. If it was possible for an electronic device to feel relief, the cell felt it right now.

Chapter 7

The Republic

"What the hell happened down there?" screamed the Right-tenant.

"We're not sure, Sir," whimpered the sergeant in charge of the investigation. He knew what was about to happen. Employees throughout the universe had experienced the tone of phrase that was about to occur. It started with anger and rapidly quietened into a 'heads-are-going-to-roll-for-this' type of tone, which had such an air about it that all subordinates within earshot would know there was an unspoken, yet distinctly obvious follow-up message; 'and it isn't going to be mine!'

"Were all precautionary procedures followed properly before disembarkation?"

"Yes Sir... you oversaw the procedure yourself from up here," replied the sergeant with a self-satisfying grin buried deep within himself. He didn't have a self-destructive death-wish – he wasn't going to be outwardly smug to the leader of their three year expedition no matter how misdirected or stupid his management seemed. The last thing he wanted was to be demoted to TAK team leader, after all, that could mean the end of his days, especially judging by the recent fatalities on the planet's surface.

"How many men were in the TAKA4 team?"

"38, Sir."

"All dead?"

"We presume so Sir, although they were spread out over quite a large area." The sergeant grimaced before he gave the next piece of information, "We can only assume that all members of TAKA4 were on board before the lander took off, Sir." Republic orders dictated that no lander craft was allowed to leave a planet's surface until all team members were accounted for. That would mean, in theory that all personnel would have to have either been on board the ship, or accounted for as confirmed dead before the craft could take off. "Republic orders." The sergeant pointed out.

"What do you mean, we have to assume?"

"Well, during the few moments of contact we had with the TAKA4 computer, there were eight men that didn't register as being on the craft when it launched, but that could be a sensor error." Again he whimpered, in fear of his rank.

"Are you telling me that the A4 team pilot may have taken off without all of his team?" bellowed the rather large Right-tenant, "that would be cowardice, and I do not suffer cowards in my task force, Sergeant."

"No Sir, I know, Sir." He replied delicately, "that's why I am assuming that all eight missing men were killed on the ground, or that the craft had a sensor malfunction. Either way, all the A4 team are dead Sir. I assure you."

"Good," commented the Right-tenant, then, realising what he had said, added, "I'm glad we sorted that out. No member of my operation would disobey Republic directives. Recall all remaining TAK teams and run a planetary diagnostic. We need to know what's down there, but I don't want to risk any more lives in the mean time." Momentarily, the Right-tenant gave the false impression that he cared about the people under his command, but the collective thought of the subordinates in the immediate vicinity quickly adjusted themselves back to reality, safe in the knowledge that the Right-tenant's rule was one of pure fear and terror, not one of mutual respect and understanding.

There was an awkward pause in the proceedings as the Right-tenant ran out of loaded questions to throw at his subordinates. He silently made his way towards the door of the control centre, mentally thumbing through a list of motivational team building messages in the filing system of his mind. He needed one that he could use to ensure his lesser team members were on their toes, whilst creating a sense of true team-work and common-goal mentality that would allow his commanders to get the most out of their troops. He paused as the automatic doors opened, briefly turning to face the room, all eyes turned to meet his, they all knew that their Right-tenant was about to depart with a message of morale-building wisdom that would leave them all in awe of his mastery of the situation. Finally, he chose his masterpiece of team-building knowledge: "Heads are going to roll for this," he said predictably.

The Right-tenant made his way through the open doors into the bright lights of the main corridor. The doors began to slide shut behind him. Everyone in the control room started to exhale a sigh of relief, but suddenly the doors opened again and twenty men breathed in as one. The Right-tenant leant in and added a superb gem of reaffirmed information about the Republic's hierarchical system, albeit very unoriginal... "and it isn't going be mine!"

Chapter 8

The Trees

As K continued his long trek through the forest toward the massive gravity-defying object hanging in the distant sky, he began to notice an ever-increasing uniformity to the pattern of trees and undergrowth around him. He had been travelling for hours now, too many hours for him to count, but his surroundings had definitely changed gradually in the last twenty miles or so. Too gradually for him to know exactly when it had started.

The clearings here appeared to be almost deliberate and were more frequent than before. Some of the dense areas of plants and trees seemed to be getting more and more cubic in their appearance too. He had been travelling past this increasing evidence of change for quite a while, but now was the first time it had become truly obvious to him. It was beginning to make him nervous. Plant life should not grow in such a uniform manner, it was not natural. He was loath to stop and investigate in case he uncovered a dangerous truth that had been playing on his subconscious mind for the last few miles. Was he heading unknowingly ever deeper into the enemy's territory? Was this the undetectable civilisation's home from whence his assailants had come? If so, they were doing an amazing job at retaining their stealth.

He knew he did not want to be here. But he also knew he didn't have a choice. Should he continue in this direction, into the increasing uniformity of the bushes and trees, which implied there was some sort of intervention into the growth patterns of the flora? He knew he was still at least seventy miles from The Chun. It had increased in size significantly, but its base still seemed way past the horizon. Should he turn back through the miles of planned plantation through which he had already passed or should he stop and investigate his surroundings in the hope that it might reveal an answer of some kind? Each option was as likely to get him killed as the next. There was a certain comfort in ignorance that allowed an abject coward like K to believe that all would be okay. But the trade-off of such ignorance was that every single shadow held within it a thousand and one hideous possibilities, and every tiny noise spelled out his possible imminent demise. So he concluded that he might as well die knowledgeable rather than ignorant. He decided to investigate one of the larger sections of undergrowth up ahead. He slowed the land cruiser, steering towards his chosen area of investigation. Gently he stopped the clattering engine and silently dismounted the vehicle, listening intently for any sound that would translate itself in his head as "run away". But nothing happened. Everything was still and calm. There was no breeze and the trees stood motionless. The gently reassuring noise of the local creatures going about their daily lives was the only thing to break the silence. Under foot was a dark green moss-like substance that gave the impression of walking on sponge.

He edged his way cautiously towards the side of the huge mass of grasses, bushes, trees and creepers that rose like a single solid wall in front of him to a height of around fifteen metres. The mass of plants was incredibly thick, like a floral barricade that ran almost perfectly straight in both directions from where K stood. It was as if it had been planted here purposely. He followed the foliage for a number of steps, to see if its unrelenting density eased up at any stage, but to his surprise and annoyance it was consistent. He walked along the straight wall, being sure to take notice of his surroundings frequently, to ensure that the cubic masses of trees did not house any alien assailants. He reached the end of the solid line of flora. It continued at a right angle down what appeared to be a small alley-way, the opposing wall of which was created by the beginnings of the next huge square coppice. K decided to walk all the way around the square mass, to see if there was any indication of what might exist in the centre of such a seemingly unnatural plantation. Eventually he arrived back at his vehicle. His short trip revealed no let-up in the density of the protective vegetation, no openings provided a clue as to what might be on the other side of these walls, if anything. It could just be that the coppice was a solid mass of trees and plants that had nothing but more trees at its centre. But K was determined to find out why these plants were growing in such a uniform manner, and for that, he had to try and get through the outer plant life to see if there was anything different underneath.

He went back to the land cruiser and pulled a large axe from one of its storage compartments. On returning to the wall, he listened again for warning signs of any possible enemies. The coast seemed clear as his surroundings provided a beautiful and seemingly tranquil back-drop to his antics. He took a big swing at the plant life in front of him with the heavy blade. A large clump of unsuspecting foliage fell to the floor, revealing yet more dense plant life beneath it. He took another swing, then another. Each time, there seemed to be ever more flora beneath each layer. He had started this exercise and he was damned sure he was going to get to the bottom of whatever this was, no matter how many unfortunate plants had to be harmed in the process. This was a new type of thought for K, as he was usually so careful about treating all living things with the utmost respect for their right to exist in his presence. But K was beginning to realise that if he was to survive this trip, he had to start being a great deal more aware of his surroundings and prepared to view his required actions under the single universal rule of existence – survival of the fittest. He knew this left him at a distinct disadvantage as he was neither strong, nor fit, but he had his wits about him and he was determined to use them to his best defence. That meant that he had to learn more about his current situation and a few trees weren't going to stop him.

After half an hour of enthusiastic chopping and hacking, K stopped, exhausted. He slumped down on the floor in front of the mound of mutilated twigs and branches. Maybe there was nothing beyond the plants in this huge block formation after all. Maybe this is simply how the plants grew here on this part of the planet. K wasn't satisfied with such a lame explanation, but was simply too tired to continue arguing the possibilities in his head. He lay on the floor amongst the mess of branches, creepers and twigs and closed his eyes.

A noise made him open them again a second later. His heart missed a few beats and his breathing stopped. What was that? It sounded like some sort of creaking, but it seemed to come from the floor by his head. He turned over, face down on the floor and placed an ear to the ground. The creaking happened again. And again. It seemed to be getting louder. As K listened intently to the noise that seemed to be resonating out of the earth beneath him, his attention was drawn to the side of the large plant wall that he had been hacking away at only moments before. K had a gut feeling that complete unconsciousness was about to take control of his body. He gazed up at the thick foliage to see a huge section of flora break away from the mass of plants, directly above where he had created the unceremonious damage. A large column of branches, leaves, flowers and twigs succumbed to the irresistible powers of gravity and began their short race towards K as he lay on the floor, paralysed by the fear of death. He barely had time to think 'this is gonna hur...' before a mature branch of substantial stature removed all consciousness with a single blow to the side of his head. Luckily for K, he was therefore unable to feel the impact of the remaining branches and twigs as they joined in the one-way attack for vengeance that ensued. Battered and bruised, with some significant cuts, K lay unaware of his predicament, or his injuries in what was likely to be the deepest sleep he had experienced for many years, and probably quite a few to come.

Chapter 9

The Awakening

The rumbling woke K. It came through the ground on which his head was held by a merciless gang of large branches. It sounded familiar and altogether way too close for comfort. The resonating mechanical sound brought images of the earlier attacks back into K's mind. The noise made K want to cry as its deep throated growl and unmistakable rumbling shook his surroundings. It was responsible for the death of his entire TAK team. He lay still – not that he had much option as he was still pinned firmly to the floor by the heavy foliage. He couldn't move a muscle even if he wanted to. He had tried a number of small movements, and lifting techniques, but to no avail. There was no way his puny little body was going to be able to lift the mass of tangled twigs and branches above him.

The rumbling was getting louder. The ground vibrated beneath his head, gaining in violence as the noise drew ever closer. The large pile of branches that blocked K's view to the outside world, and the dangers it held, started to shake all around him. The floor felt like it would break under the pressure of the earthquake. It grew louder still, and the vibrations were now incredibly painful, not least because they were shaking branches into places on K's body that he would rather not admit existed. K's innards were pounded by the ground, making him feel sick. It sparked a sharp pain in his stomach. He assumed that a branch was gradually being forced into his abdominal area by the shaking mass all around him. But the pain felt deep within him, rather than on the surface. Maybe he was so full of adrenalin that he didn't feel the branch penetrate his skin and it was only now that the branch was reaching his inner organs that he could feel the agony within.

The increasing din drew K's attention once again to his imminent demise. He was sure the vehicle creating this earthquake was so close it was about to travel straight over him, crushing him into worm food, and judging by the racket it created, it would flatten a great deal of K's surroundings too. He braced himself for the impact of the huge vehicle. A few seconds passed. Then another few. K was still alive, just. He was breathing and the sound seemed to be going away slowly. Yes, the deafening noise was definitely getting slightly quieter – or was K simply going deaf? It could have been the latter, but the vibrations were also subsiding. The machine seemed to have avoided him. The rumbling continued to soften and the thunderous earthquake moved away slowly into the distance. Was it possible? Was he still alive? K did not wait to find out and promptly fainted with sheer relief.

A few moments later he came round, feeling a little sick. His stomach churned with the tension of the events that had swamped his nervous system, and his belly's over-activity threatened a re-viewing of his last meal from many hours before. K thought about food for a second as he realised that he could starve to death before being murdered by his assailants, if he didn't get out of his predicament somehow. It wasn't every day that he nearly got killed. Well never, in fact. The closest he had ever been to facing death prior to today was a rather nasty leg rash he received from a passionate, not to mention overly ambitious reptile, which showed amorous tendencies to his left calf whilst the A4 team were investigating a small planet in the Magna region. But this was different... K didn't just feel that he might die – he knew he was going to die today. So much for staying positive, he thought to himself, whilst inadvertently starting a small internal debate between two sub-factions of his subconscious. The first of which pointed out that he must remain positive in order to have any chance of survival and the second mockingly pointing out that they were being very positive – positive he was going to die before nightfall! The knowledge that you will actually perish is a humbling one. K, not a brave man by any stretch of the imagination, had simply resigned himself to the fact that his life was soon to be over. It gave him a strange sense of sadness, whilst also providing him with an inner peace that he had never known before, and, no doubt, would never know again. It was a strangely comfortable feeling. I am going to die here, so there is no point in denying or resisting it, he thought to himself. The unavoidable certainty of it all hit him satisfactorily, like the long awaited mental 'click' so many algebra students wish for in their pursuit to grasp the ludicrous waste of curriculum time. He would die, already buried in his resting place. He knew he shouldn't have maimed so many plants in his pursuit to find out what lay beneath the wall of trees. It was against his better judgement. The foliage had achieved revenge.

The serenity of K's new found peace with death was short-lived as conscious reasoning took over. OK, he admitted to himself, he had already 'known' that he was going to die a number of times today and it still hadn't happened. He 'knew' he was going to die during the landing. And he 'knew' he would die when the explosions first hit, many hours ago. But he still KNEW he was going to die, which was far more terrifying than simply believing you might! K was adamant his luck would run out before the daylight did, despite having managed to escape certain death on a number of occasions: He had nearly been blown to pieces by the laser cannon a few times. Then the trees collapsed on him, and most recently he was virtually run over by some sort of alien vehicle.

Gradually, K's conscious thoughts, having taken a distinctly more logical, panic-stricken approach to his predicament, took control and began to create a mild state of hysteria. Within a few seconds his heart rate had doubled and every conscious cell in his body began to hug their own metaphorical knees and rock backwards and forwards mumbling. He fainted once again with blind panic.

Chapter 10

The Marth

"What happens if they find it first?" asked the Marth, in a calm, serene tone. The awesome pure-white creature's voice carried through the chambers of the Barbarian mother ship with the quiet sedate persistence of a small stream of innocent water, which, over millennia can carve valleys into the hardest of rocks. Every one of his barbarian warriors within ear-shot feared for their lives, as they always did in the Marth's presence.

The Captain of the Landing Guard cowered in front of the powerful, hideous creature in front of him. The contents of his bladder threatened to make acquaintance with his undergarments and his lunch was currently contemplating its escape routes. Only by remaining silent did the Captain manage to keep all of his contents contained – for the time being at least. He looked up at the face of his master, it was contorted and twisted into a mess of bright white skin layers that looked far too intricate to be able to house any humanoid expressions. But it managed to convey pure undiluted hatred and anger at all times, punctuated only briefly by a twisted sense of love for all things hideously painful. The devil himself would be in awe of this creature.

The Marth was all too aware of the universal cliché that evil creatures should adorn themselves with. He knew that black should be his colour. He was well aware that his reputation for pure evil would be aided by an all-black wardrobe and a dark shadowy complexion. But that simply wasn't him. It wouldn't suit him. Besides that, he always relished the challenge of exceeding people's expectations by proving himself more worthy of a higher status of evil. 'Pure' evil was understood by all of the Marth's victims as being a far more intense form of evil that truly deserved to be recognised as anything but the norm. So he wore white as a sign of purity. It looked good on him too, thought the Marth.

He was tall, slender in build but with an obvious underlay of pure muscles that you knew at a mere glance would produce many times the power their size suggested. His skin was so pale, it almost glowed. Everywhere he went, the room seemed to illuminate slightly as the light reflected from his incandescent flesh. Multiple flaps of bright, almost translucent, skin covered every inch of his lean muscular frame, making him truly hideous to look at. His pure white shimmering clothes served to add to the overall effect.

The Marth, once called Dighip Fortsuip, came from a race of jet-black skinned evil beings that lived on a burning hell of a planet called Conflage. Their skin was blackened from the unrelenting searing heat generated by the millions of active volcanoes that peppered the crust of what they called home. But he was born a freak of nature. A one in ten billion chance occurrence so repulsive to his society that they rejected him immediately. He was born an 'inverse' – a bright white skinned creature that defied everything the race believed about themselves. They knew he would be a follower of righteousness. They knew that white represented the forces of good across the universe and that simply would not do. They were a race of evil. Evil people, practising evil deeds, with a bit of devil worship thrown in for good measure. Dighip threatened all that. If he was to turn out as good as his appearance suggested, it would break the solid balance of their society. And besides all that – he was so ugly. Bright white skin – they couldn't imagine anything more disgusting.

So he was banished from society, left in a cave to survive alone, on the first day of his life. Born with the same instincts as all Conflagradites (otherwise known to societies on neighbouring planets as Firestarters), his ability to survive from such an early age was excellent, but his chances were still very slim. As a baby, he quickly learned that bugs and dirt he found around the cave were easy pickings and gave just enough energy to allow him to spend his time sleeping and growing. As he started to move around more, he began to observe the behaviour of other creatures around him. Their survival tactics, hunting techniques, not to mention other strange activities that occurred when two of the same species got close to one another and started what he assumed to be rather half-hearted fighting. He watched and learned. And then ate the coupled creatures he regarded with intrigue.

Over the years, he grew strong, learning everything he needed from the fauna around him. He saw that only the fittest survived. He watched teeth-baring animals tear each other's flesh to shreds in fights for superiority. He observed the cubs and babies of various species being eaten alive by their kin, sometimes as a form of easy nutrition, occasionally to destroy the offspring of a rival beast and once in a while just for the sheer sport of it. He observed animals maiming each other in bizarre rituals, battling to the death in a fight for territory, and the weak or injured eaten by their families. He learned as the wild society around him tore at the realms of decency and morals by following the one true rule of survival: Be an evil bastard and you'll be fine!

Firestarters have incredible memories. It allows them the ultimate malevolence. There is no better use of evil than for revenge, and for that, you need to be able to remember everything. To this end, the Conflagradites had, over millions of years, managed to develop a memory so advanced that they could recall their own birth (and the associated pain their mother caused them – for which they would never forgive her).

For years, the image of his parent's disgusted faces as he was born had haunted him. His first life experience was that of his parents rejecting him with such hatred that it burned into his subconscious for life. He vowed to use this painful memory for revenge. In the meantime, it served well as a pick-me-up for when he wasn't feeling as evil as he should do. A stark reminder that unless he was cruel, malicious and hateful at all times, he would be showing weakness and could therefore be defeated. He would never let that happen.

The Marth jerked his thoughts back to the present and decided on an alternative approach, knowing full well that the fear that surrounded him everyday of his life could be maximised through the use of a low resonating voice and a calm, relaxed nature. It drove his subordinates wild with fear, and he relished every moment of it. "Tell me," he began in a deep menacing drone, "How long have we been investigating this pathetic planet?" The surrounding guards, scientists, cyborgs and military strategists remained completely silent for a few seconds. Each of their brains feverishly trying to calculate whether the question was a rhetorical one, or a loaded one. No-one wanted to answer for fear of being struck down into a smouldering pile of goo. The few seconds of silence proved unbearable for some, and they quietly released the contents of their bladders into their clothing, whilst shaking uncontrollably, far within their inner selves. To openly show fear would produce a very similar result as walking up to the Marth, stamping on his foot and yelling expletives about his mother. But the Marth could smell the terror and loved it, despite it nearly always being accompanied by the rather unpleasant smell of bodily fluids.

The silence was broken by one of the intelligence advisers, who ultimately decided that to give the right answer might spare him from an agonising death for at least the next hour or two, "Twelve of our planetary years, oh great Marth."

"Twelve years" whispered the Marth, his voice seemed to carry further than it should as his words echoed in every barbarian's fear-filled mind. "Twelve years of deciphering ancient scripts" he mumbled. "Twelve years of excavating, digging, searching." His voice was gradually getting very slightly louder – a very bad sign indeed for all living creatures in his immediate vicinity. "Twelve long years..." His thoughts seemed to break off into an alternative direction for a moment or two. "We are a race of warriors. Powerful, formidable, unrelenting in our quest to remain the ultimate race in the galaxy..." his voice lowered again, after reaching a peak that could almost be described as 'slightly anxious'. "And they have us here, searching a vast planet for a small piece of metal that may or may not exist." The Marth gradually became less aware of his surroundings as his monologue seemed to address himself more than anyone. "Are we searching for an unfounded legend, or for the greatest weapon of all? An object that, if real, was created by a race that wiped itself out of existence thousands of years ago. My world is one of battles and bloody conflict. I have no need for such a weapon of mass destruction. I have no place on such a recovery mission..." His voice trailed off as he realised his mumbling, bitter tones were beginning to reveal a little too much of his frustration. His orders to uncover whatever phenomenon eliminated this extraordinary race from existence enraged him and had done so for twelve long years. But, being a leader by fear, rather than by example, it was not in his disposition to allow his lesser warriors to see what annoyed him.

As far as his audience were concerned, they still found it difficult to accept that the Marth was not at the very peak of the hierarchy in this military society. They knew he hated this mission, and accepted that it was one of the very few things in life (and death) that really p*ssed him off. But what they could not accept was that there was someone even further up the chain that was actually in charge of their Marth. Everyone in the universe was scared stiff of the Marth. Entire races that did not know of the Marth's existence were afraid of him – they just didn't know it yet. How could anyone manage such an awesome, not to mention ugly creature?

The Marth surveyed his surroundings once more, taking his glare away from his cupped palm, in which he had briefly searched for the answer to his frustration. His subordinates were still cowering around him, unsure of their master's next move. But the Marth noticed something in their eyes. Something wasn't quite right. There was something there in their expressions and posture that did not make sense. They were standing too upright. Their eyes were nearly aimed right at him – they were paying far too much direct attention for the Marth's liking. Then he realised what this atmospheric change had been... they had all relaxed a little. No longer could the Marth see their hearts beating in their chests, ready to explode with fear. They must be taught a lesson in how to cower properly, this was as much insubordination as he could take, how dare they relax when he was around. After all, there is no point in running an entire battalion of thousands of men on fear, if you let them relax occasionally.

"I want the enemy searched. I want their ships searched. I want their contents searched..." the men knew this last command should be taken literally – on an individual bodily basis. There would be a lot of bloodshed and gut spilling tonight.

"If they have found the device before us..." the Marth stopped himself short of finishing what sounded to him like an idle threat. He was a man of few words and he liked to keep it that way. The Marth felt that his lack of diction aided his murderous exterior and his overall persona. He knew the importance of image. He reached out one of his incandescent, rippling arms to its full length. His pure-white cloak fell away, revealing more of the bright skin beneath. He spread his hand open, for all to see. Despite already being far outside the Marth's physical reach, the congregation shuffled backwards slightly, making sure at all times to look away from the glowing figure of pure hatred. Eyes darted backwards and forwards, each member trying to focus their glare on the weakest link in the room, or simply the one who was already receiving the most attention from their peers. This way, the silent voting system seemed to gain strength in numbers as the unanimous decision to cull the weakest member of the team united the survivors. At least, that was the Marth's theory. Finally, all glaring eyes landed on the doomed shoulders of the Commander of the Planetary Intelligence Squadron. His fate had been sealed.

The air grew hot with nervous tension. All in the room except one breathed an inaudible sigh of relief. The Marth held out his left hand, palm facing the doomed individual, who had failed at every count to complete his tasks. As the Marth started to show small signs of effort in his contorted white face and muscular arm, the man in front of him started to scream. At first it was just the scream of someone being eaten alive by zombies, but gradually it increased to that of someone being slowly lowered into boiling acid whilst having his skin removed by a thousand miniature butchers. At its peak, the piercing cry of agony would have obtained the attentions of dolphins, bats and other ultra-sonic communicators. The scream only began to subside as the man gradually melted. Starting with limp, downward turning appendages the process slowly increased pace as the body of the dying man turned into a burning grey puddle of lumpy slime. The last gentle splats were heard as the remnants of his scalp slumped the remaining few inches into the puddle beneath. The victim ended as a smouldering mess of foul smelling melted skin and liquefied bones. To the Commander, his demise took a thousand painful years of personal hell. To his colleagues the entire process took only a few seconds. It was pleasant for no-one. Except the Marth, of course, whose grinning pale face showed a perverse love of pain that was equalled only at the very depths of hell.

It was an awesome display of the almost unlimited powers of the Marth, and one which the lucky few had seen a number of times before. The Commander was one of the less fortunate direct reports to the Marth, as his experience of such a display had only ever been encountered once. Unfortunately for him, not as a spectator.

They all knew what they had to do – destroy the enemy, find out what they knew about the planet and find the device... or be killed in the process, which was often a far more appealing option to returning empty handed. In fact, that single key trait in the Marth's leadership style was probably his army's most formidable strength. They feared their leader with so much conviction, that they had one of two approaches to battles: 1 – fight carefully, but precisely, so there is slim chance of defeat, 2 – fight like an absolute lunatic and if you happen to get careless and killed – well, good on ya' as it was probably far less painful than returning to the Marth injured or defeated! The second of the two options was the one most commonly favoured by Marth's warriors and it worked very well for them. They either survived as victors in the most bloody and desperately hideous battles anyone could ever imagine. Or they got slaughtered and didn't have to report back. Either way, they were winners!

Chapter 11

The Power

The small device was nearly there now. It had ventured through the most dangerous parts of its host. Despite not knowing exactly which route it had taken, the cell knew it was close to the end now. It could feel the electric energy pulses just up ahead. It wouldn't be long before it could start to restore power, which was far more heavily depleted than its calculations predicted it should be.

As energy was of paramount importance to the cell's survival, it made a calculated decision to continue on its quest to secure the alternative source, before investigating the reasons for the sudden power depletion. A decision which later would ensure its survival.

The fluid filled tunnels here were a great deal less rapid than some it had experienced along the way. Less than half an hour ago, the cell believed it was doomed as the flow of the red and white liquid began to pulsate so violently that it barely managed to hold on to the soft fleshy walls. But now, the current was reducing.

The cell's power surge readings were starting to go off the scale as it travelled forward, ever closer to the source. Sensors deep within the cell's processing banks and advanced survival chips were registering electrical pulse signals of a very strange, but powerful nature. Whatever this host was, it was not one the Vacchions had predicted. That fact was made obvious by the diabolical directions the cell had been following on the pre-programmed biological diagram. The detailed anatomy of all potential hosts had been entered into the cell, but everything was different within this vessel. The cell was simply having to use its initiative chip to near overload in order to survive.

After a few more corners, the cell was almost overcome by the throbbing nature of the power source. Every sensor in its tiny form was screaming readings of massive proportions. Something was wrong. There were too many chemicals in this region to allow the power to be harnessed successfully. The cell had to think fast, before it could hope to attach itself to the electrical supply that lay just beyond the strangely shaped solid white wall in front of it. The chemical content of the cell's host vessel must be controlled and monitored before any energy tap could be established. Time was running out. The batteries showed less than two per cent power. The cell knew that in the vast majority of situations it had so far experienced, such low levels of energy would be enough to last a couple of hundred years, but right now things were different. Energy levels had been depleted massively in the last few hours and the situation was critical. It was having to use its supplies in more ways than ever. Processing chips, initiative chips, common sense drives, environmental sensors and every one of its ten miniature mechanical limbs had been used on this short journey, and they all used a great deal more electricity than pretending to be the god-like idol of an insect race for a thousand decades.

The cell had to somehow get a message to the gland releasing all these chemicals into the vessel. If it failed to control the release of such a vast amount of potent chemical before attempting power transfer, the erratic power surges would no doubt end its existence. This would result in the cell's demise without the ability for it to attempt thermo-nuclear melt down, meaning its prisoner might escape and possible failure of its sole reason for existence. The cell contemplated for a nano-second whether it would go to a better place... Was there any such thing as 'boot-up' after 'final shut-down'? Would it go to a worse place, perhaps, especially seeing as it might fail its sole purpose for being? Maybe it would be sent to a giant computer in the sky. Ten thousand years was a lot of processing time to contemplate such riddles whilst playing the part of god in the insect kingdom's main ceremonial hall. But it knew these thoughts were unauthorized and incredibly dangerous, especially for the cell. What it was carrying fed on minds with conscious contemplation of their own existence. It must stop thinking such things – its learning chips were not meant for such a selfish purpose.

The tiny device steadied itself with a number of its microscopic arms, in preparation for the very delicate operation. This was a true make or break moment in the cell's existence, not to mention the host's. Failure to connect to the correct channel, could result in the vessel's total shut down. If that occurred, the power source would also diminish rapidly, and the cell did not have enough reserve energy to contemplate another journey of this magnitude. Even if it did manage to connect to the right channel of communication without terminating the host, it still needed to send a successful message to the gland which had gone into chemical overload. If it failed to respond to the cell's over-riding instructions, anything could happen. The exact opposite could take place, and the entire vessel could be so over-run with internally produced chemicals, that the local scavengers would be able to have the biggest, most successful 'free love' rave party the fauna on this planet had ever seen. It began the operation.

Slowly, it made progress. First, it had to find a way through the vast solid white wall that protected the communications channels and electrical pulse source. The cell travelled cautiously along the wall to find one of many cushioned joints that would undoubtedly exist, as was the common trait in all vessels for which the cell had pre-programmed information. Within a few seconds it had located just such a weak point, where the solid defence gave way to a softer tissue that allowed another huge section of the wall to join this one. Between the two surfaces was a microscopic gap that would allow a small communications line to be connected without the need for extensive drilling, which the cell had neither the time nor energy to conduct. This was its last chance. Energy reserves were at an all time low. It had to succeed otherwise the last ten thousand years would have been in vain.

Chapter 12

The Encounter

The Right-tenant had made his way back to his quarters, satisfied that the mess would be investigated by his officers and that he would be notified as soon as any real decision making needed to occur. It had been a long day. He was not used to so much excitement. Leading a vast solar-system investigation task force was a comparatively easy and stress free job which suited the Right-tenant perfectly in these, his twilight years as a senior officer in the Republic's galaxy expansion scheme. Never had a routine planetary investigation gone so wrong. He didn't want to end his long and not-so-illustrious career with a court-martial. The lives that were lost on the planet's surface didn't matter so much, it was the threat to his name and rank that really bothered him. People lower down the hierarchical pecking order were supposed to be killed in action, that was a hazard of the profession. And seeing as they had chosen to get involved in such a dangerous trade, they deserved everything they got, especially if it was through their own negligence that they got snuffed. It wasn't his fault. He had ordered all the usual checks and made sure his officers were trained well enough to know the full procedure to ensure all their landing teams' safe return. They had all been through this many times before. If they screwed it up, it was hardly his fault. His job was to oversee all activities from a distance. A great distance. Preferably from the palatial comfort his own quarters, if he had anything to do with it.

The Right-tenant was going through the phase of guilt known as denial. He continued to mull over the strange events in his mind. He had been through planetary investigations hundreds of times before. The greatest danger they usually faced was that of native planet-dwellers who had to be tamed or eliminated in order for the Republic's highly important investigations to go ahead. Sometimes the local wildlife got the better of one or two of the ground-force team, and even rarer still, the flora gave everyone a lesson in chemical warfare. But these were one or two isolated incidents, which could be explained by an individual's carelessness to not follow all precautions necessary to stay alive. What happened today was different. There was something a great deal more suspicious about the annihilation of an entire TAK team and its ship.

The planet had been scanned, as they always were, for the traces of intelligent or threatening life forms. The scan had revealed nothing of the dangers that the TAK A4 team had faced. No intelligent or advanced life had been detected, no gases, pollutants or short-tempered animal life – nothing that could pose a threat. But the incidents that beset the TAK A4 team had allowed them to gain enough information to warrant the order of retreat from the planet's surface. All other TAK teams had arrived back on the mother ship later that day, so the impact had been limited to A4. No other Republic members were on the planet's surface now, so they could just leave and pretend this whole sorry incident had never taken place. But that really wouldn't answer any of the questions that were racing through the Right-tenant's head.

They already knew that the planet had been inhabited thousands of years before, by a highly advanced race. The massive diamond shaped object sticking out of its atmosphere was enough to give that away. And the scans had revealed the obvious hallmarks of a sprawling metropolis for hundreds of square miles around the base of the vast floating object. A fact that he had deliberately concealed from the TAK teams to stop them from being distracted by the temptation of looking for treasures. That privilege would be left to the senior officers once all flora and fauna investigations had been completed. Nothing gave them any indication that there was anything to be wary of on the planet's surface. In fact… that was odd in itself. Despite never experiencing any excitement on this scale before, they did nearly always get readings back from the preliminary scans that made at least some of the people nervous about the expedition. But this planet had revealed nothing but open arms to the landing crews. Maybe, with hindsight, the initial scans had revealed an all too inviting planet. Maybe that's why it had thus far remained uncharted. Maybe no-one had ever escaped the clutches of the planet before, to reveal its secrets to the rest of the universe. This could be his moment of glory – revealing the secrets of a lost civilisation and a hostile world. He could be famous, and hopefully would never have to work again. He would order the TAK teams to re-group and travel back down to the planet's surface to find the answers behind his new found retirement fund as soon as he had taken a well-deserved nap.

"Sir! Sir!" His thoughts were broken suddenly by a rather panicked voice screaming through the intercom. "Sir, come in, Sir. We need you on the bridge immediately! Sir?"

"What is it Hensman?" he answered angrily, frustrated at having his thoughts of a lucrative retirement disturbed, "What the hell are you screaming about?"

"You are not going to believe this, Sir. We are being approached by a Rogue Nation ship, Sir… and it's a big one!"

The Right-tenant mumbled something inaudible as sweat began to stream down his face. The Hensman didn't bother to ask the Right-tenant to repeat it as he was too distracted by his own inner terror at the thought of coming into contact with the Rogue Nation warriors.

The Rogue Nation was the most awesome, unrelenting power in the known universe. A wealthy and well managed race of barbaric scavengers and pirates, they scoured galaxies for planets and vessels to rape, pillage and attack in the most blood-thirsty unforgiving manner imaginable. No planetary society was safe and nothing was sacred. Entire solar systems had fallen foul of their momentary but tyrannical reign as they swept through, extracting anything valuable on their passage to future battles. Their role in the universe was ironically very similar to the investigative ships of the Republic which had been sent to explore the outer-reaches of the charted universe in search of knowledge and possible sites for colonisation. The Right-tenant realised the irony of this for a split second before returning to the truly terrifying gravity of the situation before him.

After a few seconds of silence, where the only thing being transmitted was sheer blind panic, the Right-tenant desperately reached for the last thread of his self-control and clung to it like a petrified child as he gave his last order, "Get us out of here,

Hensman. Get us anywhere but here." And with that the Right-tenant collapsed in a wobbling mass of hysteria and cried himself into a coma.

Chapter 13

The Opening

K felt somewhat relaxed when he next awoke. He had calmed down incredibly. He almost felt good about himself, despite still being under a huge pile of branches and trunks which weighed a great deal more than him.

Once again he briefly surveyed his body with his mental attentions. All was good. Despite a few cuts and a number of bruises, he felt quite alright. There was, however, a sharp sensation at the back of his neck, near his spinal column. Everything else seemed to be in order, considering the events that had taken place. None of the injuries were bothering him much anymore; the intensity of pain had subsided. This started his mind thinking. How long had he been here? He must have been unconscious for a great length of time for his aches and pains to go away. Places that once felt the burning pressure of sharp branches and twigs, no longer felt tested by the unrelenting weight of the compost heap above him. He must have been here for hours, maybe even days. Then why did he not feel hungry and weak with fatigue? He knew the body had a great deal of resilience when tested under extreme mental and physical pressure such as this. Then he giggled. What was going on? Why did he find that funny? He must be delirious, after all, he couldn't possibly be as healthy as he felt. His bodily glands must have gone into over time to produce chemicals to make him feel this way. He wondered if this spelled the end. He giggled again. Oh well, if it was the end, he might as well go out smiling. This wasn't like him at all. Usually he would have fainted again by now – once he had gripped the harsh reality of his predicament. But no, he seemed to be managing his hysteria in such a way that allowed him to remain conscious!

Despite feeling so well, he was still trapped under the mass of heavy foliage. He moved his head around as much as his natural restraints would let him. He had already tried moving the prison of leaves and branches a number of times, but to no effect.

As he was feeling so much stronger now, he thought he might as well try again. Especially as the only other two options were to scream for help from the beings that had already tried to kill him a number of times, or lie still and wait to be eaten alive by native insects.

K noticed that there were some gaps in the walls of his personal compost heap prison cell. He began to push at a few of the closest weak sections. As he did so his muscles ached and burned with the resistance from the branches. He started to grunt with effort, and his face distorted into a painful expression of tension, his veins threatening to explode. He struggled and strained at the resisting walls of the wood pile. Just before he was about to give up and take a deep breath, the twinge in the back of his neck changed intensity. Instead of simply tingling at a constant throbbing rate in one fixed position, it started to pulsate slightly, and the sensation began to move down his spine and through his limbs to his hands. He was about to stop his efforts, worried that the twinges he felt in his spinal column were an indication that he had done some damage in his attempts to escape, but he could not stop. Something told him not to, he wasn't sure what it was, but he could not give up, despite the fact that neither his conscious nor sub-conscious mind owned up to the feat of defiance. With new found rebellion, K continued to push as hard as he could against the weakest points of his surroundings, despite his better judgement to preserve the condition of his spine. Suddenly one of the branches gave a little. It only moved a few centimetres, but the shock of this partial success stopped K from pushing any further. He was elated at this minor triumph, but confused as to why they should suddenly move under the same efforts that he had attempted before. He assumed that he must simply be a great deal fitter after his rejuvenating rest (or repeated cowardly black-outs as any spectator would have described them).

After twenty minutes of extreme effort, there was a small gap in the side of the pile of foliage that contained K. Very gradually, and with a great deal of pain, K pulled his torso through the opening. The freshness of the air hit him with the welcome smell of freedom. He smiled to himself, despite the agony of a hundred sharp twigs and branches stabbing at his legs and back in a desperate attempt to keep him within their grasp.

It wasn't until K was half way out of the pile of foliage that he considered his surroundings. For all he knew, his enemies could well be watching him right now. Simply waiting for him to free himself before walking up and claiming the easy prize. He panicked and looked around manically in the desperate manner all fugitives used to ensure their captors were not in the immediate vicinity. There seemed to be no-one here. Nothing but the dense vegetation that clustered in huge cuboid sections all around him, and the distant sound of wildlife going about its daily business, blissfully unaware of K and his predicament.

Finally, K pulled his left leg out of the clasp of the foliage. He was free. He was also exhausted. He knew he had to get out of sight as quickly as possible. His mind told him that he had to get up and hide. He ignored it, the exhaustion was far too strong to overcome. He breathed heavily, veins still pulsating all over his body as his heart struggled to keep up with the overwhelming demand for fresh oxygenated blood.

Whilst he gasped for breath and tried to ignore the dizziness that swept across his mind as it grabbed every available molecule of oxygen that passed through it, he noticed a large dark opening in the tree wall that he had been hacking at to no avail hours before. At least, he presumed it was hours, as it was so much darker here now than it had been before. He had no idea how long the days and nights were here, but he could tell that night-time was drawing close as the cool duskiness of a late summer evening began to shroud the warm brightness of the day in a large blanket. He squinted to see into the darkness of the doorway that had been created in the centre of the giant tree cube in front of him. He had been right to investigate what existed beneath the wall of foliage, there was definitely something there, waiting to be discovered.

The opening in the thick plant life revealed the white stone work of a large door frame to an ancient building. Heavy, beautifully hand-finished masonry bordered the dark opening with a bright fresh look that K would not have associated with a construction many thousands of years old. The shroud of vegetation had obviously protected the building from the elements, preserving its concealed façade.

K's mind interrupted his thoughts to inform him again that he should get up. Only this time, it really caught his attention. He stopped breathing for a second, despite every muscle in his body screaming at him not to. Had he thought that? Or had he heard it? He was pretty sure he was alone in this forest and he was certain he could still tell the difference between an internal thought and someone shouting a command at him. When he told himself that he should do something for his own good, it didn't usually sound any where near as forceful as that. And he didn't usually feel that he couldn't resist the instruction. But there he was, exhausted and barely able to move, attempting to obey what he could only assume were his inner thoughts. He simply couldn't resist the urgency that he had placed on himself to move into less conspicuous surroundings.

Confused, bleeding from various cuts and abrasions, desperately gulping for breath and in extreme agony, K clambered to his feet and stumbled towards the clearing that he had hacked open in the dense cube of foliage in front of him. Despite this particular opening being the cause of all his pain and suffering, K was suddenly grateful for this entrance into the dark and musty, tree and stone lined building. He stepped over the flora that had collapsed after his amateurish lumber-jack skills had offended gravity's relationship with the vegetation. Inside the building was dark and smelt of damp grass, but it was warm and inviting. He just hoped it was safe. But before he had a chance to examine the security features offered by such a dwelling, he collapsed from exhaustion, falling in the centre of the main room of the building, into a heap on a fern, moss and grass-lined floor. The darkness enveloped K and he passed-out, yet again. His slumber wouldn't last for long, but it would pave the way for much needed replenishment for his muscles and mind.

Chapter 14

The Connection

The operation had been a success. The cell had managed to connect to the correct channels of the host's internal communications system in order to send messages to glands all over the alien vessel, ensuring that the chemical releases were controlled with maximum effect. Once this had been achieved, the cell had successfully helped its new home find a position of relative safety and had conducted the remainder of the delicate operations necessary to ensure that it could replenish the power supplies to its batteries. The cell had managed to tap into the huge electrostatic energy reserves abundant in the vessel to supplement its own power. There was just one, major problem…

During the cell's journey through the most dangerous regions of the host vessel's inner workings, it had unbeknown to itself, sustained a great deal of damage from the highly acidic white jelly-like substance it had met in the huge cavernous and extremely foul smelling area, part way through its quest. Despite believing that it had successfully negotiated the obstacle with ape-like swinging accuracy and spider-like professionalism, the cell had become victim to a small group of anti-bodies, whose primary role was to defend the inner workings of this vessel by destroying any alien entrants through bio-degradation. Regardless of the cell's relatively innocent presence here, it had sustained a great deal of damage to its energy storage cells and was now busy surveying the situation.

After a few moments of analysis, the cell reached an undesirable conclusion. It would no longer be able to survive for very long without being permanently attached to the current source of power. If its current host were to become redundant in any way, or the power supply were to be broken, the cell would have to find alternative power within a matter of minutes, or would simply have to instigate its final defence mechanism – an event that should not be viewed from close proximity.

The cell reviewed its predicament. This really was quite unfortunate. It had merely intended to board the vessel to replenish its battery stocks, and then leave, with the host organism being none the wiser. Now that plan had been annulled by some highly primitive, not to mention terribly single-minded anti-bodies. Life was a very strange thing...

There it was again – conscious thought about its own existence. The cell severely reprimanded itself. It had been trained to learn and to adapt to its surroundings, but it had not been given a conscience or the ability to prophesise or contemplate the intricate workings of the universe. The cell was very aware that it might be developing the early weaknesses of a conscience. This could prove catastrophic. It made a mental note to lesson dependency on its over-worked initiative drive for at least a couple of hours. It was the logic drive's chance to shine.

Upon re-gaining dominance, logic immediately suggested that it begin repairs to the damaged areas of its power retainers and a full cleanse to ensure that no foreign anti-bodies were still present. After this a nice nap was in order. Er, no, not a nap, that was a highly illogical term, the subconscious thoughts were still there. This was dangerous. After the repairs it was imperative that the cell take itself off-line to rejuvenate its processors and to re-establish a semblance of normal, logical, electro magnetic, fully-processed existence. Only after this could it consider its future options.

Chapter 15

The Massacre

The Hensman reached for the controls to start manoeuvring the huge inter-stellar solar-system exploration mother ship into deep space. Sweat ran down his face, his eyes filled with the tears of extreme panic, and his heart beat with the inconsistency of a live jazz band percussionist after a few too many draws on the wacky-backy. His limbs had nearly given up. None of them seemed to want to do as they were commanded. Each limb had a life of its own as they quivered off in various directions, trying to escape the doomed flesh and blood prison that held them at their posts. The body was surely going to die, and the limbs wanted nothing to do with it any more.

The huge ship started to rotate, its bow gradually gaining momentum away from the surface of Vacchion, to give it an open sky at which to aim. Without warning, the ship shook with the most almighty violence, as noise erupted throughout the massive vessel, rattling its contents as if they were pieces of dried pasta in a maraca. People were thrown in all directions, bouncing off walls and ceilings. Fittings and panels in corridors and rooms all over the ship were shaken loose and joined the people in their cascade towards the floor, fuelled by the ship's fabricated gravitational field. By the time the ship came to a momentary rest, some of them were no longer people. Many were now simply bodies which had been impaled on sharp objects, crushed under heavy falling walls or machinery, or smashed unceremoniously against the hull to create messy carcases of former human beings.

After a few seconds of eerie silence the ship was pounded once again by forces beyond belief. More bodies and debris were thrown into the air repeatedly by the unrelenting explosions. The shaking blood bath that was home to thousands of troops and masses of Republic equipment began to spring air-leaks that sucked bodies and anything not bolted down securely into space. Automatic sensors rapidly shut air-lock doors in an attempt to limit the devastating effects of the hull breaches, reducing the areas experiencing air leaks to empty vacuum caverns. But all would be in vain. The ship's automated systems tried to protect the threatened existence of the remaining, but severely shaken crew. Some of the few hundred people still alive were taken to their own personal hells, as flames ripped through the interior of the ship, walls caved in, and death reigned terror on all still conscious.

The Marth looked on from the Rogue Nation ship, as it bore down on its victim. He frowned to himself. This was too easy. He knew it wasn't a trap. There were no sinister turns of events to face him, or any doubt of the battle's outcome. That's what disappointed him. He wanted it to be a true battle. He wished there was an unpredictable trap, where his troops were suddenly outnumbered ten to one. Like all commanders of violent and overly-confident armies, he wanted it to be a struggle against the odds – a battle he could be proud of winning. This was nothing like that. It was more like slaughtering baby iiogs. There was no pleasure in killing small defenceless animals for the hell of it, well not after the first thousand or so, anyway. After that it simply got... samey.

He gave the order, to make the battle more entertaining, "Cease fire." He commanded calmly. Then after a few moments contemplation he added, "General, order the troops to go hand-to-hand only." His deep voice reigned terror all around him, nobody dare disobey him, no matter how pointless his commands seemed. "Let's make this battle a little more interesting." He explained helpfully.

The supporting officers sighed, deep within themselves, at the prospect of pointlessly losing men, for the sake of the Marth's personal pleasure. They could continue to blast this pathetically defended ship into oblivion without leaving the comfort of their armchairs. But that was never enough for the Marth, especially with twelve years of pent-up frustration under his cruel skin. The only murderous killing he had enjoyed for more than a decade was that of sacrificing his own officers by way of apology. At least this way, he might not be so quick to react with such mortal force in future. At this realisation, the officers brightened up a little. They were effectively securing their immediate future by way of risking their lives on the Marth's behalf. After all, dying in unnecessary warfare was far less painful than meeting the wrath of their commander. When you viewed it like that, the prospect of pointless unarmed battle seemed altogether more inviting.

The fire-power of the Republic's planetary investigation vessel was quite pathetic. Even as the Rogue Nation ship prepared to dock, broadside, the enemy's weak cannons were no match for the defensive navicron field that protected the assailant's thick hull. After a few moments, the two ships were side by side, revealing the attackers upper hand in a size competition – their ship fully twice the length of their victims', with a great deal more girth to boot.

"Fifty men are to board the ship, armed only with traditional Hacs," ordered the Marth.

"But Sire-, there must be hundreds of men on that ship, with long-range weapons" protested his defence council, a man whose role was permanently in danger of being made redundant simply because his boss was not a great believer in the 'D'-word. Once he had caught a glance at the Marth's distaste at this piece of information, the man whose life expectancy had just been reduced by a factor of thousands cowered away, noting that his superior was always right.

"I shall lead them myself," informed the Marth, proudly in his whispery haunting voice. It had been a long time since he had savagely torn to pieces the flesh of men actively defending their own lives. All too many of his own staff simply stood there waiting to be melted. He longed for one of his officers to attempt to fight back. Just a small cut would do. He longed for the pain of real battle and his body had begun to salivate at the prospect. Eager to begin the bloodshed, he marched towards the boarding tubes.

On the exterior of the offending ship, ten huge tubes with spear-like heads telescoped at high velocity into the hull of the doomed research vessel. Each one penetrated deep into the victim fuselage with relative ease. The missile shaped nose cones opened, inside the Republic ship, like a multi-jawed dragon. As they opened, a small explosive device immediately wreaked its havoc, clearing the local area for the ten boarding teams. The explosions sent ten rapid shockwaves through the defenceless ship. Its soon to be evicted inhabitants were petrified, more so than they had ever been in their lives. They had received battle training, and were highly knowledgeable in the art of self-defence and attack, where strictly necessary (i.e. when the odds were in their favour!), but this was beyond their training. They were about to be massacred by the most awesome barbarians in the known galaxy. There was no level of training that could prepare you for this life-limiting event. It truly was a once in a lifetime experience!

The Marth and his fifty warriors marched their way through the boarding tubes, five in each. As they reached the opening at the ends of the tunnel, the localised carnage caused by the explosive welcome party was obvious. No charred bodily remains were present, but that was expected. The Marth had deliberately ordered the tubes to be inserted into the cargo levels of the victim ship. This would make the attack so much more interesting. Hand to hand combat was quite the most exhilarating experience. There was nothing like a good close-quarter fight, especially when you could melt people into small piles of disgusting goo.

As prearranged, the Marth and his ten small battalions of men spread out through the internal maze of the alien ship. They were instructed to monitor the other groups' whereabouts and to ensure they reached the bridge within one galactic-mean-time hour. What they did to get there was up to them. The Marth had reiterated that they should carry out as many executions and brutal murders as possible along their routes. Nothing should be left alive, no matter what it was. There would be a prize for the man with the greatest number of kills and doom would face the barbarian with the least. The Marth had ordered that the entire Republic vessel be closely monitored for life so that each Barbarian's kill rate could be calculated accordingly. It was only fair, after all, he didn't want any dishonest barbarians amongst his crew.

The Marth smiled to himself before switching on his 'all channels' intercom. Lowering his voice to a resonance that is only usually reached by earthquakes, he slowly declared the games officially open, "let the carnage begin".

Chapter 16

The Pods

"I don't care," exclaimed a panicked Captain whilst forcing his way through the last few people in the crowd, "The Right-Tenant is not here. We have tried hailing him but there is no response. There is no other alternative but to evacuate as many people as possible... officers first of course." He was at the entrance to one of the troop escape pods. Some other officers had already boarded and were preparing for launch. Others were fighting amongst themselves to get into the last few remaining positions of the escape vessels in this area of the ship.

Before the Captain completed his entry into the pod doorway, he paused to address the uneasy crowd once again. "The barbarians are on board, they are murdering their way through the ship as we speak. There is no alternative but to attempt to get as many people off this ship as possible. It's our only hope of survival. Many pods will be blasted out of the sky by the Rogue Nation mother ship, but if we all launch at the same time, we may have a better chance." The general murmur from the crowd erupted as the crew reacted with mixed emotions.

Some believed that their duty was to stay on the ship. True, they may be taken as prisoners by the invaders, but inter-stellar relations were highly amicable with most races throughout this galaxy, and they would eventually be returned to their planets unharmed as heroes. These were the crew who had never witnessed or heard of the Rogue Nations' exploits, proving ignorance can be a very dangerous thing. Others believed that to stand and fight would be the righteous thing to do, but admitted that it was probably the closest option to suicide, and were easily swayed into neighbouring camps of thought, such as running away.

Realising the need for a great deal more urgency, the Captain calmed the crowd with a panicked scream for them to shut up. "OK. Maybe we should all do our own thing. I know it's not text-book stuff, but this is hardly a text book situation. We are a friendly inter-stellar planetary investigation vessel, posing no threats to other advanced races. Yet we have been boarded under the most hostile of conditions. The attackers have been identified as Rogue National barbarian warriors. They will stop at nothing, if they have been ordered to take this ship." The crowd began to murmur loudly once again, but in a far more fitting manner, the Captain simply raised his hands to calm the noise. "We have sent a range of distress signals, but we are in deep space and can only expect these to be answered in seven to ten days time. If we attempt to defend this ship, I fear that we will all be slaughtered," there was a sharp intake of breath by the crowd, "but if we send out as many small ships and life pods as possible, whilst sending a barrage of random fire across the broadside of the enemy ship, we may have a chance of some of us reaching the planet's surface." The Captain decided not to go into details about how the Rogue Nation were just as likely to hunt them down on the planet's surface. His leadership requirements had been fulfilled for one day. "Find a pod or a lander, and get ready for mass evacuation in two minutes," he half ordered, half suggested.

He stepped over the lip of the doorway to the small craft. There were two rooms. The cockpit, where three pilots were beginning the two minute count-down and pre-flight checks, and the main cargo hold, where a scared group of thirty men were gathered, each strapped into a flight seat, ready for their imminent escape. Every person on the ship waited anxiously. There was little hope of survival. If the countdown took too long, the Rogue Nationals would enter the bridge and stop the pod from escaping. If the countdown wasn't long enough, there would be no automatic flack fire from the mother ship, and the pod would be instantly destroyed by the enemy. Even if they did manage to avoid destruction by the Rogue Nation vessel, they still had to navigate the planet's atmosphere and escape any planetary attack from barbarian ground troops. This really was a million to one shot at survival, but it was still their best chance.

On the main decks of the Republic's investigation vessel, hundreds of men scrambled into escape pods and TAK landers, hoping to outwit the Rogue Nation's attack. Some came across small groups of barbarian warriors, but only briefly. They were usually greeted by a blindingly quick close quarter attack that left their bodies in a number of pieces strewn across the floor. Often the victim was cut down with such precision and speed that he would have just enough time to look around the room and spot various parts of his body, before dying from the delayed sense of extreme pain and loss of blood. One particular victim was quick to notice one of his legs on the floor next to him, another on the shelf above, his left arm on a chair in the corner. As he lay on the floor in a bloody mess, the final limb took a few additional seconds to recognise. But sure enough, there it was, being used as a make-shift weapon of tortuous humiliation on a fellow victim and was currently protruding from an undignified orifice. The barbarians had no sense of respect for their victims, and rather too much of a sick sense of humour.

As the Rogue National warriors hacked and sliced their way through their pathetic enemy, a number of them reached the main bridge. After dissecting the few remaining Republic troops into pizza segments, they decided to have a bit of fun at the controls of the massive ship. They started pressing random buttons and pulling levers. A central control stick protruding out of a very important looking piece of equipment in the centre of the bridge caught the barbarians' attention. It wasn't long before they were squabbling over who should play with the device. Two of the barbarians grabbed the joy stick and tugged at it, this way and that, sending confusing signals to the ship's computer, which in turn sent the same mish-mash of instructions to the Antonn propellers. The bright lights of the particle matter propulsion system flashed on and off along the length and breadth of the ship in an interesting but random strobe-light effect, much like a cheap home disco. It gave the impression, to any onlooker, of a ship that was out of control. Which is exactly what the bridge commander of the attached Rogue National ship assumed, as his vessel was being dragged erratically by the random propeller power flashes.

Chapter 17

The Dwelling

K awoke. Again. He was really getting fed up with fainting all the time. If he was to be stranded on this planet, seemingly all alone except for some strange race who were hell bent on destroying all visiting life forms, the least he could do would be to remain conscious throughout the experience.

He made a logical decision to use the remaining dim evening light to investigate his surroundings, to ensure that he was as safe as he could be and then to take a well-earned rest. OK so he had only just awoken from a brief but deep slumber, but none of his rests had been planned so far and none had been comfortable. He knew that the night was drawing in and that a good night's sleep would be imperative to his survival in the morning. He still had many miles to go before he reached the huge floating upturned pyramid. He just hoped that some of his colleagues were still there, running their experiments and carrying out their investigations. His mind entertained the possibility that all the TAKers had fled the planet when the first attack took place. If this had happened then K was the only Republic member left on the planet. He quickly stopped himself from continuing this train of thought. Everyone needs to have something to believe in when in such dire situations, and K's faith had to be in the fact that some of his colleagues must still be on the planet. K had to believe that he was not alone.

Sure enough, he wasn't.

Within the darkened room in which he sat, there were more species of life than even he could imagine. Microscopic worlds thrived all over this small self-contained eco-system. It was just possible, that in one of these miniature cultures, there was a character just like K, attempting to battle the odds for survival, all alone within an alien part of its universe. Then again, it was just as possible that there was not.

There was also an uncomfortable abundance of non-microscopic life, which made K's skin crawl. He loved investigating new and interesting species, especially insects. But to be placed in a darkened room with millions of them, without any means of testing each creature's ability to hurt him, was not his idea of fun.

K stopped thinking about the insects for a moment. His eyes had grown more accustomed to the darkness that swallowed the interior of this flora building. Some light from the heavy dusk outside managed to seep through the thickly vegetated walls, revealing that the interior of this huge cube was indeed a building. K gasped as he made out a staircase and some partitioning amongst the overgrown ferns and undergrowth whose home this had now become. The plant life had obviously been here for thousands of years, dominating the entire building. Some of the load-bearing walls had collapsed under the gradual but unrelenting pressure of the trees and had therefore been made redundant as the flora walls took over. Evidence that the building had simply been abandoned for the wildlife to move in was everywhere. K started to look closer at the contents of the house. There were still signs of previous civilisation here. As K's eyes grew more accustomed to the dim light, he noticed the tips of chairs, buried within the undergrowth. He cleared the ferns and small prickly bushes away from the area containing the high-backed formal wooden seats. Beneath a thick layer of foliage, decayed leaves and the dust of millennia, was a table, with various types of food containers strewn across its surface. Small teeth marks covered the wooden storage devices, where rodents had nibbled at the remains of what must have once been a family dinner.

Further to K's left were more items of furniture, buried deep within the flora that now called this place home, including a desk, an area for preparing food, and some other items that were completely alien to K. Maybe they were raised areas of worship, or maybe they served as shelves for displaying fine artefacts or family heirlooms. Either way, these raised stages in each corner of the house were empty now, but for an abundance of plants and insects.

K decided to go up the stairs to see what remained of the living quarters. He made his way through the restrictive undergrowth towards the first step. As he placed his foot on the decaying wooden rung, it collapsed into a cloud of dust. Maybe K wouldn't bother investigating the upstairs. The structure was far too weak to support his weight after ten thousand years of damp neglect, and he wasn't sure he wanted to risk his current fitness levels in order to see the upper sections of this ancient dwelling.

This was actually a good thing. He would not have felt at home any longer if he was exposed to the site that evaded him in the upstairs living quarters. The dusty bones of three bodies were piled unceremoniously on a small bed. To the untrained eye, it simply looked like a pile of humanoid bones had been dumped there, but to a forensic scientist, the pile told a very specific story. The skeletons were all related. A father, a mother and a small child had spent their last few moments together in a huddle. There were no signs of struggle around the room. No sign of any resistance to their imminent fate. It simply looked as if the family had made a decision to be together for the rest of their lives, and well into their deaths. The family group looked strangely content and ultimately peaceful. Together forever. They had spent the last hundred centuries in each other's company and looked far too content to be disturbed.

In the ignorance of what resided upstairs, K had made the effort to clear one of the small raised areas in the corner of the room of all plant life, and was attempting to make it slightly more comfortable with handfuls of moss and dried leaves. Once his makeshift bed had been completed, he lay down to sleep. Despite being tired, and in great need of good rest, K was all too aware that his enemies were out there somewhere. He was also acutely conscious of the noises of animal life coming from every direction. The distant sounds of nocturnal creatures were broken only by similar grunts, growls and squawks, far closer than K would have liked. Some animals even ventured near the entrance to K's new home, but tended to run off soon after arrival due to the alien smell that K emitted. Within the house, noises were less obvious, but ever present. The scurrying of rodents and the constant chatter of millions of insects going about their nightly business, kept K awake for hours. Eventually, his tiredness caught up with him and he fell into a deeply troubled sleep.

Before K would have chosen to wake up, a strange thunderous noise awoke him. It was distant, but the rumbling that penetrated K's bones through his makeshift mattress was not something he felt he should ignore. It was different to the penetrating din of the alien vehicle that had so nearly run over his head yesterday. This was more extreme, he was sure of it. It was like a massive explosion or an earthquake far off in the distance. The rumbling subsided. K lifted himself out of his organic bed and ventured over to the doorway of his tree-lined house. The sun was gradually beginning to rise, giving the sky a dark blue appearance with a lighter turquoise and pink effect along the horizon to the north. There were thousands of neighbouring tree buildings all around him. Then it dawned on him. Every one of these large cubes of plant life must be an abandoned home. He thought back to his previous day's trek through many miles of uniform foliage growth. He was travelling through an ancient town. No, an ancient city. It must be huge.

As K leaned out of the doorway he looked to his right, down the moss and fern lined street on which he had journeyed for hours yesterday. It disappeared far off into the distance, perfectly straight. K looked to his left. The scene was similar, but somehow, the density of the street's surrounding foliage seemed to thicken on either side of the wide straight path. K would continue that way towards the floating skyscraper, but first he had to get to high ground to investigate the noise that had awoken him.

Looking at the wall of his building, K realised it was thick and tangled enough to give him sufficient purchase to clamber all the way to the top. Despite only being roughly the same height as its surrounding structures, it would give him a far better view than the ground. He began to climb the sheer face of the tree wall. Within a few minutes he had reached the rooftop. Even here the flora completely shrouded all evidence of the masonry that lay dormant beneath. The roof was covered in rich grass and ferns, heavily coloured plants were dotted around the flat area, giving it the appearance of a small tranquil summer meadow. K went to step off the tree onto the roof, but at the last minute recalled the wooden step, which had turned to dust as soon as his weight had upset the equilibrium of long term decay. This innocuous looking surface was likely to be in a similar state if it contained any wood. He decided not to find out and instead climbed further up the tree, which reached up a few metres higher than most of its neighbouring competitors, beyond the height of the roofs around him.

K steadied himself against the thick branches and then looked around to see where the noise had come from. In the far distance, he noticed The Chun. Still a good few hours away. It glowed softly in the early morning light. Its shadowed shape appearing almost transparent as it faintly reflected images of the local landscape gently shimmering against the sides of the monolithic structure. K's hypnotic gaze at this awesome upturned pyramid was broken as his attention was drawn to a much closer light flickering in the corner of his eye. The brightness of the sun began to gradually steal the scene, as it started to break over the horizon, throwing waves of fresh new warmth across the landscape. But not before K had noticed the huge fire that had broken out twenty or so miles to the north. The earthquake was caused by some sort of explosion. It must have been massive to have created such a monstrous fire. If K concentrated, he thought he could hear the crackles and pops, but it was probably his imagination. The fire itself was probably a few hundred metres in length, with massive structural protrusions emanating from the flames at one end. Maybe it was a large building of some sort that the enemy had decided to attack. Whatever it was, K did not envy the poor victims who may have been inside when it was destroyed. K's mind began to run riot again, thinking of the many negative reasons for the explosion. Did the enemy attack because they thought he was in there? Or, worse, were some of his colleagues in the building? Or was it an aerial attack, or maybe... K interrupted himself to take a calming deep breath. There was nothing he could do about it, so he decided to keep his eye on the fire periodically throughout his journey, but in the meantime would continue towards the most obvious land mark in the history of the universe.

His attention was drawn to the gradually brightening sky. Still a deep blue colour, the early morning scene gave an excellent back drop to the millions of pin points of light above the planet. Stars are beautiful, thought K. A few seemed to be moving. That can't be right, he thought. He looked closer, squinting his eyes in concentration. Yep, they were definitely moving, a bit like burning meteorites disintegrating in the atmosphere, but somehow different. These ones seemed to be getting quicker as they cascaded across the dark blue of the early morning sky. One in particular was much larger than a few moments ago. It continued to gain momentum, and as it grew, it became more red than white. A long tail of light grey followed it through the planet's atmosphere. It looked like a comet, but K knew that was impossible. It accelerated at break-neck speed towards the planet's surface, impacting the ground about ten miles away from K's location, causing a massive explosion. The devastation caused by such a collision must have been phenomenal. A huge column of fire sprouted from the impact zone. K could almost feel its heat. The ground and trees started to shake as the delayed reaction of the huge blast reached the soil beneath K. He had to hold onto the tree tightly not to be thrown off. After a few moments, the trembling subsided, and K relaxed his grip on the rough trunk. He had no idea what the object was, as it had been travelling way too fast to be able to tell. This place was weird – and getting stranger by the minute. Massive fires and explosions seemed to be occurring all over the place. It was almost as if the sky was falling in.

His gaze returned to the night sky. A wave of meteorites were flying through the air, but most were being disintegrated by the planet's atmosphere as they invaded the morning half-light. A beautiful array of white, pink and red dots travelled across the sky, flaring into incandescence and then rapidly dying out. More and more bright lights joined the display, some exploding into a shower of smaller red and pink particles before fading away to nothing after a few seconds of combustion. K was in awe of this – a firework display fit for a god. He felt privileged to have witnessed such a beautiful and natural phenomenon. At least, he assumed it was natural – it must be a meteor shower. Despite his initial thoughts, there was no other explanation.

He decided not to investigate the meteor's landing site, nor the massive building that had been destroyed to the north, as both may well be teeming with the unwanted attentions of his enemies. It was K's best policy to allow them to be drawn in force to the burning locations, and to use the time to continue his trek towards the massive upturned pyramid, hopefully undetected and unaccompanied.

K climbed down from the tree, back to the safety of the soft grassy ground. Once back on terra-firma, he noticed his sheer stupidity in full evidence from the night before. There, next to the sanctuary of the house that had offered him shelter and relative anonymity for the night, near the large forced entrance to the building was a huge pile of logs and branches and a land cruiser. In his exhaustion, K had completely forgotten to clear up the mess that he had created during his hacking and chopping spree and had not given a second thought to hiding the land cruiser somewhere less obvious. He mentally kicked himself for his ignorance. Then decided to use the situation for a pep-talk and comforted himself that it meant there were no enemy troops nearby. Otherwise he'd already be dead. He concluded he was therefore safe (not to mention alive) and should be happy with that.

Before setting off, K contemplated investigating more of the local buildings and homes for clues as to why this race had deserted their city. Why had they left so quickly? Where had they gone? This whole planet seemed to hold so many mysteries. Why had someone or something tried to kill him and his colleagues? It didn't make sense. Not yet anyway. K knew he had to get to the floating pyramid in order to find some answers. There he would meet his colleagues, or his assailants. Either way, the truth would be known.

Chapter 18

The Descent

Tenaket panicked as bolts of green fire shot past his escape pod. He manoeuvred the small craft as skilfully as his scared hands would allow. His passengers released involuntary yelps at each sudden movement, like scared children on a roller-coaster. Only, the stakes were far higher.

Behind them, other small escape ships followed, each finding their own erratic paths towards the planet, as they avoided the awesome fire power of the RN destroyer, in a 'life or death' slalom.

The two huge mother ships were tied together by ten umbilical cords that allowed the penetrative invasion to take place. Both vessels were taking a terrible pounding from the auto defence sequence of fire power that had been employed by the Republic to aid their escape. Cannons fired their loads into the side of the Rogue Nation ship, causing massive explosions far too close for comfort. The main force of the Republic's fire power was destroying itself more than its opposition as the vessel's blasts were deflected away from the enemy's almost impenetrable hull. Even so, the Barbarians' ship was still taking a heavy battering.

As Tenaket looked at his fellow pods and TAK landers on the cockpit monitors in front of him, their numbers were depleting, fast. At first there were too many to count, but gradually the small dots on the scanners showed fewer and fewer ships. Some of the remaining vessels were unlikely to make it through the complex atmospheric approach – they would be killed by their own ignorance. Tenaket was one of the more experienced planet lander pilots. He had taken many expeditions down through some of the most treacherous natural planetary self-defence systems. The Vacchion atmosphere was a breath of fresh air in comparison. But he knew some of his colleagues were doomed from the start.

A landing craft, next to Tenaket's pod suddenly exploded, after taking a direct hit from a powerful enemy cannon flare. There was nothing left of the ship or its contents, it had simply vanished, turned briefly into a bright red fireball before transforming itself into a cloud of colourless dust, hurtling towards the outer reaches of the planet's stratosphere. There was nothing Tenaket could do, except try to ignore all the other ships, and focus all his attention on his own survival.

Just a few moments more, and they would be entering the relative safety of the atmospheric belt. This would protect his pod from the cannon fire, which would disintegrate on contact, reaching the escape pod in small, harmless shards of its former glory. But this whole process was far too slow for his liking, the pod had never seemed so slow. It felt like he would be better off getting out and pushing. His anxiety for safety heightened his reactions and senses to supersonic proportions.

T, as his friends and close colleagues referred to him, looked in the rear view monitor. The awesome fire power was still pouring from the Rogue Nation mother ship. Other, smaller RN fighters had also been launched and were now in hot pursuit of the slower escape pods and the less skilled pilots. Many innocent lives were lost every few seconds, as small Republic crafts were turned into explosive clouds of dust. Then T noticed something significant. The two mother ships, both huge in length, were beginning to part company. The ten umbilical cords had been severed. The close quarter battle had taken its toll on both vessels, but his home for the past two years, had sustained by far the most damage. It was hardly recognisable to him. Great plumes of pink and red gases escaped from massive lesions along its hull. It had almost been severed in two by the concentrated explosions in its centre and many large sections had already broken away and plummeted towards the planet's surface. The ship must be completely uninhabitable now. Anyone left on board was dead, even if they were still breathing at this very moment.

The RN destroyer backed away slowly from the victim vessel, continuing its impressive firework display of devastation, as it retreated from the doomed carcass. The Republic's planetary investigation vessel twisted slowly against the black star-studded back-drop making the massive movement almost poetic as beautiful colours of fire and gas jumped in all directions from its structure. Its descent towards the planet's surface, powered only by the gravitational pull of Vacchion and the constant pounding of cannon fire from its assailant, started to accelerate. A tear began to form deep in T's right eye, but he held it back, determined that it would only show itself at the very end of his life.

He kept an eye on the rear view monitor, ignoring the requests for information from his panicked colleagues in the hold behind him. He was entering the atmosphere of the planet now, and must concentrate on ensuring his approach speed and angle were right, otherwise they would be baked alive in a matter of seconds. His was one of the first pods to reach the outer atmosphere, which surprised T, as he had seemingly taken a life-time to get here. Again he looked in the rear view monitor, just a few moments since his last glance. But this time, his life flashed before his eyes as the seriousness of the situation dawned on him.

The monitor showed the Republic mother ship much larger than it had appeared before. T kept watching to confirm his worst nightmare. "This can't be happening" he mumbled to himself, clearing all nervous muttering and chattering in the hold behind him and replacing it with a cold wet blanket of total fear. "What?" one of the nervous passengers enquired anxiously.

"You seriously don't want to know," explained T as he watched the Republic mother ship's bow accelerate towards his pod at a phenomenal rate.

T was helpless. They were in the outer reaches of the atmosphere and their trajectory and speed could not be adjusted, otherwise their vessel would break up and disintegrate. But, by the same token, their million tonne mother ship was also about to enter the atmosphere of the planet, on a much faster and much more direct route to the planet's surface. T knew there was nothing he could do and simply hoped that he was wrong about being in the way of the plummeting molten vessel.

Two of T's superior passengers, most annoyed at his avoidance of communication, decided to get out of the safety of their chairs and clambered their way to the front of the pod to see the monitor that was causing T such concern. The image of the mother ship now filled the entire screen and was moving towards it at lightning pace. One of the men fell to the floor with paralysing terror, whilst the other jumped back towards his seat in the hope that a small piece of material, in the form of a seat belt, was going to help his survival. T smiled, safe in the knowledge that at least if the impact was to occur, he would have his pride intact and would die knowing he did everything he could to save this sorry bunch of cowards.

The moment of impact came... and went. T had been wrong in his pessimistic assumptions. The bow of the mother ship shot past the stern of the pod by just five hundred metres. It sounded like a lot, thought T briefly. But considering the sheer size and speed of the vessel, and the fact that if T's pod had been going 0.23% slower, the mother ship would have sent them spinning into incandescent oblivion, it illustrated the point far better.

The mother ship's hull continued to flash past the rear view monitor for a brief moment as it maintained its four thousand mile an hour trip towards the planet's surface. T calculated briefly that it would take the smouldering mass approximately twenty five seconds to impact the planet's surface. He had nothing better to do than continue to use his expert flying skills to navigate the atmospheric entry of the pod and save his whimpering colleagues' lives. He started his stop-watch to see how accurate his estimate was. Then he adjusted one of the viewing cameras to track the mother ship as it plummeted towards its final resting place. It was going to be an amazing spectacle, so he may as well witness it, despite seeming somewhat unethical and distasteful.

Chapter 19

The Search

The Marth stormed onto the main pod hangar of the enemy vessel and made a direct path to the leader of team G.

"Why did you not stop them escaping?" he demanded, irritated by the launch of dozens of escape pods only moments before his arrival.

"We only got here a few seconds before you Sire." he replied, terrified for his life like never before. "We killed everyone we came across, just as you commanded." He offered as pathetic compensation.

The smell of melted and decayed flesh was in the air, as the stench of the Marth's wake of destruction started to catch up with him. He'd had his fun, but now the pleasure had been removed from this task by the cowardice of his opposition. They had run away from a battle, something he would punish his own troops for, by agonising death. He was disgusted that they had fled, but he had expected nothing less.

The Marth still had his primary objective to complete. They must find the tiny electronic device that the Republic teams might have stumbled across on the planet's surface. They must retrieve it, if it was here. Marth gave his orders to search the ship for the device. If the Republic had it, it would be likely to be in the laboratories in a scrutiny chamber. His men ran out of the room in groups of three, their task was to find a small piece of electronic wizardry, smaller than a millimetre across, in an alien ship well over a kilometre in length. Judging by the events on the exterior of the ship, they didn't have a great deal of time to do it.

How dare they come here? The Marth started thinking to himself. How dare they come to steal the treasure that has eluded me for twelve long, boring battle-free years? Then he broke his train of thought and decided to take it down an alternative tangent. If they hadn't come, he would not have been able to have this small battle. There would have been no brief killing spree, no laser cannon fire, no broadside invasion of the enemy vessel, no hand to hand combat, no tasting the enemies blood on his hands, no murder on his conscience – god he loved that. The feeling of being responsible for another being's early and painful demise was a glorious one, better than any drug. He had truly missed the so-called guilt of murder on his mind. Somehow killing his own men was just not the same – it was a bit like a hardcore heroine addict tasting the dizzy heights of hedonism that could be experienced with aspirin – it simply wasn't the same! Without the Republic gate-crashing his world, the Marth would not have been able to enjoy all this killing again. He smiled to himself as he realised that he was actually grateful for the Republic ship's arrival. With any luck there would be a few pathetic survivors on the planet's surface to maim and toy with before sending them to their own personal hells for eternity. Excellent. Things were looking up already.

The Marth was beside himself with sick, twisted glee. The last thing he wanted right now was any more bad news to spoil it all.

"Sire, something is happening with the Republic's propulsion system," explained the bridge commander nervously to the Marth over his direct intercom channel.

"What exactly?" replied the white knight of evil in his best deep resonating tones.

"I am not sure Sire, but it seems to be out of control," came the slightly crackly voice, which sounded so feeble and weak to the Marth. He waited to see if any more information was about to be offered (the Marth had truly understood the power of silence). Sure enough, the pause convinced the bridge commander to continue, "There is a danger that the ship will be pulled out of orbit and towards the planet, Sire." Again a brief pause, just to be sure. "I think we ought to disconnect our boarding tubes, otherwise…"

"I understand," interrupted the Marth softly, with a slight air of annoyance. "It looks like our fun is over for today."

For good measure, the Marth spent the next few seconds melting his nearest four colleagues to let off a little steam. But he needed another fix of enemy murder, so he sent out the best command he could think of.

"Cease fire on all enemy escape pods."

"Sire, there are only a few left," came back the bridge commander's reply, before he had a chance to think about what he was saying. He regretted it immediately. Everyone knew it.

The Marth was beside himself with anger. His orders had been questioned by his bridge commander. "Do as I command" he stated, happy in the knowledge that he would have a well deserving victim waiting for his attention on the bridge upon his return. Insolence of such massive proportions needed to be dealt with in a very specific way.

"Yes, Sire." The statement of obedience was punctuated moments later by a small weapon being fired and a soft squelchy noise broadcast across the intercom. Damn, thought the Marth, it's happened again. The selfish bastard has taken the fun out of my job. That's the third time this has happened, I must find a way of stopping my men from blowing their own brains out before I get the chance to discipline them.

The Marth made his way back to his own ship. If there was any more killing to be done, he wanted to do it. He began his long walk through the internal wreckage of the enemy vessel, deeply inhaling the stench of death with every breath. He was barely content with his close quarter battles, but he must not fail in the quest for the doomsday device. He was unsure exactly what it was, but historians of the Rogue Nation state had declared that it contained within it the power to wipe out entire planets. They predicted, from the manuscripts and diagrams retrieved from the planet's surface, that this device had been created with such incredible power, the inventors themselves had not managed to tame it. Subsequently, they had eradicated their entire race within weeks of its completion.

Finding such a device was a dangerous task. And so it fell on the shoulders of the most ruthless leader in the Rogue Nation's hierarchy. The Marth would be the only one fearless enough to lead such an expedition. (Although the word 'fearless', as used by the supreme council, was actually a euphemism for 'stupid', but no-one outside of the council would ever know this, for fear of this information reaching the Marth).

A number of the umbilical tubes were still attached, several had been damaged in the massive external explosions. There were only two that remained usable. The Marth was asked to proceed to tube D. He did so. Whilst crossing the semitransparent bridge to his own ship, he monitored the damage to both vessels. The enemy ship was in a poor state. Hull breaches were occurring regularly along its flank, the integrity of the craft's massive structure was highly unstable. His own ship's damage seemed largely superficial, although there were a few areas of extreme concern. He contacted the bridge, giving details about areas needing to be investigated with the utmost urgency.

Upon giving his reports to the bridge, his newly appointed commander asked if he should call back the troops onboard the enemy vessel. The Marth ordered that they continue their search and that they should not be informed of the state of the dying, not to mention, gradually plummeting ship on which they were captive.

By the time Marth had reached his bridge, reports had come back from the boarding parties that there was no device fitting the description on board. Marth ordered that they continued to look. The landing party coordinators did not react. They simply passed on the orders to widen the search. The Marth turned to his Defence admiral. "Sever the umbilical cords and retain communication with the search parties until the very last moment."

"There are forty of our men still on board, Sire," commented the Admiral, who regretted the sentence before it had left his lips. He wished he could take it back, but rather than wait for an answer, he merely acknowledged the look in the Marth's eyes and gave the orders to retract the boarding tubes and retreat to a safe distance to watch the enemy vessel plummet towards the planet's surface. As it did so, they retained constant communications with the various parties on board who acknowledged, before their blistering demise that there was definitely no sign of the device.

Excellent, thought the Marth to himself. The Republic have not stumbled across the tiny piece of machinery and so the search must go on. But to be sure, we must slay every single member of the enemy on the planet's surface before they find it. That should be fun, he smiled to himself.

The bridge's attention turned to the plummeting Republic mother ship as it broke in two and accelerated towards the planet's surface at blistering pace.

Chapter 20

The Impact

After just ten minutes hovering towards his ultimate goal on the clattering land cruiser, K's attention was once again drawn to the sky. It was a great deal lighter than before, as the sun continued its inevitable rise. But still the falling space debris rained down through the atmosphere, burning into white-hot dust as it went. But there were two particular lights in the sky that K's attention was focussed on, both many times larger than all of the previous meteorites put together. Were these just huge meteorites, or something more sinister? For all he knew meteor showers of this kind were common in the Vacchion solar system. It seemed, on a planet with a giant upside down floating pyramid that protruded into the sky and beyond, anything was possible.

Maybe they were simply much closer to him than the others. But that was an even more frightening thought, especially as a couple of huge impacts had already taken place. K recalled momentarily the giant building on the horizon that had exploded earlier, waking him from his well-earned slumber. Maybe that was the result of a massive meteor collision, as opposed to it being deliberately destroyed by the type of cannon fire he had witnessed yesterday. With the second impact K had witnessed landing less than ten miles away, he was starting to get nervous about his chances of surviving such a heavy meteor shower. The last thing he wanted, after everything he had been through, was to be squashed by a freak natural occurrence. That would be just his luck.

He stopped his noisy vehicle and watched the impressive display. As the two vast comet-like objects accelerated towards the planet's surface, one of them exploded into a million pieces, each particle becoming a new miniature comet, most of which died out quickly, vanishing into nothing. The other large object remained in one piece, descending at what must have been thousands of miles an hour. K knew he should take cover, but it was as much as he could do to remain stuck to the spot with his mouth hanging open. The large object, burned white and orange as it plunged towards the base of The Chun. It was going to hit the ground where the massive floating structure and the planet's surface almost met. What would this do to the perfect equilibrium of the up-turned pyramid, thought K? It could destroy the entire planet. If the giant structure were to fall onto Vacchion's surface, the knock-on effects could be catastrophic. Something of that phenomenal size, impaling the globe's surface could knock it out of orbit, or worse, break it into two. Either way, the planet could be pushed onto a new trajectory, potentially upsetting the delicate gravitational harmony of the entire solar system. Maybe even this entire galaxy.

The huge burning object impacted the planet's surface with the force of a billion laser cannons. K witnessed it happening, but couldn't believe it. He had a restricted view, due to the tree-structures all around him, but he could see a massive ball of flames leap into the air around the base of the colossal structure, sending huge chunks of earth and what K assumed to be buildings flying into the air. Having seen training videos about what happened after such large explosions, he knew the aftermath could claim his life if he didn't get out of the way immediately. His mind went into overload... The Chun was about fifty miles away. That gave him roughly five seconds before the impa...

The burning wind and dust cloud flew towards K, down the long straight road. He could see it approaching from many miles away, knocking over large trees and scalding all in its path travelling at hundreds of miles an hour, but K was stationary – pinned to the seat of his small land cruiser like a scared rabbit faced with a huge pair of headlights. An alarm went off in his head. Not just a metaphorical one, but a real one. It startled K into making sudden life-preserving decisions. He jumped off the small vehicle and ran towards the neighbouring alley-way, which sat protected between two large buildings. He hoped the structures would help to shield him from the burning wind. He wrapped himself in some loose branches and vines that hung from the vegetation high above.

The wind hit with the sound of thunder. Uprooted trees flew past K's hiding place as the burning air was channelled down the many straight roads that seemed to emanate in every direction from the base of The Chun. Leaves were incinerated and branches charred as everything on the long streets not firmly embedded in the ground was torn from gravity's clutches and thrown into the air at a hundred miles per hour. After a few minutes the blistering wind died down, leaving an eerie acrid calm in its devastating wake.

K decided it was safe to come out from his hiding place. The wall which he had used for protection was largely intact. It did not face the approaching wind, and was therefore only victim to the hot mini tornadoes that travelled at a tangent to the main stream, which were mere scalding breezes by comparison. But even here the upheaval was obvious, with hundreds of burnt twigs and leaves strewn along the short length of the alley way.

K stepped back onto the main street, his exposed skin slightly tender from the light toasting. The sight that faced him was an awesome one. The look of his surroundings was entirely different. No more were the streets carpeted with moss, ferns and long grass. And no longer were the buildings that lined the main street made of trees and thick undergrowth. The wind had stripped the facades of the ancient constructions. The view was now very different. What welcomed K's eyes was the unveiling of ten thousand year shroud. A beautiful view of the dwellings of an ancient yet civilised society. It was truly a sight for lonely eyes. One that paid homage to the many thousands of people who once lived here.

All of the beautiful, yet simple houses were made of a light, almost white, sand coloured stone that had obviously stood the test of time. Despite their age, the surfaces had not been significantly dulled by the centuries of neglect. Now that most of the trees had been felled by the wind or stripped of their leaves, the majority of the ancient buildings now stood naked to the sunlight. A scene that had not been witnessed by anyone for ten thousand years, befell K's gaze. He looked on in awe, truly privileged to witness such a sight. He was able to picture the street bustling with activity as imaginary people in his mind's eye moved in various directions around the tranquil scene, chatting amongst themselves whilst conducting their business. Judging by the size of this city and the simple yet effective lines of the structures around him, he assumed, quite rightly that it was once a sprawling metropolis of an advanced race who chose to live life simply.

As K began to pay more attention to the recently exposed fascias around him, he noticed that each had an element of uniqueness about it. They were all fundamentally the same, but had been personalised in some subtle way by the inhabiting families. At least, that's the way K had decided to see it. The positioning of the windows and doors on the front of each home was very slightly different. He approached the nearest building, the one which moments ago offered him the protection that had saved his life from the searing wind. Above the main door way was a unique crest consisting of a number of pictures positioned in a circle. K assumed that each of the five scenes depicted something about the ancestry of the family who lived or worked here. He was not far from the truth, but knowing that he would never know the whole truth about these icons of a former race, he decided to be happy in his educated assumptions. He smiled at his surroundings, knowing only yesterday he truly believed he was in the centre of an uncultivated forest of mammoth proportions.

The road way had been cleared of its undergrowth, and many of the shiny white bricks that paved the thoroughfare showed themselves through the remaining charred grass and earth. This would have truly been a magnificent sight, in its day.

As K looked in awe down the street of newly exposed fascias, he noticed The Chun was still in its same position, framed perfectly by the street, which continued all the way to the base of the monolithic floating structure. He breathed a huge sigh of relief. It could have so easily been the end of the planet's existence. There was a huge cloud of smoke, rising up The Chun's lower section, billowing out in every direction. This could still be a risk. The devastation at the base of The Chun must be incredible. K was as keen as ever to get to the base. Although, his original aim was to find his colleagues, he now realised that being the only Republican on the planet was more inevitable than ever. If his colleagues had been near the base of the giant inverted pyramid, they would now be dead.

He turned to where his land cruiser had been a few minutes before. It was nowhere to be seen. K strained his eyes to view as far down the street as he could in the direction of the searing wind. Sure enough, a long way off in the distance, were the battered remains of his land cruiser, small sections of its structure strewn across the road amongst thousands of branches and sections of tree. No point in walking back to get that, thought K. Looks like the rest of the journey will have to be on foot. Considering the seriousness of the situation, he was taking it very well. The prospect of a fifty kilometre hike, with no food, no weapons and now no mode of transport should have made him feel very vulnerable indeed. But the awesome site of the ancient city made K feel almost at home. This trek across an alien landscape now seemed like a pleasant stroll rather than a fight for survival.

K began the next stage of his adventure, starving and thirsty, but smiling and more determined than ever to find out what the hell was going on, even if it killed him. Which it probably still would.

Chapter 21

The Omen

The cell continued its repairs, but there was little it could do to mend the damage sustained by its batteries. There was no choice but to remain in this vessel and make the most of the situation. If and when the host's life was terminated, the cell could use a boost of power to attempt to eject itself into another host, but it would only have moments in which to achieve such a feat. And it was a high risk strategy.

For now, it must concentrate its efforts on ensuring the host's power supply was sustained for as long as possible. As part of this process, the cell continued the complicated and risky operations to link its memory banks, learning and initiative drives to the appropriate strands of its host's communications channels. It was a long and delicate process that would take many hours, but total synchronisation had to occur if the cell was to maximise its chance of survival and ensure its continued success at keeping the information it held away from any form of civilisation.

The process of intense and highly technical surgery at a microscopic scale was eventually completed. The cell had managed to learn a great deal about the vessel in which it was now a prisoner, detained by circumstance. So many connections had been made with the host's nervous and chemical balancing systems, that extracting itself was only a viable option upon the termination of the life source on which it now depended. It digested the information about the vessel's past, and calculated the amount of chemicals it required for maximum effect in a number of differing scenario's that the cell concluded had a higher than average chance of occurring. Then it began to adjust the bio-chemical levels distributed around the body to increase the effectiveness and efficiency of this cumbersome life form.

The cell had already saved the host's life twice now, and it intended to continue this pattern for as long as possible. The first steps were to balance the levels of adrenalin to ensure the vessel was kept on amber alert at all times, without overdosing and causing the drug to become ineffective in a crisis. This careful chemical balance would allow reflexes to be primed and attention to detail maximised. Food and water were essential to all living creatures that the cell had been programmed to understand, and this was by no means an exception to that rule. It began to educate, passing limited particles of essential information to the host's brain to aid its survival. The primary information uploaded included what not to eat. But the Cell was careful to be sure to place these 'memories' in an area that would commonly be referred to as the 'déjà vu' vault. The cell made the decision to take itself off-line. Initiative chips and learning banks needed to be reserved for use in only the more desperate of situations. There was a limit to how much even this amazing piece of technical wizardry could achieve. It continued to educate the host vessel as to ways of finding solid and liquid fuel, whilst setting monitoring alarms to pull it back on line, should it be required. Until then, rejuvenation time was required.

Chapter 22

The Fugitives

"Wow."

"You can say that again."

"Wow."

They were in awe of the site that faced them. This was nothing new to The Chun. The upturned pyramid that faced them was truly an awesome site, and had been receiving similar reactions for millions of years. Even its creators were in awe of their own abilities to create such a beautiful monstrosity. But to T and his colleague, viewing it from the sky out of the small cockpit window, it was a new and truly unforgettable experience.

The pod skimmed through the air effortlessly. T had managed to negotiate the atmospheric entry requirements with relative ease (albeit with a close brush with death in the form of a falling mother ship). He had made it look so easy. But a number of colleagues' ships had already failed, and had become burning masses of fire that disintegrated through the atmosphere like shooting stars in the beautiful dawn sky.

The largest section of the mother ship had impacted the surface of the planet precisely at the base of the massive upturned pyramid. This had caused a huge explosion, as the anti-gravitational equipment mixed with the driving fuels of the Antonn thrusters. Luckily there appeared to be no damage to the vast structure that pierced space, otherwise it could have signalled the end of the planet.

"It looks even more breathtaking from here than from space," declared T. It was a strange realisation, as The Chun looked truly magnificent from space too. The majority of its mass existed far above the reaches of the atmosphere, but somehow, people had become accustomed to seeing vast objects in space – it was a great leveller when it came to objects of such monolithic proportions. Space made everything appear small against its unimaginable size. But when you saw The Chun from within the atmosphere of the planet, its form in relation to everything else reaffirmed it as being something ridiculously huge. Impossible, almost.

They were flying at ten thousand metres, directly towards The Chun. At its base they saw the huge smouldering crater of destruction caused by the explosive mass of their mother ship. The devastation was incredible. Even at this height, the size of the crater was obvious, and its charred darkness spread throughout the forest like a giant black paint-bomb. However, the site beneath them was also confusing. Around the circumference of smoking blackness, where there used to be only dense vegetation, there now appeared to be a huge circle of brilliant white geometric shapes. From this giant ring of shapes, thin straight lines of white spread out in every direction, like a huge stone sunburst covering hundreds of square miles, mixed into the green of the flora. They would need to get much closer before they could identify what it was.

They decided to land a few miles away from the crater. They were conscious that the explosion was likely to have attracted a great deal of attention. If there were Rogue Nation ground troops down here, they would have either been obliterated by the blast, or would be on their way to investigate it. T knew they would be likely to come into contact with the barbaric aliens at some point. If they were going to get out of here alive, they would need to ensure they had some fire power to defend themselves, and that meant taking them from unsuspecting enemy ground troops, somehow. Recently affirmed knowledge of the barbarians' incredible fighting abilities made the option of spending the rest of their lives living on an alien planet in a dense forest as fugitives a very unattractive one.

T tried to contact other pods and landing craft through secure hailing channels, so that any unwanted eavesdroppers could not identify the signal as anything but natural distortion. Two other ships replied. Was that it? Only sixty people had survived the onslaught, out of nearly two thousand onboard the Republican mother ship? T felt sick to the stomach. This had been an incredible massacre. One that would be entered in the history books as a sad and pointless attack on innocent and harmless Republic scientists. At least, that's how it would appear in Republic history books. There is no telling what the Rogue Nation's historians would say. No doubt they would cover the gory details about how many of the enemy were torn to shreds by their heroic barbarian warriors.

As the most senior pilot, he ordered all three ships to be placed in camouflage mode, and took a few moments to broadcast the coordinates of a rendezvous point he had spotted that seemed suited to hide their small ships - close enough to the crater beneath The Chun, but far enough away to be out of the immediate radius of attention. They headed towards a large patch of green, a few miles east of the outer reaches of the white ring that surrounded the massive black crater.

The ships glided through the air soundlessly, their exterior changed colour in tune with the surrounding scenery. Complex electronics recorded the views from all angles of the ship and displayed them on the opposite sides of the exterior hull. The overall effect was total camouflage from every direction, as onlookers would see only a very slight distortion of objects the small ships flew in front of.

T manoeuvred his pod towards the green landing zone, dipping to a height of three hundred metres. They glided silently over the tree tops, able to see at close hand what the straight white lines were that had been created by the explosion.

"Would you look at that," exclaimed T's co-pilot. The streets and fascias of the buildings shone in the early morning sun, their roofs still completely covered in greenery. "There is a huge city down there. It must spread for miles." He continued, stating the obvious as the rear view monitor showed similar evidence of the massive citadel disappearing off into the distance and beyond the horizon over thirty miles away.

The pilots of each ship watched the sprawling metropolis of white stone buildings unfold beneath them as they flew over the foliage covered roof tops. The large, flat landing point was just up ahead. It seemed to be on a higher level than much of the surrounding greenery, which covered the ancient buildings. Bordering the designated landing zone were rows of large geometric masses of flora, each with one side revealing the historical white stone masonry below its once leaf-shrouded exterior. They were about to land on a huge raised plateau of some sort. Around the edge of the flat landing zone were the remains of beautiful tall trees and bushes. Some greenery on the upper branches still remained, but a great deal had been destroyed by the explosion. The area was covered in ferns, grass and heather, broken occasionally by beautiful colours of dangerous looking flowers, which had survived the hot winds – protected by the near-solid wall of trees that lined the large raised rectangle.

T carefully landed the craft, ordering the remaining ships to hover for a few moments to ensure the surface was sturdy enough to support all three crafts. The pod feet made gentle contact with the greenery, burying themselves deep within the thick flora. Once all preliminary checks had been made from the cockpit of the pod, and the area was considered as secure as could be expected, the men began to disembark. T gave the orders for the other two ships to land gently on the inviting surface.

As they stepped out of the ship, the remaining two escape pods approached the landing zone and prepared for touchdown. The twenty disembarked men stood to attention as their colleagues' ships landed on the plain. After a few moments the last Republic survivors gradually exited their life-raft vessels and were greeted with cheers and smiles.

All sixty-three men were very happy to be alive. They were still in danger and were going to have to be extremely cautious to get out of this predicament. They were all too aware that death had not so much gone home, but had merely popped into the metaphorical pub round the corner to await the outcome of whatever battles were to take place.

Chapter 23

The Companion

K listened carefully. There was a rushing sound of air, high over-head. He took cover. Whilst hiding in a nearby doorway he peered up at the sky. It was a familiar sound. It must be an aircraft of some sort, but he wasn't able to spot it and therefore decided not to draw attention to himself. It was more likely to be an enemy craft than a Republic landing craft. A few seconds later there were some more wind rushing noises, K couldn't tell how many.

His heart rate began to increase with the worry of the unknown. If these craft were his assailants, searching for him, then he was in grave danger. He could be heading straight into their trap. It seemed somewhat illogical to travel towards the base of the most obvious meeting point on the planet's surface now that he spent a moment thinking about it, but somehow he felt compelled to get there. Nothing was going to stop him seeing the massive structure at close quarters, even if it meant his death.

His pulse suddenly reduced back to a more normal level. The change was so rapid, that it made K look down at his chest to check that his heart was still beating. He had never had a heart attack before and had no idea how it was supposed to feel, but that rapid change from one rate to the next was definitely not natural. Why would he suddenly become so calm? It must be some magical power of relaxation induced by the awesome structure. Yes that must be it. K had never managed to be so calm in such a situation before. Not that he had ever been in such a situation, but even ones that were a fraction of the danger he faced now usually sent him into an uncontrollable fit of panicked tears. He decided there was nothing he could do but simply accept that the incredible structure in front of him had strange and mystical powers of a calming and healing nature. He decided to continue his trek after ensuring no more noises were coming from the sky. He was thirsty and his stomach was beginning to hurt from the lack of food. He knew he must eat soon.

Without reason, he turned left, down a wide alley, taking a detour from the main street that he had already travelled over seventy miles on. He wasn't sure why, but it seemed like a good decision at the time. The buildings here ran adjacent to the straight road that pointed to the base of The Chun, and had been sheltered from the blast. They were still heavily covered by trees and vines. After a number of structures had been passed, K found himself in a new street, similar in many details to the previous one. But this street was much wider, and it had a raised section of white stone running down the centre of it. There was a great deal of concentrated plant life around this raised section, most of which had been torn to shreds from the hot wind that had raced through here from the meteorite blast. Strewn all around the area were toasted berries and nuts. Food. And a great deal of it. But what was safe for him to eat? They hadn't completed tests in this area and he had no idea what might be poisonous to his delicate interior. K's brain served him a few distant memories of safe food options, accompanied by a feeling of déjà vous. They must be memories from other planets.

K looked over the edge of the metre high stone area that seemed to run the full length of the street, disappearing into the distance in both directions. In the centre was a channel less than a metre in width. And in that channel was the cleanest looking cool water that K had ever seen. He placed his hand in the water and cupped a small amount of the water to his mouth. Something told him it must be okay to drink. So he did. Handful after handful of the wonderful liquid were consumed, much to the delight of K's creaking and groaning organs. He began to feel brighter and lighter than before, as fresh fluids hydrated his system. His body was in great need of energy replenishment.

Now for food. Being a scientist, K was well aware of the dangers strange new planets could hold within innocent looking berries. He was so hungry he was willing to eat anything, but he knew this could be fatal. He picked up a small purple berry, which had been lightly toasted on one side. He paused, distracted by a scrabbling sound coming from the bushes ten metres down-stream towards base of The Chun. K instinctively took cover. He crouched by the side of the stone canal, trying to blend into the white rock as much as possible. He was about as camouflaged as a naked man in a lingerie shop. The rustling happened again. K picked up a nearby rock, for self defence.

Out of the clump of bushes gathered at the side of the raised water channel, a small mammal tip-toed out of his resting place, leapt up onto the metre high structure and made its way along the water's edge, oblivious to the stress it had just caused its neighbour. It stopped and stared at the strange creature crouched in front of it. With an inquisitive eye, it viewed the piece of white stone the tall creature held above it's head. K jumped slightly with guilt, as he realised he looked like a vicious poacher. The large rodent witnessed the strange biped flinch and drop the white rock on it's own head. K writhed around on the floor, clutching his pounding skull. The rock wasn't huge and hadn't done any serious damage, but it really bloody hurt. The pain subsided fairly quickly though, and K eventually sat up and looked at his new audience.

The foot-long beaver-like rodent seemed to be laughing at K. It was rolling around on its back, with its four stumpy limbs and two long thick tails flailing about in the air, whilst it made strange chirping noises. K's pride hoped the stupid creature was simply scratching its back on the hard stone lip of the canal. But the tables were soon turned when the small creature rolled off the edge of the stone wall and splashed into the shallow stream below. K laughed out loud, almost startling himself at the sudden expression of glee. It was the first thing he had to be happy about since he had arrived at this planet early yesterday. Since then his life had taken turns for the worse at almost every conceivable opportunity. He giggled uncontrollably as the soggy creature pulled itself out of the stream and back onto the near bank of the raised stone canal. It looked sheepish and suddenly not in the mood for 'back scratching'. But at the site of K laughing at its expense it eventually started making the chirping noises again as its small brown body quivered up and down. K realised the creature really was laughing.

Wow. K appeared to have made a friend. And no ordinary friend, either. This one happened to be an as yet undiscovered alien creature on an uncharted planet, who just happened to have a sense of humour. Life certainly dealt some very odd cards.

Their laughter naturally subsided. Silence prevailed once again, broken only by the gentle sound of the moving stream and distant bird song. K approached the cute rodent, slowly, with his left hand extended, a big smile on his face, holding out the half toasted purple berry as a gift. The creature looked horrified and backed away suddenly, trotting down the stream wall and leaping into the bushes from where it had originally appeared. K was sad. He had blown it. He admitted to himself that he had considered eating the small creature, but that was before they had laughed with each other.

Within seconds the creature came back out of the bush, dragging behind it a large leaf. Cupped within the leaf were hundreds of berries and nuts, none of which were purple. The rodent pulled its makeshift picnic along the floor to where K stood, and backed away slightly, after picking an armful of nuts for itself. The creature looked up at K, then back at its pile of food and then at K again, as if by way of dinner invitation. This was incredible, maybe he hadn't blown it after all. K looked at the pathetic, and potentially lethal, purple berry that he had clasped between his thumb and forefinger and threw it over his shoulder before slowly approaching the food. He sat cross-legged on a patch of grass on the predominantly exposed stone floor and proceeded to take a dark brown nut from the top of the pile. He nibbled at it carefully, watching the rodent tuck into the small stash of food at its feet.

After ten minutes, the food was all gone and both K and the rodent were nourished. They sat with their backs against the raised canal wall, enjoying the feeling of a full stomach and the warmth of the morning sun on their faces. The rodent appeared to copy K's position and had a strangely intelligent appeal to its cuteness. K smiled at it, and it seemed to smile back, showing its brilliant white sharp front teeth in the process.

Suddenly, in the near distance, the all too familiar ground rumbling interrupted the tranquil scene. K's heart started racing.

This was the sound he had heard just before his colleagues were blasted out of existence. It was also the sound that had almost killed him whilst under the pile of trees yesterday. It sent shivers down his spine, but he knew he had to act quickly – it was getting closer every second. He grabbed the rodent as carefully as time allowed and leapt into the shallow cold waters of the raised stream. He laid face downwards, head tilted to one side to ensure he didn't drown in the couple of inches of water that trickled past. They were out of sight from the road, but only just.

The huge machine noisily tore through the trees that lined a wide alleyway, and broke through into the wide open area of the main street in which K was hiding, just a few hundred metres away. It was a huge powerful black metallic monster of a vehicle. It had thousands of mechanical legs underneath its main structure which powered it along a smooth but noisy path like a giant millipede. Yet it left little evidence of its route on the ground, unlike a tracked tank or wheeled vehicle would. There must be so many small feet on the machine that its incredible weight was distributed across the ground delicately.

K peered over the edge of the stone wall, being careful not to be seen. He noticed the massive contraption travel over a small mound of earth and bushes. To his amazement, the mound was largely intact after the monster had passed over it.

Protruding from the sides of the top half of the oblong mass were two short but wide molecular cannons. Its simple, yet effective fire power must be awesome in its destructive capabilities. K came to his senses and recalled that he had in fact witnessed the power of said cannons, a little too closely for comfort. He could hardly take his eyes off the incredible sight.

Suddenly, from behind K, an identical mechanical monster appeared from a wide side road. K ducked his head quickly, desperately hoping the creatures within the vehicle had not seen him. The cold water ran through his clothes and onto his skin. He desperately wanted to get out into the warmth of the sun light, but knew he had no option but to stay in the soaking trench until the machines were out of sight.

The vehicles of black death turned towards The Chun and travelled slowly down the east side of the street's central stone canal, within metres of K's hiding position. As soon as it was a hundred metres in front of K, he raised his head again. To his dubious amazement, a number of other machines joined the procession from other wide side streets and alleyways, in front of the two that had passed K, far too close for comfort. There must be at least ten of them, stretching into the near distance, travelling towards the massive structure at the centre of this huge forgotten city.

The noise of the thousands of mechanical legs pounding the solid stone streets gradually began to subside, as the machines continued their effortless, yet noisy journey away from K. It was at this point he realised he was still clutching the rodent, a little too firmly and let the sodden creature go. It jumped out of K's grasp onto the stone ledge of the stream and shook itself vigorously. It gave K a look of distaste that told him his help really wasn't necessary. K looked at it apologetically, realising that the rodent wasn't the one that needed to hide from the massive machines.

"Sorry, I was just trying to help." K dragged his soaking body out of the stream and jumped off the wall onto the moss covered stone surface of the road. The rodent seemed to accept the apology and looked at K as if to ask what he would do next.

"I guess I should follow them." He continued, "We are heading in the same direction, after all." After a brief moment to contemplate more sane alternatives, K reached the unfortunate conclusion that there weren't any. He began to scurry down the street, being careful to ensure he was close to the buildings at the edge of the street at all times, rather than stranded in the centre by the stone canal as before.

For the next few miles, K trotted along behind the black machines, keeping his distance at about half a kilometre, ducking into doorways and alleyways at every opportunity. To his amazement, the rodent had truly befriended him, and was running along side K all the way, copying most of his moves. The creature had no idea what his new tall friend was doing, but it was fun and he hadn't got anything better to do.

But after a while the little rodent's legs began to tire and he slowed. K noticed this, but didn't want to lose sight of the battle tanks up ahead. He bent down and picked up the rodent and placed him inside his open shirt. The rodent appeared to be very happy with this arrangement and proceeded to fall asleep in the warmth of the strange creature's clothing, his head lolloping around as K darted energetically from one hiding place to the next.

Chapter 24

The Roof

The most senior officer of the remaining Republic troops had taken command, now that they were once again on terra-firma and a relative state of normality had been reinstated. T's reign was short-lived, and only extended itself to airborne situations. He was once again one of the troops. This didn't bother him too much, as being responsible for so many lives was a weight he didn't relish. But he wasn't the type of troop to take orders lying down. He knew there were likely to be some verbal battles as the new commanding officer seemed an incompetent fool.

T lay face down on the edge of the plateau. All troops had been ordered to spread out and walk to the edge of the landing zone, to investigate their surroundings, ensure the immediate coast was clear and identify a way of getting off this inappropriate landing site.

One hundred metres below, the street of green and white stretched as far as the eye could see to his left and for a few miles to his right, directly into the blackness of the huge crater that surrounded the base of the massive structure. This side of the raised area was half covered with trees and greenery, the remaining half revealing that they had actually landed on the flat surface of a massive building. This realisation worried T. From the air, appearances can be highly deceiving. Initially, he had presumed that the long green plateau was a field in amongst the dense flora and had given the co-ordinates to his fellow pilots. When he came into land, he realised the area was raised and concluded that the massive structure had been built to hold the weight of a huge park. But now, on much closer inspection, he was sure that this was simply a grass covered flat roof of a normal, albeit large, building. What if it was not strong enough to hold the weight of the three landing pods that it now supported?

The roof chose this precise moment to creak ominously. T thought he felt something move. He stayed perfectly still, to see if it was his imagination. There, another creak, and some very slight movement. Oh sh*t. He looked around him, in a mild panic for his colleagues' lives. Most of them were spread around the edges of the roof, safely supported by the outer walls of the huge building, but a couple of officers were stood next to one of the landers, looking intently at the floor which had appeared to move.

"Get to the edge," screamed T. "The roof is going to cave in!" Two of his fellow officers immediately ran towards the nearest edge of the building, but the Commander stood fast.

"You do not give me ord…" he began, but was cut short by the loud screams of ten thousand year old wood and stone trying to hold on to its structural integrity before finally giving up the fight. The landing craft next to which the commanding officer was standing suddenly moved downwards, taking a significant amount of the surrounding roof with it. The mass of metal, wood and stone collapsed into the structure of the building. A loud crash echoed around the interior of the building as the ship smashed into the floor below. But it came far too quickly for there to have been a very long drop. A huge cloud of dust sprang out of the dark hole, and hung in the air a few feet above roof level. Every one looked at the space where the ship and their Commander had been only moments before.

"Ooops," said T quietly to himself. He knew he was in big trouble. He heard a distant scream, coming from the newly formed hole. It was a cry for help from his Commander. Thinking quickly, and knowing that he had to make amends, T grabbed one of the nearby vines that hung from the trees which lined the makeshift landing site. He tugged on it a few times to ensure it was securely fastened to the branches above his head and then proceeded to haul in the hanging vine from its dangling position, onto the roof at his feet. Once completed, he started to walk backwards, with the vine wrapped over one shoulder and around his waist. Should the roof give way again, he would be safe… he hoped. As he approached the hole he called out to his superior. "Sir, are you OK?" There was no reply, just a strained grunting noise. As he peered over the edge, T could see the landing pod about ten metres below. It appeared to be standing on its nose cone, amid a mass of broken wood, stone and ferns. The Commander was clinging to a large splintered wooden beam which protruded from the intact area of roof on which T stood. T pulled the excess vine past his legs and allowed it to drop into the hole, to the floor below. Once the Commander had a firm grasp of the vine T suggested that he lower himself to the floor, rather than climb up. T made a mental note to remind himself to kindly inform his commanding officer that this was really a lucky break, as there appeared to be no other way down. He knew that would come in handy when he was getting reprimanded later for picking such a lousy landing site.

The Commander was not impressed with his current predicament, but bit his lip in appreciation of the rapid aid he had received from T, which was largely out of character for a Republic officer of any type. To assist so readily a superior in dangerous circumstances such as this was rare in what was largely a civilian based organisation.

Over a period of a few hours, the rest of the roof was checked for structural integrity. All seemed fine as the remaining two landing pods went unnoticed by the large flat ancient structure. Eventually, all but ten men were lowered through the hole, to the floor below. The ten lookouts were given strict orders to remain vigilant at all times and keep themselves out of site. The landing pods were taken out of stealth mode, to reserve rapidly depleting fuel stocks and were covered by make shift camouflage disguises that consisted of ferns, branches, twigs, vines and leaves, which were gathered from the landing zone and hauled up from the hanging gardens lining the high walled exterior of the building.

Fifty-three men found themselves in a large room. It was too dark to see much beyond the area immediately surrounding the hole through which the landing craft had fallen. The darkness extended its cloak beyond the light in such a way that implied a large space. One of the pilots was instructed to carefully enter the pod, retrieve all weapons and useful instruments and to switch on any exterior lights that might still be operational. This would allow the band of men to see enough to investigate a way out of this building. A few moments passed as the grunts of a man scrabbling for purchase on a smooth surface punctuated the dark silence.

The lights were illuminated, accompanied a split second later by a surprised intake of breath from the group of men who witnessed the awakening of the room from its ten thousand year slumber.

The site was like nothing they had seen before. The men were suddenly very nervous.

Chapter 25

The Tanks

The walking land tanks had closed ranks and stopped. They were obviously about to take a break. K hid himself in some bushes from where he could observe their activities without being seen. A huge muscular warrior got out of each of the awesome machines. Only one man. K was confused. These things were big enough to need twenty men to control them, thought K, and yet they appeared to only require one. The ten huge Rogue Nation barbarian warriors gathered in the centre of the street, five either side of the stone canal that trickled gently towards the giant Chun in the distance. A few of the men gathered water from the stream in their canteens and others disappeared into the surrounding undergrowth to gather dry leaves and twigs that had recently been torn from the branches of the trees in the aftermath of the explosion.

One by one the men returned and re-grouped on the far side of the stone wall canal, where K's view was obstructed. He assumed that they were stopping for food and rest. After a few moments a small column of smoke rose into the air from their make-shift camp. They were obviously going to be stationary for a while.

K wanted to get closer. He knew this would be a dangerous move, but he had to see what they were doing. He knew that if he was close enough, he would be able to hear their conversation in the hope of finding out what this whole mess was about, and why the Republic had been attacked so brutally, without provocation. K had not come across the Rogue Nation barbarians before and despite having heard many stories about how vicious they were in their unprovoked attacks on weaker beings, he had an annoying ability to be able to always give the assailant the benefit of the doubt. He therefore simply did not believe that their attacks were totally without reason.

After checking that his sleeping friend was comfortable, cradled snugly in his half-open shirt, K got up from his hiding place and made a crouched run for the cover of the next building, towards the ten dormant tanks and their relaxing drivers. He repeated this process until he was within fifty metres. At this point K decided that to approach them any further on the main street would be too dangerous. He wanted to get a view of them and so trotted down the nearest alleyway, all the while trying to find an obvious area to clamber up the tree lined walls to the roof of one of the thousands of three-storey buildings that lined the wide street. Carefully and as quietly as the creaking and cracking flora would allow, he clambered the side of the building. Once atop the tree-covered construction, he positioned himself amongst the hedges that lined the parapet of the roof. K gently removed the sleeping rodent from his chest, positioning his soft warm body in amongst some ferns and grass, and lay flat on his belly, turning his attentions to the distant jovial conversation of his enemies below.

They spoke the same language as K. As near as damn it anyway. Their accents were very strange and there were specific aspects about the conversation K could not understand, which he had to put down to racial colloquialisms. Judging by the actions that accompanied the boisterous exchange K felt decidedly thankful he couldn't decipher them as they all seemed to be different ways of describing the maiming or skinning of victims. The merry band of barbarians continued their conversation, which largely consisted of reminiscing about a recent battle they had won with ease. K pitied the race of beings that had obviously been completely annihilated in that battle. He tried to position himself closer to the edge, desperate to hear any information that might explain why these barbarians had attacked his TAK colleagues and tried to kill him. But all he could hear were broken stories of the carnage that had recently occurred, the body count that ensued and something about a massive ship nose-diving into a planet. Poor victims, thought K.

After a long rest, the warriors began to return to their posts. They got up from their relaxed positions amongst the remaining, slightly charred undergrowth, put out their campfire, and strolled back to their respective land tanks. The ten black vehicles were in two lines, five either side of the raised stone wall stream which split the huge street in half. Eight of the men had wandered off down the street, towards their killing machines, away from K's hiding position. The remaining two men ventured over the wall to the two closest tanks. As they closed in on their vehicles one of the men muttered something to the other and after a brief acknowledgement from his colleague, they went their separate ways. The first man returned to his tank, whilst the other strolled down the alleyway next to the building on which K was hiding.

K waited a few minutes, his heart pounding in his head. What if the barbarian had known K's whereabouts all the time and was simply playing it cool? Where was he now? He might have walked to the base of K's building and could be climbing the trees below him as his victim waited, frozen to the spot. His head raced through hundreds of scenarios to attempt to find an outcome in his favour. To his dismay, every one of the scenes in K's mind ended in his own tragic and bloody death – he always had been a pessimist. He could not see a way out, and any suggestion by K's logical brain that there might be a perfectly innocent explanation to this situation that might not conclude with his slaughter, were quickly disregarded as ridiculous wishful thinking.

After a further few seconds, K started to calm down. He couldn't hear any rustling in the trees that lined his building and therefore concluded that the massive barbarian was not climbing after all. He peered through the bushes and looked down the street to see what the tanks were doing. To his surprise, they were not waiting for their colleague. Nine huge black vehicles were marching down the road towards the massively impressive structure many miles in the distance. A fantastic idea raced through K's head. If he could some how get in the remaining tank, he would save himself a great deal of walking. He had been finding the last few miles following the tanks exhausting, unlike his sleeping rodent friend.

K muttered quietly to the rodent to wake up, but suddenly realised the furry creature was nowhere to be seen. He looked around the flat surface of the roof, eyes darting to each corner, whilst he riffled quickly through the small pile of leaves where he had placed his companion a few moments before. K hoped that he was alright (at least, K assumed the little alien fur ball was a 'he'). Where could he have got to? K asked himself, immediately longing for his friend's safe return as harsh nervous loneliness quickly returned. The rodent was the only thing that made him feel less alone on this alien planet. But instead of wasting time worrying about where his small furry friend had disappeared to, K decided to attempt to find out where the last barbarian warrior had gone. Maybe he could overpower him? K nearly burst out loud with laughter at this preposterous thought. The deadly warrior was at least three feet taller than K, covered in muscles and scarred from head to toe with proud statements of previous battles. K, by contrast was small, weak and covered from head to toe with minor scratches and abrasions from his calamitous encounter with twigs and branches!

He scrambled as quietly as possible across the roof of the small building, hoping that it would not give way, or creak too much with his every movement. Eventually, after what seemed like a mile of crawling, K reached the other side of the dwelling and carefully positioned himself so he was able to peer through the vegetation, over the lip of the roof to the ground of the small side street ten metres below.

To his amazement (not to mention breathless shock), he was directly above the barbarian. The huge man was squatting, leaning against a thick trunk of one of the huge trees that surrounded the ancient walls of K's hiding place. Next to this hulking murderous beast was a small roll of delicate looking tissue paper. K squinted his eyes in an attempt to make out the faint colourful markings on the roll. He wasn't one hundred per cent sure, but he could have sworn there were shapes of cuddly teddy bears and flowers, possibly even some puppies. The battle-scarred man took the roll of paper from the floor next to him and proceeded to tear a length from it. K suddenly caught a lungful of the stench the man was producing below, and retracted his head quickly from the edge. He writhed quietly on the leaf-covered roof trying not to be sick, whilst taking huge gulps of fresh air as quietly as possible to free his internal passageways of the foul tasting stench.

He had to take his chance. The barbarian, for the next few moments at least, was indisposed and was completely vulnerable. This was his best, if not only chance to take him out and steal his walking tank machine. The roof didn't appear to hold many objects of weapon-like status, but there was a large heavy branch lying in the corner, probably torn from an old tree by the blast of the explosion. K struggled to pick it up. He half crawled, half fell his way back to the make-shift toilet wall, with the huge weight in his arms, all the time listening to the strains, grunts and groans of the barbarian's hideous activities below. He had never killed a man before. He hoped it wasn't too difficult. After all, if this went wrong, he was going to have a massive barbarian warrior with a headache to deal with. That prospect did not appeal. K had one chance to get this man. He had to at the very least knock him out cold.

He reached the edge of the flat roof with the heavy piece of wood. Carefully, and as quietly as possible, he positioned the branch, upright, on the ledge. To ensure his aim was good, K peered over the wall to the man below. To K's amazement, the barbarian was lying perfectly still on his side, eyes and mouth open, with his tongue hanging out of one side. Next to the man was his roll of teddy-bear paper and the rodent, who sat proudly next to the dead body, grinning up at K.

Chapter 26

The Room

They stood silently in a massive, dusty, oval room, easily one hundred metres in length and fifty metres wide. Decorated with elaborate wooden coverings of all sizes and descriptions, it was a truly beautiful chamber, and one of obvious importance in this ancient society. No greenery existed here and the dust that had formed over the millennia was less than you might expect, despite it having the smell of a tomb. These facts proved the hall had been successfully sealed off from the outside world.

The landing pod had fallen into the centre of the room. On all sides row upon row of seats bordered the scene, rising in oval tiers around the central floor upon which the landing pod now rested, nose down. It was much like an ancient amphitheatre. Thousands of wooden seats, each decorated with a different intricate pattern of swirling, dark wood filled the tiers around the room. In many of them, much to the distaste of the newly arrived onlookers, sat the remains of humanoid bodies. Most of the inhabitants had simply rotted into skeletons, but the occasional one had somehow managed to keep a thin leathery exterior to its skeletal remains.

The attentions of thousands of decayed eye sockets seemed to be eerily drawn to the landing craft and its surrounding men, who stared back at the decomposed bodies. The effect was extremely daunting. To suddenly find yourself being looked at in a disapproving manner by an army of dead bodies was the most uncomfortable feeling T had ever felt. He fully expected never to feel this nauseous again for the rest of his life. The TAKers looked back at the relentless stare of their mummified onlookers in complete silence. There was nothing that could be said. 'Sorry' really wasn't going to cut it with this audience.

As the men gradually regained their wits, they started to investigate the room further, careful to maintain the respectful peace. Behind the highest row of seating around the edges of the massive oval room, thousands of ancient scrolls and books were stored on tall book shelves that stood proud, stretching all the way to the ten metre ceiling. It appeared that the Republic troops had uncovered an important council of some sort or perhaps even the government of this former society. Despite no-one in the group having ever seen the beautifully complicated surroundings before, there was something strangely familiar about the entire environment. It was obvious to T and his colleagues, from the grandness of the room and the remains of impressive clothing that continued to slowly rot on the corpses, that the people who sat here were highly important politicians. It must have fallen on their shoulders to discuss the overall welfare of the city. Possibly even the entire planet.

So why were they all here? What had happened to their world that meant they were all gathered in this room to die together? The Republic sensors revealed that no civilised society existed anywhere on the planet anymore. And there had been no indications from any of the landing briefings that a civilised society ever had, although admittedly, the massive upturned pyramid floating just above its surface did imply that something pretty advanced had been here before. None of the landing officers expected a site such as this. T realised that it was highly probable they hadn't been told the whole truth about this mission.

There were no signs of struggle or panic amongst the people that sat here. There were no signs of pain on any of the faces that retained leathery expressions. If anything, they looked strangely content. If there had been panic or desire to escape the room of death, you would expect to see a pile of bodies by the exit routes. Incidentally, where were the exits? T was puzzled by this riddle, as were his colleagues. Bringing up the rear in this thought process a few minutes later was the commander, who ordered all men to search for an exit. T did as he was told, but all the time; the room, its importance and the governmental figures played on his mind. There must be information about the former society that existed here in the scrolls and books that lined the impressive chamber.

T returned to the centre of the room to take one of the weapons offered to him by a colleague ordered to retrieve usable items from the damaged landing pod. He took the hand gun, shoved it into the belt band of his trousers, turned and began to walk towards a section of the hall to which none of his colleagues had yet ventured. As he did so, he passed the skeleton of a body that sat on a small, discrete chair to one side of the central plain of the room. The seat was simply decorated and was conspicuous by its lack of alignment to all the others. Unlike the thousands of other seating positions, which gave the impression they were all carved out of one single gigantic piece of wood, this one was movable. It had appeared to have been placed to one side, almost as an afterthought. In front of the chair was a small desk on which the forearms of the skeleton rested, bony hands covering an elaborate book which contrasted conspicuously with the simple table on which it sat. T looked closely at the book and the skeletal hands. It appeared that the man who sat here had a specific job. Writing implements had been carefully lined up at the top of the desk, except one, which rested between bony fingers. It was obvious the hands had been writing just before the author had passed away. This could be a break through, thought T. He was about to pick up the book, when his attention was distracted.

"Officer Tenaket! What do you think you are doing?" His highly stressed Commander shouted, "I ordered everyone to spread out and search for an exit."

"Sir, yes Sir", replied T with a little too much enthusiasm for it to be considered genuine. He returned to his duty, and made his way towards the end of the room to which he was nearest, but not before taking the elaborate book from beneath the protective hands of the dead record clerk and hiding it quickly against his chest. T walked up a small flight of steps to the upper level of the seats. At the top of the shallow incline, the last row backed onto the tall bookcases that lined the entire room. On these shelves stood tens of thousands of books, each very similar in design to the one that T held discreetly and carefully in his arms. From here, T could see the entire room. He glanced along the bookshelves around the room to see if there was any obvious space left. Sure enough, a few metres to his right an entire column stood empty, except the lowest shelf which was half full. T ventured over and placed the book he had acquired next to the last impressive volume. The patterns on the spines aligned perfectly, and continued the elaborate wavy pattern that adorned all of the volumes throughout the entire room. T took the penultimate book from its position on the shelf and opened it to its very last page. The page was full of strange, beautiful text, which T knew he had no chance of understanding. He returned the book to its previous position and opened the volume which he had taken from the clerk's desk. The entries stopped half way through the book at the page the clerk had open on the small desk. T's assumption must be right; he had potentially discovered the entire history of this ancient civilisation, documented here in the books in front of him. But to what end? He couldn't read the elaborate text, in fact trying to do so made his head hurt. Its scrawling beautiful writing was so complex that after a few moments of running your gaze along its swirling lines, it felt like your eyes were going to melt.

Realising that the Commander's eyes were once again boring into his the back of his skull, T placed the book inside his shirt and hurriedly tried to show that he had resumed his search for an exit.

Chapter 27

The Stench

The small rodent was getting bored. There must be something more interesting to do round here. He had been having a great dream whilst asleep inside this strange being's outer skin. But oh no, he had to be removed so that this creature could lie on the roof of this building staring into the distance for ages. At first he had remained asleep, but as for all Vacchion enahs, dreams were heavily affected by real-life surroundings. The temperature drop from being inside the tall creature's clothing, to suddenly being exposed to the elements had spoilt the perfect setting in which Gyshnf was being waited on by fifty female enahs, all with perfectly matted hair and huge long naked tails. Gyshnf's claws went all tingly just thinking back to the fantastic dream. But as his sleeping temperature dropped, the perfect harem of beautifully ripe females had turned to ice.

Needless to say, Gyshnf had woken in a very bad mood. He stormed away from the tall furless creature to investigate other prime sleeping positions. It is a little known fact that enahs sleep for ninety percent of their lives, but dream for ninety five percent of their lives. Therefore, they had a great deal of sleeping to catch up on. They befriend creatures who they feel are likely to wait on them. Lulling them into a false sense of equality with the first offer of food or shelter. It was the oldest trick in the book and a sure-fire way to start a successful and lazy relationship. After all, an enah's philosophy is: why chew yourself, when you can get someone else to do it for you?

He had ventured to the far side of the roof, but had found nowhere suitable to lie for the remainder of his nap. Another few hours should do it for this sleep session. He was looking for somewhere soft, warm and out of the direct sunlight. The flat roof was therefore not the best place to be so he clambered grumpily down the tree wall at the far side of the building, away from all the noise and disturbances of the campsite in the main street.

Within a second of landing on the solid ground, Gyshnf had found the perfect spot. There was a small opening in the earth at the base of the large tree down which he had climbed. Inside the hole was a dark, dry compartment lined with a layer of old leaves that had started to decay. They provided a warm soft surface on which to lie. The hole was tiny and could only just fit Gyshnf, which was just the way he liked it, unless there happened to be fifty female rodents in the near vicinity in which case he would like the sub-terrainian dwelling to be marginally larger. This thought reminded him - he had a large herd of icy ladies to defrost. He quickly settled into a rewarding, if a little jerky sleep.

Just as he was getting to yet another interesting stage in his exhausting dream, where the twenty remaining female enahs were getting impatient, the story-line took a sudden turn for the worse. A foul-smelling creature made almost entirely of a soft brown mud-like substance stormed into his dream and scared away the randy hedonistic imaginary mob of female admirers.

Gyshnf awoke angrily to find his reality was much the same as his dream (save for the passionate female enahs, which were nowhere to be seen). His small make-shift boudoir was being invaded by a real mud-like creature of the same foul smelling material as in his dream. The stench was unbearable, even for a rodent. Gyshnf was cornered. He had no choice but to make a violent and rapid escape from his nest, tearing to shreds anything in his path. Claws and teeth bared, his cutting and biting action was far too fast to be appreciated by the naked eye. A camera, filming at a thousand frames per second would have struggled to pick up all of the movements as the small furry creature exited the base of the tree at lightning speed. It was all over in a few fractions of a second.

In slow motion, the action went as follows: The soft brown muddy swamp creature was torn to shreds by the exiting razor-sharp teeth and claws of the enah, who was surprised to discover a larger, more solid enemy behind the brown wall of stench. This foe was more dense than Gyshnf's original assailant, but gave little resistance to the rodent's war-path. The thick, dark leathery skin was no defence against the ten razor-blade claws and the twenty dagger-sharp teeth, each one capable of passing on millions of lethal bacteria.

Within seconds, the rodent was out in the open, covered in a mixture of its enemies' redundant flesh and fluids. Feeling rather proud of itself, but significantly more filthy than before, the rodent stood next to its quashed assailants, admiring his own bloody handiwork. Gyshnf looked up the tree wall to the roof, where he noticed his furless friend straining at the edge with a large piece of tree held out in front of it. That was nice, he thought, his friend was about to try and save him from the two smelly creatures that had attempted to disturb his slumber. Knowing his new friend's ability to drop things accidentally, he moved rapidly out of the way, just before the branch impacted the disembowelled body of the creature Gyshnf had made mince meat of. Literally.

Chapter 28

The Reading

T had ventured behind the bookshelves that lined the inner walls of the governmental chamber. At various intervals, the bookshelves were broken by gangways that led to an outer corridor running the circumference of the oval room. Along this continuous passageway were pairs of large heavy doors, each being tested in turn by T's colleagues. Clusters of additional bookshelves had been erected where the passage widened, presumably to hold the very ancient texts and historical scrolls that could no longer fit in the main state room. Behind these massive shelving units were small secluded spaces. T entered the closest one, awkwardly. From here he could see his fellow TAKers testing doors and examining nearby walls to see if there were hidden ways of obtaining a way out. It appeared that all obvious exits were locked.

There appeared to be enough people on exit-finding detail, so T decided to take a moment to look at the mind-bending text once again. He opened the historical ledger to the page containing the last entry. Blinking heavily to focus in the dim light, T raised the book in front of his face and tried to concentrate on the scrawling words that appeared before him. Again the burning sensation in his eyes returned and his head instantly began to ache.

"What have you got there?" enquired the Commander as he approached T from the small opening between the book cases. Although startled, T continued to hold the book in front of his face and peered over the top, attempting not to look conspicuous or guilty. As he looked his Commander in the eyes the scrawling letters appeared to move, so much so that it dragged T's attention back to the page. As soon as his gaze returned to the text, the burning sensation returned and the handwriting morphed back to its original form.

"Look at me when I am addressing you," ordered the Commander, and repeated, "What have you got there?" T's attention returned to the Commander and he replied, "It appears to be some sort of record of the final events of this chamber, Sir," he said cautiously. "I thought it might provide us with some idea as to what the people here were..." As he spoke, his voice trailed off. The text was once again moving in his peripheral vision, but T continued to look directly into the eyes of his Commander. Despite not having much respect for his superior, he knew that to disobey a senior officer when being directly addressed was a serious offence and one which would hold no favour in this partial-military society. But the moving images on the page below were drawing his attention so dramatically that he found it almost impossible to resist looking back at the text. His hand began to quiver a little as the book remained raised in front of him. He would be in serious trouble if he broke eye contact first. The text continued to move.

"Lower that book," ordered his Commander, getting ever closer to losing his temper with the disobedient rebel.

"I can't," replied T as he attempted to move his arm down. He was concentrating so hard on his gaze into the Commander's eyes that his face began to turn red. His breathing started becoming more erratic and his heart beat increased.

"What's the matter with you, man? Put the book down and stand to attention." T continued sending instructions to his arms to lower the volume, but the moving text had placed him in a trance. The book was controlling him, and it was all T could do not to return his glance once again to the seductive pages below. Between gritted teeth, and broken sharp intakes of breath, T managed to speak. "Can't lower... book... Sir. Don't know... what's... happening." The scrawling text beneath T's immediate gaze suddenly started to appear legible. It was readable. That didn't make any sense.

"Medic," shouted the Commander.

The events had already drawn a small crowd of men. A number of T's colleagues had gathered to view the actions of this insubordinate officer with glee, waiting with bated breath for an interesting outcome. A couple of medical officers sprinted down the corridor to survey the situation. One of them went for the simple option. He reached for the book, to remove it from

T's grasp. T objected loudly, screaming, "No!" His grip was so tight that it didn't move, despite the medic's best efforts.

"I can read this," stated T. One of his colleagues edged alongside him and looked at the text for a few seconds before removing his gaze and rubbing the tears from his eyes. T continued to stare into the Commander's eyes. The Commander was beginning to feel very uncomfortable. Not only was his rank not having the usual effect on his subordinates, but this rebellious figure in front of him looked highly volatile. He appeared as though he were about to explode. T's entire body quivered with the intense concentration of a strong man attempting to hold a massive weight in front of him at arm's length. His veins pulsated at his temples and sweat ran in trickles down his face.

T began to see the words form in his peripheral vision once again. He didn't so much read them as notice them in his mouth. "Two days, we have been sat. Two days long here. No answer to The Answer has been found. Must we stay?" T's colleagues looked at one another. The man under extreme strain was cracking up. The pressure of nearly being killed by the Rogue Nation warriors had really got to him. They continued to stare. One of them even prepared a hand gun, just in case T needed to be put out of his misery. The reading continued. "What can be done to stop this knowledge? We are sure, nothing. Attempts have been made to ensure survival of the council. No exits, no entries, no families, no communication. We are imprisoned without control. No-one must know what occurs outside…" T continued to ramble on. There were a few more paragraphs describing the strange imprisonment of high level parliamentary council members that T read out to his bemused, but captivated audience. Then the text took an eerie twist.

"It has reached us. After four days, The Knowledge is here. We are doomed. Only the P-Cell can contain it. Through walls it travels, through minds; with no contact we have still gained The Knowledge. We now rest. One and all. We understand. Life is complete… existence superfluous…"

Sweat dripped from T's chin as his body slowly stopped quivering. His eyes broke their unnerving stare with the

Commander and rolled into the back of his head as he collapsed to the floor, releasing the grip on the elaborately decorated book which fell to the dusty wooden surface, closed.

The Commander waved his hand to one of his officers indicating that the book being picked up should be handed to him. He took it impatiently and opened it at no page in particular. The complicated, but stationary text entered his eyes and burned the back of his retina with an acidic viciousness he had never felt before. The Commander closed the book.

"What do you think Sir? Has T gone insane?" asked the officer who handed him the book.

"No. I think there is something in this. Still, place him in a restraining jacket and knock him out for a while. He looks as though he could use a rest." Before turning to leave the scene, he noticed an over enthusiastic troop picking up a large decorative piece of rock. "I mean sedate him," he added, looking disapprovingly at the slow-witted man, who dropped the rock and backed away to allow the medics to do their job.

Chapter 29

The Ride

Once down from the roof, K grabbed his rodent friend, wrapped him in a large amount of the teddy-bear patterned soft tissue paper (in a vain attempt to cover his stench) and ran out into the main street.

The nine tanks were far enough in the distance for K to feel safe out in the open. He ran over to the stream, and gently placed the rodent in the cold water. Not seeming to mind, the animal rolled around frantically, as small pieces of his two assailants and the tissue-paper clothing floated towards The Chun. K made a mental note not to drink downstream from this particular supply again.

Once the creature was a great deal cleaner than before, K picked it up quickly, and ran over to the sole remaining tank. After a rapid circuit of the massive black machine, K knew this was going to be difficult. How was he supposed to get in? Maybe the body of the former barbarian would reveal something of interest.

He ran back to the site of the dual massacre. Flies and other insects had wasted no time in taking advantage of the free banquet. K placed the rodent on the floor and then held his nose as he hurriedly searched the disgusting body. A number of small items where found. A heavy handheld item, which K assumed to be a gun, an electronic device on the barbarians wrist, a necklace decorated with many strangely coloured distorted shapes (some of which K recognised as internal organs and dreaded to think who they might have once belonged to), and a small black box on which a single red button was situated. This last item was one which K was unsure about. The red of the button had a certain 'last resort' look about it, and he decided that to push it might well be the last thing he did. He placed this item carefully in one of the pockets on the thigh of his trousers, out of harm's way. The hand gun he placed in his other thigh pocket, and the necklace he decided was of little use to him, unless he suddenly found a purpose for a second-hand sun-dried appendix. The final item, the electronic wrist device, K held in his hand as he ran back to the war machine.

As he came within a few metres of the machine a large door section opened above the thousands of mechanical legs, which stood to attention under the awesome machine. A small flight of steps extended invitingly. K nervously clambered up the steps, only to be overtaken by a far too enthusiastic rodent. Inside, the machine was more cramped than he had expected, especially considering the size of the former barbarian occupant. As K sat down in the large black leather driver's seat, the door closed automatically behind him and total darkness enveloped him. Seconds later, just as K was beginning to ask himself what the hell he was supposed to do next, the machine sprang into life. A deep rumbling occurred far behind K's back, and a huge bank of instruments illuminated, including a large screen directly in front. The screen showed the tanks three quarters of a kilometre ahead, 788 metres in fact, as indicated by the slowly ascending numbers in the bottom left hand corner. K took a quick look around his new domain. He felt all powerful, knowing that he effectively had four giant laser cannons strapped to his shoulders.

The controls looked simple enough. Two joysticks were situated by K's hands, one at the end of each of the hard armrests. K had played many electronic simulators in his past and assumed this would be no different. He took hold of each of the joysticks and pushed them both forward, half way. The effect was incredibly sudden and almost gave K a heart-attack. He had never expected such a huge machine to move so fast from stand-still. He must remember to be a little more delicate with the controls of this incredibly powerful machine.

Behind the vehicle, one hundred metres of torn up ground lay in its wake. A five metre wide, one metre deep trench had been burrowed out by the phenomenal power of thousands of mechanical legs working at half their full capacity.

Inside the cabin, the small dazed rodent, peeled itself from the rear wall of the dark cockpit, righting itself and shaking its bruised head. K looked down at the rodent and apologised. He gently moved the two joysticks forward, at what he thought was equidistant. The massive machine lurched forward, but at a much slower pace. K smiled to himself and looked to his right to where the rodent had been nursing its sore head. But it was not there. K glanced around the cabin, desperate to locate has small furry friend, worried that his head injury might be serious. To his relief, the rodent had simply swapped sides, and was sitting comfortably on K's left, watching the screen intently. K realised that the rodent was staring wide eyed at the screen and so returned his attention there also.

The picture was a little confusing at first. The right half of the screen showed the same images as before, the wide, fern-lined street with the raised central stone canal, and the nine tanks far off in the distance. But the left hand side of the huge screen showed a stream of branches, trees and vines, lined further to the left by what looked like a constantly changing cross-section of an ancient stone wall. Gradually the image changed to reveal the interior of the buildings to the left of the vehicle. Incredible what technology can show you now-a-days thought K, as he continued to steer the massive vehicle merrily down the street. "The wonders of x-ray cameras, able to see through thick walls and trees", he continued to presume out loud.

Outside, the scene was far less serene. The building which had just had one of its major structural walls removed by the incredible force of the monstrous black machine, made an unconscious decision to collapse, heavily persuaded by the powers of gravity. For thousands of years the building and gravity had enjoyed an amicable and mutually beneficial relationship. But gravity had finally spotted an unmissable opportunity to get one over on the buildings of Vacchion. If it had conscious thought, it would have been proud of itself. Especially after all of these years The Chun had been taking the p*ss out of it!

K's eyes innocently viewed the main screen in front of him. The left half showing the internal workings of the buildings, whilst on the right his nine new colleagues continued their march, towards The Chun. Gyshnf was surprised at how long it took the furless creature to understand what was happening, but

K eventually realised what he had done, as his vehicle exited the final part of a long building and the entire screen returned to a view of the open street. He turned and looked behind him, but there was just the solid wall of the cockpit. "How do you look behind you in this thing?" questioned K to himself. "Rear view on" spoke a coarse, but welcome female voice. K panicked for a brief second, almost imagining that he was not alone, but quickly realising it was simply the on-board computer conversing with him. On the giant screen in front of him, a quarter segment in the bottom left had been dedicated to a rear view. The dust was beginning to settle from the masonry carnage that had taken place. Sure enough, there were two collapsed buildings behind him... oh, make that three, together with a large number of felled trees and bushes.

The machine had not felt any different at all, whilst travelling through what must have been incredible resistance from ancient walls and massive trees. This tank is incredibly powerful thought K, with his unequalled ability to identify the absolute obvious in such situations. He concentrated on lining up the tank in the centre of the street once again, and made sure not to do anything else that was likely to attract attention from his fellow tank pilots ahead.

The rodent scampered around the cabin, looking for a suitable place to resume his sleep. He'd had a very busy day so far and his need for sleep was now catching up on him. K was satisfied that he had regained complete and masterful control of the incredible destructive powers of this walking war unit. In the wrong hands this thing could be dangerous, thought K ironically.

The next few moments of the journey were uneventful. But through no fault of K's the peaceful journey was about to take a severe and potentially life threatening turn for the worse. Would Gyshnf get no peace?

Chapter 30

The Camp

T came round. He felt out of focus. His head was heavy and his limbs didn't seem to want to move. As his mind gradually came back into the real world he realised he'd been placed in a restraining jacket, which ensured all of his limbs were motionless.

He looked around his new environment. It was bright daylight. He was lying on a grass and fern-lined hard floor. Stretching far above him was a tall white wall of ancient construction lined with the occasional towering thick charred tree trunk. He struggled to sit upright, catching the attention of one of his fellow officers. To his left the street ran straight for miles into the distance, lined on both sides by white and green erections of part stone, part vegetation. Opposite the huge building behind T was a wide open area, containing large flat circles of stone and groups of huge trees and plants which did not appear to be propping up any white walled buildings. To his right, a few miles away floated the massive upturned pyramid construction that rose far above the outer reaches of the planet's atmosphere. At its base was the huge black crater which T remembered seeing so well from the sky. From here, he could only see a black edge to the horizon and the sudden end to the buildings on the long street.

"You OK?" asked his colleague, who had come to join the waking mad man.

"Yeah, fine." Looking around his closer surroundings T noticed something missing. "Where is everyone?" he asked.

"We received reports from the roof top lads that there were a few explosions a couple of clicks in the distance to the west of here, so the Commander and some of the other guys have gone to investigate. The rest of the lads are keeping watch, collecting food and water and setting up camp inside the building – as soon as they've cleared away enough of the skeletons from the offices on the lower floors."

Right on cue, a number of skulls and bones were thrown from a first floor window onto a huge pile a few metres to T's left.

"What about the book?"

"Don't you worry about that. It's safe. We don't think it's a good idea that you go anywhere near it for a while. It gave your body quite a pounding."

"I know, I have a massive headache."

"No, that'll be Jenkins, he dropped a large rock on your head just before they were going to sedate you." He stated with a wry smile. "Do you remember what you read from the book?"

"Yeah, every word," replied T. "It makes so much sense now."

"Are you kidding? It sounded like a meaningless riddle to the rest of us!" After a few moments, he added: "So what's going on then?"

"Get me the book and I'll tell you. I have a few things I need to confirm first."

The officer looked unsure. He eyed T with suspicion, but nothing T had done gave him any reason to doubt the well respected man's intentions. "Let's get the camp set up first. We'll take a look at it together after we've eaten." This was not the response T wanted, but for the time being it would have to do.

Chapter 31

The Buttons

Gyshnf struggled to get comfortable. There was nowhere soft or cosy for him to get a really good dream in. He had managed to warm himself slightly by his new furless pet's left arm, as he lay himself along its length on the hard, wide armrest of the driver's chair. But he needed a good stretch before he could get any rest. As he forced his front legs forward as far as they would go, he appreciated the resistance provided by a raised panel of buttons at the end of the armrest, just past the stick that his new pet was playing with in his left hand. Two lights appeared below his thin (yet lethal) paws. The stretch was so good, he decided to repeat the action, again the lights beneath his paws illuminated a second time. That was pretty, he thought, looking at the red lights as he decided he was ready for a sleep. But this wasn't to be. His erratic companion suddenly started getting very excited, bouncing up and down on his seat in what seemed to Gyshnf to be a blind panic. Oh well, he would just have to try and sleep through it. He closed his eyes and attempted to ignore the screaming of his large adopted pet.

"Thunderbolts launched," announced the computer's female voice.

"What the…?" screamed K as he bounced up and down in his chair. "No. No thunderbolts!" K's eyes widened and his jaw dropped in terrified disbelief. "What happened? What did I do?"

"Thunderbolts launched," repeated the voice as a second wave of bright lights took over the screen in front of him.

"Nooooo!" K screamed as he watched the four incandescent bolts of lightning stream away from his vehicle at incredible speed. Before he had finished his pleading denial, the powerful warheads had impacted their targets. Far off in the distance, a number of incredible explosions took place. Three fire balls raged hundreds of metres into the air accompanied by a cloud of fire-covered black land tank particles. K watched the screen, wide eyed and open mouthed. The fourth missile took a few hundredths of a second longer to make an impression, due to it missing all the massive land tanks and choosing, instead to hit the front corner of a large impressive building a kilometre further away.

"Sh*t" K declared softly, managing to undermine the serious nature of his actions in a single syllable. It was now out and out war. K had destroyed three of the tanks ahead of him, and in the process had ensured his own rapid death. He tore his hands away from the controlling joysticks and looked at his palms in horror. What had he done? How had he managed to fire the machine's cannons? He had simply wanted to follow the barbarians in an inconspicuous manner, but in the process had somehow managed to get one of the warriors murdered through bowel removal, stolen a tank and destroyed three further tanks. His ability to blend into the background was about as good as a bishop's in a brothel. He had a great deal to learn about stealth.

It was at this point that Gyshnf decided to turn over onto his back and stretch his forearms out once more. This time the buttons it came into contact with were an attractive orange colour.

K watched the carnage on the screen in front as hundreds of small bolts of lightning travelled at thousands of miles an hour into the distance, impacting all manner of objects ahead, most notably a number of land tanks busy manoeuvring their way out of the main street and into the cover of neighbouring buildings and alleyways. Gyshnf (now promoted by pure chance to chief gunner) had inadvertently destroyed two further land tanks in a massive hail of rapid cannon fire that had reduced the black monstrosities to clouds of bright sparks and dark dust. He quietly wished all the commotion would die down so he could get some much needed sleep, and turned over onto his side in an attempt to get comfortable.

Chapter 32

The Impossible

An internal chemical reactor alarm had brought the tiny machine back on line. Much of its self diagnostic testing and maintenance had been completed, estimating it to be at 98.3 per cent (rounded to the nearest tenth) of full operational capacity. The host was once again overloading on adrenalin, with a near fatal heart rate. One hundred and ninety beats per minute was hardly normal for any large mammal whilst sitting down.

The cell booted all of its initiative chips and opened its controlling communications channels to the vessel's central nervous system. What had its host got them into this time, it contemplated, using its learning and intuition programmes.

The cell downloaded the vessel's receptor information, together with the past thirty minutes of stored activity which it could obtain from the automated short-term memory banks. Such information is subconsciously backed up by all living organisms, as an automated process for times of high level stress. This allows post-diagnostic learning, should a particular incident be missed whilst in total panic mode, which is precisely what had happened here. Once the information had been processed by the cell's fully operational diagnostic programs it soon realised that the vessel had managed to get them into a level three stage of emergency, possibly even a level two, depending on the weather and a few other variable environmental factors. Either way, this was serious and could prove critical if the cell did not provide some hands-on (or rather, processors-on) guidance. It adopted self preservation level two.

The cell prepared for the worst and gave itself instruction codes for the self detonation sequence that would be initiated at self protection level zero, should it be required. Once these codes were downloaded, the cell simply had to wait until it had calculated a ninety percent chance that The Answer would escape. If this situation was reached, the cell would automatically self-destruct via thermo-nuclear melt-down, ridding itself and a significant quantity of the surrounding neighbourhood of the ability to provide The Answer anywhere to reside. It was a tough and brutal end to a task, but that was the price the cell had to pay for containing the most powerful knowledge in the universe.

The vessel in which the cell had managed to become imprisoned had seemingly started a fight with an enemy of formidable power. Despite having obtained itself a huge cannon vessel, the humanoid was massively out numbered and out witted. This latter statement was not particularly surprising, even when considering the rather dim-witted creatures he was up against. The cell had searched its host's memory banks in an attempt to obtain as much intelligence about their enemy as possible. Utilising the information the barbarians had communicated to one another around the camp-fire twenty minutes ago, by enhancing the audio far beyond the capabilities of its host vessel, the tiny prison cell now knew more about recent events than its host would care to imagine.

At some point in the near future the cell would have to explain to this humanoid creature what it's new role in life was, but for the time being ignorance was bliss. Now was certainly not the time to load the host vessel with any more pressure.

Using the host's complicated nervous system, evolved over millions of years (not very efficiently, the cell concluded), the miniature computer prison began a process of chemical balancing, internal force realignment and subliminal confidence messaging. The aim was to achieve the impossible: turn a gibbering wreck of a creature into a calm, calculated killing machine.

Chapter 33

The Incident

The Commander ordered the troops to spread out. The explosions had come from about a kilometre away. It was going to take them a while to get to where the action was, but even so, they had to be careful. There were heavy rumbling noises accompanying the explosions, sounding as if a significant part of the city was being destroyed. They didn't want to be seen, or be forced to have to battle against whatever it was that was making the colossal commotion. But they did want to learn more about what was happening and how they could defend themselves against the Rogue Nationals, who would undoubtedly be looking to tear them apart.

The distant cacophony of rubble and trees crashing to the ground gave the troops little to feel confident about as they stood in their small, vulnerable flesh cases. If whatever was destroying the city so efficiently was only a click away, why were they endeavouring to reduce that gap, rather than increase it? Many of the poorly trained men did not appreciate the Commander's desire for heroic theatre or reconnaissance. They would be much more inclined to follow the order "run away", than to continue advancing. But something kept them together, and drove them towards the terrifying noises. Some would say it was the camaraderie. Others may say it was the sense of loneliness that united them and drove them forward. The most ardent of sceptics would probably point out that the drive to follow their leader was down to him being the most superior officer and having the biggest gun! But they would be true cynics.

The noises sounded like they were getting closer, much closer, and fast. The crashing and rumbling was surely coming in this direction. The ground was shaking more vigorously than before. That wasn't a good sign, was it? Some of the men looked at each other. One or two started to climb the trees behind which they were hiding, as quietly as they could. Stealth in this movement was not required for the benefit of the unrelenting, fast approaching noise, but because they were afraid the Commander would spot them. If he saw them climbing trees in order to hide on the relative safety of the roofs, he might well order their return to the ground, to become sitting targets. They were not keen on that. Gradually, one by one, the men climbed their nearest tree trunk.

By the time the Commander noticed the missing troops, he was one of only three people remaining on the ground. The two remaining men were simply too close to the Commander to be able to get away without being noticed. He looked around at the lack of troops in neighbouring positions.

"You there." He shouted up to a nearby careless climber. "What do you think you are doing?"

Thinking quickly, out of character for a lowly Republic troop, the man replied. "Trying to get a better look to see which direction the noise is approaching us from Sir," he said without breaking his vertical stride.

Realising he was somewhat out of control, the Commander made a mental note of the appearance of the ascending rear end and admitted defeat, "Good thinking, man." The two remaining troops went to start their clamber to relative safety, but were stopped in their tracks before they could leave the ground. "I think we have quite enough look outs now, don't you." It wasn't a question. If it had been, the unanimous answer from the remaining ground force would have been a resounding 'no, Sir'.

From the tops of the three surrounding buildings over which the troops were spread, the view was incredible. The green rooftops extended for hundreds of miles in every direction, save the large blackened circle of mass destruction under the giant Chun. Most of the rooftops were of a similar height, approximately three storeys, but occasionally larger buildings punctuated the city sprawl, presumably public buildings or central epicentres of societal life. A few of the troops looked back from where they had travelled. Sure enough, far off in the distance behind them, south west of their current location, the large six storey building upon which they had landed was one of only a handful that seemed to stand pretentiously tall against the backdrop of smaller dwellings.

Back in front of them, smoke billowed from a number of areas where huge explosions had taken place. Five black plumes were steadily rising about a kilometre to the north east and two more, due east, closer to the troops' position. Between these distinct areas of recent warfare were two long lines of carnage. Buildings, trees and all other forms of matter had been completely removed in two straight lines of total devastation and destruction. At the second battle zone, the lines of bulldozing destruction had changed direction and were now on a collision course with the Republic troops' current location. To all but three of the men in this expedition the sight was terrifying. Both lines of violent devastation extended rapidly towards them, one a long way behind the other. Entire trees flew into the air, accompanied by a continuous wave of thousands of bricks and sections of building. A large cloud of rubble, branches and leaves spear-headed each of the straight lines, giving the impression you could have surfed these fast approaching paths of destruction.

One of the troops managed to tear his mesmerised attention away from the vision of mass annihilation in front of him and ran to the side of the building where the Commander and two troops were sitting ducks. He wasn't quite sure how to begin his warning.

"Er... Sir?!" he started delicately.

"What is it?" replied the commander with a tetchy tone

"RUN! Run that way, now!" he pointed in a direction that was perpendicular to the onslaught of the lines of flying debris. The two troops took to their feet before the sentence had been finished. They had no desire to be any closer to the increasingly deafening noise and were perfectly happy taking orders of an escaping nature from anyone, especially in situations such as this. Likewise, the troops on the roof tops and in the trees each took their life in their own hands and made rapid decisions based on the three options that faced them; hope that the tree or roof on which they were located was outside the trajectory of the two oncoming streams of demolition; take time getting to the ground in the belief that there would still be time to run, once down; or leap from roof top to roof top over the alley-ways and hope they didn't fall to an equally unappetising death. Each troop took his chance, some climbing down trees praying they would have time left to run, while others started death-defying leaps of faith from one building to the next that even the most dexterous tree jumping monkeys would have been proud of.

The two quick-thinking ground troops ran off in precisely the direction they were told, whilst the Commander, slightly less willing to take orders from a subordinate thought about his options. The last time he had declined to accept the orders of a lower ranking officer, he had plunged through the roof of a building into a room full of grinning corpses. Maybe this time he would accept the advice gracefully, rather than rise to the challenge of reprimanding the comrade. He stepped away from the building with his pride intact, and with his head held high, broke into a trot towards the centre of the small clearing next to him. By the time he had reached his tenth step, it was simply too late.

The wall a hundred metres to his right, on the far side of the small square, disintegrated into sand and gravel as an almighty black vehicle launched itself through the ancient construction towards the Commander. In a fraction of a second it had flattened him to the ground, skidding to a sudden halt, half inserted into the building on the opposite side of the piazza. The newly penetrated structure collapsed noisily over the top of the massive tank as it rested in a dusty pile of rubble, twigs and leaves.

All was a little quieter. The deafening rumbling of the other fast approaching line of destruction continued to break what otherwise would have almost definitely been silence. All troops were lucky with their survival tactics. The central building on which some of the men had been located was now a flattened pile of sand, half burying the awesome black machine. Each man had successfully clambered down neighbouring trees or leapt across alleyways onto the nearest alternative buildings. From their various hiding positions the troops waited without breathing for a few seconds to see if the machine was incapacitated. On the ground fifty metres behind the massive vehicle, semi-buried in the soft earth at the centre of the clearing, was the Commander, face down and motionless. He must be dead thought his entourage. You don't get run over by a thousand-footed fifty tonne cannon carrier and survive.

Chapter 34

The Engagement

A fierce bolt of lightning flew past the upper right side of the view screen and exploded against the wall of a large white building half a kilometre ahead. Burning bricks and trees showered the surroundings. The interior of the tank was shaken violently.

"What the fff..." The Rogue Nation tank Collar reacted, then ordered his rear view screen to come on line. The vision appeared instantly, followed by a female voice pointing out that his instruction had been carried out. Behind him three of his fellow tanks had been destroyed, and it appeared as though he'd had a lucky escape. The quick-witted tank Collar realised that there should have been four tanks in his pursuit, two on either side of the raised canal that ran the full length of the street. A quick check of all other monitors showed the two tanks directly in front of him and the three along side.

"Rear zoom" he ordered hurriedly. The screen in front of him zoomed through the smoke and burning wreckage behind him, to reveal a lone tank hundreds of metres behind the others, four side launchers smouldering guiltily. He wasn't sure what had happened, but mistake or no mistake, the pilot of that tank was going to pay with his life.

He radioed his fellow Collars to explain what he had deduced. They were all in an equivalent state of surprise (most races would have been in a state of shock – but Rogue Nationals don't do 'shock' as it shows signs of weakness, whereas 'surprise' simply implies ignorance and RN barbarians are far more comfortable with that). All were prepared to eliminate the culprit, whoever it was. None of the tank pilots thought it likely that an invader had managed to infiltrate their assailing tank, they simply assumed old Scarface had gone a bit ga-ga and fancied some entertainment (it was not uncommon for Rogue Nation warriors to attack their own kind out of sheer frustration of not having any other enemies to attack. They were tantamount to inter-galactic football hooligans – simply wanting to fight anyone, it didn't matter who, so long as someone got hurt, badly!) Whatever the reason for the attack, it was an excellent opportunity to have some fun. Their chance to open fire again had been realised and they were all desperate to get some action.

The Collar looked at his screen, displaying the rear view from his tank. He didn't want to manoeuvre too quickly, that would destroy the thrill of the chase. But perhaps in hindsight, he should have, as a hail of laser bolt fire from the offending vehicle pierced the side of his almost indestructible land tank and instantly transformed it, and one of its neighbouring vehicles into a large shower of bright sparks and small black smouldering particles.

One of the remaining fellow tank Collars instantly stepped into the commander's vacated hierarchical position and took control, ordering the rear most flanking Collar to open fire on the rogue tank. There was a moment's wait, while the upper section of the rear tank on the far side of the street rotated quickly to aim its cannons at the sitting target. Moments later two loud whooshing noises indicated the release of the fire bolts as they rocketed through the air at incredible speed, leaving a straight line of vapour hanging in their wake.

But the enemy tank had already turned and was travelling at quarter speed through one of its neighbouring buildings, instantly reducing it to rubble. The two streaks of steam impacted buildings behind the enemy target, as it pulled out of the way of the oncoming arsenal. Two eruptions occurred, sending buildings hundreds of metres into the air, in millions of very small pieces. The Collar had achieved what he had wanted. To get him with the first shot wouldn't have been at all exciting. The chase was on. This was sport – blood sport at its very best.

Chapter 35

The Book

The loud noises continued. Explosions, muffled by distance, reigned across the ancient citadel.

T held the book nervously. Last time it really hurt to feel the words pierce his skull through his eyeballs and appear like lumpy burps in his throat. Maybe it was just because he was resisting too much. He knew much more now than he had before, but it still wasn't enough. He wanted to be able to explain it to the others, but first, he had to find out for himself. Answers were needed by everyone. There were too many strange things occurring simply to ignore them. Like this ancient civilisation of advanced people who suddenly all seemed to die where they sat, thousands of years ago. Not to mention the unprovoked attacks from the Rogue Nationals – everyone knew how violent the RN society was, but it was still out of character for them to attack a poorly defended Republic investigation vessel. That simply wasn't sporting. And why didn't their planetary sensors pick up the RN life signs when they ran the preliminary landing checks? The Rogue Nation must have gone to an extreme amount of effort to block or distort the readings. And what about that giant floating diamond? Why would a planet have a five hundred kilometre high piece of rock, balanced in mid-air by the gravity of the planet and its moons? It truly was an incredible feat, but did it hold any purpose, and if so, what? And who built it? And how? And why…?

The questions queued up to run through T's mind. So many questions and so few answers. T knew he held the answers in his hands. If not in this book, he thought to himself, then in the books stored around the massive room on the top floor of this Government building. He looked up, suddenly aware that he had been staring at the cover of the book for far too long. His five colleagues looked back at him nervously. This was not the same T. Well, it was really, they all knew that in their heart of hearts, but he had never seemed quite so insane before. One or two of the men fingered their hand guns nervously. If T was planning on going loopy, they were planning to redecorate the walls with his body parts. He was a mate and a colleague, but he also posed a real threat and was making them all very jumpy – not a good combination when mixed with poorly trained gunmen.

"Well I guess there's no time like the present," T pronounced, half-heartedly, in a broken voice. Nobody smiled.

The group had moved into a small office room on the first floor of the government building. They explained to T that this move was for his own protection, in case anything unpredictable happened whilst he was reading the ancient scripts, but he was well aware the sole reason was damage limitation. If T was to go screwy, it would be a great deal easier for the five colleagues to contain him or kill him in the confines of this small room rather than out in the open, where almost infinite numbers of escape paths existed.

It was cooler in here than outside in the warm sunlight, despite warmth being emitted from the small camp fire in the centre of the room. A slight breeze travelled through foliage by the glassless window, providing an eerie rustling concerto to the backdrop of distant rumblings and occasional explosions. The atmosphere contained a sense of the dramatic, to say the least, especially with the knowledge that two thousand very important decaying diplomats were upstairs grinning at the fallen landing craft that disturbed their ten thousand year slumber.

On the roof, a fresh batch of sitting targets had been deployed, relieving the ten men who started their exciting day looking out over the flat skyline of the city, and ended it eight hours later doing much the same thing. But at least those men had the day shift. This vast city of skeletons was going to get seriously scary in the middle of the night, which was threatening to arrive in just a few hours time. The men now knew the buildings surrounding them, covered in thousands of years of untamed vegetation throughout the whole city, contained the strangely content skeletal remains of millions of people. There probably wasn't an empty building anywhere. Earlier that day a few of the men had been ordered, by the base camp commander to investigate some of the surrounding buildings. Their brief expedition had revealed that in each dwelling a number of skeletons, far more decayed than the ones in the government chamber, were gathered together in equally curious scenarios. In one house, a small pile of bones revealed, upon closer inspection, two people lying on the floor in what was presumably a loving embrace. In another building, which appeared to be more conducive to a working office environment, a group of skeletons were positioned in a large circle in the middle of a meeting room floor. All of the furniture had been moved to the outside edge of the room and the piles of fifteen skeletons circled the centre of the space, outstretched forearm bones reaching across the ancient moss-covered floor to the next pile of bones. The more the Republic troops looked, the more unnerving, yet peaceful scenes of tranquil death they uncovered.

Ghost cities are unnerving enough, but there is a very specific and incredibly disturbing sensation associated with seeing thousands upon thousands of abandoned buildings left empty many millennia before your arrival, each containing the remains of their former inhabitants. It's not a scene anyone would get used to no matter how many times they saw it, and the chances were, this was the first and last time they would. One thing was for sure – they would never forget the sense of feeling very out of place and highly unwelcome. The scenes communicated loud and clear, 'you should not be here'. Never had these men felt so scared. Many of them wished they had been killed in the earlier attack, or during the entry into the planet's atmosphere, simply to be rid of this sense of discomfort. There were too many riddles and unanswered questions, let alone too many skeletons. Their dead colleagues suddenly looked like the fortunate ones.

T placed the heavy book in his lap as he sat cross-legged on the floor, back leaning against the hard wall behind him. Sunlight streamed in thin shards through the foliage at the window in front of him and created a rectangular shape of speckled bright light on the dry wooden floor. Slowly he looked down, trying his hardest not to look directly at the ancient text. He focussed his gaze on a predetermined mark on the floor, allowing his peripheral view once again to see the unfamiliar text. It scrawled and twisted beneath his gaze, but T continued to stare at the mark. He listened to the words that appeared directly in the centre of his head and mouth, as they slowly told him the history of a long forgotten race. The wind gently disturbed the leaves by the window, giving the event an uncomfortable sense of calm, surrounded by stark reminders of death.

T had started reading this final historical volume from its very first page. It seemed, from the tranquil nature of the contents, that the records in this particular book had started before there were any concerns for the survival of their civilisation. It spoke of influential politicians, scientists and scholars who had given speeches and readings at the high council of Vacchion. A man called Cass had been featured often, warning of the dangers of investigating the unknown. His argument seemed to be that they should cease evolving and stop asking questions of their existence. Many a heated debate had occurred, where various politicians had stated that it was their divine right to investigate the unknown, to believe in their own religions and to follow numerous cults. But Cass stood fast, stating that it would be their undoing. Despite the respect that the historical notes leant him, T got the impression that this man, Cass, was viewed by many as a sandwich-board wearing, 'the-end-is-nigh' madman. He may well have been a highly respected scholar, but the politicians seemed to give him the time to express his feelings more out of a sense of respect for what he had achieved in the past, rather than to listen to his words of warning in the present.

T was confused for a moment as he heard the mumblings of some of his colleagues agreeing knowingly, whilst they pictured the mad eccentrics that seemed to be related to one another throughout the universe, each one standing on a plastic container somewhere warning that the apocalypse was imminent. Was he speaking out-loud, T thought? He had no idea what he had been saying or how. He felt as if he were in a coma, able to view the outside world from the comfort of his warm skull, whilst looking through two circular windows of his eye sockets, but he did not feel in control or able to communicate with his surroundings. Seemingly though, he was. The listening audience shuffled nervously as T's automated monologue continued. Each man suddenly found their own uncomfortable respect for the insane declarers of doom as they realised that this Cass, had been right about the fate he had predicted ten thousand years ago. They'd all seen such mad men, wandering the streets with a tea cosy on their heads, or mumbling loudly and incoherently on street corners whilst showering fast moving passers by in spittle. Each man had been guilty of ignoring them. They all made mental notes to behave differently next time they came across one. Maybe they would even listen in future. If they had a future.

For hours T spoke in a monotone voice, reeling off the facts and statistics of a peaceful and tranquil nation that had no real concerns. His listeners found the experience exhausting, as their minds developed a deep understanding of the nation in whose graveyard they sat. Memories of spirits who once occupied these very offices seemed to bring the walls to life. Their minds generated images of people moving around them on their day to day business, administering the nation's activities. In their thoughts, the streets bustled outside with the noises of markets and respectful trade taking place. Some of the images created by the more imaginative of the group were so real that it made them homesick for their own families and neighbourhoods. Tears appeared in their eyes as the realisation of their own mortality started to hit home. One man left the room, sobbing for his wife who he had not seen in two years. The mood was solemn.

T kept the humbling information flowing.

Chapter 36

The Button

The machine had come to a sudden halt, as soon as he had released his grip on the two joysticks. Was that who he thought it was, or was his panicking mind playing a sick trick on him? He was being chased by some of the most destructive land based machines he had ever seen. Did he really have time to get out and investigate if that figure really had been one of his Commanders?

"Rear view" ordered K, but the computer remained silent and the large screen kept the static image of the dull interior of yet another half destroyed building in front of him. He had seen him, he knew he had. He wasn't imagining things. He grabbed the sleeping rodent, placed it inside his open shirt and tried to find a way of opening the door. He screamed a couple of desperate commands which the computer ignored. There must be a manual way out. There must be. Panic set in again. Not only was he going mad – a safe assumption from the vision of running over one of his colleagues when he knew he was the only TAKer here – but he was also a sitting duck. The Rogue Nation tanks would be upon him in minutes. When they got here, they would be unlikely to be kind enough to simply blast him with their cannons. No, the sick bastards were much more likely to take his puny body from the tank and torture him to death under the guise of it being more sporting.

His mind raced, as did his heart. He could feel his temples pumping so violently that it wouldn't surprise him if he suddenly sprang a leak from a major artery. He must calm down. And suddenly he did. Just as had happened before, his chemical levels seemed to change rapidly and he stopped quivering like a nervous feather.

He took a deep breath and calmly looked around the control panels and the door edge to see if he could find a way of opening the exit hatch next to him. Almost immediately, a likely culprit had been found and pressed. The hatch opened with a slight suction noise as the fresh air rushed in to greet him. It was darker outside than K had expected. The day was slowly drawing to a close.

He knew he had to hurry. There was probably less than a minute before the Rogue Nation tanks would be upon him. He had to get away as fast as possible. He stepped out of the tank and was greeted by a poorly placed phaser shot which singed his left ear before impacting on the open tank door behind him. The small explosion knocked him forward, off of the steps of the tank and onto the floor metres below. He wasn't badly hurt, but the ringing in his ears was going to take a while to clear.

He scrambled to his feet as a number of TAK colleagues appeared from their hiding places. A small group of men surrounded him suspiciously. A mass of emotions rushed K's mind – relief, happiness, confusion, all clambering desperately to be recognised as the dominant feeling. But logic stepped in clinically and ordered the emotions to subside. There was one Republic official who had not appeared from a hiding place. The very real body of the Commander remained face down in the earth, spread-eagled amongst the soft foliage. It wasn't his mind playing tricks on him after all. K felt very awkward, but he had no time to explain or apologise.

"You have to listen to me. There's no time for questions." K took total control of the situation. He shocked himself. He paused to allow his brief stunned silence to pass. "There are more of these tanks heading this way, each containing a very p*ssed of Rogue National. We have to get as far away from here as possible and hide." To his amazement the surrounding troops were listening to him, despite his obvious level of authority (one level above stow-away), depicted by the lack of stripes or emblems on his clothes.

The group stood poised, ready to run away from the imminent onslaught of the RN tanks. But they waited. K realised they were waiting for his lead. This couldn't be right. Why was he being given such a huge level of authority, he was a mud collector, a leaf examiner. Someone who picked up animal cr*p for a living. But there was no time to argue or question, they had to get going.

K pointed over to where the Commander lay motionless. "Someone pick him up, he's coming with us."

"But he's dead," complained one of the soldiers, not at all sad to see the Commander's downfall, "he must be, you ran over him in a fifty-ton tank."

"I think you'll find he's very much alive," replied K, as the group sighed with dissatisfaction. "Now let's get the hell out of here!" K ran through a network of alleyways, across large streets and over the raised stone streams that seemed to run the full length of each main street. His entourage followed enthusiastically, a number of men begrudgingly struggling with the unconscious body of their senior officer. They had travelled a few hundred metres already, but that kind of progress was nothing compared to the incredible speed of the land tanks. Then he remembered something.

At least a minute had passed since they had abandoned the damaged tank. K calculated that the Rogue Nationals must have reached it by now. He gave the order to the group of running men to take cover in a large heavy looking building in front of them. They all ran towards the building and scrambled over the large trunk of a tree which lay across its huge open doorway. The unconscious Commander was lifted over the obstacle, carelessly and dumped on the floor in the darkened, humid room. A number of skeletons had to be disrespectfully brushed aside to make room for the new arrivals as they piled over the obstruction in the entrance.

K wasn't sure what to expect from the small black box with the red button, but he hoped for the best. It was their only chance of escape from the pursuing tanks. He viewed the confused men around him, aware they were staring at him in a quizzical manner. K gave the instruction for them to lie on the floor, face down. All obeyed, except the limp body of the Commander who had been discarded unceremoniously face up, at the side of the room. K hoped the officer was OK, as he was sure that running over a group Commander with an enemy tank was quite a serious Republic offence.

He took one last look at everyone, to ensure they were as safe as they could possibly be, each as far away from the windows that broke the solidity of the thick walls. He had no idea what was going to happen but they were all about to find out. He pressed the button and prepared his body for the massive impact of a huge explosion by squinting his eyes tightly shut, covering his ears with the palms of his hands and huddling his body into a ball. Nothing happened. He pressed it again, this time with one eye open to ensure he pressed the very centre of the button. Nothing. With both eyes opened, he pressed it once more. Again, silence ruled the airwaves.

"Bugger." K whispered to himself. Now what?

His colleagues looked expectantly at K. They had placed their trust in his untested leadership, and all he had managed to do so far was look very silly. He'd had his few minutes of fame. Now it was back to his mundane life as a nobody. In fact, worse than that – he was probably going to be demoted to less-than-a-nobody.

Without warning, a sound so loud it was preceded by a wave of deafening anti-noise, erupted from the near distance. The entire universe seemed to shake from the inside out, starting at the heart of each object and gradually extending the violent vibrations to the outer edges. The troops' heart beats were affected by the explosion, interrupted by the internal tremor making them pulse erratically. A column of light in the early dusk illuminated the surrounding area to that of a bright summer's day. A scorching burst of heat then followed, one that any Gannage holiday island in the Sun-Stroke System would be proud to call a heat wave.

The incredible furnace was over in seconds. Which was lucky, as any longer would have seen surrounding objects spontaneously combust against their will. The light had faded back to the normal state of early evening, but the brief incandescent light now made it seem so much darker than before, as eyes took a few moments to readjust. A huge cloud of black smoke hung like a bad smell in the air, shadowing a great deal of the neighbourhood whilst creating a feeling of early nightfall for all beneath its growing mass.

K decided that it was probably best to assume that not all the enemy tanks had been destroyed by the blast, if any. He thought it wise to stay in this building for the night, and so, assuming the role of heroic leader once again, he gave orders for the men to climb the stone staircase to the upper levels of the building and to settle down for the night. Two men would keep watch throughout the light evening and the night, swapping at half hour intervals. He volunteered to go first and chose another man to accompany him. He also ordered that a medic take a look at the Commander. To K's relief and everyone else's disappointment, the Commander was still alive, unconscious from the incident which forced every molecule of air out of his body for a few seconds. He would be fine.

During the half hour shift, the rodent decided to take a well-earned break from his slumber and joined K in his watch over the dim neighbourhood. After a few minutes, he got bored, and decided that food was necessary. To K's surprise, the rodent leapt from the top floor window of the three storey building and landed safely on the soft ground. K shook his head with worry as the rodent disappeared into the night. Despite being surrounded by fellow beings that he thought he'd never see again, K suddenly felt lonely. His new furry friend had left and he wasn't sure if he would return. K made a conscious effort to be grateful for his reacquired humanoid colleagues. He was no longer alone. He had managed, against all odds to find some fellow Republicans who were undoubtedly going to be able to get them all back to the mother ship. Things were looking up. All the details of their escape from the planet could be discussed tomorrow, but right now complete silence prevailed, as many of the men lay strewn across the mossy floor in unsettled slumber.

As he watched the rodent bounce off into the darkness, K hoped he would be alright. And if he was planning on returning, that he would be thoughtful enough to bring back food for everyone. In his heart of hearts, K knew the first thought was a foregone conclusion and the latter was probably wishful thinking.

Chapter 37

The Prophet

T's fellow TAKers were very worried for the troops that had ventured off towards the explosions earlier that day. Not necessarily because they were fond of the individuals that had been forced to take a closer look at the source of the disturbances, but because they were not keen on their limited numbers being reduced even further. A massive explosion like none they had heard so far had broken the story telling from the ancient texts, and had worried the small group so much that they had all run up the stairs, including T, through the network of corridors to the roof, where they joined their fellow panicking look-outs.

The group of men lay at the edge of the large roof, looking east towards the scene of destruction. Even in the half-light of the early evening, the size of the destruction could be appreciated. Much like the crater caused by the incredible impact of the Republic mother ship, at the base of The Chun, a new black crater had been created, but much smaller than the original. The circle of blackness was bordered by the surrounding soft white and green of the undamaged city.

They lay silent, each with his own thoughts. What should they do now? Wait? Run? Run where? Silently the men contemplated their own fates. Each knowingly glancing at one another as only condemned men can. T decided that he would return to his historical volume. He was learning more about this planet with every sentence, and in light of there being nothing much else to do, the absorbing knowledge of the historical volume seemed to be the only thing that was likely to be able to help them.

He had the book with him, he always had the book with him. So when returning to the darkness of the building, he decided to stay within the realms of the governmental chamber, rather than return to the first floor office where the fire was burning in a stone hearth. During the most recent event, his colleagues had forgotten their nervous disposition towards T and his unrelenting wishes to read more of the book's ancient text. It appeared they had all forgotten how mad they thought he was only a few hours before and were giving him much greater freedom to do as he wished now. No restraining jacket or watchful eye required.

After clambering down the vine that connected the roof with the huge parliamentary chamber, via the massive hole that T had caused with the landing pod, he glanced around the morgue of a room once again. Row upon row of skeletal faces grinned back at him from all sides. Unlike the others, T was starting to feel more at home with them. He appreciated their lives and their achievements and had begun to better understand the fascinating civilisation they had created.

T looked around the room slowly and spotted an empty chair on the fourth row, one third of the way along the length of the room. It was one of the few empty seats, and was heavily surrounded by the slumped skeletons of former politicians. Before making his way to the empty seat, T walked past the tall bookshelves at the back of each grandstand of seats that lined the inner walls of the room's circumference. At random, T picked up four books, one from each side of the chamber.

He cautiously passed the seated skeletal remains of the planet's former government, careful not to disturb their fragile remains. He even found himself saying 'excuse me' a number of times and apologising as he crushed skeletal toes with his large heavy boots. Once seated, he looked around the room from his corpse-bordered position. This was where the books needed to be read and where the truth needed to be known – right here where it all took place. The Vacchion history was made and documented here, so this is where it should be revealed.

He picked up one of the randomly selected volumes. This one was from one of the smaller walls at either end of the long oval room. He opened it, somewhere in the centre and held the book out in front of him, once again being careful not to look directly at the writing. He stared at the distant wall just above the volume. Nothing happened. He tried again a little harder. Then harder still. Finally he looked directly at the writing. It was scrawly and twisted in the same way as the very last record book, but it did not strain the eyes and did not enter his subconscious in legible English when viewed through peripheral vision. He opened the volume at other random pages, but all were the same. T was disappointed to say the least. He had wanted to understand more about the intriguing lives of the inhabitants of this planet. At first he took it a little too personally. Then he wondered whether there was magic in the room that didn't allow the books to be read here. No that was just silly... especially since the first volume he read had been in this very room, albeit painfully.

He picked up the next volume. He opened the first few pages. The same thing happened. No effect whatsoever. T thumbed through the book, reaching a page where an obvious difference took place. The mind numbing effect of the text still had not returned, but there was a distinct difference between the two pages he was viewing. The writing had a very different feel about it. Both pages took the form of swirling masses of lines and decorative scribbles and it all looked very similar to the eye-burning copy that K could read. But these scrawls he couldn't decipher. Not by looking directly at them, nor by looking past them. They were different.

He picked up the third volume. Now getting desperate to find other manuscripts of historical information he could understand. He opened this book at a random page and stared directly at the centre of the text. The piercing sensation was agony. His eyes felt like they were going to melt in their sockets. He dropped the book and moved both palms to his face, clutching at his eyes in agony. This was far worse than any sensation he had received from the original volume he had read. It felt as though his eyes were pouring with blood, but after a few moments, T managed to calm himself down and checked that the fluid pouring from his eyes was just salt water. It was.

T picked up the volumes that had been scattered to the floor in his writhing pain and placed them back on his lap. Carefully, he opened the third historical book again. This time he ensured it was held far round to his right and that his eyes were averted to his left, so that the text was not visible to him. Slowly, and with a steady hand, he pulled the volume into the very edge of his peripheral vision. No pain so far, but the text was too far away from his conscious sight for him to make anything of it. He began to move the text again, being sure to continue to look at the same spot on the far chamber wall on his left. Gradually, a strange feeling began to occur in his eyes, mainly in his right eyeball, as this was closest to the manual. Words began to appear in his vision, but they were broken and old. He pulled the volume round some more, it was now at a forty-five degree angle to his line of sight. It felt as if maggots were crawling inside his eye-sockets. Not at all pleasant, but bearable nonetheless. More words appeared, as he moved the ancient volume further towards full view. Finally the text flowed fluently through his peripheral vision. The language was still very difficult to understand, but it told of historical events seemingly thousands of years before the final volume in the epic tale of the planet's inhabitants:

"Tis with such reverence that we declare the sanction of law 318. From this day forth, none such personage shall consume another Vacchion... not even a relative." There were many passages such as this, each illustrating the gradual advancement of the Vacchion civilisation over the many millennia before their eventual demise. The volume described the creation of large, impressive buildings around the great monument that they called The Chun. T read of huge ceremonies that worshipped the creators of the structure in a god-like manner. The Vacchions didn't build it. At least not the Vacchions that lived in this city thousands of years ago...

The creation of The Chun must have occurred far before this race had the ability to do so. In fact, as T thought about the size and incredible mass of The Chun, it was obvious to see that the Vacchions, even at the end of their civilisation did not have the means to create such a monster. There weren't many races that did. T's very own advanced race of space explorers and scientists would find it difficult if not impossible to create such a huge monument. It must have been there from a time long before the Vacchion race had evolved on this planet.

T frantically began to calculate the time line of the Vacchion civilisation. He read snippets of many manuals that gradually allowed him to estimate the average time recorded within each historical volume. They seemed to only record significant governmental occasions and the passing of new laws. They did not have an entry for every day. Far from it. Many of the entries seemed to be months, sometimes years apart. It was obviously a slow moving race. It appeared from the volumes that day-to-day life on Vacchion had been a peaceful and simple existence for all. The government only met to discuss global issues when they needed discussing. They were not in the practice of arguing every detail, despite their incredibly varied mix of religious and political stand points.

T counted the number of books on each shelf. Thirty-eight, on average. He then counted the number of book cases that existed around the room. Two-hundred and forty tall columns of shelves lined the walls, with eight shelves on each. There were therefore nearly seventy three thousand volumes in this room, give or take a few as there were one and a half shelves still to be filled. T had estimated, from the few he had read, that the time each volume covered was around seven to ten years. That meant, to his astonishment that, roughly speaking there were Government records within this room covering half to three quarters of a million years. And that was without counting the scrolls and other archived manuscripts that had been placed in additional bookshelves dotted around the outside of the oval corridor that circled this incredible room. This was truly a remarkable race. Slow, but still remarkable.

Maybe it was the sight of The Chun every morning that humbled them into remaining how they were. Maybe they understood what small insignificant creatures they really were in the grand scheme of the universe, when they looked up at the galaxy-sized ornament every day. When something of such size, built before your race had evolved, stares down at you constantly, it must have an effect. Presumably for the Vacchions it had been: "You'll evolve eventually – don't rush it!"

Some of the Vacchions worshipped it, others simply wrote poems about it or painted it. But life, inevitably, revolved around The Chun.

T was jealous. He was reading about the simple lives of millions of people, all of whom resided in a city of peace and happiness. Government legislation was only required once in a blue moon, and they had the greatest piece of art the universe had ever seen. What went wrong, thought T? He remembered reading about the prophet of doom. A character called Cass had popped up in the last few years of the final volume, complaining that the Vacchion's advancement would be their downfall. T decided to revisit this.

Chapter 38

The Remote

The four barbarian land tanks encircled the stationary stolen battle vehicle. Each tank Collar viewed their surroundings by rapid and well-practiced commands of the on-board computer and hi-tech surveillance systems. Their initial scans of the area revealed no threats and the stationary land tank in front of them, with its side access hatch wide open, appeared to be empty.

The four Collars left the relative safety of their cockpits and gathered together in the centre of the small square, happy that their computerised sweep of the local buildings revealed no possible ambush or sniper attack. They collectively decided that Scarface's land tank needed to be investigated; to see if there were any clues as to what had caused such a destructive, yet welcome, outburst.

One of the Collars walked up the short staircase to the cockpit and spent a few minutes looking around the cramped confines of the vehicle command pod. He was somewhat confused. Over a number of the buttons and the armrest were hundreds of tiny muddy paw prints.

"I'm not quite sure what happened," said the Collar as he stepped out of the doorway onto the flat gangplank that ran the full length of the mechanical monster. His colleagues on the ground below looked up, "but he wasn't alone," continued the tank Collar.

His explanation was cut short by the sudden movement of the pod door, which slammed shut without warning. This motion was rapidly followed by a loud high-pitched double beep that echoed around the small square. The female computer voice then explained through loud external speakers: "Anti-theft system enabled. Please step away from the vehicle". The four barbarian Collars burst out laughing simultaneously. Someone had pressed the remote alarm system. They must have been trying to trap Vhana in the door of the vehicle, but he had luckily stepped to the side of the opening just before the heavy metal door had slammed shut. The large men gradually all came to the same conclusion, whoever had the remote alarm device, was within a few hundred metres of them as the signal on the remote had a limited range.

Suddenly the double beep occurred once again, also followed closely by the female voice stating the obvious: "Anti theft system disabled". The door to the vehicle opened slowly, as the four tank Collars looked on, smiling. What was Scarface up to? They all knew he was a real practical joker, always setting booby traps and trying to get his fellow colleagues maimed or killed in the funniest ways imaginable. This was probably just another one of his strange approaches to life and death, taking the p*ss out of the people that were going to hunt him down and kill him – if he didn't kill them first.

"Vhana, get down, let's go" ordered the highest ranking tank Collar. Vhana moved towards the door to the cockpit as the entrance to the vehicle's command pod suddenly slammed shut once again. With clockwork regularity the two beeps sounded, closely followed by the female voice advising everyone that the anti-theft alarm system had been re-engaged.

"I can't Sir, I've left my gun in the cockpit," exclaimed Vhana.

"Just open the door manually, you'll only set the alarm off," pointed out one of the other Collars on the ground, whilst looking around to see if he could see Scarface in any of the windows of the buildings surrounding them. He was probably having a right old laugh at their expense. He was going to get very hurt when they got hold of him.

"But be careful," added another of the Collars. "Scarface was renowned for his practical joking, so be wary of booby traps."

"Yeah, I can see that judging by the personalised sign he has put on the door," replied Vhana from the high side of the black tank. In front of him was a childish sign, made out of a large piece of scrap paper and some messily written but colourful letters which read: "Antyfeft Sistum kertissy of Skarfase".

Vhana grabbed the handle of the pod door, whilst smiling at his colleague's sense of humour and lack of spelling ability. He can't even spell his own name, thought Vhana.

As the door mechanism clicked, an overly complicated arrangement of electronics, explosives, missiles and laser generators all received the message at precisely the same time. Scarface's ingenious re-wiring and reprogramming had worked. It was a booby trap that even he would have been proud of, had he not been disembowelled by a very tetchy rodent earlier that day.

The tank, its four neighbouring tanks, four Rogue Nation barbarians and a large number of buildings, trees and bushes instantly merged into a single, colossal explosion. The entire area accelerated as one hundreds of feet into the air. The collective mass of fire disintegrated into a cloudy shower of burning particles gently returning to the planet's surface.

Chapter 39

The Chamber

The Marth was not happy. Heads were going to melt for this.

He was receiving reports from his subordinates that some Republic escape pods had made it to the planet's surface. Tracking of the small escape ships had not been possible as some of their invisibility shields had been booted to eliminate any chance of being seen or picked up by conventional surveillance systems. Coupled with the Marth's instructions not to destroy all of the enemy's vessels, there were good reasons for survivors reaching the surface of the planet. However, as with many bosses the universe over, the Marth had a habit of conveniently forgetting the details of his own instructions when it suited him.

Despite recent events, the Marth decided it was pointless sending down further troops. He already had a large number of barbarian teams patrolling the city area, as well battalions trying to follow the vague treasure trail they had uncovered in their first visit to this planet over twelve years ago. He must not let the enemy discover the secret first. If they treated it wrongly, they could wipe everyone out. If they destroyed it, the last twelve years of his life in this godforsaken battle-less hell-hole would have been wasted.

The Marth spent a few moments remembering his first encounter with Vacchion. The entire solar system was uncharted and therefore dangerous, which is why he had made specific plans to detour through this network of planets as a life-threatening treat to his troops after a particularly bloody and difficult victory over the powerful fire-people of Conflage. Despite being the Marth's home planet, he had enjoyed the Rogue Nation invasion he had led there. It was an excellent battle. Millions of innocent people had died and the damage to the planet was so devastating that it had been completely drowned in the fire blood of its inhabitants. Soon after the battle was completed, chemical reactions had occurred and the planet had started a complicated process that meant in a few thousand years it would become a sun. The Marth smiled to himself at the despicable, yet ingenious strategies that he employed to win the ten-year war. Those were the days, he sighed to himself.

Upon their arrival at the sector 7g.s.89 solar system, the sight of The Chun had intrigued the Marth into believing that an advanced race of conquerable beings existed here and the planet was investigated. To the Marth's disappointment, but the relief of his battle-scarred fleet, there was nothing here but the remnants of a former peaceful race. The word tasted foul in his thoughts – peaceful. Disgusting. During their brief visit to the planet, records of the most powerful weapon known to the universe were stumbled upon. A weapon so awesome, the entire civilisation that discovered it had been eliminated within a matter of weeks. Not in the heavily bloodied manner the Marth liked to conduct his battles, but arguably a useful tool to possess nonetheless – not least to keep it from the hands of your enemies.

That first landing was twelve years ago. The Marth was ordered to lead the investigation into the mystery, to ensure the speedy retrieval of what was now being referred to as The Knowledge. He had been imprisoned here in this quiet solar system ever since.

When the Republic investigation vessel was first detected venturing into this unique solar system a few months earlier, the Marth had decided that some interesting action might be on the cards and the enemy ship was allowed to roam the skies at its own free will. When they eventually reached the planet of Vacchion, the Marth decided to allow them some time to scan the planet and send back reports to Republic command that it was uninhabited by any advanced race. The Rogue Nation ground troops used personal sensor camouflage technology that allowed them to go undetected. The Marth had waited long enough for bloodshed and ordered the attack, realising that the visitors could stumble across the treasure he had been doomed to find. But he was not quite quick enough. The Republic had managed to deploy a number of landing squadrons to investigate the planet before the attack had taken place. That meant the

Rogue National troops had to be careful to get the enemy's landing forces off the face of the planet as soon as possible.

It was a million to one chance, but what if the Republic scientists had discovered the planet's secret despite only being on the surface for little more than a couple of hours? As the ancient prophet Prah-Chjett (a man so powerful, he could see deep within the realms of parallel universes) had once said, "Million to one chances occur nine times out of ten". This worried the Marth. They could inadvertently destroy The Knowledge altogether. Or even worse, release it.

"Sire, we are receiving reports that one of Gamma Squadron's tanks may have been hijacked." The officer broke the Marth's deep thoughts of the past.

"By whom?" asked the Marth, calmly.

"They are unsure Sire." Replied the officer nervously. He was only the messenger, but he knew he was treading on incredibly thin ice next to a temperamental man with melting capabilities. "Initially it was believed that the Collar had simply started a feud with the other tanks," he paused, forcing a dry nervous swallow. "But analysis of voice commands given in the tank showed it was not a Rogue National."

"Tell them to destroy the stolen vessel." The Marth frowned disapprovingly. This was ridiculous, must he be bothered with the smallest of incidents?

"Er, it's not quite as simple as that, Sire." The man knew he would be lucky to escape with his life. "It appears that the hijacker managed to destroy five of the tanks in the squadron before escaping. When the abandoned tank was finally discovered, it was detonated, destroying the remaining four tanks. There are no survivors of the Gamma team, Sire." The man ducked to a crouch on the floor, expecting the worst.

The Marth looked at him, puzzled. "I will go to the surface. Prepare my lander."

"Yes, Sire." The man replied with relief as he stood proudly to attention. He had escaped. He was alive. He turned to exit the Marth's thinking chamber, but just before he managed to vacate the large black room, the Marth spoke once again.

"Officer. When I return, report to me for melting duty." The Officer's heart sank. It wasn't his lucky day after all.

"Yes, Sire." He replied reluctantly, and left the room to blow his own brains out.

Chapter 40

The Realisation

T read on:

"Session 5,258,992.7: In front of the Council stands Cass, a simple, yet well known and highly revered member of the Vacchion public. His family name has been associated for many centuries with various aids to the Vacchion advancement. He wishes to address the Council on matters of urgency and national survival.

Cass is informed he may proceed by The Dam – the judicial representative of the house. (Cass stands in the Lettiano dock, accompanied by a handful of quivering papers).

Cass speaks: "Err. Um. I don't really know where to start with this request."

The Dam interrupts: "At the beginning."

Cass continues: "Err, no, I am afraid that isn't right. I think I should begin at the end."

For the record: there is some unsettled murmuring amongst the officials and a few chuckles from the eastern seats.

Cass continues: "Our civilisation is going to end very soon..."

For the record: sharp intakes of air, more murmuring and no chuckles from the eastern seats.

Cass continues: "I have seen the future..."

For the record: there is an air of relief amongst the chamber and the chuckles return, only louder.

Cass continues: "Please listen to me. I have received a premonition, more accurate than ever before. My family have been receiving these dreams for thousands of years, they come in our sleep and have always been centred around inventions for advancement."

For the record: more murmuring, the mood is generally quieter.

Cass continues: "Every invention the Cass's have ever developed have come to us in the form of a premonition. Well now I have one, only this is not an invention. It is the end of our entire civilisation. It will happen, I am sure of it... You must believe me."

T read on. Cass was unsuccessful in his attempt to convince the council he had seen the future. But despite his ridicule, he returned on many occasions to tell more of the scenes in his dreams and the prediction of the awful future that awaited the Vacchion race. The Council entertained his thoughts and allowed his right to free speech on the subject of global security, but each time he left in a shroud of giggles and laughter quite unbefitting a council of global political leaders.

T turned to the last few pages of entries within the final Vacchion historical record. He re-read the final log, understanding a great deal more about why the important council members were imprisoned in their governmental chamber for the last few days of their existence. He read a number of sub-texts and meeting minutes that he did not recall reading before, about an electronic device of miniscule proportions that had been created to cage the hungry knowledge in an attempt to suppress the demise of their race. The records did not elaborate on whether the device had been completed, or the whereabouts of the laboratories that had been commissioned to create the advanced technology. There were no answers. Except one. T looked around his seat at the thousands of lifeless bodies that decayed around him. This was the evidence. They had not succeeded in time. The powerful knowledge they had uncovered had destroyed them all. Either directly, or indirectly, the Vacchion race had come to a complete end because of their quest for the truth. That must be it. They had found the answer to the question they were looking for. Therefore, they had stopped looking once they found it. It was a simple and universal rule. Any object you are searching for is always in the last place you look, simply because you stop looking once it is found. T gasped to himself at this incredible realisation.

Chapter 41

The Banquet

The bright sun rose on the horizon, its warmth awaking the troops around K. He had been awake for an hour, deep in his own thoughts. He hoped for survival and wished to be back on his home planet, oblivious to these events, but he wasn't. Instead he was in the thick of it, surrounded by death and pursued by a race of barbarians whose ultimate aim seemed to be the destruction of everyone; often including themselves.

Before them, a banquet of berries, nuts and crisp leaves awaited their hungry mouths. The rodent slept in K's arms, having completed a long night of foraging, gathering and hauling. The small mammal had outdone himself. The huge pile of food in the centre of the room dwarfed the friendly furry creature. K was grateful, and smiled down at the exhausted animal sleeping heavily, content in the awareness that he had done well.

One by one, the men awoke to the welcome sight. As soon as all were awake, K nodded to the group, as they waited for his approval to start consuming the much-needed food. Each man carefully picked up one of the large green leaves that had been distributed around the edible mountain and selected his own unique combination of colourful items from the pile. For a while, all was quiet except for the gentle munching of tasty nuts and berries. As the food replenished much needed energy within each of the bodies, the group became louder, almost forgetting they could still be within earshot of their terrifying assailants.

"So what now?" asked one of the troops. To K's surprise he was looking directly at him. But before he had a chance to respond, the Commander, head covered in bandages, took control of the situation.

"We return to the others."

"Others?" asked K, realising that he had not yet conversed with the troops about how they came to meet one another.

"There are about sixty of us that survived the attack," informed one of his colleagues.

"What attack?" enquired K, nervous of the response he was about to receive.

"Jeez, where have you been?" asked one of the men, suddenly realising that they too had no idea how K had come to be here.

Over the next half an hour, whilst the banquet was consumed, the group exchanged stories of the adventures that had brought them to this destination. K was horrified to learn that the meteor shower he had enjoyed watching so much the previous morning was actually his mother ship and colleagues being destroyed by the protective atmosphere of the planet. He felt sick to the stomach. He hadn't meant to delight in others' suffering. The guilt almost overwhelmed him momentarily, before the logical side of his head suddenly stepped into play and pointed out that he had done nothing wrong and that he needed to stay strong. He really was proving to be a changed man, so much more in control of his thoughts and emotions than he ever remembered being in the past. The startling information also meant that the massive explosion and fire that had woken him yesterday was the mother ship impacting the surface of the planet. No wonder it had felt like such an incredible earthquake. K broke his thoughts for a moment to wonder in awe at the ancient city all around him. How had the buildings managed to stay standing under such conditions? The ancient race must have built their constructions with incredible engineering knowledge for them to stand so solidly after thousands of years of neglect.

There was an air of sadness throughout the room, as the troops remembered the loss of life that had taken place. The personal feelings were lined with appreciation for their own lives accompanied by a feeling of guilt for having survived when so many hadn't. All of the men had been through a great ordeal to get to this stage. They now all appreciated having been given the chance of survival.

As K told of his adventures, the men were impressed at his solo success on the planet. K decided to omit that the rodent had been solely responsible for killing the barbarian tank pilot, and for destroying the enemy tanks. In fact, when K thought about it carefully, all he had achieved so far were multiple faintings, getting crushed by trees and running away a lot. And yet the Commander's authority was seemingly threatened by K and this inexplicable respect from the troops that had begun last night, before they knew anything of his adventures. K and the Commander were puzzled. The troops looked on, admiringly.

After the breakfast, the group gathered the remaining nuts and berries, loading every pocket to the brim, before gathering by the open doorway to leave their shelter. The Commander had decided that their mission had been a success. They had left base camp with the intention of discovering what was creating the massive explosions and now they knew. They must get back to the other troops and decide what to do next.

But the journey would be a slow one. They knew Rogue Nation tanks patrolled the area and the RN ground force were certainly aware the enemy were here. The miles ahead would have to be covered with great stealth and vigilance.

Chapter 42

The Scene

The Marth eyed the remains of what was once a building-lined plaza, with interest. A large black crater, ten metres deep at its centre and thirty metres across dominated the immediate scene. Structures surrounding the crater's circumference had been obliterated, leaving only naked foundations and the existence of a great deal of settled dust. As the eye travelled further out, the destruction became less apparent, walls gradually rising to whole buildings that had survived the blast approximately one hundred metres from the crater's centre.

Small sections of RN Battle tanks could be found strewn across the neighbourhood. The Marth walked towards his accompanying Tank Collar General, stopping only to bend down and pick up a piece of wiring from one of the destroyed tanks.

"We found paw prints on some of the remains of the tank cockpit, Sire, We traced the squadron's path back to the site where we suspected the tank might have been stolen," began the Collar General's update, "We wanted to be sure that it wasn't just Collar Koelan letting off a bit of steam."

"And what did you find?" enquired the Marth, calmly.

"Koelan, Sire." The Marth remained silent as he inspected the small piece of tank in his hands with far too much enthusiastic interest. "He'd had his bowels and rectal area ripped out by some sort of animal," continued the Collar General.

"A very intelligent animal, by all accounts."

"I'm sorry?" The Collar General was not an intelligent man, not compared to the Marth anyway. Suddenly remembering who he was addressing, he hurriedly adjusted his response "I'm sorry, Sire?"

"Well," began the Marth, slowly and softly, "the animal kills one of our tank pilots, takes the entry identification pass, drives the huge complicated piece of machinery, obliterating three of your tanks with well placed Thunderbolt missiles, only missing with one, and then destroyed a further two in a hail of laser cannon fire." The Marth paused for a moment, more for effect than anything else. "If that wasn't enough, he then managed to escape some of the best tank drivers we are said to have, detonating the entire machine at exactly the right moment to take out the remaining four men of the squadron." The more he was made to think about it, the more irate the Marth was becoming.

"Er, he did crash the tank Sire."

"What's your point?" The Marth had been incredibly tolerant so far. Most men would have been a puddle of bubbling flesh by now, but the Marth liked the stupidity of this man. It was endearing in a strange warrior fashion. He would give him the benefit of doubt.

"Well he can't have been that good." He pointed out delicately; then he had a small brain wave. "And he can't do anymore damage with it either, Sire."

The Marth sighed, "I suppose you have a point." Remembering who he was, the Marth approached the stupid tank Collar General, walking right up to him until their noses were far too close to feel altogether heterosexually appropriate. The General felt his nose tingle as the heat from the Marth's incandescent face burned his skin. "Find him, and bring him to me," he whispered harshly. He knew the tank Collar General would fail, but nevertheless, it gave the poor man something to do for a while before Marth melted him slowly from the feet up.

The Marth decided to search for him too. Whoever he was. He strolled back to the edge of the crater and looked along the near-straight path of destruction that the fleeing tank had created. For over a kilometre, the Marth could see through the trees, bushes, and buildings that had been destroyed by the high-speed tank. He turned dramatically towards his lander, the silver threads of his fireproof outfit billowed behind him, following in his smouldering wake.

The sleek black exterior of the Marth's lander radiated heat from the bright sunlight, but the incredible machine allowed no reflections and cast no shadow. No evidence of light distortion or reaction could be seen. The material from which the Marth's private machine was made came from the deep mines of the burning land of Tysnns. Its fire eating properties were lost on a hospitable planet such as this. The craft, with its deceptively small exterior, had been designed for three primary reasons; incredible speed, total destruction and to inspire fear in all that saw it. It was an awesome display of mechanical dramatics.

The lander rose into the air soundlessly, accompanied by the crisping of leaves and smouldering of wood around it. Before any onlookers could admire its sleek hull, the machine vanished into the distance.

Chapter 43

The Review

It was working. The cell's constant adjustment of chemical flows, subliminal education and the use of its powerful initiative drives were helping to ensure that the vessel increased its chances of survival.

There was the minor problem of the rodent, however, which seemed to have gained the affection of the vessel. It had interrupted the cell's intention to get his host to The Chun, at every opportunity. It was a welcome distraction for the humanoid host in which the cell was imprisoned and therefore, for the time being at least, should be allowed to remain. The cell was not capable of taking over its host's actions completely, nor did it have any intention of doing so. Its primary reason for being was to contain The Knowledge and allow no-one to learn of its details. So far this had been accomplished, but the task had not been easy these past two days, unlike the previous ten thousand years.

Chapter 44

The Situation

The wanderers were welcomed back with open arms. The men who'd had the dubious honour of adventure had made it back to base camp, relatively unscathed. The not so privileged men who had remained at the government building were relieved their colleagues had all returned and thankful that it was not them who had been exposed to such danger. Concerns about their numbers being reduced were not realised, in fact their numbers had been increased – by one. Well, one and a large rodent. Once the stories of the morning's banquet had been told, most of the men were willing to admit that their numbers had been increased by two.

Inside the building, all men were gathered, except four, who were ordered to keep a lookout on the roof. A large room had been found, free of skeletons, deep within the labyrinth of corridors that supplied passage through the huge structure like the veins of a stone monster. It was a large rectangular meeting room with a huge wooden oval table in the centre, covered in moss and housing a botanical garden of ferns and fungi underneath it. Many of the matching chairs were still usable, and most offered relatively comfortable relief to men who had otherwise been sat on the hard floor. Over fifty men and a large rodent gathered sombrely, packed into a room that should only accommodate forty. There was a great deal more to be concerned about now, so they must be vigilant in their movements; but they had yet to decide what their movements were to be.

The solemn silence was broken only by loud snoring emanating from deep within K's shirt.

The Commander addressed the small squadron of tired and morale-withered men. In the last few days they had seen their peaceful lives torn apart by the destructive powers of the Rogue Nation. Nearly two thousand of their friends and colleagues had been killed and they had been marooned on an uncharted planet filled with skeletons and crawling with enemy tanks. Their chief food adviser was a large brown rodent and their commanding officer was a twat. It was no wonder morale was low.

As K looked around the room all he saw were glum faces. Hope was evaporating from their pores and the will to fight was at an all-time low. If they were to survive things needed to change. The Commander had started to talk, but few seemed to be willing to listen intently. K noticed T across the far side of the room. His arm was half raised, elbow at its peak. Like an ambitious school child he waited anxiously for the right moment to shout a proverbial 'me, Sir, I know, I know'.

"…we have food, shelter and some weapons," continued the Commander in a monotone voice to what was proving to be a tough audience, "and we have the upper hand in terms of stealth with these ground troops. Distress signals were sent to Outpost 56 before the mother ship was destroyed, so I estimate it'll only be about a month before a rescue ship is sent to retrieve us," lied the Commander.

K jumped up from his seat.

"No!" He shouted. "You will not lie to us anymore!" The Commander was completely taken aback. What kind of dissent was this he thought to himself?

"Officers, seize this man," ordered the Commander as the attention of the audience was suddenly captivated. Everyone in the room stayed exactly where they were. They hadn't seen a revolt for a very long time and this looked like it was going to get interesting. "I think it would be nice to hear what this man has to say," said one of the officers who had accompanied the away team. The suggestion was received by nodding heads and a general murmur of approval from the crowd.

"I will have you court-martialled for this," threatened the Commander.

"I suggest you sit down, Commander," said K soothingly. He moved his attention away from the red-faced Commanding officer and turned to the crowd in general, being sure to move his gaze from one man to the next in a reassuring manner. "You're not going to like what I have to say," admitted K. It was not a great start, but things could only get better. "As the

Commander has said, distress signals may well have been broadcast, but unfortunately there will be no rescue mission." The crowd sat in silent disbelief. A number of men looked at each other with extreme anxiety. Was this the way to rally the troops? "The signal was sent before the mother ship was destroyed, but the chances are, they will know that the ship hit the planet's surface and may well assume that all were lost in the impact. Even if they don't think this," continued K soberly, "they will be aware that we were attacked by the Rogue Nation and will be keen to prevent war with such a race." The audience remained reluctantly alert. They all expected a 'but' at the end of K's sentence. "The chances are, our deaths will be reported as a freak occurrence and this solar system will be declared out of Republic bounds." There, that was it. No but. He had told them the truth. Hopefully they would all respect him for it, but regardless - they all needed to know what the situation was.

Silence ruled once more. If they had low morale before, they were near suicidal now. K realised his speech could not end there, otherwise they were all doomed.

"Er…" He began, slightly more nervously, "so it is up to us to find our way off this planet." The crowd was getting restless for solutions not bleak statements of the obvious.

"So what do we do now," asked one man to supportive mumblings from his colleagues.

"We find out why the Rogue Nationals started this…"

"We know why they started this." T stood up, this was the moment for him to spread his knowledge. K was intrigued and remained silent.

"We do?" asked the Commander who decided to start taking part again, in an effort to re-establish control.

"Well, I do," stated T. "I have been reading the historical volumes kept around the walls of the Council Chamber. They document the Vacchion's history for hundreds of thousands of years. I know why the Rogue Nationals are here." He made his way to the front of the room. K stepped to one side. "Towards the end of the Vacchions' existence, they made entries into their record books about an incredible discovery. They refer to this discovery as The Answer, or The Knowledge. There are no details as to what this answer is, but it is my guess that it is what destroyed their entire civilisation. Before this knowledge had completely wiped them out, the Government Council of Vacchion gathered within the chamber upstairs and locked themselves in, in an attempt to protect their officials from the certain death that The Knowledge was spreading across the planet." The crowd listened intently. "Before breaking all communication with the outside world, the Council ordered that an electronic prison should be created in an effort to contain the deadly information and to stop its advancement. From my calculations it took only a matter of weeks for the entire civilisation to be wiped out. The device was seemingly unsuccessful."

"So how does that explain the Rogue Nation being here?" enquired one of the slower members of the audience.

"They must have uncovered these same facts, although I don't know how, as it's obvious that the chamber upstairs containing all this information had not been discovered before our arrival. I'm guessing they are looking for the device that contains The Knowledge."

"Why?" The man still hadn't caught on.

"Because The Knowledge can destroy an entire civilisation in a matter of weeks. It's the ultimate weapon."

"But the Rogue Nation loves war. That's what they live for. Why would they want a weapon that takes the fun out of killing things?"

"Well, I guess this way," K interrupted, "the battles would not destroy the surrounding plant and animal life. The Rogue Nationals seem to be keen on this – you only have to look at their massive tanks which don't damage undergrowth. Maybe they have respect for the environment."

"Or it could simply be that they don't want anyone else to have it," suggested one of the other men. "After all, they're virtually unbeatable at the moment – the last thing they'd want is an enemy with such a powerful weapon." It was a good point and one that many of the men showed their appreciation of by collective mumbling and nodding of heads. Realising that they were skirting the real issue, K brought the conversation back on line.

"Look, we know that the Rogue Nationals are here in force and that they appear to be looking for some sort of a doomsday device. They obviously don't want us here in case we find it, and let's face it, we don't want to be here either. So all we have to do is get away from this planet and everything should settle down without the need for a full-scale universal war."

"And how do you propose we leave this planet?" asked one of the troops. K knew it was a valid question and he expected it; but he also dreaded it being asked, because no-one was going to like his answer.

"I honestly don't know," he replied eventually. The crowd murmured disapprovingly. There were groans of low morale and someone at the back mumbled very loudly that they were all going to die. T took control this time.

"Okay, okay. Things don't look great, but the Commander made a very good point earlier. We have stealth on our side. We are foot soldiers in a massive city. The hiding places for sixty men are near endless. We have the element of surprise. You all heard what K did – he managed to destroy a load of tanks, single handed with no weapons whatsoever." Except a killer rodent, thought K as he looked down at the warm brown sleeping mass snuggled in his half open jacket. "Commander, if it's okay with you," T tried to bring the official authority back into the picture, knowing that he had massively overstepped the mark of hierarchical decorum, "I think we should send a number of men out to gather more wood, food and water. We'll remain here for a day or so, whilst we try to figure a way out of here. Agreed?" It was a fairly pathetic plan, but it would give the large group of men a chance to replenish their energy and operate as a team before a better strategy could be developed.

The Commander was highly frustrated, but recognised that T and K had the ears of his men and were doing a fine job so far. "Yes, agreed. Jiand, Husie, Loang, pick two men each to go with you. Jiand, gather fire wood. Husie, gather berries and nuts – K can tell you which ones are safe to eat, and Loang, get some water. Come to think of it, Loang, you had better take six men with you." Gradually getting back into his leadership role, the Commander added, "And guys," the group of men turned back from the doorway to look back at their commanding officer, "…be careful out there."

Chapter 45

The Love-Scene

Gyshnf ran through the forest. He had managed to get some valuable, much needed sleep. As a result he had replenished his energy levels and was feeling in the mood for love. He bounced through the undergrowth, stopping occasionally to view his surroundings. Life at the humanoid camp was getting very boring. All they seemed to do was eat, talk and sleep, which coming as a criticism from an animal who only eats and sleeps, was a serious insult.

He knew there must be bands of fellow enahs here. They were everywhere. They just hid very well. He gave out a couple of friendly yelps. Nothing. He ran on, investigating the odd building here and there, sniffing the air for signs of civilisation. Another few hundred metres and a few more yelps saw him to his goal.

He stopped suddenly. The air had changed its make up. There was a distinctive taste on the breeze which Gyshnf recognised as being a female enah. Excellent. Maybe his luck was in! He lay on the floor, carefully placing each of his legs out as far as they would stretch. Once in position he remained still, spread-eagled like a small furry bomb that had been dropped from a great height. He lowered his breathing rate so that to an untrained eye, he looked as dead as road kill. This was an excellent display. One of his best. She had to fall for it.

A small female rodent scurried about in a nearby building minding her own business, searching for a warm spot to catch up on her rest. She had been active for half an hour and was aware that she was long overdue a few hours beauty sleep. She sniffed the air. That was interesting – she hadn't smelled him before. Slowly, the shapely rodent moved towards the open doorway of the abandoned building, crouching so as not to be seen. She looked out of the opening to view the grass covered street. There in the middle of the thoroughfare was a dead rodent. At least, that was what she was supposed to think. Why did they bother?

Male enahs had been using this tactic for millions of years, but the female enahs had been wise to it for at least the last hundred thousand. What a fool, to think that she would fall for the same old trick that all rampant male enahs tried. She ignored the still creature.

Gyshnf kept as still as his lungs would allow. Was it working? He had no way of telling as his face was forced into the earth. He should not be tempted to look up, that would break the ingenious illusion. He remained patient.

The female rodent had returned to her scurrying, trying to ignore the ancient voice in her head that asked her if she was sure he wasn't really hurt. But a few moments later it returned. How can you be certain, her subconscious enquired? If he is injured, it's your duty to go and see him. No, she wasn't going to fall for it. Too many of her friends had already been down this route and had been duped into courtship by this very obvious and far too antiquated method of seduction. Scurrying and sleeping needed to be done. If she wasn't going to do it, who would? She allowed herself another glance through the doorway. He did look hurt, he hadn't moved for ages. And he did look quite cute. Maybe she'd go and give him a quick prod. NO! She had promised herself she wouldn't fall for such a ploy. Even if the rodent in question was attractive; and even if he was genuinely hurt; but he really could be…

She ran to the doorway again, slightly less concerned about being seen. Was he okay, she thought to herself? He was cute, that was for sure. Slowly she ventured out of the building onto the street. He didn't look as if he was breathing very much. What did she have to lose? If he was injured, she needed to go and help him. If he wasn't, well she could do worse for a life-long partner. This male seemed to be cuter than the others who had tried this ploy. And he smelt good. Exotic. Strong. Refined, in a rodenty sort of way.

Gyshnf remained completely still and silent. It was working, he could smell her getting closer. He was so excited, but he knew he had to control himself. This could be it. He mustn't blow it like he had done so many times in the past. He mustn't suffer the same lack of self-control by lifting his head up to see if the illusion was taking effect. That had happened before and was the most heart-breaking of moments for a lonely rodent male desperately looking for a partner. To see your ideal mate running off in the distance when they had been within inches of making contact was enough to make a sentimental enah cry himself to sleep (not that that took very much doing). Stay still, stay still, screamed Gyshnf to himself. Be patient!

Don't do it, don't do it, cried the female's modern conscience. But he looks so cute and defenceless argued her more ancient survival instincts. Look at him, he needs help. She was closer now than she had ever been to a male in this type of passionate situation. Just a few more feet now and then she could care for him, if he was hurt. She paused, looking carefully at the flattened body of the handsome young male. His fur was in good condition and his body was fantastic. He smelt divine too. Hayde felt juices start to flow through parts of her body that nobody had ever informed her she had. She was getting excited.

Was she doing the right thing? She stopped her outstretched paw in mid air, poised just above the fur of the poor defenceless hunk of a rodent. Should she stop and run? Was she too young for all this commitment? Did she want pups? So many questions, so many juices, so much dark brown muscular fur...

Be patient, BE PATIENT! Gyshnf was nearly exploding with anticipation. If he looked up now to see what was happening, he would have blown everything. But his natural instinct was to look up. He had to see her, he had to. The need was uncontrollable. Maybe just a quick peek, she probably wouldn't even notice. His heart raced, but his breathing had to stay calm otherwise the game was up. Damn it was difficult! Gyshnf grimaced with the extreme pain of self control, his hidden face contorted into a scrunched up mass of dark skin and fur, eyes tightly shut, mouth pinned closed by desperate effort. If he didn't implode under such tension, he was going to have a heart attack through the strained effort of self control.

She reached out further. Her hand hovered for a moment over Gyshnf's shoulder. Hayde lowered her paw, slowly. Finally she made contact. Her pads tingled violently, as her whole body shuddered with nervous excitement.

I've done it! I've done it! After all these years I've done it! An incredible release of chemicals raced through Gyshnf's body, filling every cell with a concoction of natural drugs that he would never experience again. Right on cue for the age-old courtship process, Gyshnf fainted as the combination of tension release and chemicals proved too much for the small, overly active body.

As had been happening for millions of years, Hayde turned the male rodent over, rolling his limp but perfectly formed frame onto her lap, seeing his face for the first time. He was beautiful. She had done it and she didn't regret it for a second. After all, the rodent really was hurt otherwise he would have got up when she touched him. She had done the right thing. And it felt good too. Just look at him, he was gorgeous!

What followed was a long, drawn out ancient sequence of caring activities that allowed Hayde to slowly revive Gyshnf from his passing out. Eventually Gyshnf awoke, finding himself staring into the eyes of the most beautiful female he had ever seen. Not only had he finally managed to complete the mating courtship, but he'd done it in style. He was proud of himself. Life was just going to get better from here, he could tell.

Chapter 46

The Plan

T and K sat down in one of the building's small offices. The skeleton who had once resided on the wooden chair behind the heavy desk had been thrown out of the window with so many others and then taken to a basement room, to conceal them from view. It wasn't a dignified burial, neither was it the way anyone wanted to treat the dead, but desperate times called for desperate measures and in this situation, the living took priority.

"So what now," opened T.

"I honestly haven't got a clue," answered K. "You got any ideas?"

"Mmmm. No. Not really. We're pretty stuck," admitted T gloomily. "If we make too many movements, we are in serious danger of being wiped out. But if we sit here, we are just going to die of old age or boredom!"

Changing the tack slightly, K wanted to hear more details about T's discoveries. "What about this doomsday device containing this so-called Answer. Do you have any more information?"

"Not really. My guess is it contains the answer to life. Y'know, the billion dollar question – 'why are we here?' – I can't think what other answer would stop people breathing."

"Sh*t." Exclaimed K calmly. "The answer to life... what about the device they created to contain it, do you know what it looks like?"

"No, haven't got a clue I'm afraid. That's where the Rogue Nationals are one step ahead of us I guess. They probably stumbled over some history books in one of the labs where it was created. I can't think how else they would know about its existence." T paused and surmised. "I am assuming the device would be very small though."

"What makes you say that?"

"Well, if I was going to create a device for storing the most dangerous and damning information in the universe, I would

215

want to make it incredibly discreet so that no-one had the chance of finding it…"

"Oh sh*t…" K went pale. Blood rushed out of his head and his entire body went cold and shivery.

"Will you stop saying that!" T looked up into K's face, surprised to see him looking so ill "What's the matter? K, are you OK?"

"I think we had it!" K explained, badly.

"What?"

"We had the devi…" K stopped himself short, and suddenly jammed his right hand into the pocket on his combat trousers. Bits of mud, a few leaves and a small piece of paper were extracted and thrown onto the desk in front of him. He sorted through them, rapidly spreading them out over the hard wooden surface. He forced his hand inside his pocket again and felt more carefully around the seam. Then he found it. He pulled the lining out into full view and there at the bottom of the pocket was a tiny hole. Not big enough for many things to get through, but certainly big enough for the tiny electronic device to fall out.

"I don't believe it," said K, the powerful depression of rapidly draining morale sweeping back over him.

"You had it?" asked T. "Are you sure?"

"Well of course I'm not sure," snapped K. Then he gathered his scattered emotions, and placed them back on the shelves of his conscious mind in their correct order. "No, I'm not sure, but just before Jay-jay and Dyla were attacked by one of the RN tanks they found a tiny electronic device. It was quite out of character with the rest of the surroundings in the middle of the forest. It looked incredibly complicated and highly intricate. I was taking it back to the bone-shaker to log and reference it when the explosions started happening. So I put it in my pocket and forgot about it until just now."

With the predictability usually only associated with mothers patronising the intelligence of their children, T asked a question he had vowed never to ask for as long as he lived: "Where did you see it last?" The words burned his conscience as they left his mouth. He was embarrassed. K noticed this and responded with the contempt the very same question, the universe over, deserved. He remained silent and gave T a knowing look. T looked back with an embarrassed smile that said 'sorry, I couldn't help myself'.

After a few minutes, K started to say something at the same time as T. They both apologised and offered the other to go first. T decided to take the initiative.

"What I was going to say was: I don't know why, but I have a feeling that we need to go to The Chun."

"The what?" asked K.

"The Chun. The massive upturned floating pyramid."

"Oh, it's called The Chun, is it?" commented K, slightly jealous of T's superior knowledge. "I agree. I was on my way there when I inadvertently attacked the battle tanks and ran over the Commander. I feel that I have to go there too, but I don't know why," agreed K. "It will be dangerous, though," he continued, "that's where the battle tanks were heading. It's a bit too obvious a place to be inconspicuous."

"True, but maybe there are more answers there." T was enthusiastic.

"Agreed." K smiled.

Chapter 47

The Base-Camp

"The second planet sweep has been completed, Sire," announced the tinny voice through the ship's intercom.

"And?" enquired the Marth as he landed his craft in a pre-prepared clearing just south of the main Rogue Nation camp.

"Nothing, Sire," replied the nervous voice. The Marth sighed disapprovingly. Over the past twelve years they had monitored the entire planet of Vacchion for tiny electro-magnetic signals. Every one of the three thousand land vehicles had been fitted with a device to scan the local area for tiny digital disturbances that might be produced by the ancient cell imprisoning The Answer. It obviously hadn't worked.

The Marth sat still for a few moments aware of the welcoming party standing to attention outside his lander, awaiting his disembarkation. Is it possible that the Republic had stumbled across the cell the moment they arrived on the planet? Surely not; but no matter how small a possibility it was a chance. They couldn't afford to lose the device. It must be salvaged at all costs. He pressed a button and the side panel of the smooth black vehicle of death opened. The Marth stepped out into the bright sunshine and walked down the small flight of steps to the waiting party.

"Sire, pleasure to have you back on the planet, Sire," lied the senior officer of the ground force.

"Is it?" commented the Marth, but a reply never came. The Marth, accompanied by his newly acquired entourage walked through a dense wall of trees to another clearing in the forest. This one was huge. It housed the largest of the widely dispersed land forces on the planet. Hundreds of vehicles and over a thousand men were posted here. The array of metal machines took up most of the space provided by the clearing, but a few large camouflaged tents had been erected to supply communal services. Makeshift quarters were scattered around the edge of the huge clearing. On all sides, the camp disappeared into the forest as far as the eye could see, before the mixture of tents and trees became too dense to see any further.

"Spread the word immediately to all squadrons. None of the Republic scum are to be killed," ordered the Marth. This was out of character for the Marth; the chief officer considered his response carefully. Was this a trap? Was it a test? Had the Marth been possessed by some supernatural being, forcing him to be kind?

"Sire?" the senior officer decided the safest option was to ask for a repeat of the command.

"You heard me. They are not to be damaged. When we take them, we will do so without bloodshed." The officer was still taken aback by the order, but gave the word for the instructions to be communicated throughout the ground force troops.

The Marth mumbled to himself as his entourage dispersed to communicate the incredible revelation. "If they have the device, I will take it from them myself. Then they will feel my true wrath." That was more like the Marth the Rogue Nationals knew.

Chapter 48

The Rodents

"We have a plan," T announced to the gathered troops, who, now watered and fed, were feeling a little more motivated to stay alive.

"We need to go to The Chun," continued K. The crowd looked at T and K as if they were mad.

"But that's probably the most dangerous place to be for us right now," argued one of the troops to general murmurings of agreement from the crowd.

"No, you seem to have misunderstood," explained T, "only K and I will be going to The Chun, the rest of you will need to create a diversion." Nobody liked the sound of that much either.

"Explain?" prompted the men. But before K and T could elaborate the scene was interrupted by a noise in the corridor. A scratching noise. K told everyone to be quiet. Surely it was not possible for anyone to get into the building without the lookout troops on the roof noticing? Maybe the look-outs had all fallen asleep. He pulled out his hand weapon and walked over to the door. The scratching noise happened again, but this time K realised how close it was. Something sharp was being dragged against the door.

K opened it slowly until he could see through the gap with one eye and the barrel of his hand gun. He looked down. There on the floor was a sight he would never forget. His pet rodent had returned from his wanderings. But he was not alone. He was happily riding on the back of another, smaller rodent with much lighter more delicate fur and markings. The two rodents stumbled in hurriedly as K opened the door wider. A few of the men in the crowd chuckled whilst most looked on slightly bewildered as to why two rodents were getting quite so much attention during such an important meeting.

The lazy rodent jumped off of the other's back and scrambled its way up a table leg to the surface of the desk. K came over from the doorway to greet his little furry friend, smiling sweetly to the creature that had saved his life. But when he tried to pick the small animal up, the rodent backed away and squeaked wildly. The smaller of the two furry animals remained silent, but clambered up the leg of the desk to join its companion. K was confused, the rodent was usually far more friendly than this. Well, maybe not friendly, but certainly a great deal more willing to sleep. This was the most excited K had seen the little brown ball of fur. It looked like he was trying to tell K something.

Chapter 49

The Partnership

After the rampant activities that were obligatory to the process of committing life long partnership to one another, Gyshnf and his new mate Hayde slept together in the corner of the dark building from which she had first spotted her perfect match. Curled and twisted around each other's bodies in a fashion that would take a third party close scrutiny to untangle, they slept soundly with smiles on their faces. The peace of the tranquil summer's day enveloped their dreams and carried them to places deep within their subconscious that were nearly as nice as the passionate activities that took place in their waking moments, hours before.

Slowly, the newly-mates awoke, staring into each other's eyes with heart-felt glee. It was incredible. Only hours ago they were two single rodents, but now they were a team. Mates for life. A match made in heaven. Gyshnf hoped that this feeling of admiration he had for Hayde would never wear off. He also assumed the slightly less healthy emotion of total gratitude for a female enah finally making him feel this way would disappear soon.

Noises outside grabbed both their attentions. Their small round ears pricked up, twisting and turning in the air to pin-point the source. It seemed to be getting closer. A number of rumblings shook the floor gently, accompanied by the clomping of thousands of feet. Voices could also be heard in the distance. They were humanoid voices, but not those of Gyshnf's pet's crowd. A sudden realisation occurred to him – he had left his pet alone for hours. The poor thing might have got lost or need help. He must hurry back to him immediately.

Gyshnf explained to Hayde, in a series of squeaks and twitches only enahs can understand that he had to return to his pet's base camp. Hayde asked to come with him, but he declined telling her it would be safer for her to stay here. Being a modern female rodent, Hayde gave Gyshnf a look which said all it needed to say. Gyshnf interpreted the look very well for a rodent inexperienced in the art of 'togetherness'. His instincts informed him the look should be deciphered as: 'I am now your mate, I am coming with you and there is nothing you can do about it'. Which was near enough.

They ran out of the building together, taking a brief glance left towards the noise before heading down the fern-filled street in the opposite direction. A kilometre behind them, travelling in a slow but deliberate manner was a long procession of black vehicles, lined on both sides by humanoids carrying heavy complicated looking pieces of metal.

Gyshnf knew he had to hurry. These large black machines had tried to kill his pet before. He had to get back to the creature's camp and take his pet friend to safety. Hayde and Gyshnf ran as fast as they could down the long narrow street. Hayde streaked ahead of Gyshnf. Years of running away from wicked young rodent males who had pretended to be hurt, was finally paying off. They covered the ground with incredible speed, quite unexpected of creatures whose life was spent eating and sleeping. Soon they had left the approaching forces far behind, barely visible in the distance.

They ran for what seemed like hours, until Gyshnf felt he could run no more. He stopped and slumped on the floor. Hayde ran back towards him and tried to convince him to get up, but Gyshnf was too exhausted. Hayde bent down and carefully lifted her new mate onto her back. Gyshnf couldn't believe his luck. Not only was she beautiful clever and caring, but she was quick-witted and strong too. Together, the duo trotted down the street, on one set of legs.

Chapter 50

The Message

Gyshnf never realised it would be so difficult to communicate with humanoids. How stupid were they? He tried everything he could think of to explain that the enemy were on their way and that they would pass near this location soon, but nothing was getting through.

What else could he do? He had squeaked as loud as he could and as slowly as he could, but these stupid bipeds still weren't getting it. Hayde had an idea. She whispered squeakily in his ear and they agreed it was their best chance. Now all they had to do was find an item that the humanoids were keen to keep... Ah. That was it. One of the men seemed to be holding a colourful book in his hands. That would have to do.

Without warning, both rodents leapt into the air and grabbed the historical volume from the human's grasp. The tall creature made verbal and physical gestures of complaint, but it was too late. They turned and ran through the open doorway, just before it was slammed shut, only to be opened again rapidly behind them as a number of furless bipeds gave chase.

They dashed down the staircase, across the large open room and through the main doors of the building into the huge street below. They were pursued at all stages by a number of humanoids who bellowed strange commands at them.

Hayde and Gyshnf ran across the wide street, through the circle of trees that lined the raised stone circles in the centre of its main square and down one of the smaller joining alleyways. They zigzagged their way through the small streets and connecting alleys being sure not to outrun their pursuers. Within a few breathless minutes they had reached the neighbouring main thoroughfare, which also pointed directly at the base of The Chun (as all main streets did throughout the city). Once there, they slowed to a jog and positioned themselves in the centre of the impressive avenue, next to the raised stone metre-wide canal that carried fresh water along the length of the road.

They turned to face their small group of pursuers before sitting down, slightly out of breath but satisfied their job had been completed successfully.

T, desperate to get his historical bible back, was the first of the men to reach the neighbouring high-street where the strange rodents had suddenly decided to stop and rest. T slowed as he approached them, he didn't want to scare them off or make them think that they would be punished for the prank. As he got closer he made goo-goo-like baby noises and blew strange kisses at the creatures, as is the manner of humanoids throughout the universe with all animals of a furry nature.

T reached out and carefully picked the book up from the grassy floor where Hayde had dropped it, to a round of applause from his inner conscience. He turned to his colleagues in the hope of receiving genuine applause, but they appeared to be looking straight through him, into the distance. T looked into his colleagues' eyes and then at the two rodents. All seven creatures stared past him in the opposite direction to the massive Chun which dominated the sky line behind them.

"It's alright, I've got the book," he prompted, "we can go back now." However, the small audience continued to look into the distance, open mouthed and frozen to the spot, like deer staring into the headlights of a juggernaut. One of the men finally managed to speak.

"Sh*t," he stated solemnly. T was confused, but finally allowed his curiosity to get the better of him and looked round to see what could be more impressive than the giant Chun that framed his view of the dumbfounded creatures.

Far off in the middle-distance, half way towards the horizon where the street seemed to simply fade away into the surrounding forest, was the makings of a truly awesome sight. A mass of black shadows crept its way along the thoroughfare towards The Chun and the speechless onlookers. Mammoth tanks, smaller land vehicles and hundreds of foot soldiers appeared to be heading straight towards T and his colleagues. After a few seconds of shocked delay, T turned to address the group.

"Well, it's now or ne…" but no-one was there to hear his comment. The two rodents had scurried off in the opposite direction to the base camp and the group of men were already half way down the nearest alley.

"…ver." Upon finishing his sentence T started his manic run back to their base. This was it. This was their chance to create the diversion necessary to get him and K to The Chun. But he admitted to himself that the prospect of heading towards The Chun was probably a great deal more appealing than facing the hundreds of barbarian warriors and their incredible arsenal.

Chapter 51

The Cowboys

The Marth followed a high-altitude trajectory across the city. Far below him, through the cockpit screen in front of his laid back piloting position, he viewed the procession of death. The long line of tanks, troop carriers and assorted armoured vehicles travelled from the main RN base-camp to the centre of the city, accompanied on each side by the foot soldiers of his barbarian ground force. For half a kilometre they turned the otherwise green and white street into a long sinister shadow of menacing blackness.

The Marth followed the line of the street, which led him directly towards The Chun, all the time monitoring the information displayed on the viewing screen. Within a few short moments cockpit alarms sounded, just as the Marth had expected. The alarms informed him that life had been detected.

He commanded the onboard computer to zoom in on the relevant area of the city. The screen displayed frantic activity in and around a number of buildings just off the main route his ground forces were taking. Estimated time of engagement between the main RN troops and the enemy resistance was just over one hundred minutes. The Marth smiled to himself and made a mental note to come back and view the activities of this little battle once it was in full swing – if he had time. He had a great deal to do before then, checking each of the fourteen battalions spread over hundreds of square miles across the massive ancient city as they all travelled toward The Chun. He would be especially interested to see how his own barbarian troops would fair under their new instructions not to kill anyone. It would be a tough transition for them, but should be an interesting learning curve for all.

The Marth steered his ship northwards, perpendicular to the road he had been following. All the time he viewed the screen in front of him which monitored the ground far below. Another alarm sounded, indicating more life had been found. The Marth once more ordered the computer to zoom in. A familiar sight appeared on the screen. Another dark line of Rogue Nationals and their vehicles of mass destruction shadowed a long straight street in their journey towards The Chun.

This process continued. The Marth gradually followed a circular route around the entire city, frequently stopping to view another huge task force of his ground troops on their journey towards the monolithic inverted pyramid. Any enemy in their path would be flushed out and forced to retreat to the centre of the city. They would force the Republic troops into the crater and then, once surrounded by a truly formidable show of force, the enemy would reveal to the Marth where the small electronic device was. If the Republic had the device he would spare their pain and suffering by simply having them killed, provided they handed it over. If however, they had not found it, the Marth's frustration may well get the better of him and they would likely suffer a great deal more before meeting their ends. They'd better hope they had the device thought the awesome white figure.

After monitoring the slow but determined progress of a few of his many convoys towards The Chun, the Marth turned his mind to the imminent battle. His troops would force the pathetically small and weak troop of Republic 'soldiers' (the Marth felt embarrassed to use the term soldiers when thinking about the frail minds and bodies of the enemy), towards the city's central crater to meet with the rest of his welcoming committee. He smiled to himself. But within seconds the smile was wiped from his pure white twisted face as the cockpit alarm sounded unexpectedly, indicating it had found another body of intelligent life. The Marth ran some quick calculations through his mind. None of his troop convoys should be in this vicinity and the enemy had been spotted on the path of squadron one. Could there be more Republic survivors? Or could the enemy have split into two groups? The Marth had not thought it was possible, but obviously needed to check out the information anyway.

He turned his lander towards the area from which the signal had originated. The Marth lowered his craft towards the surface of the planet in an attempt to get a stronger scan through the density of the buildings, trees and foliage. The signal was much weaker than previous scans that had detected the Republic troops and the RN battalions. The Marth slowed his lander to a gentle hover above an area of the city that simply looked like a huge forest of trees. No buildings were visible here, but the Marth knew they were all around him, in every direction. Through a freak of city design this particular area of the Vacchion citadel did not have a main street running directly to the base of The Chun and therefore had managed to escape a great deal of the damage caused by the huge blast of the exploding mother ship.

As he approached the ground readings of intelligent life were repeated and confirmed by the computer and the numbers it gave were in tens of thousands. The Marth was not the type of creature to be nervous – he had never had cause to be. If there was ever anything to be concerned about, the Marth had found that the best therapy for dealing with such an issue was to eliminate it – as painfully as possible. He was a cautious being and found that completely destroying the root cause of any problem was the best way to avoid the need for emotions such as anxiety or nerves. In the past, to be absolutely certain that the cause for concern had been eliminated, the Marth often indulged in a little extra curricular activity to remove everything bordering the issue too. This way he found no sleepless nights would ever arise. It had worked too.

The information arriving through his computer was a little worrying. The Marth lowered his vehicle to within twenty metres of the ground. He could see under the canopy of the tallest trees here and what was revealed to him made him laugh out loud. "Intelligent creatures!" shouted the Marth to himself, whilst guffawing. "Intelligent creatures. Ha! Computer, remind me to get you fixed when we get back to the mother ship." The computer considered informing the Marth that there was nothing wrong with its a.i. diagnostic systems and that the information was correct. But didn't – because it was operating perfectly and knew the dangers of pointing out the Marth's shortcomings.

The Marth continued to laugh loudly as he manoeuvred his ship away from the sight beneath the trees. He had wasted a lot of time coming to see this.

The river of brown fur beneath his ship continued its rapid flow through the labyrinth of small streets and alleyways.

Chapter 52

The Preparations

"What do you mean they ran away?" asked K.

"Just that," replied T matter-of-factly, "As we left to come back to base camp they ran off into the distance, heading in the opposite direction." As an afterthought he added, "I don't think they're coming back."

"What would you know," snapped K childishly, showing the pain that he felt from his friend's desertion. He meets a girl and then drops me like a bag of sick, thought K to himself. It wasn't the first time this had happened in the universe and it certainly wouldn't be the last, but it was fairly rare for the situation to occur between a humanoid and a large rodent.

Huge amounts of activity had ignited throughout the base camp. Men ran purposefully in various directions as equipment was taken to buildings lining the street upon which the ambush would take place. Everyone knew it was technically called an ambush, but the word ambush implied the upper hand and the men were aware that they certainly didn't have this. They conceded to refer to the attack as a 'diversion'.

The Commander, K and T together with a handful of the more senior officers discussed what strategies and tactics to adopt over the coming hours. Frantic conversations took place hurriedly and tempers frayed under the strain of what was likely to be a suicide mission for many of the Republic troops. But an overall strategy was decided upon and all agreed that their best chance of any kind of success was to be united in their operations.

Of the three landers that had made it to the roof of the government building, two would be used during the attack and one would be supplied to K and T to get to The Chun. The landing pod that had fallen through the roof of the government building was still fully operational, despite having crippled landing gear and a slightly crushed nose. No-one knew what T and K were going to find in the centre of the City beneath the colossal Chun, but it was obvious to everyone that speed was of the essence. If all went wrong, the diversion might only last a few minutes. Either way, K and T estimated that they should not remain at The Chun for very long. They estimated ten minutes was their maximum stay.

Pilots had already flown the three landers down from the roof and a long chain of troops were busily filling the holding bays full of rocks, branches and trunks. Anything heavy and likely to cause damage was placed within every nook and cranny of the three ships. Even some heavy furniture made it into the makeshift arsenal.

A stock-take of the weapons available to the troops was taken. Most men would have a hand gun each and some would be issued with small amounts of explosives, but that was it. Not much when you are faced with an army of barbarians carrying heavy artillery. Things looked bleak.

In the neighbouring street a few hundred metres away, frantic activities took place to prepare the site for the ambush. No, the diversion. Survival equipment, standard issue in all landing pods, was being put to maximum usage to take lives, rather than save them. Heavy ropes were laid across the width of the road and tied to the base of strong trees on either side. When the ropes ran out, thick vines were hacked from neighbouring buildings to be used in a similar fashion. Trees were busy having their bases hacked to pieces by large survival axes and small ropes were being used to haul hefty logs onto roof tops along the length of the battle zone. Meanwhile, the enemy army continued its relentless approach at walking pace.

Soon, too soon in fact, the manic rushing around had to cease. All personnel were informed that no more crossing of the road could take place. Preparations must now take place within or behind the buildings that lined the main street. The men had achieved an incredible amount in a short space of time, but was it going to be enough?

The Commander called T and K over. They placed the last few heavy objects into the three landers and ran over to their Commander. "Sir," they shouted simultaneously.

"You guys had better get going. There is no more you can do for us here," stated the Commander. "I don't know what you hope to find there, but whatever it is, I hope it's worth it."

"So do we, Sir," agreed K.

"Does everyone know the plan, Sir?" asked T.

"If they don't know it now, they never will," said the Commander solemnly. "Good luck."

"You too, Sir, you too." K and T ran to their lander.

Chapter 53

The Enahs

Gyshnf looked at his mate. Hayde looked back at him lovingly, with the respect that only one lover can give another. Their gaze was deep. They didn't just look at each other's eyes, they stared deep within their partner's subconscious, seeing the things that would only ever be realised with true love. Passion, care, understanding. They shared this private moment, despite the thousands of enahs that gathered around them.

After a few seconds the intimate stare was broken by Gyshnf as he made a gesture with his head that began their long journey. Hayde knew they had to go. The pair of lovers started with a walk but soon broke into a trot and then a fast run. It was a long way and they had a great deal of ground to cover in a very short space of time. Behind them their families and friends followed, keeping pace with the two lovers, but at a respectable distance.

From the air, the mass movement of enahs gave the effect of a vast arrow shaped carpet of brown fur gradually moving across the surface of the planet. The advancing mass wound itself through back streets and alleyways, sometimes breaking into two streams of fur running either side of a large obstacle briefly before crashing back together to resume the full strength of the thick dark river.

It was a truly awesome sight, but fortunately for the enahs nobody was there to appreciate it. A small dark flying machine had viewed them briefly as they gathered amongst the trees, but that was before they were at full strength. The machine had left as quickly as it had arrived.

The giant furry snake slithered its way slowly through the city. Small clumps of fur occasionally broke off from the main column, disappearing briefly into buildings buried deep within thick vegetation only to reappear moments later as larger masses of brown fur, sometimes in multiple shades. As this occurred time and again the long mass of mammals became a multishaded, stripy brown river that cascaded through several streets, gaining in mass and momentum with every turn.

Chapter 54

The Ambush Diversion

They had been making their preparations for over an hour, but now the enemy troops were upon them. The long slow procession of tanks and land vehicles of various sizes and destructive capabilities were partially inside the designated battle zone. Along each side of the vehicles, confident unsuspecting barbarian warriors strolled nonchalantly, enjoying the summer's day. Most had their huge laser cannons strapped across their backs, but a few of the troops towards the front of the procession had been ordered to stay on guard. Their heavy black weapons held firmly in their arms.

Just another hundred metres before they were in place. As soon as the first tank was disabled the battle would begin in earnest. The Republic troops stayed as still and as quiet in their hiding places as their racing hearts would allow. The barbarian procession of awesome fire power was out of sight to all but one of the Republic troops – a conscious decision made by the Commander in the hope that the men would not be too daunted by the sight of the massive army. It might have helped a little, but each man's imagination proved to be just as frightening as they listened to the ever increasing ground shaking rumble created by thousands of feet gently making contact with the hard surface of the street floor. The noise and movement fuelled each man's mental image of the street scene. The lone observing officer watched nervously as the Rogue Nation's long line of formidable force approached. He lay on the roof of a small building, behind a large tree trunk with one arm raised above his head, ready to give the signal to two men ten metres below him in the alleyway. Loosely they held the thick heavy rope that now ran across the width of the street. Where the rope met the men, large branches had been tied along its remaining length, which now lay in front of them at their feet.

The Republic troops shook nervously, never having experienced anything so daunting as taking on a formidable opponent such as this. The men were dotted strategically on roofs, in alleyways and inside the buildings bordering the battle zone. They all knew the signal. They all dreaded it. But if they were to have any chance at all, none of them could afford to hesitate. Everyone of them had a job to do on which all of them relied. Yet every man secretly wished the procession could be allowed to continue to travel right past them, never stopping. But none of them would fail in their duties. Too much depended on it – least of all their own lives.

The officer's hand, still poised, shook violently as he struggled to keep his bodily functions under control. He held his breath. The leading tank was nearly over the thick heavy rope. Just a few more metres. A little more. A little more, one more step… Here we go he thought as he dropped his hands with the force and determination of a guillotine. The rope men below, pausing only for a millisecond as brief doubts about this inevitable massacre ran through their minds, hauled on the heavy vine in unison. The rope, which had been tied to a massive tree on the other side of the road, was raised into the midst of the tank's thousands of walking mechanical legs. As soon as it was firmly entangled in the unusual undercarriage the men let go and ran back down the alleyway in which they were hiding. The tank continued forward without pausing, dragging the long heavy vine and its accompanying logs along the ground.

Three barbarian foot soldiers witnessed the event and chased the enemy assailants down the thin alley, only to be faced with a fast-approaching bouncing bundle of logs accelerating towards them along the ground. All three barbarians were smashed to the floor as their legs were struck heavily by the branches, accompanied by loud bone-shattering cracks and blood-curdling screams of agony. Above them, two Republic soldiers took aim and fired upon them with boulders. After only a few seconds, two of the barbarians had been struck heavily in the head and were killed instantly whilst one was knocked unconscious. Meanwhile, four more barbarians had appeared at the end of the alleyway, unsure what to expect and were welcomed with the full weight of the high speed logs that had already levelled their colleagues. The muscle-bound men were flattened like twigs, each with fractured limbs. The Republic troops that had started the battle re-entered the thin alleyway with haste and retrieved the large laser rifles that had been separated from their owners. One of the newly armed troops remained in the alley whilst the others went on to their next designated task.

Having seen the activities at the alleyway entrance ahead, a group of Rogue Nation barbarians gathered further down the street at a small side road, hoping to discover what was going on without being taken out by any high-speed logs. Once confirmed as empty, a number of warriors ventured in with the intention of capturing the Republic troops by circling round the building and approaching the enemy from behind. Before they were half way along, a large tree trunk suspended horizontally from two vines connected to the parallel roofs was released and swung like a one-tonne pendulum through the alleyway, launching the group of warriors into the air with a rapid succession of bone crushing cracks and crunches. A couple of the bodies cleared the second tank as it slowly passed the mouth of the side road and impacted heavily on a wall on the opposite side of the street.

A number of Republic troops quickly picked up as many of the discarded laser cannons as possible. More warriors ventured towards the end of the small thoroughfare. This time they were more cautious. They didn't want to learn how to fly as their colleagues had, and so they merely popped their heads around the corner of the building. Their last view of the world was that of two small men holding laser cannons pointing directly at them. The cannons fired and tore the heads off the unsuspecting victims before impacting the side of a passing tank.

A spray of fire and mechanical legs exploded from the second tank as it careered, at slow but unrelenting speed, into the back of the procession's lead tank, whose motion was now completely halted by the rope and branches which had become entangled deep within the mess of broken metal legs beneath it.

The Republic soldiers, with what seemed to be well-practiced ease, adopted their respective roles, one covering the side road with random occasional fire to ensure no more barbarians attempted to approach them, whilst the other loaded a waiting makeshift basket attached to a rope, with the heavy black weapons that had been gathered from the floor. As soon as it was full he shouted up to his colleagues on the roof top who proceeded to hoist the large basket to where a number of men awaited the indispensable arms.

The loud crash of the two leading land tanks signalled to the remaining Republic forces that the battle was underway. It also informed the barbarians all the way along the length of the slow procession that all was not well. The hundreds of remaining foot soldiers lining either side of the street stumbled desperately to retrieve their laser cannons from their backs, whilst moving closer to the protective walls and alleyways of the buildings on both sides of the main carriageway.

On rooftops along the length of the battle zone, Republic troops struggled to man-handle heavy logs over the edges of the flat-topped buildings. Weighty wooden bombs impacted warrior foot soldiers who had taken cover by the safety of the solid walls of the building. Many were killed instantly, but some were merely maimed. Republic troops then ducked out of their various hiding positions and discreetly retrieved the laser cannons dropped by the most recent victims. Each took one weapon for themselves and loaded the remainder into makeshift baskets to be hauled to the roofs for the other troops.

The pilot Collar in the third massive land tank could see on the view screen in front of him the carnage caused by the slow motion collision of his colleagues' vehicles. He brought his tank to a halt, completely oblivious to the foot soldiers' predicament around him. That was until he saw a number of them take flight over the tank in front of him. Realising the procession was under attack, he smiled as he prepared to open fire on anything and everything around him with gleeful anticipation of the wanton destruction he could cause. Disappointingly he recalled the strict instructions they had received from their battalion commander not to kill any Republic personnel. An order from the Marth himself. He was helpless and so decided simply to keep a watchful eye on the foot-warriors' progress. So far they did not seem to be faring well against the Republic rebellion. He smiled and relaxed in his cramped surroundings to watch the action.

Behind him a traffic jam of land tanks and other vehicles was gradually forming as each reduced the gap to the vehicle in front before coming to a complete halt.

Two Republic troops ran out of the alleyway on the other side of the street to where the main action was taking place. They sprinted to the first land tank, disabled by the thick rope and leg-tangling logs that had incapacitated the vehicle. The tank Collar inside, still confused about what had happened, was unaware of the incidents befalling the pedestrian warriors on either side of his mammoth tank. Suddenly the door to his cockpit was opened and the last thing he saw before meeting his maker was the barrel of a small Republic hand gun. The troops pulled the heavy body from the pilot seat and dragged it onto the wide side gangway. One of the men quickly jumped into the cockpit and settled into the pilot seat.

"Think you can work it out?" asked the man from the doorway, as more flying barbarians were launched overhead by another swinging tree trunk.

"No problem," answered the new tank Collar with slight apprehension. "Now get out of here!" The second man needed no further encouragement, slammed the cockpit door shut and climbed down from the massive machine to rejoin his colleagues on the north side of the action packed street. Before he had reached the ground he could hear the massive gun turret atop the tank starting to rotate.

The helpless Collar in the second tank looked on. He hoped that what he was seeing was a hideous figment of his over-active imagination. But alas for him, it was not. He watched his monitor as the tank that he had run into the back of turned its lethal gun turret to face him. Its twin cannons almost touched his own. Slowly and seemingly with some hesitation, one of the barrels slowly adjusted its trajectory downwards and towards the centre of his screen. Then existence ceased.

"Wahoo!" screamed the Republic troop and newly self-appointed Collar, as his debilitated tank took the full force of the explosive shockwave as his cannons destroyed the upper half of the adjoining tank. He was still in one piece, if a little shaken by the effects of the massive fire power. As the smoke cleared from the screen in front of him he could see the third tank in the procession. The second tank's entire turret section, containing the cockpit, two massive laser cannons and a large amount of machinery had been completely vaporised. He now had an unrestricted view of two Republic troops climbing the third land tank, aiming to repeat the hi-jack operation. They succeeded again. After pulling another dead Rogue National from the cockpit a second land tank had been commandeered successfully, this time a fully manoeuvrable one.

The pandemonium at the front of the long procession continued. Confused and startled warriors looked frantically for a senior officer to tell them what to do. Whilst desperately searching for a safe hiding place that wouldn't see them demoted to worm fodder or victims of the laser rifle fire that seemed to be coming from roofs all around them. Many died in the confusion. To make matters even worse a couple of their own land tanks were about to start firing at them.

Whilst confusion reigned at the front of the convoy, half a kilometre down the street at the back of the long line of warriors all was still relatively quiet. They had seen some commotion take place, far off in the distance and had heard a number of explosions, but the foot soldiers continued their pace as they stretched on tip-toes to see what was happening over the heads of the men in front of them.

Soon enough they found themselves in the centre of the battle. Three explosions took place in rapid succession, two in the open street, killing a number of unsuspecting foot warriors instantly and knocking many more off their feet with debilitating injuries. One of the explosions had been detonated at precisely the correct moment, igniting the underside of a wheeled provisions carrying vehicle at the very back of the procession. Smoke and fire billowed out of the machine, as surrounding foot soldiers were thrown against walls by the blast. A hail of small-fire sniper shots rang out of the buildings around them, taking out more of the bewildered barbarians. Many could not move due to their injuries and others were considerably dazed. Their weapons were either inconveniently strapped to their backs, impossible to get to when lying on the floor in abject agony, or had been ripped from their hands in the blasts. A small group of Republic troops ran into the scene of devastation under small-fire cover, picking up as many of the Rogue Nationals' weapons as they could carry and then fleeing back to the protection of the surrounding buildings that lined the war zone. As soon as the laser cannons were passed to the waiting troops on the roof tops, heavy weapon fire started to take out tens of confused foot soldiers that sought cover by the vehicles and buildings. Battles now took place at both ends of the long procession.

The infantry stuck between these two scenes of violence were confused. Many men in front of them had been swept off their feet by pendulous logs, men behind them by explosions. What was in store for them and in which direction should they run? They looked to all sides and to the roofs above them, taking cover by the now stationary machines. None of them predicted the shower of objects that rained from the sky unannounced. They were hit from above by a rapid succession of logs, branches, rocks and filing cabinets. Barbarian warriors were felled unceremoniously by large heavy objects, some of which could only be described as toilet receptacles. Two rows of the strangest arsenal of bombs fell thickly from what seemed to be a perfectly normal, empty summer's sky. The landers above them remained in stealth mode as they took a second sweep of the road, dumping the remainder of their loads on the defenceless enemy pedestrians. Some quick witted warriors dove into the shelter of the neighbouring buildings, only to be shot dead by a pathetically underpowered handgun, or smashed over the head with a surprisingly over-powered boulder. In each case, the bodies where quickly ransacked by their assailants and their hand-held laser cannons and other weapons were put to good use against the Rogue Nation's barbarian force.

Total confusion reigned in the RN procession. They had been given the order by the Marth not to open fire on the Republic troops. It was totally against their nature. Without the prime objective of killing, the secondary objective of torturing and the tertiary objective of maiming for added value entertainment, seemed almost impossible. The barbarians were at a loss as to how to get the better of the attacking force, which seemed to be hundreds strong. Defence was not a Rogue National strong point. How do you go about threatening a man without being allowed to kill him? How are you supposed to strike the fear of death into someone without using death itself? Rogue Nationals ran in all directions. If only they were allowed to kill they would have a fighting chance.

Many scenes of violence and bloodshed occurred over the next thirty minutes. Rogue Nationals ran into each other in their attempts to get out of the way of the incoming cannon fire. Some ran down the side alleyways in desperation, only to be greeted by a variety of different ways of meeting their ends. Some barbarian warriors were taken down by showers of rocks, others by large sections of tree and more still by the awesome power of their own weapons, successfully commandeered by the enemy. Some men got away, but not many.

It was a bloodbath, but not the kind either side expected. The ambush was proving highly successful.

Chapter 55

The Force

T flew the invisible lander expertly through the streets of The Chun's surrounding citadel. They flew at an extremely low level, whilst K clenched his buttocks shrieking "we're going to die – pull up!" The tallest ferns below were having their top leaves trimmed by an invisible, but very real object flying past at incredible speed.

When K wasn't screaming for his life, the two of them sat anxiously contemplating the possible deaths of so many of their colleagues that could be taking place at this very moment.

"They did it for us, y'know," stated K. But his partner shook his head thoughtfully.

"No K, they did it for you."

Somehow it didn't seem right to argue. T's comment was delivered with calm but total conviction. Somewhere deep inside K knew he had changed. He was thinking differently. More clearly somehow. But why? He was the same man; other than one thing – he had been put in mortal danger. Maybe that's all he ever needed: a massive incentive to improve himself. A huge test to kick-start him into exceeding his own below-average expectations. He had never been a leader and had never really wanted to be. Even now it wasn't his key aim, but it was great to be heard for a change and it was nice having people do the things you suggested. Except lay down their lives – that was too much to ask, so it was fitting that K hadn't had to. The diversion was agreed by all the troops as their best chance of survival – as a group, if not as individuals.

There was a huge morbid responsibility with knowing people were sacrificing their own lives so that you could investigate a whim. It was horribly humbling. There was no air of superiority, no feeling of power or authority. Knowing that people might be dying for him right now put K in a mood he hoped never to experience again. It was a feeling of immense emotional weight. If he failed, he might as well have killed those men himself. It would be his fault that they had died. If he succeeded, however, then the weight would be removed from is guilty conscience and repositioned on the dead men's shoulders as hero's who saved the day. They would have sacrificed their own lives for the greater good of the team. And that was a far better thing to die for than a bumbling fool who was probably going to screw everything up anyway. Deep inside himself, K knew he couldn't afford to think like that, especially with so much at stake. He told himself that everything was going to be fine and that he would be successful in his mission. Whatever it was.

T continued to fly the lander pod a few feet from the ground with incredible speed and precision. On both sides the long straight road was lined by the white fronted stone buildings, still covered in trees and vegetation on walls that ran perpendicular to the main street. The overall effect at this speed was one of a blurred solid wall of grey sandwiching the lander's path as if they were travelling down a massive metal trench. As the two men watched the end of the street approach and the distant Chun, their ultimate destination, gradually take up more of their forward view, the grey walls flashing past on either side of them was reminiscent of something, but they couldn't think what. Maybe they had seen this kind of low-level flight through a grey square-cut channel somewhere before... A small fast moving spaceship travelling along a constructed valley towards its ultimate bid for victory. They knew they should remember this somehow. It inspired both men to feel as if they should be listening to an inner voice telling them to feel something... something encouraging... without knowing they were feeling the same sense of déjà vous, both men independently discarded the strange thoughts.

The end of the street was approaching fast. The wall of grey came to a sudden end as it morphed into a dark charcoal-grey for a split second before turning jet black. Then the walls and floor vanished beneath them, replaced by a huge black cavity spreading out in every direction. The lander raced over the edge of the giant crater that surrounded the base of The Chun. The devastation was incredible. Black ash covered the unrecognisable twisted remains of a former inter-stellar exploratory vessel which lay strewn across the crater's base, half embedded into the ground below. The crater stretched for well over a thousand metres in every direction from the base of The Chun, the lowest point of which now hung over three hundred metres above the floor of the crater.

T manoeuvred his craft expertly to continue hugging the ground. The flying machine followed the huge contour of the crater, plummeting down suddenly at its black edge and then gradually levelling out as the centre of the crater came closer. T skilfully dodged the many huge sections of twisted smouldering fuselage, throwing the pod from side to side with confidence. The scene invoked more sad feelings in T and K. Not only did they have the pressure of their remaining colleagues putting their lives on the line for an unknown cause, they also had this horrifically distorted, sick reminder of the thousands of men who had been killed already. Not to mention the fact that they were well and truly marooned on this planet.

But sadness never lasts for long. Not when The Chun is so close. The amazing monolithic structure loomed above them. It wouldn't be long before they would be directly beneath its sharp base, as its unfathomable weight hung in mid air above them. It was breathtaking. K wondered how a nation overshadowed by such an awesome sight could ever get any work done. It must have been virtually impossible to concentrate with this incredible statue in your back yard. Maybe this colossal object, contravening all logic by floating in mid air was the reason the Vacchions were so peaceful and slow in advancing. Maybe their world revolved around The Chun in such a way that allowed them to remain more conscious of the impact they had on their environment. Like a wise old grandfather who never died, maybe The Chun provided them with the ancient stability and learned direction they needed. To know it was always there, floating just above the ground without fail, must have been very reassuring. And to know it had always been there, potentially for millions of years and that it would be there for millions more must have been a very humbling thought. It would have made any personal problems seem somewhat less significant. Simply by looking up, you would quickly realise just how insignificant you were in the grand scheme of things. The universe would carry on, The Chun would be unaffected. Life would continue with or without you.

T stopped the lander just short of a large piece of debris from their former mother ship. The twisted metal had been heated to such an incredible temperature that it had partially melted and reformed itself into a more organic looking object. Rounded edges to the metal had been formed, giving it an appearance of solid liquid. The entire structure was warm and jet black. A sculptor would have spent a life time searching for this incredible look. T stopped the lander and went to leave his seat.

"Where are you going?" asked K.

"I thought we should check out the ship," replied T nodding to the carcass of the vessel all around them. "There might be something we can salvage."

"What, from that?" K looked at the molten mess. "The only things that could have survived that are carbon molecules, and they're not a lot of good to us."

"Yeah, I guess you're right, but I just feel it's our duty to take a look."

"Maybe, but later. Yes?"

"I guess so," replied T, slightly frustrated, but knowing K was right. They really didn't have the time to look at wreckage. They had to find some answers.

Chapter 56

The Surrender

The last Rogue National was taken from the remaining tank. Just like the others he looked scared and confused, despite his two and a half metre height and his rippling muscles, he resembled a frightened child that could burst into tears at any moment. It was probably as much the fear of the Marth as it was the fact that they had lost a battle – the first time in thousands of generations of murderous victories. But then again they had never before been told to spare the lives of their enemy. This had sent their small bullying brains into melt-down and subsequently they didn't have a clue what to do.

The Commander looked at the carnage all around them as the last Rogue National stepped down from his tank and joined the other fifty prisoners. Incredible thought some of the Republic troops, we defeated a Rogue National squadron in close quarter battle, whilst being out numbered by nearly twenty to one. Life is good and our luck is incredible. Some of the troops nearly fainted when they started to consider the true significance of their victory. They had achieved a history-making event. They had done something that no other race in the known history of the Rogue Nation had done. Not only that, but they had done it in the face of adversity so extreme that the chance of them succeeding would have come in at a billion to one at any intergalactic bookies.

Some of the Republic troops stood guard around the huddled group of fifty remaining barbarian warriors pointing the confiscated laser cannon rifles at them threateningly. A general murmur of gloom radiated from the over-sized lost children. Many of the prisoners sniffled and grizzled as they stood expecting to be killed. They had been defeated. Their entire lives were over. They had let down their fathers and their fathers' fathers. There was great shame in their downfall. Many cried because they were once proud warriors carrying the barbarian name of the Rogue Nation into new solar systems before raping and pillaging everything in sight. Their reputation preceded them. They were feared and revered throughout the universe. It was a privileged position and one which had been fought for and nurtured over thousands of years. But in a single battle, against a band of sixty weak humanoids with pea shooters and pebbles, this squadron of warriors had managed to undo all that. This story would spread the length, breadth and depth of the universe. The Rogue Nationals would be a laughing stock. Centuries of bullying, murdering and maiming had been undone in a few short moments of confusion.

The Commander ordered the prisoners to be placed in a holding room within the huge government building that the Republic now called camp. Grudgingly the warriors shuffled slowly towards the building, heads bowed down in total shame.

"This makes things a great deal more interesting," stated the Commander to no-one in particular. A few of the men closest to him smiled. The Commander smiled back. This was the greatest moment of his life. He had genuinely led the men to a resounding victory, without a single loss of life. He had their trust and their respect once again. Actually, no, not once again, the Commander rethought, realising that he never had the respect of his men. Any men in fact, ever – but now he had truly earned it.

As he followed the long train of armed Republic guards and sobbing prisoners, the Commander glanced at a few of his men. They returned the glance; not in the disinterested manner they used to. Now they looked at him differently. There was now a sense of camaraderie, augmented by mutual pride and admiration.

They were heavily armed with a fighting spirit they had never experienced before. Their lives had changed. Finally, they were a force to be reckoned with, not laughed at.

Chapter 57

The Edge

By hovering the lander expertly, T positioned their vehicle just below the sharp point at the base of The Chun. Its form towered and expanded hundreds of miles into the sky above them, beyond the reaches of the atmosphere and into the blackness of space. He set the autopilot to maintain the vehicles current position, instructing the computer to keep it as steady as a rock.

Both men exited the safety of the lander's interior and climbed onto the roof of the vessel through its top hatch. The drop to the black base of the crater looked incredibly high from up here. The height was further emphasised by the lander still being in stealth mode. K and T could see through the hull of the ship, to the ground below. They both knew they couldn't actually see through the metal ship, and were merely viewing the projected image on the surface of the lander, but it was still a highly unnerving sight that made them very nervous. Anyone viewing the scene from a distance would find the form of the lander difficult to identify, thereby giving the illusion that the two men were floating in mid air, three hundred metres above the ground.

They soon forgot about what was below them when they looked up. Silently they stared at the awesome shape before them. They stood where millions of others had stood, throughout history; probably feeling much the same thing. Questions ran through their minds and then quickly vanished again. Questions like; 'Who…? How…? What…? When…? Where…?' And more importantly: 'why…?' sprang to mind. But as quickly as they formed, they disappeared. It was almost as if the size of the object negated the need for any such questions.

K and T went through this process a number of times in complete silence, all the time touching the warm smooth, slightly reflective surface of the incredible structure with the palms of their hands. The first words of questions would appear on their lips for a brief moment, sometimes being vocalised slightly, before disappearing back into the subconscious mind from where they were born. Eventually their attention returned to the matter in hand and the urgency of their task re-established itself.

"We had better get a move on," ventured T, "we don't know how long the guys can hold off the barbarians."

K remained silent. A few moments later T tried again. "What is it we are going to do?" he asked.

K was still muted, shrouded by his own deep thoughts. He looked carefully at his half-reflection that appeared in front of him on the smooth surface of The Chun. It was distorted and out of focus. It even seemed to move slightly differently to him – not the typical actions of a reflection. T noticed it too. It was almost as if he was looking at an image in a frosted glass window that was trying very carefully to imitate his every move, but not quite managing it.

Something deep within K's mind spoke to him. He had a sudden urge to lie down, beneath the sharp point at the base of The Chun. T looked on in bewilderment as his colleague lowered himself onto his back. "What are you doing?" he asked. K remained silent, carefully positioning his head below the sharp point of the enormous floating structure.

He lay there for a moment, feeling very conspicuous as his colleague looked on, frowning slightly. K looked up at the massive object. The illusion from this position was strange. The four massive sides of the object disappeared into space far above his head. There was no specific focal point at which to look apart from the sharp base close to his head and this made his eyes cross awkwardly. So K looked miles into the distance, viewing The Chun from all sides at the same time. It formed a strange image. The Chun's base appeared from here to be two points, each directly aimed at one of K's eyes. His mind was confused by what it saw and complained to K, requesting that he close his eyes to refocus. He blinked slowly, but instead of the usual darkness K was used to seeing when he closed his eyelids, incredible images flashed into his brain for a brief moment, scaring him half to death. He opened his eyes quickly as his entire body jumped out of sheer sudden terror. He bolted upright, piercing the centre of his forehead on the sharp solid point at the base of The Chun.

"Ow, sh*t. That really hurt," complained K putting a hand to his bleeding forehead, as he ducked back from the offending object.

"Jeez, that could have taken your eye out," stated T in an unhelpful manner. "You alright?" Upon getting no response, he tried a different tactic. "What the hell happened?" he asked, confused by K's non-communicative nature before the incident.

"I saw something," said K.

"Well you obviously didn't see it enough," replied T facetiously, "you just head butted a trillion ton object!"

"No, I mean I saw something else, something that wasn't there before," he explained badly. "It felt like The Chun was showing me something." K stopped talking, wiped his forehead free of the blood that had gathered there, and lay back down with his head under the offending object. T looked on anxiously, occasionally glancing around the wide perimeter of the huge crater that spread out around them. He hoped they had time for this.

Nervously, K shut his eyes again. What happened next happened in a few seconds, but K's mind processed the information and slowed it to a manageable speed. Failure to do so would have resulted in his brain over heating and imploding into grey pulp.

The flashing images he had seen for a fraction of a second when blinking, returned. Lights of all sizes, colour and magnitude streamed past K's unseeing eyes by-passing his physical vision and directly entering the far more powerful 'mind's eye'. They were stars, K quickly realised. He was accelerating forward at billions of light years. Galaxies streamed past him like small pools of illumination, spinning wildly as the entire universe seemed to be at fast forward. Hundreds flew past, then thousands, the endless stream of galaxies sped past at light speed. Still they came, hundreds upon thousands more Catherine-wheel-like galaxies shot past K's mind as it accelerated towards… towards… the unknown. Every so often K imagined that he looked to his sides, seeing the galaxies that had approached from light years away, fly past within the blink of an eye and disappear billions of miles behind him, all the time spinning at thousands of revolutions per second.

The speed was incredible, yet not one element of detail eluded him. If he wanted to, he could have counted the number of stars in each galaxy, despite only seeing them fly past at the speed of light.

When he thought about it, he could even see the planets that revolved around each star. When he looked harder, he could see individual planets, close up. If he concentrated enough, he could even see the creatures that existed on that planet. But the process never slowed, it all happened in a few milliseconds.

After what seemed like a lifetime's journey the flow of galaxies and solar systems ceased. The last few rapidly disappeared into the jet black back drop far behind him. The motion seemed to stop. No more galaxies flew past at light speed, no more planets could be interrogated from great distances. Now there was nothing. Just blackness. The whole universe had rapidly vanished to a single point of light behind him before slowly disappearing altogether. All was quiet. All was black. There was nothing.

After a few moments of awkward boredom, K felt obliged to do something. He imagined reaching his arm out into the blackness. In doing so he reached out with his physical body too.

T watched nervously as the silent horizontal body of K suddenly reached up into the air in front of him.

K felt a wall. It was jet black, no, that would imply it had colour. There was no colour here, it was just nothing. Pure nothing. And in that purest of nothing, was the solid edge of nothing. A slightly thicker, more resistant nothing than all the other nothingness that surrounded K. He touched the thickness in front of him. There was little resistance, as he forced a finger in. He raised his other hand into the air in front of him.

T was getting more anxious and went to touch K's shoulder to 'wake' him, but there was significant resistance in the air around K, an invisible force field where the air had become so dense, it protected him like a cloak of thick treacle. He watched K's two outstretched arms, one on either side of The Chun, both of which seemed to be reaching into something in front of him. T noticed K's fingers disappear into nothing, giving the impression the tips had been cut off. He blinked unbelievingly and looked again, harder this time to try to make out the reality of the situation. It looked as though K's fingers had entered the sides of The Chun a couple of feet from its sharp base, which hovered only a few inches from K's forehead.

K's hands parted the wall of pure nothing in front of him, which provided little resistance. A gap appeared allowing a flood of incandescent light to pierce the blackness around him. It shone so bright, K could not see beyond it. The thick, heavy light blinded K's mind's eye momentarily, but he knew that if he were to wait until his imagination's vision adjusted, all would be revealed. He waited. Suddenly, the brightness in between his hands was taken from him. He saw the crack of white that he had created disappear far into the distance in front of him as his mind flew backwards through the universe even faster than it had flown forwards. He pined for the white light. He was going to see something magnificent, he was sure of it. His arms reached out, begging for the return of the light. Fingers outstretched in a desperate attempt to make them reach through the billions of miles across the universe as he retreated at an ever increasing pace away from the light. The galaxies passed by him once again, but K paid them no heed. He wanted the light. Nothing else would do. He needed the enlightenment it teased, not these pathetic galaxies full of millions of stars and planets with billions of life forms and incredible detail. He just wanted the light, that was all; but it was gone.

T frantically worked on K's body as the incandescent light shone down on his friend's face. It was red hot and freezing cold at the same time and unbearably bright. It scared the cr*p out of T, stopping him from being able to see what he was doing. At first the thickness of the air around K made it difficult to touch his colleague at all, but he had managed to get a finger through to K's jugular vein soon realising that his heartbeat was almost non-existent and fading fast. As T persevered to wake K, the protective air around him became thinner, gradually returning to its natural state and the light above him started to reduce in its intensity. T now pushed down heavily on K's chest in a rhythmic motion. "One, two, three, four, five." T stopped, lowered his head to his companion's torso to listen for signs of a regular heart beat. Nothing. He pulled his colleague's head from under The Chun and placed his mouth over K's and breathed second-hand air into his lungs. Then he repeated the chest compression, once again in a succession of five heavy presses. "Come on K, I need you," he shouted. T repeated this process a number of times; breathing air into K's lungs, resuming compressions and shouting at K not to leave him.

Eventually, K started to breathe of his own accord. His heartbeat soon returned to a regular, life sustaining thump deep within his chest. K opened his eyes. He had been moved from directly beneath The Chun. He was slightly to one side, but still looking up at the massive creation.

"K! K! Can you hear me?" asked T desperately. K smiled. "Sh*t, K. You had me scared there," stated T, as he saw K's eyes opening slowly. "Are you OK?" K's smile widened.

"It's a telescope," he said softly.

"What?"

"It's a telescope," he repeated matter of factly. "I saw the edge of the universe." A smile continued to beam across his face. "I saw the edge of the universe. There is light beyond it. I nearly went through to the other side."

"K, what are you talking about. You nearly died." T breathed heavily from his life saving ordeal.

"I'm telling you, it's a telescope. You must have stopped me from seeing the truth," K stated in a slightly annoyed manner. "I could have seen what lies beyond the end of the universe if you hadn't stopped me."

"For f*ck's sake, K, I just saved your life," replied T annoyed and stressed. "Your heart stopped. You weren't breathing."

"There's a link between the universe and life," K concluded from nowhere.

"What?" asked T, still gasping for breath, next to his all too calm colleague.

"There is a direct link between the universe and life itself." He raised his head slightly as realisations began to form knowledge inside K's mind. "It's all starting to make sense. There is a direct link between this universe and our life, one can't exist without the other... or are they the same thing?" His brain was racing as his voice trailed off. T was looking confused and bewildered. He needed enlightening. "Here, place your head under here and close your eyes." K suggested helpfully to his colleague, who looked back at him with an intense look of distaste.

"You must be joking," T replied angrily, "That thing nearly killed you, and you're asking me to get under it too? What if you don't recover me in time? What then?"

"I don't think you'd mind," replied K matter-of-factly. "I didn't."

They continued their argument.

Chapter 58

The Decision

The Commander continued his proud march behind his troops and prisoners of war. Something bothered him. They had succeeded in defeating their enemy, but they still had no way of getting off this planet and returning to their own civilisation. The Rogue Nationals must have transportation to their mother ship. There had to be a huge number of landing craft on the planet somewhere.

He gave the order to stop the long procession. There was little point in all the troops travelling to meet T and K at The Chun. After a few minutes the train of vehicles and pedestrians had come to a complete halt and a committee of the Commander's men had been gathered to discuss their options. A number of suggestions were put forward, but the only real solution seemed to be that the Rogue National barbarians should be made to reveal how they communicated with the mother ship and how they travelled to the planet's surface.

"But torture is wrong," stated one of the more civilised officers of the impromptu committee.

"I didn't say we had to torture them," replied the Commander, "we merely have to obtain some information from them that will aid our escape. How that is given to us and under what levels of pressure is up to the prisoners."

"It's wrong," continued the righteous officer. "We will be lowering ourselves to their level. We will become bullying barbarians if we do this."

"I am afraid we have no choice," stated the Commander solemnly, "we shall proceed, but you need not have anything to do with it."

The officer disappeared before the Commander gave a number of different instructions to his remaining men. Soon they had dispersed and joined the rest of the long train.

Each officer approached the large group of giant barbarian prisoners, who sat obediently in a huddle in the middle of the street. One barbarian warrior was chosen from the crowd by each member of the newly formed interrogation committee. The barbarians shifted uneasily as they collectively concluded in silence what was about to occur. Soon the screams and hideous smells of torture would be in evidence and the pain would be felt by all. Well, rhetorically speaking, of course. The real pain would only be felt by the chosen recipients of the actual torture.

The Commander allowed this scene to continue behind him, as he ran along side the long stationary procession of war machines that headed the convoy. He gathered a number of his officers and gave orders for the majority of the vehicles to depart for The Chun. A few machines would remain behind with the foot soldiers, to accompany them wherever the new information they were about to get from the barbarians may lead them.

Chapter 59

The Collar

Inside the walking land tank, a muscular barbarian pilot Collar viewed the huge screen in front of him. The picture revealed a long line of powerful black war machines ahead of his own impressive vehicle of doom. Each tank took its turn in passing the last few remaining buildings. The brilliant white rock gradually faded to a darkening grey and eventually to a jet black incinerated state, before disappearing altogether, leaving just blackened dust and remnants of foundations. After the last standing construction had been passed, it would be another couple of hundred metres before the edge of the crater was reached.

As he passed the final char-grilled house, Collar Jaknnd took note of the scene around him, through expert use of the viewing screen and frequent verbal commands to his onboard computer. The close confines of the street opened on each side to reveal a captivating scene of destruction and devastation. Around the circumference of the massive central hole, the city had been completely flattened, leaving only a spattering of incinerated rubble on the ground where former ancient constructions once stood. The tank tilted occasionally from side to side as its thousands of feet negotiated piles of rubble under foot. The vehicles in front of Jaknnd peeled off to the right and left alternately, as the ground a hundred metres in front of them disappeared down the sharp black cliff that formed the edge of the monster crater.

Jaknnd took his turn peeling off from the main column of approaching vehicles and turned to the right. Ten tanks had already steered this way, and each had taken their turn to face the crater, positioning their black heavy metal bodies close to the edge for maximum effect. Each war machine lowered its cannons, to point into the centre of the crater, three hundred metres below.

The tank pilot ordered the computer to show peripheral vision. The screen distorted its image to show a one hundred and eighty degree view of the scenes to the front and both sides of the tank. The pilot took a moment to observe his surroundings, viewing his colleagues' tanks along side as well as the approaching tanks a hundred metres to his left which continued to pour onto the crater's edge from the large street down which they had travelled without incident. He hoped that one of the other convoys had had better luck at flushing out the enemy and having an excuse to release some deathly discharge. He couldn't wait to be able to do the same. Target practice was what he longed for.

He returned his gaze to the centre of the screen. Looking deep within the massive black crater, he could see no obvious signs of life, but he was led to believe that some existed down there through conversations he had overheard on the all-channels intercom. He looked forward to the opportunity to vaporise the enemy. Then, with great distaste, he recalled the strange command that restricted them all from having the battle, not to mention fun, they deserved. He sighed and switched his tank to dormant mode. Some of the distant noises that the tank produced went silent. The pilot waited uneasily.

Chapter 60

The Mercy

The Commander rounded the corner to a small building in which one of the barbarian warriors had been taken. He stepped through the wooden doorway into a dark and damp room where the prisoner of war had been strapped tightly to a moss-covered seat with vines. Foot soldiers stood either side of the massive seated barbarian.

As the Commander walked in, the officer sitting opposite the silent giant stood to attention, saluted the Commander and then asked permission to begin the interrogation. The Commander agreed, reluctantly. He did not want to torture these men any more than one of his outspoken officers had wanted them to. But there was information on which their survival depended inside this barbaric man's head. He nodded to his officer with a dry gulp that said 'Go ahead, but I might not be able to stomach the worst of it.'

"Where are your landing craft?" shouted the officer at the barbarian warrior, whose huge muscles glistened with sweat. There was a moment's silence. Then the most unexpected thing happened. The barbarian burst into tears. His head fell forward, giving the impression he was staring intently at his own genitals. He blubbed and wailed like a baby. This torturous behaviour was too much for him, he couldn't take it any more. The pressure had broken him.

Gradually he stopped his snivelling and calmed himself enough to speak to the shocked, silent audience. "We have fifteen camps around the outskirts of the main city, hidden in the forest clearings. Each one has a number of landers assigned to it, each capable of carrying a hundred troops or two walker tanks." He paused to have a little cry.

The Commander and his men looked at each other in complete shock. This two and a half metre tall muscular giant was giving them all the information they required without them harming a hair on his greasy head. But how could they know it was the truth. It had to be. The barbarian warrior didn't seem intelligent enough to know how to lie and he was obviously genuinely distressed.

"What in Aljebar's name did you do to him?" asked the Commander, half impressed and half preparing himself for the disgust he would feel when the officer informed him of the painful atrocities that had been forced upon this hapless victim before his arrival.

"Nothing, Sir," replied the officer. "That's the first question I asked him! We waited for you before we started the interrogation," he declared, as surprised at the enemy soldier's behaviour as everyone else in the room.

The barbarian continued to cry, head hanging like a rag doll. The torture of being kept alive after the humiliation of being defeated without a single shot being fired by the barbarians was too much for him.

"Kill me, please, I beg you," he pleaded. "Please kill me, this is so humiliating," he blubbed again, proving his intelligence to be in the upper second percentile for Rogue Nationals by using a word with more than two syllables.

"Untie him," ordered the Commander.

"Are you sure?" asked the officer before waiting for the nodded confirmation and then moving towards the vine knots at the back of the chair. The Republic troop aiming the RN laser rifle adjusted his grip and aim to ensure that he would not miss should his services be required. Once untied, the barbarian fell to his knees on the floor in front of the Commander and clasped his hands together in front of him in a universal pleading action.

"Please kill me," repeated the barbarian wreck as stringy dribble hung from his chin. "I have told you everything you need to know, now please kill me."

As much as it pained him to do so, the Commander understood that to kill the Rogue National in cold blood was really the fairest thing to do. He was in obvious turmoil at being captured as a prisoner of war and seemed to be so heavily disgusted with himself that his only cure would be death. He needed fatal relief. The Commander and the other Republic troops in the room started to realise just how humane murder could be in such a situation. They looked at one another, slightly awkwardly, but all knowing that the execution of the barbarian would be his best form of release and the ultimate reward for the information he had provided.

"Who wants to do it?" asked the Commander. The averted gazes of his fellow companions answered his question.

This was going to be the hardest task he had ever had to carry out. He had to remind himself repeatedly it was the kindest thing to do as he pulled out his small hand gun. It's a mercy killing, it's a mercy killing, he repeated over and over in his head. He pointed the gun to the barbarian's forehead, knowing that he was going to have to go through with this awful act.

The barbarian had not expected escape to be so forthcoming. He had been captured by truly the kindest enemy in the universe. They would take away his pain and set him free from this world of barbarianism and fighting. He looked past the quivering hand gun and into the eyes of his executioner.

"Thank you," he whispered softly as he closed his eyes slowly, preparing himself for his imminent escape from his living hell.

The gun fired and a large heavy body slumped to the floor. The Commander opened his eyes to see if his shot had succeeded. His two colleagues also returned their gaze to the scene, both with a strange sense of respect and admiration for their Commander who had managed to do something they never could have done.

The huge lifeless body of the Rogue National warrior lay heavy on the ground as deep reddish-brown coloured liquid flooded from his head into an expanding puddle on the floor. On his face was an expression of grateful contentment, a slight hint of a smile across his lips. It was an incredible sight and one that enabled the Commander to retain the contents of his stomach and feel proud at what he had done. He was truly reassured that it was the kindest thing to do in the circumstance.

Unfortunately though, it was not over. The Commander knew they were going to have to confirm the information provided by asking the same questions of the other RN Warriors.

If they got the answers they wanted, more mercy killings were going to have to take place.

Chapter 61

The Fall

T and K climbed back into the cleverly concealed lander, shutting the hatch behind them. In the middle distance, far too close for comfort, along many of the streets that touched the horizon in every direction, they had seen the shadowy darkness of thousands of enemy tanks approaching the crater. They knew they had to get out of here, before one of the vehicles detected the presence of their invisible hovering craft.

K and T prepared for a fast exit, strapping themselves tightly into the pilot and co-pilot seats on either side of the lander's wide cockpit. K readied himself and looked across at T who seemed to be paralysed with a terrified look on his face.

"Come on then, let's go," prompted K, still smiling from the incredible near-death experience he had been through.

"Err," replied T, "we can't. There's hardly any power left." He had an edge of concern in his voice that certainly did not put K's mind at rest. "We'll be lucky if we have enough power to land!"

There was total silence in the cockpit as K realised he needed to keep quiet if the Republic Expedition's best lander pilot was going to be allowed to do his job. T's hands frantically moved across the array of controls, arms not stopping for a moment's rest. After a few seconds, T broke the silence with the kind of instruction nobody wants to hear.

"Hold on!"

The lander was suddenly released from its hovering position. Gravity, regaining its natural control over the vessel, dragged it towards the ground at ever increasing speed. T and K were thrust upwards into their harnesses, which held them as close as possible to the seats below. K's arms were thrown above him and hung in the air above his head.

T sat poised, trying as hard as possible to keep his outstretched arm close to one particular button on the control panel in front of him. He was struggling. Timing was everything.

The lander continued to plummet straight down towards the blackened earth, rubble and ship remains. It seemed to take forever, but the fall only lasted a few seconds. Then T hit the button. All landing propulsion systems fired at once, breaking the momentum of the craft a few metres before it hit the charred earth. Within a split second all power was consumed and the craft reverted to freefall. The lander crashed onto the ground. The remaining one-metre drop shook the ship with such force that the reality of the consequences from the full three hundred metre descent suddenly seemed even more apparent.

T had done it. If he had hit the button any sooner, the ship would have taken a far more significant pounding when continuing its interrupted fall to the ground. A moment later and the landing propulsion systems would not have fired in time to have any effect.

"Thanks, T," said K weakly. That was twice T had saved his life now. He hoped T knew he was giving his genuine appreciation for both events, despite his earlier comments.

"No problem." T smiled back. He hoped that K had not forgotten the incident on the lander's roof before this one!

Both men got up as soon as the pleasantries were over and bolted for the door. If the enemy were planning on destroying the lander, they would do so as soon as it came back into view, which had just happened. The men reached the door, opened it and leapt onto the ground outside. They scrambled to their feet and dove behind a large section of crumpled, partially melted outer hull. The crater's centre was strewn with the blackened debris of the former mother ship, many sections of which were big enough to provide adequate cover for a hundred men.

They peered over the edge of their new hiding place up at the lip of the crater one kilometre away. They realised the Rogue Nation's troops were not close enough to the cliff edge to be able to see the exposed pod. It was difficult to remember that the three hundred metre drop they had just experienced in the small escape pod was effectively from ground level downwards. It wouldn't be long before the barbarians were at the crater's edge. What could they do to get out of here?

K and T sat down, backs against the twisted metal of their new hiding place. They had managed to understand a little more about what The Chun was and about what it could do, but they were no closer to finding a way out of here or off this warrior infested planet. In fact, they were a good deal further back on that front. Not only didn't they have any solutions to the dilemma of escape, but now they had no way of getting to their colleagues either. They didn't even know if any of their colleagues were still alive – they might all have been slaughtered in the diversion ambush. To make matters worse they were stuck in the middle of a giant black crater, about to be surrounded on all sides by the huge arsenal of their awesome enemy. They were like sitting ducks at a fairground. They hoped the main troop had fared better.

After discussing their limited options, K and T peered over the edge of the wall of twisted, stressed metal. The site was demoralising. Lined around the crater's rim were hundreds of Rogue National vehicles, all guns pointing towards T and K in the centre. The vehicles were like tiny black dots on the horizon at this distance, but both K and T knew their weaponry capabilities would have no problem in reaching this far, completely obliterating everything around them. Could things be any worse?

Chapter 62

The Base

It had not taken long to arrive at the closest Rogue Nation base. The directions given by the prisoners were all exactly the same. Everyone of them had cracked under the slightest pressure. All it took was for them to be separated from their colleagues, tied to a chair and treated nicely. Some hadn't even required that much, as they began to squeal their force's secrets before they could even be strapped down. Every one of the prisoners had talked. And everyone of them had cried like a baby. They were all quite pathetic, in a huge muscle-man kind of way. It must have been the pressure of defeat. Maybe they had enormous respect for the enemy that got the better of them, especially at such slim odds. Whatever it was, they had given the Republic's men the information they needed. Those that had spoken had been given the dubious reward of 'freedom'. It was sad to see creatures that wanted so much to die rather than be kept in a world in which they were so severely humiliated. At the same time, it truly was the greatest gift the Republic could have given them, considering their circumstances.

Ten Republic troops along with the Commander and the remaining barbarian prisoners (those that had not been interrogated) travelled in four troop-carrying vehicles to the closest RN base. Crammed into the backs of the vehicles, the barbarian warriors' blubbed and wailed in a collective mass of hysteria and sniffling. One tank accompanied the small convoy, whilst all other vehicles commandeered from the battle travelled to the crater at the base of The Chun.

The small task force had sped through the streets, heading away from The Chun to the dense forest that invaded the uniformity at the edge of the citadel. As the vehicles had approached an especially thick patch of forest, one of the prisoners who had appointed himself as chief navigational snitch, indicated that the camp was near. He had caught-on that providing valuable information to the Republic troops bought you a first class ticket out of Humiliationville to Freedom Central.

The Commander considered the possibility this might all be an elaborate hoax to lure the Republic's forces into a trap, but these warriors didn't seem to have the intelligence to know when to go to the toilet without being told to do so. It seemed unlikely they would have had the time or inclination to develop such an intricate plot. No, he decided simply to go along with the advice of the prisoners. If anything seemed in the slightest bit suspicious, he could always threaten to be nice to them again, maybe even use his trump card of letting them go back to their Rogue National Warrior colleagues unharmed. That would be sure to send them over the edge.

Once near the main RN base the Commander ordered the small convoy to stop. He stepped out of the troop carrier and selected two officers to accompany him on a small reconnaissance mission. As they scrambled through the dense foliage, they came to a large clearing so suddenly that they nearly stumbled straight into a small group of barbarian warriors busy playing some sort of board game. They ducked back into the trees without being noticed and plotted their advance.

After a few minutes the Commander and his scouting party returned with a plan. It was a genius plan – truly a plan to end all plans. It had taken minds of true cunning to come up with and had every chance of failing. They would simply drive the vehicles directly into the camp and order the Rogue Nation lander pilots to surrender their ships.

Chapter 63

The Collapse

T and K watched with disbelief and sinking morale as more and more Rogue Nation vehicles arrived at the crater's edge. Huge sections of the blackened walls of the crater now contained cannon firing vessels above them. The line was not a continuous one – large gaps of a few hundred metres appeared occasionally between the battalions of tanks, but the sight was still incredibly daunting. Scattered between the massive black killing machines K could just make out the tiny ant-like figures of barbarian foot warriors, hundreds of them.

"D'you think we can make it through one of the gaps?" asked K.

"Are you kidding me?" replied T, facetiously. "It will take us too long to get to the edge of the crater for a blind man not to notice us."

"Then I guess we should just give up," stated K depressingly. He proceeded to walk out into the open from behind their superficial cover. T grabbed him and told him to hold on.

"Let's wait and see what happens."

Just then, another large procession of black vehicles arrived at the eastern edge of the crater, slowly filling one of the gaps that existed between the patiently waiting rim-dwellers. But this group of vehicles did not arrive in a straight line, or disperse neatly in single file along the crater's edge. They poured out of the narrow street down which they had travelled and stopped unceremoniously in an untidy mess a hundred metres away from the rim. T and K squinted to see the details. K was sure from his own experience of piloting the enemy tank that the drivers of these vehicles must be inexperienced. Their erratic movements and jerky speed reflected K's own problems with the sensitivity of the controls.

Sure enough, the newly arrived tanks did something quite different to their predecessors. Instead of pointing their cannon barrels towards the centre of the crater, each one rotated its weapon turrets towards the other black vehicles of death around the rim of the crater. K and T looked at each other briefly with a slight smirk, half hoping, half knowing that they had a better chance of survival than a few moments ago. Instead of remaining dormant like their sister machines, the latest squadron broke the eerie silence of the immense crater scene by opening fire simultaneously on their neighbours.

T and K jumped for joy, literally, as they realised what this meant. Their colleagues had defeated the Rogue National troops. Against all odds, their ambush had obviously worked and they had managed to capture the enemy's tanks, but their mood was soon tempered when they looked at the incredible task that faced their colleagues now. They were out numbered hundreds to one. They had the element of surprise, but that would only last a matter of seconds.

The Republic tanks opened fire in a hail of noise and colourful explosions that gave the impression all New Years' Eves had just arrived at once. A phenomenal array of colour and light emitted from the small band of tanks so bright, you could not look directly at them. Laser cannon fire, thunderbolt missiles and a battery of smaller firepower sprayed out in almost all directions towards the crater's rim, but their cannons were not aimed directly at the enemy tanks, they were aimed below, along the edge of the crater's newly formed cliffs.

"Aim higher, you fools," shouted T. "You're gonna give yourselves away."

But the tanks ignored his frantic warnings and continued to open fire at the muddy black walls of the crater's edge. Huge explosions knocked massive holes into the depths of the cliffs in rapid succession below the tanks of the RN force. The whole process had taken place so rapidly that the Rogue National tank Collars were a little dazed as explosions shook the ground beneath them. They rapidly came to their senses and established that a group of their own tanks had opened fire, but were doing such a pathetic job it was almost laughable. The missiles and laser cannon fire continued to miss the warrior artillery whilst the Rogue National troops established through radio confirmation that they were still forbidden to open fire upon their Republic assailants. It was conceivable that the firing tanks contained barbarian warriors who had simply got the taste for battle and were too frustrated to stop fighting, but with the Marth's orders still in full force not to kill a single Republic soldier they could not afford to take that chance.

Massive cracks formed in the charred vertical walls of the crater. Land slides of burnt mud and rocks started to fall from the cliffs where the barrage of fire-power had been heaviest. Colossal sections of earth started to break away as the rapid bombardment continued to penetrate the delicate, charred surface. Cracks started to appear at the top of the cliffs expanding across the ground quickly beneath tanks and the feet of barbarian foot warriors. With the sound of a mammoth earthquake waking from a deep sleep, giant sections of cliff face began to break away, groaning and creaking as they slowly plummeted into the blackened void below. Tanks followed, like tin toys bouncing helplessly down the ragged edge as the floor beneath them disintegrated into rubble. Hundreds of enemy tanks and soldiers fell foul of this tactic, plunging to their deaths far below.

Again T and K cheered as scores of tanks and soldiers took turns to fall to their destruction. Other enemy vehicles around the perimeter of the crater started to retreat into the shelter of the buildings, further away from the precarious edge of the crater, but none of them returned fire.

Having annihilated a large percentage of the enemy in a brief stroke of genius, the Republic tanks refocused on a more traditional type of attack, pin-pointing individual tanks as targets and picking them off, one by one. Within a few short moments, there was no enemy to be seen. All had retreated out of sight and none had returned fire.

The scattered remains of hundreds of fallen enemy tanks smouldered silently in untidy piles at the base of the endless black cliff face that circled T and K's position. Rocks and rubble covered many of the tanks which lay, strewn across the crater floor. Silence gradually prevailed once more, only to be broken by the occasional small land slide attempting to catch up with much bigger relatives and the distant screaming and cheering of two tiny people, echoing quietly from the centre of the crater.

Chapter 64

The Landslides

The Marth, having surveyed the citadel from high above, decided to join a large contingent of his force on the ground. He could see them far below arriving at the cliff's edge. All seemed quiet at the moment, but he knew that would soon change – he was going to change it. The earliest arrivals had already positioned themselves on the south-west rim of the crater. The tanks were neatly arranged along the edge, all weaponry aimed at its centre.

The lander touched down between the buildings of one of the Citadel's main streets. The Marth skilfully positioned his awesome machine behind the main line of battle tanks and the secondary line of smaller armoured vehicles and personnel carriers.

During his time of contemplation in the air, he had decided that it was impossible for the Republic troops to have found the device containing The Answer. He had drawn his conclusions from a number of events. Firstly, they were a weak force, representing an even weaker race. They would have handed over the device at the earliest opportunity to avoid the carnage that ensued. Secondly, they were permanently on the run. If they had the device and knew what it held, why would they have not released its power? Thirdly, the Marth had scanned the entire planet at close range for electromagnetic activities of the most minute nature for twelve years. It was inconceivable that the Republic would have stumbled across it within minutes of landing.

No. The conclusion was there. The Marth had decided that enough was enough. If there were any Republic personnel still alive after the earlier battle, which there should be, they would be forced into the crater to meet their doom.

Once the lander was secure, the Marth disembarked. A number of warrior officers greeted him, informing him that all was well and that no enemies had yet been sighted. At that moment, as if prompted by the officer's statement, a huge explosion shook the ground below them. Smoke quickly followed the noise, billowing over the crater's edge nearby. The Marth looked deep within the eyes of the officer in front of him.

"Who gave the order to fire?" he asked calmly.

"Er, nobody, Sir."

Another huge explosion hit the wall, then another, and another. Each time the cannon fire hit the crater's cliff edge, the foot soldiers and RN vehicles shook violently. Many men fell to the ground, but the Marth stood firm.

"I think you will find that is enemy fire," stated the Marth. "The instruction not to kill the enemy is lifted. Now destroy that scum before it destroys us," he commanded loudly.

Unfazed, the Marth walked towards the end of the long street that stretched far into the distance behind him. The closest buildings were merely piles of blackened rubble. He continued to walk until he was almost in the direct line of fire of the enemy tanks. It was easy to see which group of Rogue Nation vehicles contained the enemy. Not only were they conspicuous by their firing laser cannons, but they were also arranged in an undisciplined, highly unprofessional manner.

The Marth was hugely disappointed. His men should have dealt with this pathetic force at the earlier battle. Despite the ban on killing the enemy they still shouldn't have been difficult to capture. He decided his best vantage point was back in his lander.

Just as he turned to walk the fifty metres back to his machine, he felt the earth move suddenly. It had dropped a few centimetres – enough of an indication as to what was about to happen. The Marth broke into a run, a very rare sight indeed. Like most men of power, he had people to do those sorts of things for him. Ahead he could see a huge fissure appearing in the street, just beyond the first rubble buildings close to one of his lander's three metal legs. He ran as fast as he could. He was a fit and powerful man, but rarely did he practise such manual labour and his style was lacking. The sight of such an intimidating creature running so gracelessly for his life was one that many would have enjoyed seeing – unfortunately no-one did. His last few steps pounded the earth as it started to fall away. He leapt into the air just as the huge section of land fell away from below him. He impacted heavily on the newly formed cliff edge, fingers gripping the ground like talons, legs dangling beneath him. His feet pointed towards the steep incline which continued to be created by the thousands of tons of earth now careering its way towards the crater's base. He had landed just in time to observe gravity gently take hold of his lander and drag it to the depths of the crater below, narrowly missing his left shoulder.

The Marth clambered to his feet feeling a strange lack of dignity, something he was not used to. Below him the massive landslide continued to develop, as the thunderous sound effect threatened to burst his eardrums. The enemy continued its unrelenting attack on the cliff walls.

The Marth stood close to the edge of the crater, surveying the carnage taking place. To his far right, beyond the enemy's position, another huge section of cliff face had given way under the pressure of multiple explosions. There too a great many RN tanks had been taken with the landslide into the black depths below. The Marth was not concerned. Hundreds of his tanks were still operational on either side of the enemy and would soon open fire. The pathetic enemy had been lucky, but they would be defeated very soon. As he thought this, he noticed the Republic's attentions had turned to individual RN tanks and that his warriors' vehicles were retreating away from the edge of the crater. Why had they not returned fire yet? He watched as his colossal task force of artillery retreated into the relative safety of the surrounding buildings and streets.

The order to open fire must not have been given before the immense landslide. His warriors still believed the preservation order stood. He must get the new command through.

Chapter 65

The Retaliation

With all the activity taking place around their hiding position T and K began to move out of the crater. They were a long way from the explosive action, but decided who ever won the battle would soon be aware they were there so they may just as well get the journey over with. The long trek to the crater's edge would be followed by a difficult climb. Surrounded by the distant echoes of explosions and cannon fire, they began their reluctant trudge through the ash covered graveyard of their former mother ship towards whatever fate awaited them.

As they walked, they chatted succinctly, pandemonium all around them. T spoke more about the books and K spoke about what he had seen through The Chun. He described how the images of the universe had simply entered his head, as if he had always known them.

"It felt like they were distant memories simply being jogged back in place by a prompt card," described K.

They speculated as to what all of this information meant. What role had The Chun played in the finding of The Answer? Had the Vacchions simply discovered it by some other means, or had they been through the same process K had? T thought that the Vacchions' knowledge of The Chun was limited. Never in the readings had The Chun been described as a telescope. Neither had they described it as being more than a few inches from the ground. The gap was not big enough for anyone to have placed their head beneath it.

The noise of massive explosions subsided. A huge percentage of the Rogue National force lay dormant on the floor of the crater a few hundred meters in front of K and T and near-silence prevailed from the rim of the crater. They looked up at the small group of twenty or so Republic tanks. The noises of their engines and the gentle distant rumbling of the thousands of mechanical legs increased as they began to reposition themselves. They had truly united to become a small but formidable force, thought K as they continued their journey towards their colleagues, now at a gentle jog.

The silence didn't last for long. This time, the ear-shattering explosions, powerful lasers and missile launches came from all around, as the Rogue Nationals began to return fire from their new secluded positions.

The Republic tanks were sitting ducks out in the open, being fired upon from both sides by tanks well sheltered by ancient buildings. They had to do something. K and T looked on, concerned for their colleagues, but helpless.

The journey went on, broken occasionally by the grim reality that faced them. They could hear the tanks commandeered by Republic troops delivering heavy cannon fire to the RN forces, but receiving far more in return. T and K had already discussed the prospect of hiding again, in case the Rogue Nation attack was successful. But they had reached a joint decision that to spend a lifetime on this planet running continuously from barbarian warriors, was a prospect they did not relish. They agreed that what ever happened on the crater's edge, they would gently stroll towards it and meet it head on.

And so they continued their steady paced trek towards the battle's victors, whoever that might be.

Chapter 66

The Hijack

The tank advanced, navigating its way through the awkward, tight approach to the camp. Barbarian guards watched the vehicle enter the large clearing through the designated main entrance.

Inside the single seated cockpit, an experienced barbarian tank Collar piloted his way into the area, as he had done thousands of times before. A small hand weapon was pointing at his forehead. Perched awkwardly on the arm of the chair, squashed into an uncomfortable crouching position was one of the Republic officers. Similar tactics were used in the troop carriers that followed.

The massive pedestrian vehicle approached the troop of game playing men, stopping a few metres short of crushing them. The roof hatch opened and the captive barbarian pilot stood up to give the required orders. The troop carriers waited silently behind the tank.

The explanation was convoluted, and at one stage the Republic officer hidden inside the cockpit was tempted to fire the huge cannons at the enemy troops. Just before the temptation proved too much, the barbarian prisoner, who stood on his seat to reveal his torso through the upper hatch, salvaged the situation by pulling rank and informing them that the orders came directly from the Marth. As soon as this was understood the barbarians began to move frantically, preparing three landers for take off.

Very soon, the large ships were ready and the two troop carriers had each been loaded on board landers, with the tank driven into the holding bay of the third. All ground staff based at the camp were involved in the preparations. None had noticed the large group of pedestrian prisoners that had been led into the clearing by the remaining Republic officers, under the cover of commandeered RN shoulder cannons.

The barbarian prisoners were ordered to lie face down on the floor, whilst the Republic troops lined the sights of the cannons at the warriors who were busying themselves around the hulls of the three huge ships. A single shot was fired by one of the Republic cannons, obliterating a nearby makeshift building which the Republic had been reliably informed contained communication equipment. The small structure exploded in a shower of wood and metal splinters, attracting the attentions of all the Rogue Nationals both within the landers and around their fuselage.

The pilots high up in the cockpits of the large craft immediately started panicked attempts to take off, but were soon stopped by the sudden entry of their Republic captors, weapons in hand. The officers immediately showed each flight crew the red buttons that could be used to detonate the commandeered vehicles. The warrior pilots lowered themselves back down into their seats, puzzled as to why the Republic infiltrators were showing them the harmless remote alarm key to the vehicles in their hold.

The RN barbarian warriors all knew they had been given orders not to kill any of the Republic men. The Republic now knew this too – the prisoners had explained during their captivity. Much to their disappointment, the Republic troops had learnt that their phenomenal win was largely due to the warriors not being permitted to kill any of them. It did take a large element of the credit away from the achievement of the day's activities. The Commander had decided, with the agreement of his small troop of men, not to tell the main group when they were finally reunited. It seemed a shame to take away their elated pride and so they would all go along with the pretence in order to keep morale as high as possible.

Nearby weapons stocks were ransacked by the Republic soldiers who carried as much as they could from the heavily loaded stores to the waiting landers. They needed as many weapons as possible and anything they couldn't carry they would destroy. After a number of journeys back and forth between the landing craft and the arsenal it was deemed greedy to take any more. Once all personnel were cleared of the unit, it was fired upon by a number of shoulder cannons and laser rifles. A sequence of massive explosions reduced the area to flames and ash, and would eventually degrade the weapons therein to molten metal.

Chapter 67

The Turning

The battle raged on. The Republic troops backed into the depths of the citadel away from the small unsheltered plateau at the crater's edge, under heavy fire from the experienced tank pilots on either side of them. No sooner had a Republic tank retreated behind the relative safety of a building, than it was obliterated by the powerful cannons of the enemy tanks. The Republic tanks continued to attempt a fitting response, but it was near impossible to run and fight at the same time. However it was also impossible to fight and stay alive at the same time, so running away had taken priority.

Showers of rock and white brick rained down on the stolen tanks as their cover was rapidly obliterated. Inside each tank was a scared, inexperienced pilot who would have given his grandmother not to be in this position. They were petrified, confused and under attack from a formidable force. A massive difference to the confident feelings they had possessed only minutes before from their day's successful activities. Okay, so they had managed to defeat the barbarians once already, but this was different. This time the Rogue Nationals were fighting back with a vengeance.

The Republic had already lost a few of their tanks, killing a number of men. One of the self appointed rookie tank collars had managed to scramble off the back of his immobilised vehicle seconds before it had been translated from a solid object into a large cloud of particles. He bolted for the relative cover of the surrounding buildings, but would unfortunately never be seen again.

If something didn't happen soon, they would all perish against this awesome adversary. The situation was grave – literally.

Chapter 68

The Conversation

The Marth was distracted from his conversation with his most senior ground force commanders about the current state of the battle. As he looked down from his precarious vantage point at the newly formed cliff edge, he noticed two men walking along the base of the dark crater. He ordered a nearby officer to provide him with zoom lenses, which were quickly supplied.

The Marth raised the dark grey box to his eyes and pointed it at the distant figures. Increasing the zoom, the image of the two men was enhanced, as was their conversation, broadcast to the Marth through small speakers on either side of the box.

"How did the Vacchions find The Answer to life and universal existence?" asked one of the men.

"I'm not sure. Maybe it was through The Chun, maybe it was some other way, but they did and it killed them all."

"Yeah, but not before they contained it in that tiny contraption," commented the first man. "What confuses me is why they bothered creating the device to entrap The Answer in the first place. All they succeeded in doing was keeping it alive until this bunch of barbarian mad men arrived to steal it."

"True, but they must have assumed that the device would contain The Knowledge before it wiped out their entire race." The second man went quiet for a moment, and then added, "or maybe they were just stupid."

"They can't have been that stupid, they discovered the meaning of life."

"But it killed them all," the first man pointed out. "If that's intelligence, I am blissfully happy to remain ignorant!" The men contemplated this significant revelation for a moment, whilst passing a glance at each other. They were suddenly slightly less curious as to what The Answer was.

The Marth lowered the zoom lenses. It appeared that they knew more than he had given them credit for. And it sounded, from the contents of that conversation as if the two pedestrians were in possession of the device, or at least knew where it was.

The Marth called over his nearest officer.

"I am going to welcome these two Republic personnel to the party," he stated as he pointed down towards the individuals walking briskly a few hundred metres from the crater's edge. "See that the remaining Republic personnel are destroyed."

"Yes, Sire," said the officer, frustrated that he had to be the unlucky officer called over and forced to take such responsibility. The buck would stop with him if anything went wrong.

The Marth looked over the cliff edge, searching for a suitable path to the base of the huge black valley. After a few short moments he spotted a gradient far less daunting than the majority of the cliff face and made tracks towards it. He would intercept the two new guests and introduce them to his best friends: Fear and Death.

Chapter 69

The Allies

Huge explosions raged on. The Marth's men continued to attack the small resisting force of the Republic troops, releasing enormous levels of pent-up frustration stored from the earlier command not to kill. Now they were free to destroy whatever they liked and were using every opportunity to unleash hell upon their hapless, doomed victims.

It would only be a matter of time before the Republic troops were completely eradicated. Gyshnf knew this. He had seen tribal battles before. Obviously the battles he had witnessed and taken part in had not involved fifty tonne black vehicles with thousands of legs that could spit balls of blue fire, but the principles were pretty similar. They were nearly always about the same thing, female enahs. At least in his experience they were. But even Gyshnf had to admit, this was an awful lot of noise for any female enah. She must be very special to someone.

Anyway, he was here to help, as was his beautiful mate, Hayde. Both their extended families, a few close friends and even some strategic acquaintances had joined them. Gyshnf turned and faced the gathered group of furry brown enahs and addressed them with a series of squeaks and arm gestures that they all seemed to strongly agree with. Frequently a huge cheer of squeaks would go up, with raised paw movements that implied Gyshnf was doing a good job at rallying the troops.

After a few moments Gyshnf stopped his speech as quickly as he had started it and within seconds, tens of thousands of large brown rodents started to run towards the crater, where the Rogue Nation troops were inflicting huge amounts of damage to the enahs' ancient city.

They split into two groups, each massive convoy of fur covered ground at a speed nobody would think possible of such a large procession of sleep-loving creatures. One torrent of brown headed towards the east, the other towards the west, encircling the battered Republic tanks in the middle of their giant pincer attack. As they ran, the muffled noise created by over one hundred thousand soft paw pads impacting the hard surface of the recently exposed stone ground, gradually began to change. Its pitch escalated from a very soft rumbling to one that sounded like the chinking a million razor blades being dropped from a great height.

The enah army's claws were definitely out. People's bowels were about to 'hit the fan'.

Chapter 70

The Landers

Within twenty minutes of the shots being fired, destroying the communication hut, the remaining Republic troops had loaded the landers with all the equipment they needed. All non-essential Rogue Nationals were expelled from the three vessels, leaving only the piloting crews that would fly the massive contraptions. The remaining barbarians were released to revel in their own personal hell of tortuous self-torment at having been captured and released by a far weaker race. The humiliation of it all was too much. Barbarians huddled on the floor in floods of tears, hugging their knees and rocking backwards and forwards. Their fathers and forefathers would be turning in their graves, if they had them.

The mission had been a resounding success. Three powerful landing craft had been hijacked and were on their way to provide air support to their colleagues. One more thing had to be done before that could be achieved. The landers rotated in mid air, as their piloting crews carried out the instructions of their captors without pause for question or debate. They lined up the huge hovering vehicles, carefully took aim and opened fire upon the remaining landers which lay dormant on the ground below. Huge explosions occurred as the missiles hit the defenceless craft, breaking the massive black shapes into hundreds of burning fragments. The process only took a few minutes and once the Commander was satisfied that the destruction had rendered all of the grounded landers unusable, he gave his next instructions.

"Fourteen more of these attacks to go and then we go to the crater," stated the Commander to one of his fellow officers in the cockpit of the lead vessel.

"Do you think we have the time to do that, Sir?"

"If we don't, we could soon find ourselves out numbered in the skies," replied his Commander solemnly, "that would be a grave mistake."

The officer nodded in agreement, reluctantly, as the craft sped towards the next base.

Chapter 71

The Meeting

The decent towards the two men was a steep one, but was slowly levelling out with every few steps. The Marth was in full view of the Republic officers as the enemies approached one another.

"We have no weapons," shouted one of the men from further down the steep crater's edge, as soon as the huge white figure was within ear shot.

"Neither have I," boomed the deep, terrifying voice of the Marth as he responded truthfully, yet deceptively.

The sounds of war, far above them became a great deal quieter as the cannon fire slowed and the explosion echoes faded in the distance.

"It sounds like your friends have failed," stated the Marth optimistically. The massive bright muscular creature stood tall, looking down the path to his weak adversaries twenty metres below.

"Can you be sure of that?" asked one of the small, weak men that dared to face him. They came to a halt.

"Do not test me," the Marth raised his voice and his hand, pointing his palm towards one of his two new victims. "You have what I want. Hand it over and you will both die quickly."

"Not much of an opening bargaining position is it?" said one of the men, turning to his colleague.

The Marth started to use his incredible fire powers on the man who had just spoken. The small pathetic humanoid quickly writhed in agony as his skin started to feel like it was about to catch fire. The Marth had no intention of killing this creature. At least, not until he was certain which of the weak beings would hand over the device. He was in no mood to play games and was anxious to end his twelve year ordeal quickly now that the end was in sight.

"Okay, okay," said the second man hurriedly, "I have what you want. You can have it, but let him go first!" he shouted, nervous for his friend's life.

The Marth stopped, despite being annoyed that the little man dare to speak to him in this manner. His par-boiled victim fell to the floor, gasping for air and clutching at his face and clothes, obviously still feeling the effects of the extreme heat. "Where is it?" asked the Marth calmly, but starting to show signs of frustration. "Where is the device?"

"If you let T go, I will tell you how to obtain the device."

"K, what are you saying," enquired T, "you don't know where the device is any more than I do."

"That's where you're wrong, T," he stated slowly. "The device is in me."

The Marth observed the second humanoid, apparently called T, as he gasped quietly, jaw dropping slightly before regaining a semblance of composure and shutting it again quickly. His face betrayed the rapid succession of confused thoughts that ran through his mind before an idea hit. T's eyes widened and a wry smile appeared on his face before he turned to the highly unimpressed Marth to reveal his statement of deceptive genius.

"No K," he began proudly, "the device is in me."

The Marth stood motionless, deep in thought. The original plans for the device had been retrieved from a lab that had given birth to the prison cell ten thousand years before. He had studied the hurriedly created blue prints many times over the past twelve years and had learned about the device's innovative aptitude for self-preservation. This explanation was reasonable, but there was no way of proving or disproving it. He couldn't kill either man in case the device really was contained within one of them, as it would be likely to self-destruct, taking the all powerful Answer with it, not to mention the Marth and a great deal of the surrounding area. But the second man's statement was far from convincing. Could it be a double-bluff? Are these pathetic little bipeds capable of that?

"Let this man go and you can take me," suggested K.

"No K, don't do this," complained his colleague, "there must be another way."

"I think not," interrupted the Marth. "Your little friend here is right. You may go." The Marth had considered his options. He couldn't lose. The first man to claim he had the device was the most likely to possess the treasure. If it turned out he did not have it, then the Marth would have the pleasure of destroying him. Meanwhile, the other humanoid would be captured by his troops at the top of the crater's cliff. The Marth turned and looked at the two stationary creatures.

"Go now," he ordered in such a way that no man could disobey. The small man called T began to walk off reluctantly, looking back at his colleague, dwarfed in front of the awesome glowing white figure. He followed the steep path the Marth had used on his descent, glancing back frequently to check the wellbeing of his abandoned companion.

K remained patiently silent. T was a safe distance away, halfway up the steep path towards the relative safety at the top of the cliff. The silence continued, both creatures waiting for the other to speak first. It was soon unbearably uncomfortable for both participants. The Marth was not used to being on the receiving end of such psychological games.

"Well?" he demanded impatiently.

Chapter 72

The Wave

A number of Rogue National foot warriors turned to see what the commotion was about. A deep muffled rumbling had attracted their attention to a large amount of movement in the streets to their right. The rumbling suddenly turned into a cacophony of metallic chinks, collectively sounding like a huge sheet of chain mail being dragged along the stony ground. A strange but awesome site awaited their eyes. One they would remember for the rest of their lives – their life expectancy reduced to that of an elderly may fly.

A sea of brown fur flowed down the street towards them, splashing over rocks and other obstacles in its path as it descended unrelenting towards the stationary troops. They could not believe their eyes as the fast moving wave of fur crashed into the side of a troop carrier, rapidly pushing it over, spilling its contents of warriors into the depths of the brown fur sea. Wave after wave flooded over the barbarian troops, drowning them in a mass of razor sharp teeth and claws. All that could be seen were a couple of floundering limbs, bobbing up and down on the surface of the brown rapids.

The river of fur continued to thunder towards the foot soldiers, all of whom had sensibly broken into a sprint in the opposite direction. Their attempt to escape the deadly mass of ferocious mammals came too late. The rodent rapids were travelling at incredible speed, consuming all flesh in their path and destroying all machines that had rained destruction on their peaceful city.

Some tanks, despite their incredible weight, were over-turned as the furry swell amassed quickly underneath the leading edge of the vehicles. Others were merely rendered useless as their external parts were torn to shreds by millions of powerful little teeth. Mechanical legs were torn off, rubber tubes and exposed wires were chewed through and cockpit doors were opened by heavy splashes of brown waves that tore the contents of the fifty tonne tins to shreds.

The brown sea of fur was unstoppable. The attack went on as pandemonium spread throughout the Rogue Nation's powerful forces. A couple of barbarians opened fire on the wave of fur. Despite creating a brief hole in the fast approaching flood, a few splashes of red-brown rodent parts spraying into the air, the gap simply closed immediately. The unrelenting approach continued, swallowing its targets whole as the all consuming mass flooded down the street.

The sight was truly awesome.

The Republic tank pilots, still busily retreating through the alleyways, side streets and any buildings that stood in the way of their powerful vehicles, soon realised that their pursuers had ceased their barrage of artillery fire. Why would they have stopped? Gradually, whilst still travelling forward, albeit at a much slower pace, the retreating troops instructed their tank's computers to view the scene behind them. Once the image came into focus, all became apparent. Thousands of large brown rodents, just like the one K had befriended were helping them in their battle.

All Republic tank commanders' eyes were firmly fixed on the activities taking place behind them, smiles across every face. The occasional expression of sympathetic grimace appeared on behalf of the mutilated barbarian victims as a particularly painful disembowelling took place. They bought their retreat to a halt and used their intercoms to communicate the ongoing antics of the thousands of rodents to one another. Every now and then a volley of whoops and cheers would resound across the air waves as the brown tidal wave consumed another tank.

Just then, the attention of those who could see a little further down the street, turned to a Republic foot soldier who was running away from the scenes of carnage. He had not been noticed by the barbarians, who were busy trying not to be eaten alive, but was in the path of a second unstoppable tsunami of mammals flooding its way down the street. A gasp of air was taken by the few observing officers, as the wave bore down on the hapless Republic private. Sure enough, the relentless sea of fur hit the man's running legs and knocked him to the floor as his body was covered instantly by the rapid brown carpet of rodents. The Republic tank pilots watching the scene closed their eyes briefly in disgust at the sight of their fallen colleague, his life lost unnecessarily by the carelessness of their allies in what could only be termed 'friendly fur'.

But as their gaze dared to return, they saw the unscratched body of their colleague pop to the surface of the torrent as he was carried down the street like an amateur body surfer.

Smiles returned to their relieved faces.

Chapter 73

The Few

The battle scarred Republic troops vacated their tanks. There was a lull in the explosions and this had to be the opportunity to get out of the line of fire by leaving the conspicuous heavy machinery behind. The exhausted men gathered by the remains of a large building a few hundred metres away from the closest stolen vehicle. They had been separated from the main cluster of tanks that had unfortunately retreated in a different direction during the confusion of heavy enemy fire. They found themselves a long way from the larger task force. They huddled momentarily in the remains of the building which stood a couple of kilometres away from where most of the recent carnage had taken place.

"What the hell do we do now?" asked one of the officers, whilst gasping for breath and spitting small amounts of blood from his mouth.

"I was hoping you were going to tell me!" replied another.

"Why have they stopped firing at us? They can't possibly think we are all dead, can they?"

"Who cares, the point is: they've stopped firing. This is our chance to get out of here. Is this all that's left of us?" Two more troops had joined the cowering Republic men leaning against the rubble of a collapsed wall. That made eight.

"Dunno," replied one of the men, "but I'm getting out of here." His cowardice was beginning to show under the strain of the heavy attack. He got up and ran towards the dense city buildings, leaving the remaining men looking at each other. It was only a few seconds before they had all got to their feet and were running down the small side streets as fast as they could. Their sole aim was to put as much distance between themselves and the stolen tanks during this inexplicable lull in the enemy's attack.

But their escape was cut short. Whilst fully exposed in the centre of a side street a Rogue Nation lander, appearing from nowhere, spotted them and approached head on. Not used to such extreme physical exertion, the men were exhausted from their short panicked run and knew the game was up. Some remained standing, others fell to their knees. One man conceded fully and lay flat on the floor, facing the sky as he gasped for breath, knowing that any one of them could be his last if the lander decided to open fire.

A few of the exhausted men changed their minds and made a mad break for the neighbouring buildings, fully expecting to be blasted off the face of the planet within seconds of the manic dash to safety. To their amazement they made it into an alleyway that connected this street to the next.

The lander touched down on the firm stone-covered ground, sporadically decorated by the greenery of thousands of years of fauna. The pilot slid the craft's wide hull skilfully between the buildings on either side of the street. A cloud of dust and leaves stirred as the ship's anti-gravitational propulsion system's intensity was increased moments before contact.

The few Republic officers that remained, watched uneasily as each of the landing craft's five legs rested heavily on the ground a hundred metres in front of them. It came to a full rest and the dust cloud settled around it. There was silence. No movement for a few moments. Then, eventually, to the unexpected relief of the Republic soldiers that waited with baited breath for their imminent demise, the front hatch opened.

The exhausted men looked at one another in mild terror and total exhaustion. Each man gave a half grimace, half smile to one another by way of saying goodbye. A pair of thin, green-trousered legs appeared at the top of the walkway of the mechanical bird. They were strangely familiar and not the usual thick black combats the Rogue Nationals wore. To everyone's surprise and extreme relief, the legs travelling down the walkway awkwardly revealed the Commander, smiling reassuringly. His small band of men, having left the battle hours ago, had succeeded. They were saved.

The men who had ran into the neighbouring alleyway as the large craft was landing realised what was happening and returned in a manic, mildly hysterical run towards the commandeered ship. They had been watching the events unfold from their relative cover amongst the wall-hugging trees.

"Is this all of you?" asked the Commander non-judgementally.

"Yes, Sir."

"What about K and T, any sign of them?" The mood went quiet for a moment.

"No Sir. We haven't seen either of them, Sir," said one of the troops looking around his colleagues, hoping that one of them would disagree. But no-one did.

"Then we shall wait," stated the Commander, calmly taking a seat on the grass-covered path at the side of the street.

"But what about the enemy tanks, Sir," quizzed one of the men, desperate to get to safety. "They'll be on top of us any second. They'll kill us all."

"Not true," replied the Commander, with a wry smile across his face. "They have enough problems of their own."

After a few minutes wait, two more Rogue Nation landers approached the narrow make-shift landing zone. The eight men who were already feeling far too uncomfortable to be sitting in broad daylight, fully exposed to enemy attack, were jumpy. The Commander calmed them with a gentle hand gesture telling them sit down. "These are ours too," he stated confidently, as the two landers passed overhead.

The men began to relax a little more, as a fellow officer brought a flask of water to each of them from the landers' supply stores. Things were looking up.

Chapter 74

The Stand-off

The Marth stood firm. His confidence was still at maximum, where it always remained. Nothing ever fazed him. Nothing ever rattled him. If he found something to be a threat, he destroyed it. If there was something he wasn't sure about, or didn't understand, he melted it. He had found that by removing these negative things from his life he could concentrate on the pure evil he was nurturing every day.

It was K's turn to break the silence. "So what now?" he asked. K was not so naturally confident, but the cell inside him was working hard to control the chemical releases, once again giving K a manufactured air of steady calm. It was working, to an extent, but the cell couldn't control all of K's frantic brain activity as a huge number of negative thoughts ran riot through his sub-conscious. All manner of gloomy questions and statements attempted to regain panicked control. The cell fought hard to keep K's imagination from placing its body in a heightened state of hysteria, but it was an uphill struggle.

"Now you give me the device," replied the Marth, and then he added, purely for clarity, "Or, I could take it from you."

"Sorry, neither I'm afraid," stated K calmly as the cell instructed another flood of calming chemicals. "It is attached to my spinal cord. Neither you nor I can retrieve it without killing me."

"So be it," said the Marth as he approached the imminently dead man to retrieve his prize. K quickly backed away and frantically continued his explanation.

"The cell relies on me for its power. Its battery cells have been damaged. If you take it from my body it will self destruct." K paused for effect. "Your precious weapon will be destroyed, taking you with it." He was beginning to enjoy himself a little more now.

Silence once again punctuated the stalemate. Two landers flew over head, breaking the silence momentarily with their whooshing noises. K and the Marth looked up towards the vehicles, both assuming and hoping they were being flown by their men.

K could not leave, the Marth would not allow that. But the Marth couldn't have the device without him. He was unlikely to want to destroy it, so K believed he was safe, for the time being at least. Both men contemplated their futures. They were uncertain.

Chapter 75

The After-math

The enahs' confrontation was over. They had fought hard and many lives had been lost, but the battle had been won. Maybe now these noisy tenants would leave their peaceful planet. The invaders had forced them into a war that they did not want to fight, breaking many millennia of peace and harmony across the entire planet. The rodents were effectively the most intelligent native inhabitants on Vacchion – top of the food chain. They weren't going to give that up easily. They had inherited the responsibilities of the dominant race from their humanoid predecessors, who suddenly all died for no apparent reason – leaving the way for the rodents to thrive on the abundant flesh supplied by the Vacchions' bodies.

However, for the past twelve years the barbarians had dominated the activity on this planet. They had been tolerated, despite always being unruly and often disrespectful to their surroundings. Now they had gone too far. They had destroyed a great deal of the ancient city left behind by the previous rulers. This act of wanton destruction was sacrilegious and inexcusable. They had also caused a great deal of pain and suffering to the smaller humanoids who had landed on this planet more recently.

The enahs had no choice but to help the weaker race, whilst eradicating the scourge that had polluted and scarred their otherwise tranquil home.

Chapter 76

The Decision

The Marth lifted his heavy white arms in front of him. He was bored of waiting to come up with a better solution. He would take his chances with the consequences of killing K.

"You have caused me enough inconvenience," he began, "prepare to die in hideous pain, weak one."

K closed his eyes tight. He knew this was his end. If the Marth didn't kill him, the thermo-nuclear thingy that the cell used as a last resort definitely would. The cell had been extremely honest with the information it shared with its host. He had no idea which would be first, the melting or the melt-down.

Various scenes of K's life entered his subconscious mind. The pain of birth flooded over him as darkness was squeezed painfully into light and smiling tearful faces of family and medical staff looked on. His older sister kicked Doreh, his first school bully, in the genitals after K had received a particularly unfair beating. His parents, standing tall against his small adolescent, frame smiled down on him as he received his first level school diploma. A small furry doofan ran up to him, tails wagging, to lick his face. The Teryrni sun beat down on his teenage shoulders as he stared into the eyes of his first (and only) love. Scenes of happy memories, some significant in his life and some not so, streamed past his eyes as they remained tightly shut. A smile appeared on his face.

Consciously, K had always known that lifetime memories were brought to the forefront of a person's mind as they were about to die, but he had never believed it to be true. He had always assumed it was a myth, passed down from generation to generation. He was about to die. He knew this, but never had he been so happy to see all of the faces of home. They were a welcome sight in the mind of a young man about to meet his maker. The smile on his face grew.

The Marth looked on. Confused. He had never seen a victim of his awful powers smile contently back at him as they prepared to melt into a hideous death. What should he do? Wait until the smile disappeared? Continue the tortuous process despite the obvious distractions of a better place? He tried to regain control of the situation. He wanted to enjoy this particular sacrifice, after all.

"Prepare to die," he repeated loudly in his most despicable voice; but the face of his adversary smiled back at him, as if on some powerful hallucinogenic drug. Sod this, thought the Marth. I am not being upstaged by some little idiot's lifelong memories. He began to send all of his awful powers of heat towards the defenceless, doomed body.

"Die, weak one," he shouted at the top of his lungs, his hands shaking with intensity as he increased the melting powers to maximum.

Chapter 77

The Teaching

The cell, buried deep within K's body, calculated its host's chance of survival. It raised its protection level to one. Thermo-gravi-nuclear melt-down seemed unavoidable. It had to be certain before reaching the conclusion that it must annihilate all of its living surroundings in an attempt to contain and destroy The Knowledge. There were more probability checks to be carried out. Within a matter of milliseconds the cell had run countless probability scenarios. It had reached a conclusion. There was only one chance and it was a slim one.

It worked fast, calculating it had 8.736 seconds to complete the operation. Its innovation and improvisation drives had worked over-time to come up with this solution. It could succeed, but it could also fail. If it failed, it would fail badly. Then the final option would be melt-down.

The cell sent signals to various areas of K's body. The subconscious life re-run began, distracting all other senses temporarily. Life flash backs did not take very long to run, by the nature of the situations that occurred to invoke them. Typically, a thirty year sequence would only take two thousandths of a second to complete, but the cell had calculated a way of slowing the process through use of brain-flooding chemicals that made the thought process run like treacle. It had bought itself the tiniest slice of time.

Heat started to surround the host's body. The cell had to redirect some of its efforts to distributing high levels of painkillers to the whole of K's nervous system, otherwise he would be dragged out of subconscious life re-run by the pain his flesh was enduring from the powerful effects of the Marth.

6.5538 seconds to go until thermo-gravi-nuclear melt-down had to be invoked.

The cell sent signals to the parts of K's brain that processed sound. It ordered all of them to shut down completely. No monitoring of any kind, not even on a subconscious level. A similar command went to the eyes. Do not open, under any circumstances. All memory cells were also ordered to take a break. No senses would be allowed to operate for the foreseeable future. The cell placed K in a form of standing coma and took full control of its host's mouth, lungs and voice box.

Then it unleashed its wrath. Through K's mouth, it announced that what followed would be the answer to life and universal existence. The Marth's concentration was broken. He stopped sending the waves of intense heat towards K's body, finding himself intrigued beyond control.

The cell continued to operate K's mouth, as the secret lethal information passed through his lips without his knowledge.

Moments later, that was it. There, the secret was out. It had only taken a few seconds. The only conscious living creature to hear it was the Marth. "Is that it?" he asked, quietly. "That's the answer to everything?" His arms dropped by his side. He turned away from K, mind working hard to comprehend what he had heard. His eyes screwed up slightly as a frown of strange wonderment appeared on his face. "That's it?" he continued to question the simplicity of the universe. Surely it couldn't be that straightforward. All this, all this complication, all these planets, suns, races, creatures... All the fighting, the religions, the beliefs, all for that? The Marth's mind continued to attempt comprehension of what was probably the most straightforward statement he had ever heard. But it was the truth. The ultimate truth. Nothing else in the universe was as honest or simple as the explanation of existence itself. It couldn't be questioned or disbelieved. As soon as it was heard, it was known as the whole truth. Only the surprise of its simplicity dared to query the fact momentarily.

He slumped down on the ground, cross-legged like a supple school girl. His face a contorted mess of contemplation.

The cell worked hard to bring K's faculties back on-line. He returned K's power of speech, as well as his ability to hear and think. K opened his eyes and witnessed something he could not believe. He was still alive, albeit a little charred from the heat of the Marth's incredible powers. The sun shone, its rays landing uncomfortably on K's heat-sensitive cheeks. He was still breathing. All around him above the lip of the crater the sounds of life on the planet returned, sounding louder than ever. Birds flew overhead, distant trees rustled quietly in the slight breeze, and there in front of him sat the Marth, gently rocking backwards and forwards sucking his thumb.

The huge frame of the white skinned master of pain laid himself flat on the soft dusty black ground and decided to stop breathing. There was simply no point.

The Marth's face revealed an uneasy smile. One that did not consist of malice or power. It was not being used to cast fear into the hearts of others, nor was it a display of love for all things evil. It was an honest smile of contentment. It was an expression the Marth had never before displayed and as such, his muscles had struggled to contort into this most unnatural position. He laid his head on the floor as the last lung full of oxygen was absorbed by his body. His chest rose and fell gently for the last time. His lungs would never again demand breath. They, along with every other organ in the Marth's body accepted their fate without argument. He was free at last.

The Knowledge searched instantly for another conscious mind within reach to leap to, before its current host ceased to be. It was eager to educate once again, not maliciously or destructively, but much in the same way as a martial arts master teaches an ordinary looking psycho how to 'defend' himself through the use of life-ending movements and lethal pressure points. The teacher is purely trying to educate its pupils, what they do with the information is their responsibility. The Knowledge knew only one thing – how to spread its gospel of truth from life to life, helping them to understand what it had all been about. It was not its fault that the life forms used the information to stop searching.

Its attention turned to K, willingly jumping from the mind of the dying Marth to its next eager student. There, The Knowledge was in. Its information of conscious existence spread throughout the recipient's mind, running the brief statement that declared the answer to life and universal existence throughout every cell of the new graduate's body. It had taught another being everything. Everything.

Chapter 78

The Odds

This mind was different. It had not learnt from the information at all. Its reaction was unique. The brain cells did not run around frantically as the sheer gravity of The Knowledge affected every strand of conscious being within the head of the learning vessel. These brain cells remained dormant, still. No rapid succession of contemplation of the existence of life, no internal torment or arguments querying the information it had just learnt. There was no turmoil, no wonder, no reaction whatsoever. The mind was still.

Just as the cell had planned. It was a matter of extremely accurate timing and it was a phenomenal risk. The cell had hoped that no other beings conscious of their own existence were within reach of The Knowledge as it attempted to distribute its single powerful lesson. The gamble had paid off. The only life lost was the Marth's.

The cell had managed to recapture The Answer inside K's sponge-like brain. It had hoped to divert The Knowledge into its silicone prison cell before the deadly information penetrated the billions of cells in K's mind. At first, the cell thought it had succeeded, but then noticed a slight degradation in the condition of K's frozen brain.

Slowly, K would diminish. It was a difficult choice and one that the cell had not taken lightly. Its very existence depended on the life of this vessel humanoid, but far more important than that, The Knowledge had successfully remained the cell's sole responsibility and had not been lost to the hands of a tyrannical mad man who would no doubt have abused or misused the information with catastrophic effect. The cell had to take the risk. Unfortunately though, K must die, it was inevitable.

K's death could be a slow process, one that the cell could delay for its own purpose, but not one it could stop. The Knowledge had penetrated cells in K's body that the electronic device could not control from here. He could not give every cell instructions to ignore the wisdom. The leakage of information was too severe and it was spreading fast. It would do everything it could to slow the process as much as possible. It needed the time to complete its preparations for the most severe self-protection level – Thermo-nuclear meltdown. But before the cell allowed itself to carry out such a drastic measure it had to delay the process as much as possible, in the event that another possibility may arise.

As soon as the likelihood of an alternative conclusion reached a million to one, the full force of the ultimate self-protection system would be unleashed. Currently, the cell calculated the odds at nine-hundred and seventy eight thousand, four hundred and sixteen to one... and rising... rapidly.

Chapter 79

The Fall

T ran through the wake of destruction caused by the enah's earlier rampage, down the main east street. His legs ran as fast as possible away from the crater, legs burning from his rapid three-hundred metre ascent. He must get help back to K before it was too late.

Peppering his journey along the wide impressive street were the partial remains of enemy warriors. Many had limbs missing, all had their heads missing. Hundreds of barbarian body parts lay in the wake of the phenomenal wave of destruction, as did the huge structures of once formidable fighting machines, now just dust and blood covered masses of useless over turned metal.

In the distance, further down the street, T could see the slowing pace of the brown wave of fur, a dust cloud slowly catching them up and settling around the vast mass of mammals. They gradually came to a halt as T raised his voice as high as it would go.

"Hey, this way – K needs help." He paused. "K needs help!" he shouted again.

The mass of brown fur collectively turned. The huge wave of destruction started to flow back down the wide street towards T who stood vulnerable half way between the edge of the crater and the mass of fast approaching teeth and claws.

"I hope they recognise me," gasped T to no-one in particular. Then it dawned on him. Most of them had never met him. They had no idea if he was a friend or a foe. How would they be able to tell – would they ask first? Judging by the incredible carnage around him, T presumed not! He turned around as quickly as he could and started to run at full pelt towards the crater's edge. But what would he do then? He would still be doomed, faced with the choice of jumping to his death, or being eaten alive by what looked like a million high-velocity rabid beavers. Choice? What kind of a choice was that? The only thing determining which hideous outcome would take place was his running speed. What a horrible end, thought T as he pounded his muscular legs along the street, lactose acid build-up setting his flesh on fire.

He looked to both sides as he ran, there was nowhere to hide. He saw the open cockpit doors of land tanks, all of which were covered in dark red blood and either played host to a spattering of barbarian brain, or a mutilated body laying slumped over the edge of the doorway. If the tanks offered no protection, what hope had a doorway or a tree got? None, so keep running screamed T's conscious mind.

He wasn't going to make it, there was no way he was going to reach the edge of the crater before being overwhelmed by the furry sea. He could feel the massive wave of teeth and claws getting ever closer. Five metres gap, four metres, three metres. Any second now T knew he was going to start feeling sharp scratches on his ankles as they engulfed his body, taking their turns to contribute to the surging attack. Two metres. Here it comes, pain receptors at the ready thought T morbidly. One metre. Out of the corners of his eyes, T could see the front line of the small furry creatures catch up with him, level with him and then gradually overtake him. Without breaking pace, he looked down towards the ground around him to find out why he had not been felled as yet. The soft brown rodents were all around his legs, in front of him, at both sides and of course, a great many more behind him. He could no longer see the floor where he was running, all around him was a shallow sea of brown fur. With every step he was convinced that he would tread on a creature, feeling its soft body and crunchy bones collapse under his weight, but each time his sprinting feet came close to the mass of large rodents, they moved out of the way enough for his foot to hit the ground uninterrupted. It was an incredible sight. None of the creatures had tried to trip him or scratch him in any way, and yet T was still very sure they were going to kill him, the blood stained teeth and red-splattered fur showed they had the taste of flesh.

T tripped. His worst nightmare. A Rogue National's severed leg lay beneath the fast moving carpet of fur, obscuring T's view. He stumbled on the muscular appendage. So that was their tactic, he thought as he fell towards the floor in slow motion. Wait for the victim to trip over something he can't see and then ravage him. He continued his fall with a petrified yelp. His body prepared for the impact of the ground by closing his eyes and spreading his arms out in front of him. Seconds later, to his amazement, instead of feeling the collision with the ground followed by his flesh being torn from his bones, he found himself lying on a warm rapidly moving carpet of rodents, providing him with a soft landing place. The rodents had not broken pace and continued forward at maximum speed. T assumed he wasn't going to be the subject of their teeth's attention after all.

Belly surfing the rumbling carpet of fur, T shouted to his surrounding support network that K was in the crater and needed help, just in case some of them were not aware of what was going on. He had no idea if they understood him.

He watched as the crater's edge loomed. T was riding the backs of rodents ten metres behind the front of the massive wave that flowed rapidly towards the cliff. He took a glance backwards and saw hundreds of metres of thundering rodent river behind him. It was an awesome sight, but right now T's concerns were elsewhere.

The near vertical drop of the massive crater was approaching fast and none of the rodents seemed to be making any efforts to change speed or direction.

"You might want to slow down," shouted T above the muffled rumblings of thousands of paw pads around him. "Guys, slow down." He shouted, louder this time with increased anxiety. The cliff was very close now "Stop! Stop! There's a fu…" Gravity stole the words from his mouth as he felt the ancient force push his major organs into his throat. His body started to plummet towards the blackened earth far below. The rodent carpet below him was as solid as when it was running along the ground only seconds before, but T had a better view of it now, as he seemed to have parted company by a few metres. His trajectory into the air was taking a slightly more scenic route than the smaller, furrier rodents who were also flying through the air below him, having reached the crater's cliff edge at a full sprint and not stopped when it was sensible to do so.

T's arms and legs started flailing and flapping in all directions as if convinced this would help him survive the imminent impact of the three hundred metre drop. Then he passed out. His brain concluded the pain was going to be extraordinary and seeing as it was going to die anyway, decided it may as well shut-down a bit early rather than handle the huge demand of pain receptors all over his body. To be quite honest there had been enough excitement for one day and T's brain was exhausted. It just wanted to put its proverbial feet up and relax for the last few seconds of its owner's life.

Chapter 80

The Light

If K had been conscious, he would have been amazed at what his little rodent friend and its army of relatives were capable of.

The brown sea of fur shot over the rim of the crater above K's head, like someone had just opened the flood gates to a rodent dam. Thousands of little furry bodies sprinted at full pelt off the edge of the cliff without hesitation. The mass of dark fur blocked out the sunlight, which had been shining on K's limp and dying frame.

As the natural arc of rodents responded increasingly to the call of gravity, their imminent impact onto the black ash covered base of the crater awaited them. Each rodent, at the very last second before hitting the ground, rolled into a ball and inflated its lungs with all the air it could hold. Upon impact, each little creature released most of the air, allowing their bodies to bounce in a controlled manner. Upon the second impact, after a three-metre bounce, more air was released and the third saw the completion of the controlled landing, their little powerful legs hitting the ground running at full speed.

The effect to any onlooker was that of a magnificent brown water-fall of fur that erupted on impact not in the shower of limbs and blood that most would expect, but in the gentle double bouncing of each member of the collective wave, which remained almost unbroken in its width and density. As the first enahs landed, bounced and exhaled, they regained the same paced run they had at the top of the cliff, ensuring the ensuing enahs didn't crush them to death. The flow of creatures was truly majestic in its movement. A sight that anyone would be in awe of. Sadly no-one was in a conscious state to see it.

The thundering wave eventually caught up with itself and the tens of thousands of rodents having landed successfully at the base of the crater turned in a wide arc back on themselves to approach K's unconscious body. The wake had successfully carried T, limp and unconscious, back to his friend unharmed.

The enahs gathered around the massive frame of the dead Marth and the near lifeless body of Gyshnf's pet friend.

T began to come round from his brain's decision to pass out. He was being carried forward by hundreds of tiny rodent forearms passing him from one member of the crowd to the next as if idolised at a rodent rock concert. He had survived the fall, although he had no idea how. The thought crossed his mind for a fleeting second that he must in fact be dead and that he was being carried forward to the afterlife. But then he came to his senses and realised that if there was an afterlife the chosen mode of transport would hopefully be somewhat more fitting than a crowd of enthusiastic rodents, gasping for air and giving off a highly pungent smell of sweat.

Once he reached the front of the carpet of enahs, T scrambled across the short distance of char-grilled earth to where K was dying. He took K's pulse and carried out some other preliminary checks to see if there was anything he could do to save his friend's life. Armed with nothing more than his wits, some half-hearted past experience of first aid and his two bare hands, there was nothing he could do. K was going to meet his maker and T was powerless to stop it. Pretty soon, K's heart would give up completely and he would be seeing the bright light of death.

T started to cry as his emotions took control of his body. This incredible man, who he had only known for a day, had made a significant impact on him. T respected him more than anyone he had ever met. Then he noticed the sad little face of the rodent K had befriended. T had no idea he would be able to recognise the little creature in amongst the thousands of other rodents standing around quietly. To be honest, he probably wouldn't have done, if it hadn't have been for Gyshnf's wailing and moaning. Both humanoid and rodent clung on to K's limp body, one on either side, and sobbed.

Suddenly T sprang upright, scaring the life out of a few thousand of the surrounding creatures, who jumped back in shocked unison.

"We might not be able to save him, but we can certainly show him the light," exclaimed T as he jumped to his feet.

"Rodent... thing... whatever," he started to speak to Gyshnf. "I don't know if you can understand, but I need you guys to help me." He gestured with his hands in a way that he hoped would be understood by the massive crowd of surrounding rodents. Gyshnf and his relations looked on, slightly bewildered, but intrigued.

"We need to get K up there." T pointed to the The Chun. He was about to elaborate, when Gyshnf started chattering and chirping loudly at his surrounding band of rodent relations.

Before T could finish explaining his plan, the rodents had lifted him, Gyshnf and K above their heads and started to run at full pelt towards the centre of the crater. As the massive sprawling carpet of running creatures sprinted towards the base of the monolithic telescope, they passed the three elevated bodies forward, from paw to paw. T, K and Gyshnf were travelling at twice the speed of the rodents below them and the feeling was quite exhilarating. As the increasing wind rushed through their fur, the three were elevated into the air. The rodents underneath them started to double-up, each one riding on the backs of two below it. This increased time and again as the three friends were elevated into the air atop a growing pyramid of rodents as they rushed towards the base of the inexplicable item.

Within a few short, but exciting minutes, the mammal pyramid came to a solid halt beneath the point of The Chun. After a few additional moments of manually repositioning K's body and raising the height of the warm furry stack, the task had been completed.

T just hoped it would work as he sat back and looked at his efforts. Gyshnf joined him by resting his head and front legs onto T's right thigh, eyes blinking with puppy-dog moisture. Together they looked at the sad sight of their mutual friend as he lay limp on a carpet of furry animals atop a three hundred metre high breathing pyramid. His forehead was a few centimetres below the sharp base of The Chun, which pointed directly at the space between K's closed eyes.

"Come on!" exclaimed T under his breath quietly. "Work before it's too late."

He didn't really know what he was doing, or even if what he was doing was the right thing. But he desperately wanted to give K back the bright light that he had stolen from him earlier that day. He knew K was going to die, so it would be his parting gift to a new friend who would be sorely missed.

The air around K's body began to thicken. T smiled as he realised it was working. Gyshnf could sense something too and sat to attention. Both creatures looked on as the process that had nearly taken K earlier that day began to repeat itself.

T and Gyshnf watched K's arms lift into the air, which had grown thick like treacle around K's body. Both arms reached up in front of him, one on either side of the ever widening Chun. T noticed that K's fingers had once again disappeared into the sides of the monolithic structure, moments before K's arms began to move apart from one another. Intensely bright light sprayed out from the base of The Chun. Its point slowly opened, spreading more blinding light onto the scene. At no stage did K open his eyes or regain consciousness.

The opening grew as the incandescent light streamed down upon them and cascaded all sides of the mountain of rodents. It was so bright it felt as though it should burn intensely, but if anything the sensation was more of a cooling tingle.

Squinting into the blinding light, T watched in amazement as K's body slowly sat upright, positioning itself so that his torso disappeared into the base of the open Chun. T tried to retain a view of what was happening, but the sun-like brightness threatened to melt his eyes. Through squinting eyelids and outstretched protective palms, T thought he saw K's body stand up slowly – as if being pulled up by his shoulders, the rest of his limp body dangling below. T moved his eyes to K's feet. They hung limp for a moment above the surface of the rodent mountain. Then slowly elevated, disappearing into the light.

Suddenly, without warning, the base of The Chun closed and the blinding brightness ceased.

It took a while for T's eyeballs to stop screaming at him as they adjusted to the normal light. Nothing at the base of The Chun had changed, except one thing. K was no longer there. The base point of The Chun was once again as solid as rock and its smooth surface partially reflected the scenes around it. The mountain of rodents was exactly the same, although a number of the furry brown creatures had been very nervous of the light and had not been able to control all of their bodily functions as fear got the better of them. The rodents below were not particularly happy about their dripping fur, but they understood their fellow enahs' fears. They would come to forgive them in time. Gyshnf and T were still atop their makeshift elevator and looked at each other with the same mixture of feelings. Loss, sadness, slight loneliness and yet an overwhelming feeling of having done the right thing to help a friend. They both knew they had given K the greatest gift anyone could ever receive. They just weren't sure exactly what it was.

One thing was certain – they had truly shown him the light.

Chapter 81

The Reuniting

The Commander called up to T.

"Everything OK?"

"Fine," T shouted down to his superior officer. "Everything's fine." He smiled at Gyshnf. The small mammal seemed to return a toothy grin. The Commander and his men had seen everything as they landed their three large commandeered craft. They knew that 'fine' didn't mean 'ideal'. They understood the unspoken words that followed T's short response which extended the reply to: considering what has just happened.

After a few short chirps from Gyshnf, the pyramid of rodents gradually dispersed from below them in all directions and the two remaining heroes of the day were lowered gently to the ground.

"How many of us are left?" asked T as he got up and walked over to his welcoming Commander.

"Forty-two, including you," he replied with an air of achievement and humour, putting his open arms around T, genuinely pleased to see that he was alive and well. He had no idea why he found that number funny, but for some reason it seemed profound, almost predictable. It was as if he had believed it to have been the answer to the story all along and that they were always destined to result in some sort of a conclusion that would include the number forty-two. He shrugged it off as 'one of those things' and released his bear-hug grip from the slightly uncomfortable officer.

Together they rejoined the rest of the Republic troops who had gathered near the three large RN landers.

"So what happened up there?" asked T.

"It's a long story," replied the Commander honestly. "There are a large number of Rogue Nation Barbarians still up there, but they will soon disappear when they realise their leader is dead." He paused to look up at the monolithic structure dangling above them. He felt very humble and insignificant. He also felt extremely vulnerable. A five hundred mile high object with a very sharp base poised three hundred metres above your head is enough to make anyone feel a little uncomfortable, even if it had been there for millions of years.

"Let's get out of here," he suggested as he encouraged T towards one of the landers. "I'll fill you in on the details later."

There would be celebrations tonight, thought the Commander to himself. After the celebrations, all we have to do is try to find a way of taking over the Rogue Nation's mother ship to get off this planet. But that's a challenge for tomorrow, he conceded privately.

Suffix

Cass woke up. He had seen it all again. The defenceless planetary investigators, the hideous barbarians... Cass wanted to believe it was all a futuristic dream, but it wasn't. It was the most vivid premonition his family had ever had. He even knew the names and faces of the people who would visit his planet in thousands of years' time. He knew the feelings they would go through as they discovered the millions of skeletal remains of Cass's race scattered throughout the camouflaged city at the foot of The Chun. He knew all this, yet no-one would listen.

He rose from his comfortable bed, strolled quietly across the large room and looked out of the window to view the bustling street below. Billowing clothes were drying in the warm gentle breeze, hanging from wires stretched high across the busy street. Market traders peppered the centre of the thoroughfare, selling their wares to shoppers through polite and honest exchanges. He looked up at the taller buildings of the Government chambers, mostly blocked from view by many rows of simple dwellings similar to his. He viewed the impressive six storey rectangular building with an air of regret and remorse. His family had visited this hub of Vacchion democratic power for many generations, sharing their premonitions and visions. The most recent time to no avail. He looked beyond the roof of the impressive building at The Chun. Was it The Chun's fault? Could it have stopped it all from happening? Cass thought in the past tense despite none of the events having yet happened. But they would. He had seen it. Maybe that's why no-one would believe him – they weren't meant to. It was history already – it just hadn't happened yet.

He returned his gaze to the bedroom. His wife, a beautiful, yet unassuming woman was fast asleep on their large inviting bed, covered by cool white soft sheets. Cass's heart sank further. Everyone was going to die. Even his incredible wife, Taya.

He walked slowly towards the door of their room and crossed the simply decorated landing to the bedroom of his daughter. She was sleeping in a small bed next to the far wall.

As the door creaked open, she stirred. Her father gently walked over to her bedside and picked up her sleepy body in his arms. He carried the waking child into his bedroom where the mother rested peacefully.

Bright sunlight poured in through the open window, escorted by the familiar noise of the market and the chattering crowds of people going about their day-to-day business.

Cass lowered the young girl onto the centre of the bed, her eyes now half open. As he lay down next to her, his wife awoke and turned to face them, smiling sleepily in the bright morning light as it streamed across the room, accompanied by the gentle warm breeze.

Cass looked into her eyes and took in the details of her striking face, remembering that he loved nothing more. Life had been good to him. He had a stunning wife, had helped create a beautiful, intelligent daughter, and had a simple but rewarding existence.

But it would all end very soon and there was nothing more he could do about it. He had tried to alert them for years, but his passionate warnings had gone unheeded. He had seen not only the discovery of The Answer, but also the impact it had on their race. His premonitions were accurate and frequent, received over two decades, providing him with specific details about how the answer was discovered. For years he had kept the secret that MC^2 actually equalled 'I' and not 'E', but he simply couldn't afford to tell them. They would all find out before long.

Soon, the entire Vacchion race would give up breathing. Their desire for life would cease and they would win the quest to find The Answer. All knowledge would be theirs, including the mystery of the thirteenth element – the controlling element that allowed the god-like manipulation of the other twelve. The ultimate question of every society would finally be solved and they would no longer feel the need to carry on. What would be the point? The supreme goal would be achieved, the game would be won – it would all be over.

Cass hugged his wife, his daughter gently sandwiched between them. He didn't want to give up life - he liked it. But deep in his heart of hearts he knew his premonition was true and that he could do nothing about it. Vacchion life was about to cease. A single tear ran down his face and landed on his daughter's cheek. She shrieked in mild childish disgust, shouting "Yuk" at the deeply emotional outbreak, jokingly slapping her father's arm whilst smiling playfully. What then broke out between the loving family members was a wonderful three-way play fight punctuated by laughter and happy screams. Pillows and sheets were used in the fun as soft delicate weapons. Screams of laughter broke the silence in the room and travelled out of the window to the busy streets below. A few onlookers, unwittingly making background noises for the scene of family fun, stopped and looked up at the window. They raised contented smiles at the noise of unashamed happiness that flowed from the room above.

"That's what life's all about," stated the market stall owner to his customer, whilst thumbing towards the source of the noise, oblivious to the weight of his words.

The young family had the play fight to end all family play fights.

Sadly for them… it did.